Praise for Kevin McGee

For Prentice Pendleton and the Ghost Ship of Capron Bay

"Great read!!!
I had heard about this book from a friend but thought…this isn't the type of book I would normally enjoy and thought it was just for kids anyway. I decided to read the introduction anyway. I was completely hooked and couldn't believe how creative the author was and it grabbed my attention. I finished it pretty fast enjoying every bit of it. I highly recommend it for all ages. Great read!!!— MC"

For Prentice Pendleton and the Ghost Ship of Capron Bay

"We struggle to find books for our kids to read that are interesting, as well as good spirited and kid friendly. Our eleven-year-old has not put this book down, unless told to do so to complete other chores, and schoolwork. He will finish it by tomorrow for sure. He loves reading it, as well as sharing the story with us. Highly Recommend. Have ordered the second in the series and cannot wait for him to start it". — Brian

For Prentice Pendleton and The Boo Hags

"Another Great read. Great sequel to Prentice Pendleton Ghost Ship…more action, the only thing that slowed him down from finishing is he didn't want to finish before the third one came out. Highly recommend for any readers but especially great for high energy boys who don't like sitting and reading" — Tammy

Also by Kevin McGee

<u>Prentice Pendleton and The Supernatural Squad of Capron Bay Series</u>

Book #1: Prentice Pendleton and The Ghost Ship of Capron Bay

Book #2: Prentice Pendleton and The Boo Hags

Book #3: Prentice Pendleton and The Haunting of Minuteman Cemetery

<u>United States of Scare: Tales of Terror From The Fifty States</u>

Book #1: The Gamecock Creeper

Book #2: The Witching Tree of Smithfield

Book #3: Coming Soon: The Black Agnes

PRENTICE PENDLETON AND THE ETERNAL STORM

A Prentice Pendleton and The Supernatural Squad of Capron Bay Adventure.

For every kid who ever felt small in a world too big.
For every spark of color in a storm of gray.
And for those who still believe that courage lives in the quietest hearts.

This is your story too!

PROLOGUE

Inuit Fishing Village
Anjukani Lake, Canada
January 5th, 1924

Joe LaBelle tied his sled dogs to a tree just outside the village. The team had stopped abruptly, refusing to go any further, and Keto, the lead dog, stood rigid, his fur bristling as he stared at the cluster of snow-dusted buildings ahead. The unease in his dogs unnerved Joe. Something was wrong. The silence in the village wasn't natural, it was the silence of a world holding its breath, waiting to scream. Fresh snow had blanketed every hut, every boat, and every inch of ground creating an illusion calm that would soon be shattered.

The fur trader adjusted his hood against the bitter wind, stepping cautiously onto the ice-covered path leading into the village. He'd visited here dozens of times trading furs and supplies. But this time was different.

Anjukani was usually alive with activity—a thriving fishing village where Joe traded furs, found warm food, and enjoyed a brief respite. Now, an eerie silence blanketed the settlement. A dense fog slithered across the ground, creeping between buildings like a living thing.

No smoke rose from the huts. No children laughed in the twilight. No dogs barked warnings of a stranger's approach. Even the ever-present wind seemed to hold its breath, afraid to whisper through the haunted quiet.

He slung his rifle from his shoulders and cocked the gun. He wasn't sure the weapon would even work. The bolt-action rifle hadn't been fired in a long time and was partially frozen from the blizzard over the last few days. Even though it might not work, it reassured him as he approached the gates.

It was cold, almost too cold for this time of year. He sighed, knowing he couldn't leave. The night was fast approaching, and the dogs couldn't stand being out in the wilderness another night. He had to get some shelter for them.

11

"Hello?" he called out, hoping someone would answer him.

Nothing.

He swallowed hard.

"Hello?" he called out again. His words were louder this time, but a terrifying thought popped into his mind. Maybe he didn't want to be heard. Maybe there was someone or something in the village that would mean him harm.

No response.

Joe hesitated, his breath fogging in the cold air. He glanced back at his dogs. They stood watching him, ears flat and tails low. His instincts screamed to turn back, but the approaching night and the bitter cold left him no choice. His dogs needed shelter.

He stepped inside, tightening his grip on the old rifle and raised it, ready to fire if needed. His military training kicked in, and he moved one foot in front of the other with his rifle, scanning the buildings as he moved.

Something was wrong here.

The cold felt sharper here, unnatural for the season. Each step was careful, deliberate, as his instincts sharpened, and his senses heightened. His eyes scanned the small houses, his grip tightening on the rifle. His heart pounded away like a war drum preparing for battle. His blood pulsed with energy as his body went into combat mode.

Clang!

The sharp sound shattered the silence—a pot or kettle tumbling to the ground, distant but deafening in the stillness.

He quickly moved down an alley to his right, moving towards the sound. The fog scattered as he did so. As he sped down the alley, he passed Amka's hut. Amka had been his partner in the fur trade for a long time.

Joe wanted to go into his friend's home to see if he was okay, but he knew he had to get to the location of the sound first. He would check on his friend after.

"Eeeeyahhhh!"

A blood-curdling scream tore through the fog, freezing Joe mid-step. It was inhuman, primal—something ancient and malevolent. His pulse quickened. His legs weakened at the sound.

He had seen the worst war had to offer, but the scream struck fear in him. It was something prehistoric and evil.

Then came another scream, higher pitched. A child.

Joe put his fear aside and ran towards the sound of the scream. He turned corner after corner too quickly. If someone had been waiting for him, they would have soon taken him out, but he was lucky there was nothing ready to pounce on him.

He came to a three-way fork in the village paths. He stopped and listened for any more sounds. As he stood listening, he tried to calm his breathing and slow his heart rate.

Nothing.

He moved down the middle alleyway, passing the village worship house. It wasn't a church. It was just a gathering place for the villagers to come and worship however they wanted. Joe tried to glance inside the small building to see if anyone was there, but the fog was thick, and he couldn't make out anything.

High above, unnoticed, colors flickered across the dark sky, ribbons of energy twisting and dancing. A spectacle beautiful and terrifying, their power ancient and uncontainable.

A sudden flash of movement in the street ahead caught his eye. Joe stopped and raised his rifle, aiming right where the movement was. He waited for something else to move, but nothing did.

He forced his legs forward slowly, his finger resting on the trigger. He came to the end of the alley. He flattened against the last hut, putting his back on the wooden frame. Something crackled just ahead. He took a deep breath and swung around, rifle raised.

Nothing.

A large kettle sat atop the flames of a community-wide kitchen and firepit. He knew many of these local Inuit villages had large communal kitchens where they could cook for the entire hamlet.

Joe swung his rifle left and right, scanning for potential threats, but there was nothing. He crept towards the firepit. The flames were still raging underneath the bubbling kettle. The large cast iron cover had fallen from the kettle. That was the clanging he had heard earlier. The cover was pushed off from the bubbling of whatever was inside.

The cooking kettle scared him. It meant that whatever had happened here had occurred recently and was right in the middle of what the villagers were doing.

"What is going on?" he whispered to himself.

"Ruff, ruff, ruff!"

Barking erupted in the distance.

"Keto," he cried out and ran back towards his dogs. He ran as fast as he could through the village's alleys and paths. Shadows loomed in the alleys as the sun sank lower.

He came to an intersection and hesitated for a moment. He needed to figure out which way to go. That's when he heard it. A faint but unmistakable creak. A door moving.

"Grrr," a deep guttural growl echoed through the silent village. Then another and another.

Joe froze in place. Unable to move.

"Ruff, ruff, ruff," more barking from his dogs.

He tried to move but couldn't. His legs froze in place.

His eyes searched the village's alleys, but the darkness of the approaching night crawled towards him.

"Eeeeyahhhh!" came the scream again, tearing through the darkness.

Something was coming for Joe.

"Ruff, ruff, ruff!"

He took a deep breath and willed his legs to move. They finally obeyed, and he raced towards the sound of his dogs. He still wasn't sure if he was headed the right way, but he ran at full speed, moving away from the growling.

He turned the corner and saw the front gates of the village.

Bang!

Something crashed behind him.

"Grr"

More growling.

He didn't waste any time looking back. He ran on, powering towards the gate. He could still see some sunlight on the other side of the wooden doors and was desperate to get to it. A shutter crawled along his spine, but he kept looking forward. He knew something was chasing him, and he knew he would see it if he turned around. Part of him knew he would slow down if

14

he risked a glance, but the other part was terrified to see what was chasing him.

He was almost at the gate.

"*Grrr!*"

The growl was louder now and closer.

"*Ruff, ruff, ruff,*" Keto cried out as if he was telling Joe to hurry.

Joe closed on the gate, but he would have to slow down before going through. He knew there was a sharp left turn to make as soon as you went through. He also knew the ground was full of snow and ice. Any attempt to stop suddenly and he would be on his back, and whatever was chasing him would be on him.

He couldn't slow down.

"*Grrr!*"

He could feel it now. It was close.

Joe exploded into the gate, holding his hands out as he bounced off the wooden door. The hinges groaned as he hit the old structure with all his body weight. Using his momentum, he pushed himself off the door as hard as possible to continue exiting the village.

It was the only way to keep his speed, and when he hit the door, he spun around and caught a quick glimpse of his pursuers. It was only for a brief second, but what he saw would haunt him for the rest of his life, and it spurred his legs to move faster. It was tall, impossibly thin, its elongated limbs ending in wicked claws. Its pale, taut skin stretched tightly over bones, and its hollow eyes glowed like embers in a skull-like face crowned with jagged antlers. It stalked forward with a hunched, predatory gait, moving silently despite its grotesque frame.

Even though he used the door to propel himself through without losing speed, he felt his feet begin to slip as they hit a patch of ice underneath the snow. He dove forward, tucking his shoulder and rolling. He didn't miss a step as his feet caught the ground. He was up fast, and he ran on. There was a loud crash behind him as the things chasing him slammed into the gate.

Joe didn't look back. He looked at Keto and his sled dogs.

They weren't alone.

A young girl stood beside them.

15

She looked familiar, but Joe was in too much of a hurry to figure out who she was. He heard the creatures behind him. There was no way he was going to make it. He might get to the dogs, but by the time he could get them ready, the creatures would be on them.

He lifted the rifle and was about to spin around and make a stand when he saw the young girl raise her hands. A golden glow began forming. At first, he thought it was growing around her hands, but he quickly realized it was spreading from her hands and getting brighter and brighter.

Swoosh!

Her hands sparked and exploded as fiery energy flowed from them. A wave of colors shot from her fingers and arced toward the beasts chasing him. It was a flaming rainbow of energy. The sizzling power tore through the air right by his face, and he felt the heat on his skin. He stumbled to the ground and slid through the snow. He looked back towards the village. He never got a good look at the lead creature because it was ripped to shreds when the girl's rainbow power slammed into it.

The other beasts screamed in fear as they turned to run back into the village, but the wave of energy was relentless. It swung towards their fleeing bodies, cutting three of them down in crackling explosions. The remaining monsters could escape the gate, disappearing behind the village walls.

Then everything went quiet.

Joe turned to see the girl collapse on the ground.

He didn't hesitate. He was on his feet in a moment and ran to her. He scooped her up and placed her on the front of the sled. He secured her as quickly as he could. Keto and the team were well-trained. As Joe put the girl onto the sled, they readied themselves to move.

"Hike!" he shouted. "Hike"

Keto and the team knew they needed to get out of there quickly. The dogs worked in unison and drove the sled through the snow with powerfully perfect speed Joe had never seen before.

As the team sped away from the village, Joe could hear the screeching cries of whatever those things were. Even though the screams were terrifying, he was glad to hear them because they drove Keto and the team to move faster and faster until they were far enough away from whatever evil had befallen the village.

A few hours later, they stopped to rest. Joe had no choice but to start a fire. The temperatures were too low, and they all had to warm up. The girl had awakened during the flight from the village but had said nothing.

They sat silently by the fire, warming up and eating whatever the trader had in his packs, which wasn't much. Joe gave Keto and the team most of the food and offered the rest to the girl. The sled team needed to eat and regain their strength after their escape.

Joe scanned the tree line surrounding their small camp as the girl and dogs ate. He kept his rifle ready even though he knew the weapon wouldn't do much against those things. There were no sounds out there, which made him very nervous. There should have been some sounds from animal life, but tonight, there were none.

"They have not followed," the girl suddenly said.

Joe looked at her, not sure how she knew that, but he said nothing.

"They are afraid," she said.

"What is your name?" he asked her.

"Nanurjuk," she told him.

"Star," he whispered.

She looked at the white man with surprise.

"I understand some of your language. Your name means star," he smiled.

She nodded.

"What happened back there?" he asked, still checking the tree lines.

The girl stared into the flames for a minute before answering.

"The storm. The adults all...become siku," she said.

"Siku," Joe whispered, trying to figure out what the girl meant. Siku means ice. Did the adults become ice? Did they freeze?"

She nodded.

"Then the...ninngappoq come," she said.

17

"Ninngappoq?" he said, trying to remember if he knew the word.

"Mon…monsta," she spoke the word slowly.

"Monster?" he repeated.

She nodded.

"Those things?" he asked.

She nodded.

"What happened to the…kids," he asked.

"Taken," was all she said.

"The…frozen adults?" he asked her.

She hesitated.

"Smashed," she answered.

He felt bile rising in his stomach. He wanted to vomit

"They're looking…for me," Nanurjuk said.

Joe looked at the young girl.

"You? They wanted you?" he asked.

She nodded.

"Why," he asked, but he realized the answer before he finished.

"I am…kataujaq angut," she mumbled.

Angut means man, Joe thought. But it also could mean a soldier or something like a guardian.

"Kataujaq…" he whispered, trying to think of the word.

"Color," she added.

"Color…rainbow. Rainbow soldier, no rainbow guardian," he asked.

She shook her head slowly, her eyes flickering with uncertainty.

"Rainbow warrior?" he mumbled, searching his memories. The phrase stirred something deep within him—a half-remembered legend whispered by the villagers around campfires. Stories of guardians who fought ancient darkness with the power of colors. He'd always dismissed them as folklore, myths to entertain children, but now those stories felt disturbingly real.

Nanurjuk lifted her gaze, meeting his eyes. Slowly, she nodded.

Joe stared at her for a long moment, heart thumping in his chest. Then, managing a gentle smile, he handed her some

18

food. She accepted it quietly and ate without another word, the silence heavy with the weight of unspoken truths.

The young girl looked at him and nodded. He smiled and handed her some food. She took it and ate in silence.

Far away, hidden in darkness, something ancient awakened, sensing the ripples of power. The storm had begun, and the world would never be the same again.

1
TRAINING

North Bimini Island
Bahamas
December 31, 2024

The fishing boat swayed gently on the turquoise waters, the rhythmic waves lapping against its weathered hull. Sunlight danced across the surface, illuminating schools of colorful fish below. I leaned on the railing, scanning the vibrant sea life. A stingray glided along the ocean floor, its graceful movements mesmerizing.

"Beautiful, isn't it?" the old man asked me as he joined me on the deck.

"I can't believe this is the ocean," I answered. "It's clearer than the fish tanks at Mystic Aquarium."

"These are some of the most beautiful waters in the world," he said.

I nodded, closing my eyes, feeling the gentle breeze against my face, and taking in the smell of the sea around me.

"I can feel the power of the water," I said.

He nodded slowly, gazing thoughtfully across the vibrant water.

"There's power here. Ancient energy. The colors flow stronger in some places, and this is one of them."

I studied Jon quietly. His bronze skin and weathered face revealed years spent under the relentless Caribbean sun, and his imposing physique hinted at strength hardened by a lifetime of hidden battles. Yet, in his Bermuda shorts, sandals, and cutoff Tom MacDonald t-shirt boldly declaring *No More Snowflakes*, he hardly matched the "wise mentor" stereotype Grammy had planted in my mind. I'd expected someone who looked like Gandalf or Obi-Wan Kenobi, not a sun-tanned beach bum who could bench-press a motorcycle. But appearances, I'd learned, were deceiving, especially when dealing with masters of the colors.

He did not look like your typical Old Wise Man teacher. We had all come down to the Bahamas for Christmas break. Dad said it would be good for us all to get away for the holidays after the year we've all had. I knew that was just a story, though. The real reason for coming here was to meet Jon Kane, the Jedi master of the colors. Grammy said he was the best and the last master of colors she knew of.

When she told me that, I expected an old man in a brown cloak or grey pointy hat carrying a long, ancient-looking staff. I certainly didn't expect a sun-tanned, beach-going sandal-wearing guy. Not that I have anything against those things. It's just that the stereotype is more of a Gandalf-looking wizard than a Tom MacDonald fan.

"See the dolphins," he said, pointing towards the ocean.

I squinted as a pair of fins sliced through the surface, vanishing as quickly as they appeared.

"This is where dolphins get their stereotype," he laughed.

"I didn't know there was a stereotype for dolphins," I replied.

"Movies and television make it seem like they are social animals, and they want to be around people," he said.

I stood waiting for him to finish.

"That is not true. They shy away from people most of the time," he grimaced.

"I didn't know that" I said.

He nodded as he looked at me.

"Here, they like to be around people. They seek human interaction out for some reason," he said, shaking his head.

"Is that why you're here? To seek out human interaction, Master Yoda?" I laughed. I had spent two weeks with Mr. Kane, and I knew it was the exact opposite. He came here to avoid people.

"I can see why the bad guys want to get rid of you," he laughed, shaking his head.

"They just want to get rid of me because I'm better looking than all of them," I said, trying not to laugh.

"Modest, too," he said.

21

"Don't forget sarcastic," I added.

"How could I," he laughed, turning his tanned face towards me.

I shrugged.

"Show me," he ordered.

Just as I had gotten to know he was sarcastic and disliked people, I also knew it was time to work once he wanted to get to work.

I licked my lips, tasting the salt from the ocean air on them.

"Easy now," Jon said softly. "Calm your breathing. Find your center."

I inhaled deeply, focusing on the sensation of the ocean air filling my lungs. Memories of our first training session two weeks ago came rushing back, the storm, the relentless rain, and Jon's booming voice cut through it all. His massive arms folded across his chest as he stood unflinching in the pounding rain.

"Focus," he commanded. "Focus on the colors. They can be overwhelming. Start with blue. It is the color of peace and tranquility."

I tried to focus that first night, but the wind and rain assaulted my senses. Red and black swirled in my vision no matter what I did.

"Do not let the environment dictate to you what you feel," his voice booming over the whipping wind. Control your emotions. Maintain your feelings."

I focused on white, desperately grasping at anything pure and calming fresh laundry, crisp bed sheets, untouched snow. But the image of snow brought unwanted memories—*Do you want to build a snowman?* It echoed in my mind, and suddenly Olaf flashed before me, smiling like my sister once did in the car leaving the hospital when I thought for a moment that she was a talking Olaf stuffed animal. Her laughter quickly darkened into screams, twisted metal, cold water, Poppa's lifeless face.

Anger surged, red and black erupting through the purity. Energy surged through my veins, unstoppable and furious. Before I could stop myself, it burst from my hands, a fiery bolt slamming into the ocean, sending up a plume of boiling mist.

I opened my eyes, breathing heavily, and looked at Jon. He stared back, expression unreadable, the rain pelting his massive frame.

"You must control it, Prentice," he said firmly, his voice cutting through the storm.

"I ended up seeing the car accident and Poppa," I grimaced, trying not to cry.

"No matter what memories come, no matter how much they hurt, you can't let the past control your power."

Two weeks later, I stood on the deck of the fishing boat, feeling the gentle sway of the ocean beneath me. I had learned many things during these training sessions, but it always came back to one simple truth: controlling my emotions.

I closed my eyes and reached inward, feeling for the colors. They flowed around me like the ocean itself, sometimes calm, smooth, and inviting other times turbulent and unpredictable. Each color held its own power, waiting patiently beneath the surface, ready to surge forward at my call.

I exhaled slowly, picturing the colors as gentle currents, smoothly intertwining. Blue, the calmest and strongest, rose clearly in my mind. Its peaceful power spread through me, mirroring the serenity of the waters below.

I reached out with my mind, calling gently to the dolphins swimming below. Their movements paused, sensing me, curious yet cautious. At first, their apprehension was palpable, a rush of fear rippling through their minds. Gently, I reassured them with waves of calmness, soothing their fear until curiosity replaced caution.

Their sleek bodies turned gracefully toward me, cutting effortlessly through the clear water. I sensed their intelligence, their wonder, their trust. Without hesitation, I dove from the boat, slipping beneath the surface to meet them, drawn by the shared bond of energy and understanding.

The swimming duo stopped moving and turned back towards me. I felt their energy and their emotions. At first, their fear was loud, but they quickly calmed down as I called out to them. My inner voice assured them they were in no danger, and they relaxed. Their muscular bodies turned towards me and answered my call. The dolphins were coming to me.

23

I felt them glide through the water as they closed in on me. Their muscular bodies slicing through the water with ease. I could sense their intelligence as they wondered what I was.

"Prentice," Jon shouted to me, but I ignored him focusing on the dolphins.

"Prentice," he yelled louder, and I could feel some tension rising in him, but I still felt the excitement of the two princes of the sea cutting my way as I called them.

"Eeeeeee," a sharp, high-pitched whistle broke the calm of the waters surrounding the dolphins. I felt the echo tear through my mind simultaneously as fear ripped through the dolphins.

I clutched my head, agony slicing through me as their fear echoed painfully through my mind.

"Prentice! Lookout!" Jon shouted, trying to break my connection with the dolphins.

The speedboat sliced through the ocean like a missile, bearing down on us. The laughter of the boys in the boat twisted through the roar of its engine. My rage flared like fire, energy burning in my hands, begging for release.

"Aaaht!" the boat's horn roared as the ship exploded past our anchored fishing boat. My connection with the two dolphins broke, and they dove deep into the ocean, barely avoiding the bottom of the speedboat. The ship roared past my face by inches. The displaced water crashed over me, trying to drown me.

"Hey!" Jon screamed at the occupants of the speeding vessel as it narrowly missed our boat. The powerful waves desperately tried to capsize our boat. There were a lot of people on that boat. I couldn't make out faces other than the two in the back. They were shirtless, but both had Bermuda shorts and sandals. Their sandy blond hair blew in the wind, covering their face. The one on the left had a long scar along his cheek. I could see it clearly in the sun. They pointed at me and laughed as the rest of the people raised their glasses and yelled back at us.

Anger sparked deep within my chest, flaring instantly into red-hot rage. Red surged uncontrollably, consuming the tranquility of blue. I fought it, trying to force it down, but the anger was too strong, too vivid.

24

"No," I whispered desperately, but the colors surged violently out of my control.

A blazing wave of red energy erupted from my hands, shooting across the water directly toward the distant black speedboat. It slammed into the hull with an explosive force, rocking it violently, almost capsizing it as passengers screamed and scrambled for balance.

My eyes snapped open, horror-stricken at what I had done. Jon's strong hand gripped my shoulder tightly, grounding me back in reality.

"Control yourself, Prentice!" he shouted, anger and worry mixing in his voice. "Focus! Or you'll hurt more than your pride."

I closed my eyes and took a deep breath. A moment later, I felt the anger cool down, and I tried to read the name of the black boat with a purple stripe down its side, but it was too far. I looked up at my teacher.

Jon's hands grasped the boat's railing. The thick muscles on his arms bunched in anger. I got the feeling he could rip the handrail off the boat if he wanted to. I watched his jaw clench with frustration but quickly relax as he forced his emotions to calm down.

"That was not part of the lesson," he grimaced as he looked at me. His eyes full of anger and rage.

"You have to control your feelings," I smiled.
His nose flared, and his green eyes roared with fury. I joked one too many times.
He nodded his head over and over.

"You are right, Prentice. No matter what," he said calmly now but stared off into the distance, trying to follow the path of the speeding boat as it moved further and further away from us.

Crack!

Thunder exploded in the distance.

"Let's get back in before the skies open on us," Jon said.

Twenty minutes later, the boat slowed to a stop along the dock. Jon's deckhands quickly tied it off and unloaded some bags from below. I hopped over the railing and started looking for Dad. He was supposed to be waiting for us. There was a lot of commotion on the other side of the marina. A large group of people gathered around a huge yacht that sat dockside, taking up several spots generally reserved for the fishing boats of the locals.

The boat's name, "Late Night King," was plastered on the side of the monstrosity in big white lettering. The owner wanted everyone to know who he was, even though I did not know.

"Late night, king?" I said out loud to myself.

"Just another rich guy who thinks he can own the island," Jon sneered as he hopped over the railing. I followed him as we made our way toward the landing.

"Dad was supposed to be here," I said.

"He's probably waiting out in the lots. Look at the circus over there," he grimaced.

He was right. People were running in every direction. I saw a lot of cameras and cell phones out.

"He must be some kind of celebrity," I laughed. "Look at everyone trying to get pictures."

Jon just shook his head.

"Now, you seem like Master Yoda," I laughed.

"Call me Yoda one more time," he threatened.

"You're an angry...Yo...," I began to say.

"Hey! You! You almost capsized us," came a loud voice.

I looked up towards the landing. The two kids from the speedboat were walking my way. There was a third kid I hadn't seen on the boat following behind. The one with the face scar was leading the way. He was my size with broad shoulders. His sandy blond hair was now tied back in a ponytail, revealing his facial scar even more. He was probably my age or a year older.

I glanced at Jon.

He stopped walking standing in front of me. His Oakley glasses covered his eyes, but I knew they were angry behind the dark lenses. His jaw muscles clenched as he squeezed his teeth together.

"Prentice," Jon said.

"I got this, Yoda," I laughed. "They're my age. You can't hurt them. It would be child abuse."

He looked at me.

"Yo...da," I smiled.

26

"I'm going to feed you to the sharks," he grimaced.

I laughed.

"Control your emotions," he said.

I winked at Jon and turned to face the approaching trio. Scarface led the pack, his unbuttoned beach shirt fluttering slightly in the ocean breeze, clearly intended to show off his annoyingly defined abs. The other two guys trailed behind, wearing matching Vineyard Vines polo shirts with their collars popped aggressively upward, expensive Bermuda shorts, and pristine boat shoes that probably cost more than everything in my closet back home combined.

Scarface squared his shoulders, trying his best to intimidate. I sighed inwardly, already annoyed by his ego-driven bravado. I glanced back at Jon, who had settled comfortably onto a nearby crate, folding his muscular arms with a grin that told me he was more than happy to watch this unfold.

"Hi," I said, forcing a polite smile.

"You almost tip-sized our boat out there," Scarface sneered, his voice dripping with arrogance.

I heard Jon groan softly behind me.

"You mean *capsized*," I corrected, trying to suppress my grin. "And actually, you're the ones who almost ran us down."

"We blew our horn," one of Scarface's buddies snapped, crossing his arms like he'd just stated the obvious.

"Sorry, I didn't catch your name," I said casually. "Was it Chad or Brad?"

The kid stared blankly. "What?"

"I'm Chad," the other one jumped in eagerly. "Do I know you?"

Jon laughed quietly behind me.

"No," I replied slowly, struggling to keep a straight face. "It was a joke."

Scarface stepped closer, puffing himself up again. "Do you even know who you're messing with?"

"Nope," I said, turning to Jon with mock seriousness. "Should I?"

Jon just shrugged, thoroughly enjoying himself now.

"I'm Prentice," I said calmly, offering my hand in an attempting to ease the tension.

27

Scarface slapped it away with surprising force. The unexpected aggression ignited something primal inside me, and red flashed violently through my mind. My anger surged, hot and raw, energy crackling dangerously through my fingertips, begging to be unleashed.

"Prentice," Jon's voice echoed sharply in my mind. "Don't let it control you. Breathe."

I closed my eyes briefly, forcing myself to exhale slowly. The red began fading, replaced by a steady, soothing blue. My hands relaxed, the burning energy receding.

I opened my eyes again and sighed deeply, regaining control.

"You don't know how lucky you just got," I muttered softly, looking directly at the kid.

Scarface turned abruptly at the sound of a girl's voice. Two young women stood atop the landing, watching us curiously. Both wore bikinis, clearly comfortable in the tropical sun. They were pretty enough, I suppose—but neither compared to Lena.

"Trent? Are we heading back to your father's house soon?" one asked impatiently.

"Yes, Ashley. We'll be right there," Scarface responded, clearly annoyed by the interruption.

"Oh, so you're Trent," I said, finally piecing things together. "And let me guess—he's Chad, and the other guy must be Hunter or Kyle or some other generic frat-boy name."

"Do you even know who I am?" Trent demanded, puffing his chest out dramatically.

"Uh…no," I replied with exaggerated seriousness.

"I'm Trent Kellerman," he declared proudly, his voice rising so the girls could hear. He waited expectantly, clearly expecting awe or fear.

I widened my eyes in mock amazement. "No way. Trent Kellerman?"

His chest puffed out further, and a smug smile spread across his face.

"Incredible," I said, letting a pause hang in the air. "I didn't know who you were thirty seconds ago, and honestly, I still don't."

Jon chuckled behind me, making Trent's face flush deep red with anger.

"Dude," one of the frat boys interjected, clearly offended on his friend's behalf. "His dad is Clayton Kellerman, host of Kellerman Live."

I stared blankly at him. "Yeah, still no idea who that is, Chet."

"Whose Chet?" he asked, genuinely confused.

Jon laughed again, shaking his head.

"My father owns this island," Trent declared loudly, clearly irritated.

"Oh, so he's the one ruining the place," Jon muttered dryly from behind me.

Trent's glare snapped toward Jon. "Who are you supposed to be?"

Jon stood, sighing heavily. "Prentice, hurry up. My patience is fading fast."

I turned slightly toward Jon, offering him a playful grin. "Control your emotions," I teased softly.

He sighed and raised his hands apologetically.

"Okay, Trent, Chad, Brock—or whatever your names are—you nearly ran us down, but I'll let it go," I said calmly, moving past them toward the dock.

Trent's hand shot out, grabbing my arm roughly.

"Who the hell is Brock?" one of the other guys asked, genuinely puzzled.

I shook my head in disbelief and looked at Trent. "Seriously? You trying to impress the girls with this tough-guy act?"

His grip tightened painfully, anger sparking in his eyes. My patience snapped. I seized his wrist, twisting until his fingers peeled away, forcing him into an awkward spin. He stumbled, and with a satisfying shove, I sent him sprawling off the pier and into the water below.

"Hey!" Chad shouted, rushing at me with his fist cocked back. I sidestepped neatly, letting his momentum carry him forward. With a slight push, he tumbled in after Trent, hitting the water with a loud splash.

I spun around to face the third guy. "You are next, Brent?"

He stared at me wide-eyed. "How do you know my name's Brent?"

Jon chuckled behind me. "Lucky guess," I replied dryly.

"Brent!" Trent shouted angrily from the water.

Before I could fully turn back, Brent sucker-punched me. I staggered, red surging through my vision as fury ignited deep inside. My fists clenched, energy humming dangerously through my veins.

"Easy," Jon whispered urgently, sensing my struggle. "Control it."

I exhaled slowly, forcing my anger down, replacing it with the cool, calming blue. Dolphin blue. Brent charged again, but this time I was ready. I snapped a quick left jab, feeling his nose crunch beneath my knuckles, then followed with a sharp right hook into his gut. Brent doubled over, gasping for breath as he dropped to one knee.

"Took you long enough," Jon said, smirking slightly as he stood and joined me on the pier. We walked past the two girls, their wide eyes and shocked expressions almost comical. I gave them a quick wink but said nothing.

Dad appeared from around the corner, casually munching an apple. "Hey guys," he said with a mouthful.

"Hey, Dad," I replied.

Jon nodded briefly. "Robert."

Dad nodded curtly in return. Their exchange was brief, loaded with the tension of two men who respected each other, but perhaps didn't fully trust one another yet.

"How'd the lesson go?" Dad asked, looking between us.

Neither of us answered.

A group of people were running our way, and they were angry. The lead guy was massive. His muscles bulged at the sleeves of his tight-fitting polo shirt as he ran. I couldn't be sure, but it seemed he was staring at me the whole time. Three or four clones of him were running right behind, followed by a couple of guys who looked like older versions of Trent, Chad, and Brent.

"Friends of yours?" Dad asked, eyeing the approaching group skeptically.

"Prentice's," Jon replied dryly.

"Uh... no," I protested quickly.

Dad raised an eyebrow at me.

"They're not my friends," I clarified.

Dad sighed heavily, turning to Jon. "Let me guess—these guys are the dads?"

"Bingo," Jon said, clearly amused despite the situation.

The big guy in front came to a pounding halt in front of Dad. He towered over Dad by a good four inches. He was even bigger than Jon and probably Hog back home.

"Hi there, big guy," Dad said as he stepped to his left, putting himself right in the middle of the pier.

The rest of the group came to a stop behind the big guy.

Jon stood next to Dad but said nothing.

"I want that young man arrested for assault," the big guy said.

"Who? Him?" Dad asked, pointing to me.

"Yes," the man replied.

"What for?" Dad asked him.

"I just told you," the man said, moving closer to Dad.

"And you are?" Dad asked him.

"Captain Michael Byrd," he answered.

"Branch?" Dad asked.

"Army," he replied, eyes staring at me.

"You serve in Iraq or Afghanistan?" Dad asked him.

I noticed the man's eyes glance toward Dad.

Another man wearing cargo pants and a perfectly fitted polo shirt stepped beside the big guy. Dakota must have been rubbing off on me. I instantly pegged him for a Fed.

"What is going on here, Mr. Byrd?" he asked.

Dad sighed loudly. I'm pretty sure he, too, realized he was a Fed. They tend to carry themselves with a confident attitude.

One of the adult Chads stepped up. He was a soft-looking man with a perfect beard. I could tell this guy never worked a hard day in his life.

"I know you," he said to Dad. "How do I know you?"

"Not sure," Dad shrugged.

"I want him arrested," the big guy said again, pointing to me.

31

"Why is that Mr. Byrd?" the Fed asked.

"I watched him assault Trent Kellerman and his friends," the big guy replied.

I started to say something, but Jon beat me to the punch.

"Did you see those boys grab hold of Prentice first?" he sneered, sliding his glasses to the top of his head. "Or did you see Late Night King here drive his speedboat and almost capsize us on the water?"

The big guy, Byrd, took a half-step back as he looked into Jon's eyes.

"It's true. I am the late-night king Clayton Kellerman," the adult Chad said. I try to keep a low profile, but you know…when people love your show, it's hard."

"Don't even know who you are, but I figured you're the moron driving that yacht around these waters," Jon said.

The man seemed insulted more at Jon not knowing who he was than the moron comment.

"Why is the FBI in Bimini with a Hollywood celebrity?" Dad said, interrupting the conversation.

The Fed smiled.

"Special Agent Joseph Liang," he said.

Dad said nothing.

"I'm afraid that would be because of me," a man said, coming through the growing crowd. He was a short, heavy-set man with glasses. He was sweating badly as he struggled to breathe in the heat.

"Senator Bradler," Dad said, acknowledging the short, fat man. Do you have a personal FBI escort?"

"I'm sorry, who are you?" Agent Liang asked.

"You're that Police Chief from the small town with the statue riot," Clayton Kellerman said proudly, smiling because he figured out who Dad was.

Dad said nothing.

"Chief Pendleton," Senator Bradler said.

Agent Liang's eyes flicked to Jon and then back to Dad. The agent's gaze lingered on Jon just a moment longer than necessary, and I noticed him swallow nervously, betraying recognition or perhaps fear. He clearly knew something. Something big. Something dangerous.

32

"What you did with the statue and the riots was excellent work," the agent commented.

"Excellent? He ticked a lot of Hollywood off," Kellerman laughed.

Dad said nothing.

"Agent Liang, please arrest that young man," Byrd insisted

"You didn't answer me," Dad told the big guy.

"What?" Byrd asked.

This was getting good. It was hard to follow but good.

"Did you serve in Iraq or Afghanistan?" Jon asked again for Dad.

Byrd hesitated. He was searching for an answer, meaning he didn't serve in either place. He answered the question by not answering the question.

"I…," he began.

"Agent Liang has no jurisdiction here. We're not in the United States," Dad added, making sure to lock eyes with the big guy.

"Then we'll go to the local police chief," the big guy replied.

"That would be me," came an accented voice.

Everyone turned toward the voice. A short, stocky man with deep brown skin and a commanding presence calmly strolled through the crowd. He wore a crisp blue button-down police shirt tucked neatly into dark cargo shorts, proudly displaying the embroidered patch on his chest read North Bimini Police. His casual stride radiated an easy confidence, and despite his stature, he carried an authority that immediately silenced the murmurs around him.

"A midget?" Clayton Kellerman snorted loudly, amusement clear in his voice.

The short man casually took another bite of his apple, completely ignoring the insult. Instead, he looked calmly toward my dad and Jon.

"Chief," Dad greeted him with a respectful nod.

"Chief Pendleton," the small man replied in his rich Bahamian accent, returning the nod. He shifted his attention to Byrd. "Now, what's the problem here?"

"That young man assaulted Trent Kellerman," Byrd said angrily, pointing aggressively toward me.

The Chief took another deliberate bite of his apple, eyes fixed steadily on Byrd.

"You're Chief Sands?" Agent Liang interrupted, clearly surprised by the diminutive officer's stature.

"I am," Sands answered evenly, unbothered.

"He's a midget," Kellerman laughed again, clearly amused by his own wit.

I rolled my eyes, amazed by the man's cluelessness.

Chief Sands glanced briefly at Kellerman before looking straight at Byrd. "I saw the entire incident clearly. This young man," he said, gesturing toward me with the half-eaten apple, "was defending himself."

"But...," Byrd started to protest.

"You heard the Chief," Dad interrupted firmly. "Now, please leave."

Byrd's eyes narrowed dangerously, anger simmering behind his gaze.

"Consider carefully how this ends, Byrd," Jon warned, his voice low and even.

Byrd hesitated briefly, looking from Jon to Dad, clearly weighing his options.

Chief Sands turned casually toward the dock, eyeing the enormous yacht. "Who owns that monstrosity?"

"That beauty is mine," Kellerman announced proudly, puffing out his chest.

"Of course it is," Sands replied with a faint smile. "I'll be impounding it."

"Impounding it? On what grounds?" Kellerman shouted indignantly.

"Oh, several," Chief Sands said nonchalantly, walking calmly toward the yacht. "Code violations, reckless boating, disturbing the peace...take your pick."

"Chief Sands," Senator Bradler interjected smoothly, "I'm sure we can find a reasonable solution."

"I already did," Sands replied coolly as he signaled to the officers nearby. A small army of blue-uniformed Bahamian police immediately began boarding Kellerman's yacht.

Byrd glared one last time at Dad before turning away with a frustrated growl. Kellerman scrambled after Sands, shouting protests as Bradler followed, sweating profusely. Agent Liang lingered behind briefly.

"You've made powerful enemies today, Chief," he warned Dad.

"Not the first time," Dad replied, shrugging calmly. "Won't be the last either."

The agent shook his head, then reluctantly joined the group retreating to the yacht.

Dad turned toward me, clearly exasperated. "Trouble finds you wherever you go, doesn't it?"

I grinned sheepishly. "Just lucky, I guess."

Jon snorted. Dad turned to him.

"Hey, I didn't raise him to turn out exactly like you," Jon laughed.

"Oh, nice one, Yoda," I teased Jon.

Jon glared at me and then turned back to Dad. "Permission to hit him?"

"Permission granted," Dad replied immediately, smiling. "Ouch!"

2
THE FIRE WITHIN

Jon Kane's House
Bimini, Bahamas
December 31, 2024

"Dad, your phone has been buzzing over and over for hours now," I told him.

He shrugged, not really caring.

I picked it up and read the text message out loud.

"It's from Hog. It says, what did you do down there? I'm getting calls from the FBI and Senator Hopper's office."

Dad laughed.

"I thought that guy's name was Liang on the dock?" I asked him.

"It is. Hopper is a Massachusetts Senator. Liang's office must have called him," he replied. "Hog's going to love dealing with this."

"You know he'll take it out on me when we get back," I told him.

"Well, you are dating his daughter," Dad smirked.

"Oh wait, nobody told me our little crayon had a girlfriend," Jon said as he entered the room.

"Little Crayon? Geez, it's like you've been talking with Franklin," I said. "He calls me crayon man all the time."

Dad spit out the water that he was drinking.

"No, he does not," he laughed.

"Oh yeah, and much more than that," I said.

"I like that kid," Jon added as he slid open the back door and stepped onto the patio. Dad and I followed.

It was a crisp Caribbean evening. The moon hung high in the starry sky like a ghostly orb of night. It cast a little bit of winter white over the backyard, accompanied by the chilly Christmas winds of the islands. His house overlooked a quiet island cove where the tourists didn't go, so you could enjoy the beautiful scenery peacefully.

Jon led us to a group of wooden lawn chairs in a circle around a stone firepit. He leaned down into the pit, about to set a fire, when he stopped and looked back at me. He smiled and sat down in a chair.

"Go on...crayon man," he said.

"Wait, what?" I said.

"I'm pretty sure he's telling you to start a fire," Dad added, taking a seat.

"A fire?" I asked.

"You know. The orange flames that give off heat and light," Jon smiled.

I looked at Dad.

"C'mon, rainbow Jedi," he smiled.

"I really wish you never knew," I sighed and stepped up to the firepit.

I heard the familiar pinging of a FaceTime call, but I didn't turn around.

"Crayon Man, island life treating you good?" Franklin's voice sounded.

"Seriously, Franklin?" I groaned, turned to see Jon holding my phone. He had a grin from ear to ear.

"Oh, c'mon. You're literally a walking color wheel. You should be grateful I didn't go with Sherwin-Williams or 'Rainbow Brite."

"You must be Franklin," Jon said, looking into the phone.

"That depends on who is asking," Franklin said, now on edge because a strange guy was using my phone to call him.

Jon smirked. "I liked this kid before. Now? Not so sure."

"He has that effect," I shrugged.

"I'm with...crayon man here, and he needs some encouragement with his homework," Jon told him turning the phone towards me.

"Franklin, what's up?" I said.

"There you are, crayon man," he replied. "Who was that old guy?"

"Old?" Jon asked.

"Oh, that's Yoda," I smiled. "He's my teacher."

37

"Ahh…your Jedi master," Franklin replied.

I nodded.

"Cool. He's like a surfing Jedi master, like Crush from Finding Nemo. Let's catch some waves, dude," he said into the phone.

"I don't like this kid," Jon said.

"Relax, big guy," Franklin chuckled. "You're basically Crush from Finding Nemo anyway."

Dad laughed.

Jon glared at me.

"Well," I shrugged, "at least he didn't call you Squirt."

Dad laughed again but Jon said nothing.

"You just said you like him, and I quote. I said he calls me crayon man, and you said I like this kid," I said, trying not to laugh.

Jon stared at me.

"Now he called you a big green surf turtle, and you don't like him," I laughed.

"If he's Crush, that makes you the colorful clownfish Marlin or the forgetful dummy Dory," Franklin added in the phone.

Dad laughed this time.

"Actually, I like this kid," Jon chuckled.

"You're not helping me, Frankie," I said.

Everyone laughed.

"Okay, start the fire," Jon said.

"Wait, he has to start a fire using nothing?" Franklin asked.

"He does, and he better hurry up. It's getting a little cold," Jon said.

"Sweet. I can call him Firestarter now," Franklin laughed.

"Okay, shut up, snowflake. Let's watch Crayon, man," Jon said.

"I'm no snowflake, man. No way," Franklin laughed. But I'll be quiet. I want to see Crayon Man go all Smoky the Bear."

"You know that bear puts the fires out," I said.

"Okay, yeah… you're right," Franklin laughed, realizing Smoky was the poster bear for stopping forest fires, not starting them. "My bad."

"Okay, Prentice, go ahead," Jon said.

I took a deep breath and turned back to the firepit. A group of dried-out branches was set up like a pyramid inside the middle. There were black char marks along the bricks from previous fires and a load of ashes from burned-out wood around the edges.

I focused on the bottom of the branches. I imagined a burst of sparks followed by flames catching the dried-out sticks, which resulted in a complete campfire.

Nothing happened.

I imagined a blast of red lasers erupting from my eyeballs and setting the sticks on fire. I knew I couldn't shoot lasers from my eyes... but I didn't think I could.

Nothing happened.

I sighed and looked up.

"Focus your mind and energy," Jon whispered.

Dad said nothing, and Franklin remained silent for once.

I leaned over, willing my eyes to stare at the bottom of the pit. My jaw muscles clenched, and my head began to throb. I clenched my fists, willing the fire to obey, but the flames refused me. I could feel the energy coiling inside, taunting me, demanding anger as its fuel. Is this all I am? I thought bitterly.

"You're straining your body. That's not going to work. Use the colors. Use your mind," Jon instructed.

I glanced at him

"I know," I whispered.

Jon exhaled loudly, shaking his head. "You know what your problem is?"

I clenched my jaw. "Please, enlighten me."

He smirked. "You're fighting fire instead of speaking its language."

I turned back to the pit. "And what language is that?"

"What's the first thing fire does when it's born?"

I frowned. "It sparks."

He leaned back in his chair, arms crossed. "Then stop trying to command it. Spark it."

I sighed and looked around the area. Colors. What color is fire? Red and orange. I scanned the area, searching for something to use—something red or orange. A light flashed out in the bay. A boat, a flashing red beacon. I focused on the distant red light.

I zeroed in on the colored light flashing. My heart began beating in rhythm with the light. Blood flowed through my body, and I felt a wave of red heat rising from within. My eyes turned back to the pit and tunneled in on the bottom of the branches. Focus.

My mind flashed to every moment my powers had worked. The rage at Macey, the chaos in Freetown Forest, the fury when those thugs tried to run me down. Fire only answered to hate.

I took a deep breath as the wave of heat rose and rose within.

I held my hand, ready to fire a blast of red fiery energy, and set the pit ablaze.

Nothing.

I took another deep breath and focused one more time. My fingers arched and spread wide.

Nothing.

"Darn it!" I shouted and walked away from the pit. Anger and frustration rose inside me.

I felt their eyes on me as I walked to the yard's edge overlooking the cove. The waves quietly slapped against the rocks below. I expected Jon or maybe Dad to walk over to me, but they didn't.

I can't even start a fire. How will I ever be able to control this? I remembered the fiery rage I felt when I soared out of the water and onto the deck of the Ennis. The power and energy I felt were tremendous when I picked up the crew and slammed them all down to the deck.

My mind drifted to the woods of Freetown Forest and the fight with the Boo Hags. The moment my friends needed me was when the angry energy grew and exploded from within. I rode the rainbow then. Just as I did when Macey was trying to hurt Rachel in the Minuteman Cemetery.

My powers came to me when I was angry and full of rage and hate. The fiery, profound red energy was always building through anger. What did that say for me? Was I going to go to the dark side? Was I going to become some rainbow version of

40

Darth Vader? I looked towards the sky, my eyes drifting to the bright moon, which hung in full glory.

Fire was red and angry so why can't anger spark it. Wait, that wasn't true, was it? Fire doesn't exist just to destroy. It's warmth. It's light.

Nobody said anything behind me, but I could feel them all staring at me. I could even sense Franklin from his cell phone. I closed my eyes, trying to think and figure out what was going wrong, but nothing came to mind.

My eyes lifted to the full moon, its silver glow painting the cove. I twisted my head, studying the orb. It was beautiful, powerful, bright, energetic, and white. I lifted my head.

Fire counters the darkness. It illuminates and brightens the night.

Fire is caused by a spark, often not red, orange, or yellow. The sparks are white, and white is a brilliant, energetic light full of goodness. Angels are usually shown in white because they represent purity and light against darkness. And just like that, the energy inside me shifted.

My eyes closed, but I still saw the moon hanging in the night. Its brightness held the darkness away. Fire is born of sparks. Sparks are white, not red. Energy sparked inside me. I felt it flowing from my toes through my body as warmth and calmness washed over me.

I spun and fired a glowing white fireball toward the firepit. The sizzling and crackling ball soared through the Bahamian night. I twisted my hand, and the ball arced upwards and then quickly sloped down, exploding into the firepit. The white-hot fire sparked at the bottom, which turned into flowing red-orange flames crackling away in the pit. The yard slowly illuminated with a warm, fiery glow of fire.

"My crayon, man," Franklin said on the phone.

Dad sat back, relaxing in his chair, sipping his lemonade. I looked at Jon.

"Well done, Prentice," he smiled.

"Okay, who got the marshmallows," Franklin asked.

***

41

Jack floated silently in the cove, barely disturbing the water's surface. The Caribbean heat clung to him, heavy and suffocating. *Too warm,* he thought. I won't last long here.

But he hadn't come for comfort. He had come to see if the rumors were true. A few months earlier, rumors spread in the non-human world about another kid that could harness the rainbow. Prentice Pendleton. Whispers that he was not only a mighty Rainbow Warrior but a powerful human, even for a boy, and he was surrounded by friends who were just as strong.

It was a coincidence that he learned the boy was in the Bahamas. He had come to the islands following a lead on the Winter King and wasn't looking for the boy. However, he had felt the surge of power earlier when the kid reached out to the dolphins and found the boy just as the confrontation was happening on the dock.

And as he watched Prentice ignite the fire, not with anger but with something else entirely. He knew he was powerful. The two men standing with him were also strong, but they didn't see the whole truth. The boy is more powerful than they realize

A shift in the water. A dolphin, circling. Jack barely registered it.

They'll come for him soon. This much power couldn't remain hidden for long.

He took one last glance at the boy and launched himself from the water, vanishing into the night.

3
THE GATHERING STORM

Capron Bay Middle School
Capron Bay, MA
January 3rd, 2025

"The fire pit burst into glowing flames. It was awesome," Franklin said as he took a bite from his sandwich.

"What changed?" Adam asked.

"I don't know. He said he'd tell me when he got back," Franklin replied.

"I talked to him last night," Lena said. "They were stuck at the Miami airport, and flights were backing up."

"Yeah. Have you seen what they're saying about the storm?" Dakota added.

"Storm of the century," Adam said.

"I've seen reports of up to four feet of snow," Franklin gasped.

"The biggest storm in the last hundred years," Dakota marveled.

"It's supposed to start Thursday night into Friday morning," Lena added. "Dad and   Captain Lynch are stressing out preparing for it."

"We've already got about eight inches left from last week's storm," Adam mentioned. If we get two or more feet, there will be nowhere to put the snow."

Ronnie Lynch appeared and sat down next to Lena at the lunch table. Everyone looked at him, not sure what to make of him. He seemed more friendly over the last few months, but they still didn't trust him.

"Hey, Ronnie," Lena said.

"Hey," he said, looking around the cafeteria.

"You hiding from something," Franklin asked him.

43

Ronnie looked at each of them, not saying a word. He seemed nervous.

"Ronnie?" Lena asked him.

Ronnie hesitated, his eyes flicking toward the cafeteria doors like he expected someone to walk in at any second.

"You guys need to be careful around Peter," he muttered.

"We haven't even seen him since Halloween," Dakota said.

Adam snorted. "Well, *I* saw him—right before I introduced his no-no squares to my fist."

Franklin nearly choked on his sandwich laughing. "Dude, that *never* gets old."

Ronnie gave them a half-smirk but quickly sobered. "I'm serious. He's got *family* here now. Two cousins. And they're not like him—they're worse."

"Worse *how*?" Lena asked, frowning.

"One of them is some kind of black belt," Ronnie said. "And the other? Let's just say... *I don't think they fight fair.*"

"What's their deal?" Adam asked, growing uneasy.

"Bo and Hu Sun," Ronnie said.

Franklin snorted. "*Who?*"

Ronnie exhaled sharply. "Yeah, yeah, I know. Their names are Bo and Hu. Spelled H-U."

"Wait, so their last name is *Sun*?" Adam asked, narrowing his eyes.

Ronnie nodded. "Peter's aunt married some rich Chinese guy. They just moved here from Beijing."

Dakota frowned. "You think they're tied to that new Chinese tech company in Boston?"

Ronnie shrugged. "No clue. But I do know Peter has been hyping them up for weeks. Like, way more than usual."

"How bad can they be?" Franklin said, still smirking.

Ronnie leaned in, voice dropping lower. "I met them once. There's something... *off* about them."

"Off like 'weird' or off like 'dangerous'?" Lena asked.

Ronnie hesitated, scanning the room again. "Both."

Before anyone could respond, the cafeteria doors swung open. Peter Brown strolled in, a smug grin already plastered across his face. Flanking him were two unfamiliar figures, a boy

44

and a girl, their matching ice-blue eyes almost glowing beneath the fluorescent lights.

The group fell silent.

"Okay," Franklin muttered. "The eyes? That's creepy."

As if sensing their stares, Peter turned toward them, smirk widening. He whispered something to his cousins. The boy gave a slow, mocking wave.

Capron Bay Police Dept.
Emergency Management Office
Capron Bay, MA

Detective Hog Sheridan exhaled heavily, resisting the urge to slam his head into the table. He had been listening to these so-called "experts" bicker for three hours.

Biggest storm in a century, and they were still arguing over whether to call it a "bomb cyclone" or a "historic blizzard."

Across the room, Brother Kiernan caught his eye, smirking as if he knew exactly what Hog was thinking.

The door swung open. Doc Eddings strolled in, wearing his usual top hat and thick wool scarf, as if he had stepped straight out of a Charles Dickens novel. Without a word, Hog slid the latest weather report across the table.

Doc picked it up, eyebrows lifting. "I don't like the term *bomb cyclone*."

Hog smirked. "Snowmageddon?"

"Mega Blizzard?" Brother Kiernan offered.

"Bombageddon!" Brother Kiernan giggled.

The Priest chuckled.

Doc just sighed. "You two done?"

"I vote 'Frozard'—frozen blizzard," Hog added, barely keeping a straight face.

"Detective Sheridan," Doc warned.

"Sorry," Hog sighed. "I'm just *really* tired of this meeting."

"So am I," a new voice interjected.

The room fell silent as Chief Pendleton walked in. He moved through the room with purpose, dropping into a chair

45

beside Hog. As he passed, he casually reached out and yanked Hog's ear.

Hog grunted but didn't react.

"Finally, back from your Bahamian vacation, huh?" Hog muttered.

The Chief didn't even glance at him. "Dropped Prentice off. Came straight here." He winked.

The mayor leaned forward. "Okay, people. Enough nonsense. Where do we stand?"

Silence.

The Chief turned to the Harbor Master. "Jason, is the Coast Guard on standby?"

"Yes, sir," Jason Rivera confirmed. "They're recommending we clear the harbor completely."

"Make it happen," the Chief ordered. He shifted to the town's emergency manager. "Ortiz, what's the latest forecast?"

Ortiz scanned his notes. "Storm begins Wednesday night at 10 PM. Winds building up to 75 miles per hour. The bay will see the worst impact first."

Captain Lynch nodded. "Those waves are going to be dangerous."

"Then we make sure no one stays on their boats," the Chief said. "Jason, Lynch, coordinate that."

The room moved quickly from chaos to order. With the Chief giving direct assignments, plans got made instead of debated.

"Mr. Lawrence, how are we on plows and salt trucks?" he asked the Town Transportation director.

"Our full fleet is ready to go. Luckily, our salt supplies have built up over the last two years, so we haven't needed to use them very much," Adam Lawrence answered.

"Okay. I want a complete parking ban. Detective Sheridan, you and Mr. Ortiz, ensure the media promotes a full parking ban beginning tomorrow night at 10 PM. I want split shifts for every department, from the Police to the town recreational department, beginning tomorrow at noon. Each shift comes in four hours early," he said.

Everyone nodded.

"Where is Fire?" he asked.

"They're prepping all their equipment to ensure everything is working properly," the mayor replied.

"Okay, I want them involved in going around the town enforcing the parking ban and knocking on doors," the Chief said.

The mayor nodded.

"We're going to need the school department as well," the Chief said.

"We've canceled school Wednesday, Thursday, and Friday," Mark Vickers replied. Mark was the town's superintendent.

"Okay, but I want the high school and middle school complex fully prepped for emergency shelters. Work with Mr. Lawrence to prepare the complex," the Chief said.

"If we have to pay staff overtime to help out, that's fine," the mayor added.

Mr. Vickers nodded.

"Thomas," the Chief said to Brother Kiernan. "You and Doc go to Hope Manor. Meet with staff there and determine if we need to act early and move the patients," the Chief said.

"Where will we move them?" asked Theresa Morgan, the Town Council President's assistant. She had attended the meeting for Ms. Sorenson, who was tied up at other meetings.

"If we have to, we'll move them to the schools," the Chief replied.

"Why would we do that?" she asked.

"The nursing home is old, and if the power goes out, they will not be able to repair it quickly," Brother Kiernan interrupted. The schools are equipped to handle the patients if need be."

"Okay, but how are we going to move them?" she asked.

"We'll get their families to help out," Brother Kiernan began to say.

"That is a liability we're not ready to handle," Ms. Morgan interrupted. "We should just leave them alone."

"Captain Lynch," the Chief said.

"Sir?"

"Make a note that Ms. Morgan, who is representing the absent Town Council President, advises leaving Hope Manor

47

residents at the facility so they can possibly die," the Chief ordered.

Captain Lynch was typing on a tablet.

"I didn't say leave them to die," Ms. Morgan protested.

"That's what could happen if they are left there. Do you want the liability for that?" Doc interjected angrily, which surprised everyone at the table.

Ms. Morgan said nothing. She just shook her head.

"Thomas and I will handle the nursing home," Doc added. "We'll make sure they are safe. Right Thomas?"

"Yes, sir," the Priest replied.

"Spread the word to everyone in town; if they need to, they can go to the schools for shelter," Mayor Travis added.

"The grocery stores are already depleted," Hog added.

"Hungry?" Brother Kiernan asked him.

Everyone laughed.

"Well…yes, but that's not what I meant, sunshine," Hog replied, and Brother Kiernan smiled.

"Can we purchase more supplies in the next few days?" the superintendent of schools asked.

"I'm sure supplies are going to be tough to come by up and down the East Coast," Mayor Travis replied.

"Restaurants in town and nearby will be closed for several days," the Chief said.

"How will that help us?" the Harbormaster asked.

"We need to contact them and tell them the town will purchase all of their supplies if they bring them to the school," the Chief said. It will help us and them."

"We'll pay for them to help prepare it if need be and for their staff to help out," the mayor added.

"This is going to be a big bill," Ms. Morgan said, her words sounding annoyed. "How are we going to afford this?"

"We can get rid of your position," Hog laughed.

Doc Eddings kicked him under the table.

Ms. Morgan glared at the big police officer.

"Since the Governor has declared a state of emergency, the state will provide state and federal funds, Ms. Morgan," the mayor added. "I'm sure you are aware of that."

"Of course," she lied.

The Chief smiled at the minor insult the mayor had just thrown at his rival's assistant. Her boss, Penny Sorenson, was the President of the Town Council and wanted to become Mayor.

"Let's get this done, people," the Chief said.

"Will we meet again later?" Ms. Morgan asked.

"No. Meetings waste time. Let's get to work," the Chief replied, leaving the room.

Hog, Doc, Brother Kiernan, and Captain Lynch followed the Chief out of the room. Everyone else remained at the table.

Ms. Morgan sat stiffly in her chair, watching the departing figures of Chief Pendleton, Hog, and Brother Kiernan. She turned toward the mayor.

"Mr. Mayor, why is the Priest included in decision-making?" she asked, voice cool.

The mayor met her gaze evenly. "Thomas volunteers his time to the town and actually gets things done."

"And why is he always with Chief Pendleton's son and his friends?"

The mayor's eyes narrowed. "Thomas isn't much older than them. And with his skin pigmentation disorder, he's been shunned by plenty of adults. Or..." He let the silence stretch. "Is his condition something you have a problem with?"

Ms. Morgan's face flushed. "Absolutely not."

The mayor nodded, pushing back his chair. "Good. Then let's not question people who are helping, shall we?"

4
RIVALS, RAINBOWS AND FROSTY

Capron Middle School
Capron Bay, MA
January 3rd, 3:30 PM

Dakota dribbled left before faking a shot. Franklin took the bait, leaping to block it. The second his feet left the ground, he knew he'd been played. Dakota smirked, shifting to the left for the easy bucket.
Whack!

A mittened hand came out of nowhere, swatting the ball into the frozen grass. Rachel landed just in front of him, balancing carefully on the slick court.

"Get that fluff out of here," she gloated.

"I didn't see you there, or I'd have faked you out too," Dakota huffed.

"Yeah, right," Adam snorted, rolling onto the court in his all-weather wheelchair.

"Please, you'd have bricked it anyway," Lena teased.

"Dude, you couldn't hit water if you fell out of a boat," Franklin laughed.

"What?! Are you nuts?" Dakota shot back.

"Nah, they're just being nice," Adam smirked.

Dakota spun around, looking for the ball to prove them wrong—

Crack!

The basketball slammed into the side of his head, sending him stumbling.

Laughter erupted from the edge of the court.

They turned to see Peter Brown, flanked by his new sidekicks, grinning like a pack of jackals.

50

"What was that for?" Dakota growled, still holding the side of his head.

"Not nice!" Franklin snapped, taking a step forward, Rachel grabbed his arm, stopping him.

"Oh, come on, Dakota. It's just a game," Peter smirked. "Right?"

Lena crossed her arms. "Is that what you told yourself when you cried like a baby on Halloween?"

Peter stiffened, glancing at his cousins. His smirk faltered for a split second before snapping back into place.

"Did you tell them about that, Peter?" Franklin started— Crack!

An ice ball struck Franklin just above his right eye. He dropped to a knee with a grunt, a thin trickle of blood running down his temple.

Hu Sun, still packing another icy projectile, snickered.

"That wasn't nice, you jerk!" Lena shouted.

Hu's eyes darkened. "Watch your mouth."

His sister, Bo, stepped up, her cold gaze locking onto Lena. "He won't hit a girl. But I will."

Lena didn't back down. "Funny, I thought he was the girl."

Adam choked back a laugh.

"Told you they were wise guys," Peter muttered to his cousins.

Hu grabbed Franklin's foot and yanked him back.

Rachel lunged to stop him—Bo shoved her, sending her crashing into Lena. Both girls hit the ground hard, Lena's face scraping against the ice.

Peter moved in, giving Franklin a quick kick.

"Tip him over," Peter sneered, gesturing at Adam's wheelchair. "Let's see him try to get up."

Hu stepped toward Adam, grabbing the chair's armrest— Snarl!

A golden blur leaped into Adam's lap, bared fangs snapping inches from Hu's hand.

Druss.

The Golden Retriever's growl was low and dangerous, eyes locked onto Hu like a predator scenting prey.

51

Hu staggered back, his face draining of color.

"Making friends, Franklin?" I called, strolling onto the court, my hands deep in my pockets.

Peter stiffened. His cousins turned to size me up.

"This him?" Hu asked, sizing me up.

Peter nodded.

"Druss, with me," I said.

The golden hopped down from Adam's lap but stayed close, still watching Hu.

I stopped a few feet away, locking eyes with Peter. "How many times are we going to do this?"

Peter clenched his fists but said nothing.

"He's not so tough," Bo said, tilting her head, her dark eyes studying me. Then she smirked. "Cute, though."

Lena shifted slightly.

"Oh, I see. You two are a couple," Bo said mockingly, making air quotes.

Lena bristled. "What's that supposed to mean?"

Bo just laughed.

"Who are you?" I asked.

"No, that's not Hu. That is," Franklin interjected, pointing at Hu.

Peter suddenly lurched forward, landing face-first in the snow.

"I've had enough of you, Peter," Dakota growled, fists clenched.

"Is everything okay here?"

We all turned to see Mrs. Ryder approaching, hands in her winter jacket.

"Hi, Mrs. Ryder," I said casually.

"Prentice, we missed you in school today." She eyed Peter warily.

"Just got back, ma'am. Flights were delayed everywhere."

"I see." Her gaze swept the court. "Everything alright?"

I looked at Peter, who was just pushing himself up. "Just a competitive game of basketball, ma'am."

She didn't look convinced but nodded. "Peter, let's not start your cousins off on the wrong foot."

Peter forced a smirk. "Of course not, Mrs. Ryder."

"Alright then. Let's end the game here," she said.

"Who is?" Franklin asked.

Rachel burst out laughing.

I shook my head with a grin. "See you tomorrow, Mrs. Ryder."

She lingered for a second before walking off. The rest of my friends followed.

I paused for a moment longer.

Bo was still staring at me, unblinking. "We'll be seeing each other soon," she said, her voice smooth as ice.

Something about her sent a chill up my spine.

"Looking forward to it," I said flatly before turning to leave.

Headquarters
Sheridan House
4 P.M.

We all sipped from the hot chocolate Dakota made for everybody as we sat around HQ. As soon as we got out of the cold and snow, Dak set himself to making hot cocoa. None of us knew what he did to it when he made it, but it was always better than when anyone of us made it. I even gave Druss some in his water bowl, but he only took the occasional lap with his tongue because it was too hot.

I put my mug down on the table and looked up the group.

"So, what was that all about? I asked them.

"Those two are Peter's cousins," Franklin muttered slurping away at his whipped cream topped mug of cocoa.

"I gathered that from Mrs. Ryder's questions," I replied.

"Ronnie came to us at lunch today," Rachel informed me.

"You think we can trust him?" Adam inquired, interrupting her.

"He did come warn us about these two," Lena mentioned.

"What did he say?" I asked.

"He told us these two were Peter's cousins who just moved here. Their Dad is working for some new tech company. My Dad said there is a new company starting up and everyone isn't hapy about it," Adam stated.

"He said they were bad news and told us we should be careful around them," Dakota added.

"He did seem genuinely concerned," Rachel agreed.

"And scared," Adam mentioned.

"I can see why," I told them. "I sensed something off with the girl."

"That's Bo," Franklin said. "Her brother is Hu."

"And that's what Ronnie said," Lena added. "That something was off with Bo."

"We'll have to keep an eye on them," Adam remarked.

We all nodded in agreement.

"Forget them for now," Dakota declared. "What happened in the Bahamas? Franklin said you met Yoda."

Everyone giggled for a minute.

"I kind of did, I guess. His name is Jon Kane," I grinned.

"Was he like some mystical immortal?" Adam laughed.

"No, not really," I laughed. "He was more like mix between a surfer and skateboarding dude."

"Yeah, he did remind me of someone who likes to say hang ten dude," Franklin laughed.

"Did he teach you anything?" Lena wanted to know.

"He did. He taught me quite a bit actually," I nodded.

Everyone waited for me to explain more.

"He taught me the true power of the colors comes from emotions," I told them all.

"No duh," Franklin shrugged.

"Yeah, we already knew that" Adam smirked.

"I know, I know," I nodded. "But he showed me ways to control it, use it, harness it so I can be better and stronger with them."

"Did he talk about you being Atlantean?" Lena wanted to know.

The mention of Atlantis got everyone's attention, and it brought me back to the moment I learned of my connection to Atlantis. After we had freed the crew of the Capron Bay ghost ship, Doc had been researching everything he could about the colors and the legend of the rainbow warrior.

He had discovered the possible connection to Atlantis and Grammy reluctantly confirmed that legend was true but what the world believed about Atlantis was not accurate. History tells us Atlantis is a ring of islands somewhere in the Atlantic Ocean and the society was far more advanced than perhaps even current society.

It was destroyed by an earth-shattering eruption of a volcano. Historians and Archeologists have searched for it since the Greek philosopher Plato first wrote about it. It is one of the most famous legends throughout human history and nobody knows if it ever truly existed.

Then Grammy told Lena and I the true story of Atlantis. The island chain was called Oypanio which means rainbow in ancient Greek. The islands served as the base for Atlantis, which was a highly advanced ship that travelled the world keeping. The ship contained Rainbow Warriors who used the power of the colors to keep peace throughout the world's many civilizations.

The enemies of the rainbow warriors launched an attack leading to the volcanic eruption destroying the Atlantis and almost all the rainbow warriors with it. Survivors would band together around the globe trying to hold on to their culture and history but eventually, those who can control the rainbow disappeared into history.

"So, what did he say?" Adam asked, drawing me back to the moment.

I sipped some more hot chocolate and placed the mug down and nodded for Adam to pull up the Atlantis details we had worked on for months. A picture of the Oypanio Islands appeared on the big screen.

"As we know, the Rainbow Warriors were from all over the world. They came from every culture and society. I don't know for sure where I'm from, but the family traced its roots back to at least ancient Ireland," I told them.

"We already knew that" Dakota said.

"I know, just trying to level set since we haven't talked about this in a long time," I answered.

Everyone nodded and waited for me to explain some more.

"It seems a lot of the warriors' history since the Atlantis was destroyed is lost. As the numbers grew smaller and smaller, the truth about them disappeared too," I told them.

"Makes sense," Adam interrupted.

I nodded and continued.

"There are legends about who could harness the rainbow, but nobody knows for sure if they're true," I added.

"Like who?" Dakota asked.

"We already knew about Leonidas and his 300," I replied. "Jon believes that is true. There is evidence to nearly confirm that. He mentioned King Arthur."

"Wouldn't it be cool if you were a descendant of King Arthur," Franklin interjected.

"It's Uther," Adam clarified.

"Who is Uther," Franklin asked.

"Arthur's real name is Uther," he informed Franklin.

"What?" Franklin looked shocked at this revelation.

"Its true. His name was Uther. Through the years, it became Arthur," Adam said.

He looked like we had just shot his puppy. Mollie rubbed his arm trying to reassure him everything was okay.

"It's okay, It's just his name. Everything else about the legend is the same," Adam whispered rubbing his other arm.

Franklin yanked his arm away when everyone broke into laughter. His face turning bed red.

"The last rumors of someone who could harness the rainbow circulated at the beginning of the 19th century. It was a young girl but the rumors faded away and it was assumed she either didn't exist or was killed," I interrupted the laughter.

"Who is the group going around killing them all? I mean is there a Darth Vader hit squad out there?" Rachel inquired.

"Nobody seems to know," I shook my head.

"And these forces have already tried to take you out," Lena grimaced.

I nodded.

"But you have the Supernatural Squad by your side," Franklin bellowed.

Pendleton House
Capron Bay,
January 3rd, 9:00 PM

"School is canceled for the rest of the week," Dad told us. Carolyn let out a tired cheer as she lay her head on her pillow. Druss, lying on her bed, wagged his tail as if he understood that school would be closed for at least three days.

"Is it going to be that bad?" I asked him.

"Right now, this is the biggest winter storm to ever come this way," he replied.

I nodded, not sure what to expect. I hadn't seen too many snowstorms in my life.

"And it's going to hit us head-on," he grimaced.

"What can we do to help?" I asked.

He glanced at me and smiled.

"What?" I asked.

"Most twelve-year-olds would be looking to have fun during the storm," he said.

"We will at some point," I said. "But, if it's going to be that bad, everyone will need to help."

"Yes, sir," he said. That's why the government has already declared a state of emergency, which allows the use of Federal resources to help."

"What does that mean?" I asked him.

"It means Agent Mason is arriving in the morning to supplement the police department," Dad said.

"Cool," I said. "He'll be able to help a lot."

His cell phone rang, and he opened it. I couldn't tell who was on the other end, but Dad nodded in agreement to whoever it was.

"Can we get enough beds in time?" he asked.

He waited for an answer.

"Okay, I want it done tomorrow," he said, glancing at me. And add a bunch of kids who will help him."

He turned towards me when he hung it up.

57

"You have your task tomorrow," he said.

I waited for more information.

"You and your...squad," he smiled. "You guys are going to help pack up the residents at the nursing home and get them to the high school. We don't think the home can withstand the storm, so we're getting them out ahead of time."

"All of them?" I asked.

He nodded.

"It's not going to be easy. We have some memory care residents and some hospice patients," he said.

"What's hospice?" I asked. I knew the memory care patients were those with dementia who needed extra care because they didn't remember many things. Mom worked with many of them.

He sat down on the couch and looked at me.

"Hospice patients are those in the end stages of their lives, and people are just there to make their lives a little easier during..."

"The end," I interrupted.

He nodded.

I looked at Carolyn and Druss lying on the bed. Both could help us do that.

"We can help. All the guys will be glad to," I said.

He nodded.

"I'll ask Anyika to help, too," Dad added. "She's really good with that stuff."

"And you know she'll keep us in line," I laughed.

"Oh, I know she will," he laughed. "Doc and Brother Kiernan will also be there to help you guys. Rachel and Adam's parents are helping us organize the food and other needs at the school."

"What about the Reservation?" I asked.

"Chief Tackna and Agent Mason will get that all squared away," he said. "The Chief thinks it is best if they come to the high school, too."

"So, the whole town will be at the school?" I asked him.

"Pretty much," he nodded. The expression on his face looked odd.

"What else?" I asked.

58

He looked at me and shook his head in anger and frustration.

"I may need you to be Rudolph at one point," he said.

"What?" I asked.

"If something goes wrong and someone gets left out there in the middle of this mega storm, I may need you to..." he began.

"Play Rudolph the red-nosed reindeer and get them," I said, smiling now that I got his reference to Rudolph. He wanted me to use my abilities if I needed to.

He nodded.

"I can do that," I said.

"But you shouldn't have to," he replied.

"You said it's only if things go wrong," I said.

He looked at me.

"Things always go wrong."

The small, nimble figure crouched on the oak branch, watching the boy inside.

Prentice Pendleton. The rumors had been true. A boy who could harness the full power of the colors.

And Chernobog wanted him dead.

Jack Frost had come to see the truth for himself. Now, as he clung to the frozen tree, the reality settled into his bones like the winter wind.

He had never feared anyone before.

But something about this boy...

Something about his power...

Jack exhaled, mist curling in the night air. He needed to make a choice.

Would he follow orders?

Or would he risk everything—

For a war that wasn't his.

A kid who was a rainbow warrior? No way. He was several hundred years old and had never encountered a kid with that kind of power. There had been rumors about a girl with the powers a century ago, but she was never found. Chernobog had crushed the village with a brutal winter storm and sent the creatures of the winter God to finish the survivors off.

He shuttered at the thought of Chernobog. He went by many names: the King of Darkness, the King of Winter, and even the King of the Dead. He was pure evil. He heard the name Prentice Pendleton being whispered among the fairy folk, but he didn't believe the rumors. He didn't believe them until he heard Chernobog wanted the boy dead. He decided to come see the boy for himself.

As he entered the skies above the town, he felt tremendous energy and power in the air. It was like a raging sun burning bright in the rainbow world. The power sparked in many places throughout the small community where the kid spent a lot of time, but the energy pulsing from the kid's home was a beacon in the night, drawing him. As he came closer to the house, he got the bad feeling he was being drawn in like a moth to a bug zapper, but he had to see for himself.

Now, as he crouched in the tree, the ice flowing through his veins felt the sudden warmth of the rainbow warrior. The rumors of a boy being a true warrior of the colors weren't rumors anymore. This human kid was the real deal. He swallowed hard and, for the first time in a long time, felt a wave of fear wash over his body.

Or was it something else? A pang of guilt mixed with hope. He looked at his hands and, for a moment, thought he saw the icy skin shimmer in the moonlight. He looked up, and the boy was now staring out the window right in his direction. There was no way he could see him. Humans could not see his kind. They could not see him unless he chose to reveal himself to people. Even the kid's power could not break that barrier. He knew that, but he couldn't shake the feeling Prentice Pendleton was looking right at him.

He steadied himself, trying to control his breathing. He knew Chernobog would be sending for him. Even though he despised the King of the Dead, he was one of his assassins. The executioner that winter always brought with it. His victims would wake up to a garden silvered with ice where crystalline white replaces the browns and reds of fall. Tree branches would glisten and shine like diamonds, and their victims would slowly turn to ice with them. They would freeze in their last moments, not understanding what was happening. Once the ice formed over their entire body, they would burst into thousands of pieces, never to be seen again.

He always felt for his victims. He didn't think what he did to them was painful. At least, he hoped not. It wasn't his choice to kill them. He never wanted to kill anyone, but it was a bargain struck a long time ago. He had no choice.

Whoosh! The sound brought him out of his trance, and he returned to the house. The boy had opened the window and was sniffing the air. The winter warrior froze in place and held his breath. He didn't want the boy to see his breath as it left his mouth, but then he realized it wasn't like the humans. He had nothing warm inside him to meet the cold air. He was numb inside, he realized, as sadness crept over him now.

Howls erupted in the distance, and inhuman cries of rage and hunger began to sound in the surrounding forests. He shivered, knowing the creatures of winter and darkness were on the move. They were all coming here. They would use the cover of the coming storm to tear the city apart and everyone in it. It had been done with a cold, calculating strategy numerous times before, but it may take work this time.

Prentice was powerful. An idea began to form in his mind. His small eyes and smooth, cold skin shifted as a dubious smile appeared across his face. It was a long shot, and he wasn't sure he could pull it off, but he had to try.

He leaped from the tree and soared into the night sky as fast as he could. He wondered if the kid had seen him leave the tree as he glanced back at the house. If he had, there was no sign of it, so he turned and flew towards the stars to make some plans.

WHAM!

Something slammed into his body, sending him into a wild spin. The stars swirled around in all directions as he plummeted back to Earth. He closed his eyes, focusing his mind and body, and lifted his arms, slowing his fall. He came to a complete stop, hovering fifty feet above the ground. He spun around to look down at what had hit him.

"Why are you spying on me?" a voice asked from the ground.

A figure appeared from underneath the trees. His mind struggled to understand what he was seeing. The Pendleton kid was standing there glaring back at him. The boy's breath formed a misty cloud in the cold night, but he could see the fire in the kid's eyes.

"You can...you can see me?" he asked.

Prentice said nothing.

"How is that possible?" he whispered to himself. His mind raced, trying to figure it out. No human could see him. They've never been able to see a fairy unless they wanted humans to. He glided to the ground and landed in thick snow. His feet made no sound as they crunched into the hardened snow.

"I mean you no harm," he said, holding his palms up. He felt the rainbow warrior's eyes studying him, which made him nervous.

"I'm not so sure about that," Prentice replied. "You wouldn't have been spying on me."

"I wasn't spying," he answered.

"Hiding in a tree and watching me through a window isn't spying?" Prentice asked.

He thought about that for a moment.

"I...I see how that looks, but" he began but stopped talking when he noticed a small red ball of energy building in Prentice's open palm.

"You really going to shoot that at me?" he asked.

"Who are you?" Prentice asked. "And why were you spying on me."

"I wasn't spying on you," he said again. He thought about fleeing into the night again, but he wasn't sure if he could without Prentice knocking him out of the sky again.

The glowing energy grew larger in Prentice's hands.

"Who are you?" Prentice asked again.

He flung his hands up towards Prentice. Ice blasts flew from his hands, cutting through the cold night.

Prentice fired the glowing red energy, which quickly shattered the icy projectiles and slammed into him. He felt his feet leave the ground as he was thrown backward, slamming into a thick tree. He slumped to the ground, trying to breathe through the pain. The rainbow warrior reared back, ready to fire another blast of power.

"Jack," he yelled.

Prentice stopped and glared at him.

"What?" Prentice asked.

"Jack," he grimaced, struggling to his feet.

Prentice stood ready to fire again.

"My name...is Jack Frost."

5
THE KING OF THE DEAD

Syracuse, NY
January 3rd, 2025
9:30 P.M.

The heavy wooden doors groaned on their iron hinges as the man pushed them open, allowing the winter wind to howl through the entryway like a spectral wail. Snow swirled around his boots as he stepped inside and slammed the doors shut, cutting off the shrieking storm.

A deep, frigid silence settled over the castle's stone halls. He inhaled the icy air, letting it seep into his bones like a long-lost lover. This was home. This was power. Syracuse had been his domain for centuries—not because of the people or the history, but because it was the coldest, snowiest place in America.

It suited him.

He adjusted his thick woolen coat and moved forward, his heavy boots echoing across the stone floors. The castle, Crno Castle, had stood here longer than history remembered.

As he ascended the winding staircase, a golden glow flickered to life with each step, cast by ancient torches mounted in iron sconces—except they weren't torches at all. Modern light bulbs, disguised to maintain the illusion of the old ways. He sneered at the thought. A necessary compromise.

The world had changed, but fear...fear was eternal.

He reached the third floor, stepping into a vast chamber unlike the rest of the castle. Rows of sleek monitors flickered, data scrolling across them as teams of operatives worked in silence. The walls were lined with high-tech surveillance equipment—a jarring contrast to the ancient stone that housed it.

A short, overweight man sat slumped on an expensive leather couch, sipping a steaming mug of hot chocolate. He looked up and offered a half-hearted wave.

Chernobog's lip curled in disgust.

"Senator Bradler. To what do I owe the displeasure?"

64

The Senator scrambled to his feet, his face slick with sweat despite the chill. "I—I thought it best to bring the news in person."

Chernobog stepped forward, handing his coat to a silent servant. "I'm listening."

Bradler wiped his forehead. "Agent Liang's nephew has already contacted the boy. We now have confirmation that Prentice Pendleton will be in Capron Bay when the storm hits."

Chernobog's expression remained unreadable. "I already knew that."

"Y-yes, but we also discovered something...useful." The Senator licked his lips nervously. "He has a...love interest."

That got his attention. Chernobog's piercing gaze locked onto the sweating politician. "Go on."

"Lena Sheridan. Daughter of a Detective. It appears she is...important to him."

The room fell silent. Then, slowly, a grin spread across Chernobog's face.

Bradler's voice grew stronger, emboldened by the King's reaction. "There are also his friends. A tight-knit group but they can be used as leverage."

Chernobog nodded. "And the government response?"

"The Governor has declared a state of emergency. The FBI is sending a disaster response team, led by Agent Liang."

Chernobog turned toward the massive screen on the far wall. Satellite imagery of the looming blizzard filled the display. It would be the perfect cover. The town would be isolated. Cut off. Trapped.

A sultry voice interrupted his thoughts.

"The creatures of the frost are already in place. Some have arrived in the woods. Others will come with the storm."

Bradler flinched as a tall, willowy woman glided into the room, her hair as white as frozen mist, her eyes like shards of ruby. She wore a luxurious fur coat, tied at the waist, and carried herself with the grace of a winter storm in human form.

Chernobog's expression softened. "Akka."

His sister. The Queen of Ice.

She ignored Bradler completely, stepping toward her brother. "We are ready."

65

A shrill ringing shattered the moment. A servant answered, listened for a brief second, then hesitantly handed the phone to Chernobog.

"My lord," a voice crackled through the receiver.

Chernobog sighed. "Alpha."

Senator Bradler visibly tensed. He and Alpha despised each other.

Chernobog listened for barely five seconds before hanging up.

"I am tired of his excuses."

Akka folded her arms. "I told you to dispose of him after the Boo Hags failed."

The King of the Dead merely poured himself a glass of ice-cold water. "We have Alpha. The demon army. Agent Liang. The creatures of frost. The worst storm in a century. The Pendleton boy doesn't stand a chance."

"I sent Frost just in case," he added.

Akka stiffened. "Frost?"

Bradler looked between them, confused. "I thought Frost worked for you."

Chernobog swirled the water in his glass. "He does."

Akka's expression darkened. "He has no loyalty."

"He does what he is told," Chernobog replied evenly.

"He obeys only because you hold his sister hostage," Akka spat. "One day, brother...he will turn on you."

Chernobog laughed.

"When that day comes, dear sister, I will crush him."

Bradler shifted nervously. "If he's that much of a threat, why not just...kill him?"

Chernobog took a slow sip of water. "Because nature forbids it."

The Senator's face twisted in confusion.

The King of the Dead set his glass down and smiled.

"But if he fails? Well...our Frost problem solves itself."

Pendleton House
Capron Bay,
January 3rd, 10:00 PM

"Wait a second." I narrowed my eyes at the kid standing in the snow. "Did you just say your name is Jack Frost?"

He nodded.

"Like, snowy Jack Frost?" I asked him as I closed my hands, pushing the energy away.

"Snowy?" he asked me.

"Yeah, the flying snow and ice wizard?" I asked him.

"I'm not a wizard," he replied.

"So, you're not Jack Frost then?" I asked.

"Yes, I am Jack Frost," he answered.

"You just said you're not a wizard," I stated.

"I'm not," he said.

"Then, you're not Jack Frost," I added.

"Where did you ever get the idea Jack Frost was a wizard?" he asked me.

"I don't know," I shrugged. "Just always thought Jack Frost was an ice wizard."

He shook his head.

"Well, he uses magic to create snow and ice," I added.

"Are you a wizard?" he asked.

"No," I declared.

"Neither am I, and I never have been," he said.

I stared at him.

"You really, Jack Frost?" I inquired.

He nodded.

I crossed my arms. "Prove it."

Jack smirked. WHAM.

A bolt of blue-white ice blasted from his fingertips—a streak of pure frozen energy. I barely dodged as it slammed into a pine tree, shaking snow from the branches.

I glared at the kid in front of me.

"You trying to kill me?"

"Just a demonstration," he laughed.

"Really?" I exhaled. My hands flickered red-hot for a second, but I forced myself to stay calm. "So...why were you spying on me?"

"It's not magic. I harness the temperature around me, and I can influence the creation of snow and ice in the air," he said. "A lot like the way you use emotions and colors…Prentice."

"You didn't answer my question?"

"I wasn't spying," Jack said, shoving his hands into his pockets. "I was…studying you."

"Studying me?"

He nodded. "Didn't believe the stories. Thought they were exaggerated."

"What stories?"

"Rumors really. Of a boy who can control the rainbow," his icy blue eyes locked onto mine.

I said nothing.

"Come on, Prentice," Jack smirked. "You knew I was here. You flew after me and knocked me out of the sky." He tilted his head, studying me. "I think your little secret is out. At least…to me."

I clenched my fists, forcing down the sudden flare of red energy itching at my fingertips. "Who's spreading the rumors?"

Before he could answer, a low, eerie howl echoed through the trees. The sound rippled through the night air, unnatural and stretched too long to be anything normal. My skin prickled as I instinctively turned toward the noise.

"That's…not a wolf," Jack murmured.

A chill crept down my spine—and not from the cold.

Jack's smile widened. "Don't you want to know what it is?"

"Nope." I turned back to him, forcing my voice to stay steady. "I want to know about these rumors."

Jack's expression turned thoughtful. "There's an unseen world out there, Prentice."

Another howl. Closer this time.

"Not human," I muttered, my pulse quickening.

He gave a slow nod. "Humans. Monsters. Fairies. And a whole bunch of other things."

Another howl—this one joined by a second, then a third. The woods seemed to tighten around us.

"And that?" I asked, keeping my stance firm.

Jack exhaled, his breath curling in the icy air. "An ancient creature of pure evil. And it's coming—to kill you." He paused, letting the words sink in before adding, "Not alone. They're all coming—with the storm of the century."

Awesome.

I let out a slow breath. "You're really not making me feel great here, Jack."

He laughed—a sharp, unsettling sound that sent my instincts into overdrive. Was it amusement? Or something else?

I narrowed my eyes. "Still trying to decide if I believe you."

Jack met my gaze, his smile never faltering. "Relax, Prentice. I'm not here to kill you."

I tilted my head. "Then what are you here for?"

Jack's grin stretched wider.

"Oh, I was sent to kill you."

And then, he laughed.

6
JACK IN THE SQUAD

HQ
1 P.M.
Capron Bay
January 4th, 2025

"We have the entire house covered in cameras," Adam announced, his voice tinged with pride as he gestured toward the monitors.

The display against the wall flickered with a grid of live footage. The treehouse, which had been transformed into HQ, was now outfitted with security cameras thanks to Adam's dad, who had scored some used ones from a company overhaul. My dad had helped, too, donating police department monitors to complete our surveillance system.

"Nobody is sneaking up on us again," Dakota declared, leaning forward with his arms crossed.

I glanced at Lena since it was her tree house we were using as our headquarters. I wasn't sure how she felt about her house suddenly becoming Fort Knox.

Lena felt me looking at her and turned towards me shrugging her shoulders.

"What about the watch communicators?" Rachel asked Adam.

"Dad is getting them today," Adam replied.

The watches were another gift from Minute Man Tech, the company Adam's dad worked for. The new tech would sync directly with each of us and even connect to the cameras.

"Does the watch really sync to us individually?" Franklin asked.

Adam nodded.

"And you can track us on the monitors?" Lena asked.

"I can even track Mollie?" Adam said, looking at our ghostly friend.

We all turned toward him.

"How?" Dakota asked.

"I spoke with Anyika and Brother Kiernan," Adam smiled. "I was going to keep it a surprise, but I'm too excited about it."

"And?" Rachel inquired.

"They gave me a warding symbol that Dad will have engraved into Mollie's watch. It will allow her to go further distances from the house and stay in physical form a little longer," he said.

The watches were another gift from Minute Man Tech, the company Adam's dad worked for. The new tech would sync directly with each of us and even connect to the cameras.

"That's awesome," Lena cried out.

Rachel high-fived Dakota.

I forced a smile, but a weight pressed on my chest. We all knew this couldn't last forever. Mollie wasn't supposed to be here. She was dead, a wandering spirit who'd been tied to this world ever since her father was killed. Anyika and Brother Kiernan had warned me about keeping her here. They were still searching for a way to help her move on without losing her. But until then, she was part us.

Knock, knock.

Everyone froze.

"Adam, what is on the monitor?" Lena asked.

Our wheelchair-bound friend looked over all the monitors and shook his head.

"I got nothing showing on any of the cameras," he said.

Knock, knock.

We glanced up toward the ceiling of the clubhouse. The knocking was coming from up there.

"Dude, do we have a camera on the roof?" Dakota asked.

Adam shook his head.

"Why not?" Franklin asked.

"How is someone supposed to get up there?" Adam replied, looking confused.

"Uh, dude. They can fly," Franklin added.

"Nobody can fly," Adam scoffed.

"Crayon man can," Franklin laughed.

71

"Oh, yeah," Adam said, reminded that I could at times…fly.

"Let me go see who it is," Mollie began to say. She could remove a warding and become her spiritual form.

"No," I shouted louder than I meant to.

Everyone turned towards me.

"I know who it is," I sighed.

They all looked at me.

"Jack?" I shouted.

Silence.

"Jack? I shouted again.

"Do you know of anyone else who can fly and knock on the roof?" came a sarcastic voice from above.

I shook my head.

"I can't get in because the place is warded. You'll have to invite me in," Jack added.

I looked at my friends.

"Uh, Prentice. Who is that?" Lena asked me.

"I didn't get a chance to tell you guys yet," I said.

"Tell us what?" Adam said impatiently.

"Who is that?" Dakota asked.

"Someone who was sent to kill me," I smiled.

"What?" Lena cried out.

Franklin shot up ready to fight.

"Relax," I told them all. "He has already warned me that he was sent to kill me," I added. "He wants to help us."

"Jack, come down to the back door. I'll let you in," I shouted.

A moment later, there was a knock on the door. I walked over, wiped a ward off the wall, and opened the door.

Jack stood there wearing the same clothes he was wearing the night before. He nodded at me.

"Come on in, Jack," I said.

I felt a wave of pressure release in the air as the warding disappeared and Jack walked through the door.

"Hello, everyone," he said, waving gently to my friends.

Nobody said anything back.

"Guys, this is Jack," I said. "Jack Frost."

"The storm's moving faster than expected," Ortiz, the FEMA liaison, informed the room.

The Chief nodded.

"Okay, we need to get moving then. Brother Kiernan, you and Doc get moving on the nursing home," the Chief ordered.

"Roger that," the Priest replied and quickly left the room.

"Hog, get over to the schools and make sure they are ready to handle everything," the Chief said.

"On it," the big Detective said as he left.

"Mayor, we need the media to advise anyone in the town to head to the schools if they think they can't ride the storm out," Chief Pendleton advised.

"Already on it. My staff is on the phones with them as we speak," Mayor Travis said.

"Good," the Chief replied.

The door swung open, and FBI Special Agent Mason entered the room.

"About time you decided to come and work with the real police," the Chief smiled shaking Agent Mason's hand.

"Well, I figured you needed my help since the entire media world hates you," the FBI agent laughed. "It's Good to see you, Chief."

"You too, my friend," the Chief replied.

The mayor gazed out the window. The marina waters were already restless.

"I just want to get through this without any loss of life," he murmured.

"Mayor Travis, I have Captain Lynch already setting up a command post down at the middle school gym. I think you and your staff should head down there and settle in. It will be a long couple of days and nights," the Chief said.

The mayor nodded as he stared out the window overlooking the marina.

"I just want to get through this without any loss of life," he said.

"We will, sir," the Chief assured him. We have some of the best people around to help us out here."

The mayor looked at him and nodded. Then he turned and left the Chief's office.

"You like him?" Agent Mason asked the Chief once the mayor was far enough away from the office to hear the question.

"He's a good man. He's navigating small-town politics, but his intentions are good," the Chief said.

"This storm could be nasty," Agent Mason said as he sat down.

"You think?" the Chief said sarcastically.

Mason sat down. "The storm isn't the only thing we need to worry about."

The Chief frowned.

"I felt something on the way into town," Mason continued. "A negative energy in the woods. It's waiting."

The Chief exhaled. "Can we handle it?"

Mason shook his head. "I'm not as strong as Prentice. But if I can feel it… that means it's bad."

"You can feel that stuff?" the Chief asked.

Agent Mason nodded. The FBI agent possessed some of the power of the rainbow. He couldn't harness all the colors like Prentice could, but he did have some ability.

"Something we can handle?" the Chief asked.

"I'm not sure," the agent replied. I'm not as strong as Prentice. I can't quite grasp what it is, but there is something out there."

The Chief nodded.

"Where is Prentice?" Mason asked.

"He's probably with his friends. I asked him to help Brother Kiernan and Doc get all the nursing home residents down to the school," the Chief said. "I was hoping you would stop by the nursing home first and then go to the reservation and help Chief Tackna get all his people down to the school."

"Will they go willingly?" Mason asked.

"I don't know. But I know they have grown to trust you and might listen to you," the Chief said.

Agent Mason nodded.

"Okay, I'll head up there, but first, I want to stop and talk with Prentice for a minute. Get an idea of what he is feeling. If I can sense something, I'm sure he can," he said.

The Chief nodded.

"I'll call him right now. Let him know you're on your way over there," the Chief said.

"I also have some help coming," Agent Mason added.

"We can use all our help," the Chief said.

"I figured. I'll touch base with you shortly after I talk to Prentice," Mason said.

"Can you check on Doc and Brother Kiernan?" the Chief asked.

"Will do," Mason answered as he left the room.

Chief Pendleton looked out the window. A bad feeling was starting to build in his stomach. He didn't know why, but he felt things would get bad.

HQ
2:30 P.M.
Capron Bay
January 4th, 2025

"What's up, Jack," Franklin finally said as he approached the new kid and shook his hand.

"Hello," Jack replied.

"Dude, we need to get you some gloves. Your hands are cold," Franklin smiled.

I looked at my small blond-headed friend in amazement.

"Prentice, are you saying this is Jack Frost," Adam asked.

"Did you not listen, Adam?" Franklin asked. "He said his name was Jack Frost."

"The Jack Frost?" Adam added.

I nodded.

"Adam, his name is Jack Frost," Franklin said, shaking his head. Do you have an issue with your ears?"

75

"Franklin, don't you know who Jack Frost is?" Lena asked.

"Duh, it's this guy right here," Franklin replied.

"Really?" Rachel sighed.

"What?" Franklin looked puzzled.

"Franklin, Jack Frost is a fairy," Mollie said as she looked Jack up and down.

"Mollie, that's not nice. We don't even know him. Why are you calling him a fairy? I'm sorry, Jack," Franklin patted his shoulder. "Dang, you're freezing. Someone get him a sweatshirt."

Whack

"Ouch," Franklin rubbed his head where Rachel slapped him. "What was that for?"

"Dude, Jack Frost is a winter fairy who brings snow and ice to the world," Adam said.

Franklin thought momentarily, his eyes widened as if a light bulb had gone off in his head.

"Wait a second. Are you saying like…the Jack Frost? From the movies?" Franklin asked the group.

Everyone nodded.

"What do you mean he was sent here to kill you," Lena demanded, interrupting Franklin's sudden revelation.

"Take a breath," I told Lena.

"Don't tell me to take a breath if this kid was sent here to kill you and is now standing in our HQ," Lena growled.

I noticed Jack take a step back from Lena.

"Let me explain," I said.

"You better," she stammered.

"Can I explain?" Jack asked.

Lena glared at him, and I noticed Mollie step closer to Jack.

"Let him explain," I sighed.

"Wait," Franklin said. "Can you create snow and ice at will?"

"What?" Jack asked him.

"Can you just make snow out of nothing?" Franklin asked again.

Jack nodded.

"That is so cool," Franklin smiled. "Do you want to build a snowman?"

Whack!

Rachel hit him again.

A piercing screech shattered the air.

Everyone froze.

"Get that ward back up," Jack said running to a window.

"What is it?" I asked.

"Get that ward back on the wall by the door," Jack said. "Do you have a marker?"

I quickly drew the ward next to the door again and threw the marker at Jack. He drew some symbols near the window and then ran to another window and drew another one. The ward looked like a number four with antlers and fangs.

The piercing screeching growl roared again. It sounded a little closer this time.

"What is that?" Rachel asked.

"A snow demon," Jack said, putting the symbol near another window.

"A snow demon?" Dakota asked.

Adam was already typing on the keyboard, and a picture appeared on the big monitor. It resembled a mix between a dragon and a big prehistoric monster cat. The head looked like a dragon with rows of sharpened teeth and long sharp spikes protruding beneath its mouth. Razor-sharp horns rose from the head and pointed back towards a thickly muscled, scaly back. The legs bulged with muscles and were capped off with razor-sharp claws. Its physical nature was terrifying, but it was made worse by deep, dark black eyes that dripped with hatred and anger.

"That is a winter demon?" Mollie asked.

Jack looked at the screen.

"Close. The horns are much longer, and the claws are serrated. It makes it easier to tear flesh apart," he said.

"That is a comforting thought," Franklin grimaced.

"What does it want?" I asked.

"That," Jack said grimly, "is here to kill Prentice."

7
FIRST ENCOUNTER

HQ
2:45 P.M.
Capron Bay, MA
January 4th, 2025

"The snow demon is an advanced scout," Jack said, pressing up against the window, his eyes scanning the tree line beyond the Sheridan's' fence. "They always arrive just before the storm, like bloodhounds tracking their prey."

"You mean the blizzard?" I asked him.

"Wait a second," Lena interrupted, her voice sharp with frustration.

We all turned toward her.

"What is going on?" she demanded.

"Yeah," Adam added, crossing his arms. "Because we don't know you, Jack."

"His name is Jack Frost," Franklin said. "Does anyone listen?"

"Franklin, stop." Lena shot him a glare, the kind that made even Franklin shut up at least for a second.

Her eyes flicked between me and Jack.

"Prentice, you're going to explain right now."

I sighed. "I was going to. Then Jack said we had a snow dragon-cat-monster outside, which kind of took priority."

"Then talk. Now." Rachel cut in, her voice edged with concern.

I looked at Jack.

Another high-pitched howl tore through the trees, closer this time.

"Tell us then," Rachel interrupted.

Another high-pitched howl sounded somewhere in the trees. Only this time, it was closer.

"I don't think we have time," Jack warned.

"I'm not talking to you, Frosty," Lena snapped.

Jack raised his eyebrows but stayed quiet.

"Okay, fine," I said. "Last night, Jack was outside my house… spying on me."

Franklin stiffened. "Wait, what?"

Jack exhaled, his breath misting in the cold. "Because I was sent here to kill him."

The room fell silent.

Franklin took a step back, eyeing Jack warily.

"Well," he finally said, nodding slowly. "At least you're honest."

"Why?" Lena demanded.

Jack hesitated.

"I'm Chernobog's assassin," he admitted.

A quick tap of keys, and a picture of Chernobog popped up on the monitor behind Adam. His monstrous, skeletal face glared back at us from the screen.

"He's ugly," Rachel muttered.

"Who is he?" Mollie asked, staring at the image.

"The God of the Dead. The King of Winter. And pure, unfiltered evil," Jack replied. "When he gives an order, you obey. Or you die."

"So, you just do it?" Lena shot back, her voice trembling with restrained fury.

Jack didn't answer right away. His shoulders slumped slightly.

"I have no choice," he said.

"Everyone has a choice," Lena growled.

Jack finally turned toward her. "Not when Chernobog has your little sister locked in a dungeon," he whispered. "For two hundred years."

Lena flinched.

BANG!

The entire treehouse shook.

"What the hell was that?" Rachel shouted.

BANG!

The walls rattled again, and a guttural growl rose from below—low, ancient, and hungry.

Jack spun toward the window. "It's here."

80

"Can it get up here?" Lena asked.

"The warding should hold," Jack said, but his tone wasn't confident. "But it won't leave until its master calls it back."

"And when will that be?" Adam asked.

Jack didn't answer.

"Is the master Chernobog?" Franklin asked.

"No," Jack muttered. "It's something *worse*."

Franklin snorted. "Crayon Man, you got some real interesting friends."

"Does that include you?" I shot back.

"You know it does, Crayola," Franklin grinned. "You know it does."

He grabbed one of the modified water cannons we'd filled with holy water, pumped it, and racked it like an action hero.

BANG!

The treehouse shook again.

"Will holy water even work on this thing?" Adam asked.

Jack hesitated. "I... don't know. Never tried it."

Franklin grinned. "Let's find out."

He shoved open the window and leaned out.

"Here, kitty, kitty, kitty..." he whistled.

"Is he always like this?" Jack asked.

"You have *no* idea," I muttered.

But the demon didn't take the bait.

Another howl split the air. And this time, it wasn't alone.

"Prentice!"

A voice.

A *familiar* voice.

My blood ran cold.

"No," Lena gasped.

"Prentice!" the voice called again—this time, followed by a sharp, vicious bark.

Jack's head whipped around. "Who the hell is that?"

"My little sister, Carolyn," I whispered. "And our dog."

I turned just in time to see Carolyn step into the yard—Druss right beside her, his golden fur bristling.

Then the beast stepped out from behind the tree.

"Grrrrr..."

Druss placed himself between Carolyn and the demon. The creature snarled, its massive jaws dripping with thick black ooze, its sunken eyes narrowing as it studied its prey.

Then...

YEOW!

The demon lunged.

"AHHH!" Carolyn screamed.

BARK!

Druss leapt.

I leapt.

BOOM!

A crackling ball of red energy slammed into the beast's side, sending it crashing into the snow.

Druss landed and slid, then looked at me, his ears pinned back.

"Go with Carolyn!" I ordered.

For a moment, he hesitated. Then he sprinted to her side.

The demon rose, its grotesque mouth stretching into a wicked grin.

"That thing just smiled at you," Jack whispered.

"Yeah. I noticed."

The beast crouched, muscles rippling.

Then it *charged.*

I fired three more blasts—each hit home, but the monster barely flinched.

"What the hell is this thing made of?" I yelled.

"Bad intentions," Jack muttered.

Then—

SPLAT! SPLAT! SPLAT!

Holy water-filled paintballs exploded against the demon's face.

 screeched, shaking its head violently, clawing at its own burning skin.

I turned—Franklin was grinning like a madman, holding up the empty cannon.

"Say hello to my little friend!" he cackled.

The demon roared, whipping toward him.

"Uh, Franklin?" I called. "Shoot it again."

Franklin grimaced. "Yeah… about that… kind of out of ammo."

"Are you kidding me?!" Jack groaned.

"Jack!" Franklin shouted. "Do your thing! Freeze it or something!"

Jack hesitated.

"I can't," he admitted. "Winter magic can't harm another creature of winter."

Franklin's jaw dropped. "If you tell me you 'give warm hugs,' I swear to God, I'll punch you."

But I wasn't listening anymore.

I focused.

My hands glowed.

A surge of red energy burst outward.

I let it fly.

And just as the blast hit the demon.

Jack hurled a frozen sphere of winter magic straight into it.

A fiery pink explosion erupted.

And when the smoke cleared…

The beast was *gone*.

Or rather…

"Hey, guys," Dakota called, stumbling from the bushes, holding up something in his hand. "I found its head."

Franklin clapped his hands. "Welp. That's a whole new crayon in the box."

I sighed. "Don't say it…"

"Frosty Rainbow," Franklin grinned.

Jack exhaled.

"That," he said, "was level One."

Lena's face paled. "How many levels are there?"

Jack hesitated.

Then he looked at me.

"Eleven."

8
THE MAHAHA

Sunset Lake Nursing Home
Capron Bay, MA
January 4th, 3:30 P.M.

Brother Kiernan slid another heavy box into the back of the van. The cold bit through his jacket as the wind howled past the nursing home, sending ice crystals swirling in the air. Across the parking lot, Doc Eddings was busy helping oversee the transfer of elderly residents onto school buses, their fragile forms bundled in thick coats and scarves. The town had rallied together, with fire departments sending ambulances and surrounding communities sending extra personnel to ensure every patient made it safely to the emergency shelter at the high school.

Doc approached, adjusting his glasses as he surveyed the remaining supplies.

"Thomas, there is some food in the back of the building we must get," Doc uttered.

The Priest nodded and went to the back of the nursing home. Doc followed.

"We should have plenty of food for the residents at the school," Brother Kiernan said examining the remaining boxes.

"That is true, but this is special dietary needs for some of them," Doc added.

"Gotcha," Thomas nodded.

Brother Kiernan was about to pick up the boxes when a chilling sound cut through the air.

YEOW!

The unnatural howl echoed from the forest beyond the parking lot. It wasn't a coyote. It wasn't a wolf. It was something else.

Thomas froze as his eyes scanned the trees for any sign of what made the noise.

84

Doc came up beside him. "Thomas… did you hear that?"

Kiernan didn't answer. He didn't have to.

A shadow moved in the trees.

It was massive—easily the size of a bear but its silhouette was wrong. Too long. Too predatory. The shape slithered between the branches before stepping into the light.

"Thomas?" Doc whispered. "That… that is not a coyote."

Kiernan swallowed hard. "Nope."

The creature emerged fully into view, its head tilting as it studied them. It resembled a panther, but its elongated snout, dagger-like horns, and glowing yellow eyes marked it as something far worse. A forked tongue flicked out, tasting the air. Then, its lips peeled back in a grotesque, hungry grin, revealing rows of jagged, dripping teeth.

"Oh, fantastic," Doc muttered. "I think it likes us."

"Doc," Kiernan whispered, never taking his eyes off the beast. "Get inside. Now."

The librarian didn't argue. They backed up slowly toward the door. The creature twisted its head trying to understand what he said. Then it widened its mouth, revealing rows of razor-sharp teeth dripping with saliva.

"I think it wants to eat you," Doc said.

The beast lowered its body, muscles tensing. A long, sinewy tail swayed behind it, tipped with something sharp.

Brother Kiernan glanced at his friend.

"Maybe it's your skin. He likes your skin," Doc whispered.

"Really?" the Priest replied.

"Well, you would make a better meal than me. I'm too skinny," Doc said, trying to calm his nerves.

Then, it pounced.

"RUN!" Thomas bellowed.

They sprinted for the door. The snow slowed them down, but the demon didn't struggle. It thrived in it. Thomas heard the heavy thuds of its footsteps closing the distance. He made a snap decision and shoved Doc forward, sending the taller man tumbling into a snowbank just as the beast's jaws snapped shut inches from his head.

The monster let out a furious screech as it overshot its mark, its talons skidding across the ice. Thomas barely had time to react before the creature whipped its tail forward.

SLASH!

The demon stopped. It lifted a clawed hand and tasted the crimson streak with its tongue. The yellow demon's eyes flared with rage as it stood about twenty feet away from them. It wanted more than just cutting the Priest. It wanted to kill them.

Then it smiled.

"Oh, that's bad," Doc muttered, still half-buried in the snow.

The beast roared angrily as it swung back around to face its prey.

"I think it is angry Thomas," Doc said as he struggled.

"You think?" Brother Kiernan replied.

"I do. I think he's angry," Doc said again.

The pale Priest glanced at his friend, amazed that he could be so simple for someone so brilliant. He smiled.

The beast grunted, bringing Thomas' gaze back to it. He eyed the creature who stared back at him.

"What are you?" he asked.

"Thomas," the beast hissed as it took a step closer.

"It knows your name," Doc said.

"Lucky me," Brother Kiernan replied, slowly moving a step to his left. The beast's eyes followed him.

"What's my name?" Doc asked it.

The creature said nothing.

"What's your name?" Doc asked it.

The creature said nothing.

"That's disappointing," Doc said, shaking his head.

"Uhm…Doc, do you have any idea what this is?" Brother Kiernan asked the professor as he took another step to his left.

"Thomas," the creature hissed again.

"That's…me," Brother Kiernan replied. "But that's Doc Eddings. He…tastes better."

The beast glanced towards the professor.

"That's not amusing, Thomas," Doc said as his friend tried to smile.

Brother Kiernan suddenly darted to his left, trying to draw the creature away from the professor. The beast leaped after him. Thomas dove to the ground, rolling away from the beast as it skidded to a halt on the snowy grass. Its immense tail lashed at him, but the Priest rolled away, avoiding the razor-sharp tip.

Thomas was up and running into the tree line quickly as he could. The creature hesitated for a moment, looking at Doc. Then, it decided the gangly librarian was not the bigger threat and took off after the Priest.

The priest knew he had one chance. He bolted for the tree line, hoping to draw it away from the residents. Behind him, Doc was already scrambling to his feet, watching helplessly as the priest disappeared into the woods.

The demon pursued.

Thomas sprinted down the snowy hill, ducking between trees as branches lashed at his face. The howls behind him never faded, the monster kept pace.

He burst through the snow-covered trees and slid down a steep hill. He glanced behind him but couldn't see anything through the thick trees. He reached the bottom of the hill and stood up, wiping the snow from his clothes and glancing around the area. He knew he was behind the nursing home but was unfamiliar with the terrain.

A deep, guttural snarl rumbled from the ridge above, vibrating through the frozen air like a war drum.

Thomas slowly sank to the ground and slid behind thick shrubs. He let out a slow, deep breath, calming himself. He knew his only chance against this creature was to be calm. Fear caused mistakes, and this beast would pounce on a mistake.

The beast snorted above as he searched for Thomas. Its warm breath shot from the snout, making a thick cloud in the cold air. It distracted the creature for a moment, allowing Thomas to scurry into the thick tree line, where he could hide more easily.

He moved deeper into the woods, trying to distance himself from the thing chasing him. Thomas jumped as his pocket buzzed. It took him a second to realize his cell phone had vibrated. He slid the phone from his pocket and glanced at the screen. It was a text from Doc.

"It came after you," the text read.

"Thanks, Doc," Thomas whispered, shaking his head at the Doc's obvious observation.

Another growl erupted from behind him. He couldn't tell if it was close or not, and the thick trees made it difficult to hear.

Then, he heard something worse.

Laughter.

It was high-pitched, shrill, and wrong.

Kiernan slid to a stop, his breath coming in short, ragged gasps. His eyes darted around the trees.

Something else was here.

"HAHAHAHA!"

It came from everywhere and nowhere all at once.

The priest's gut twisted. The laughter wasn't random. It was guiding the demon to him.

The beast burst through the trees, nostrils flaring. Kiernan ran.

CRACK!

Something slammed into his chest. He hit the ground hard, the impact knocking the wind from his lungs. Dazed, he turned his head and found himself staring at clawed, human-like feet.

The creature grinned down at him.

Its skin was pale blue, stretched tightly over a sinewy, emaciated frame. Elongated arms ended in fingers too long for comfort, each tipped with needle-sharp claws. Its bare feet, twisted and clawed, dug into the snow, leaving no imprint. Strands of stringy white hair clung to a gaunt, elongated skull, its grinning mouth filled with jagged, ice-coated teeth. But the worst part? The milky-white eyes that stared at him with gleeful malice.

"It can't be," Thomas whispered to himself.

"HAHAHAHA!"

He rolled to his feet, ignoring the agony in his ribs. He swung a punch at the thing's ribs but it barely reacted. Then, it swiped.

Pain exploded in his side as he was sent flying into a snowdrift.

More laughter.

The Mahaha stalked forward.

BAM! BAM! BAM!

Gunfire erupted through the trees. Agent Mason.

The bullets slammed into the Mahaha's chest, staggering it, but no blood spilled from the wounds. It turned its head toward Mason and grinned.

BAM, BAM, BAM, BAM!

Four more rounds pierced the icy blue skin, driving it backward some more. Holes appeared in the chest, but again, no blood flowed from the wounds. Thomas glanced behind the fiendish man and saw the ground drop away.

"Sunset Lake," he whispered to himself, realizing the small lake was at the bottom of the drop-off.

"You just can't stay out of trouble, can you?" Agent Mason said as he was knelt by the injured priest.

"I have him right where I want him," Thomas gasped through the pain.

"Hahahahaha," it giggled again.

"I put eight holes in this thing," Mason said.

"Water," Thomas squawked.

"What?" Mason asked.

"The lake. Push it into the lake," he groaned. 'Push it into the lake."

Mason nodded, but before he could move—

A scream.

Something sprinted into the clearing.

Doc.

And he was running straight at the thing.

Mason barely had time to react before the gangly professor drop-kicked the demon in the chest.

The Mahaha screeched as it was knocked off its feet. It tumbled over the ridge and into the frozen lake below. The ice shattering upon impact.

"Hahahahaha," it screamed in a creepy giggle as it plummeted to the frozen lake beyond.

Mason ran to the drop-off and peered over the edge. All he saw was a jagged hole in the ice below.

"It's dead," Thomas said softly. "The water kills it."

Mason let out a long breath. "That's... one way to do it Doc."

Doc dusted himself off. "What can I say? A well-placed boot is a universal solution."

Kiernan groaned. "You… are insane."

"What was that thing?" Mason asked.

"It was a Mahaha," the Priest replied.

"Wawa?" Mason asked.

"My dear Agent Mason, Wawa is a gas station located in the Pennsylvania area. I don't think that was a walking gas pump," Doc said as he got to his feet.

Agent Mason stared at his friend.

"That was a joke, sir," Doc laughed.

Mason looked at Thomas, who was trying not to laugh. The pain was too much.

"Did you just hear him?" Mason asked.

"Hey, he's learning," Thomas shrugged.

The snow crunched behind the three friends. Mason turned just in time to see the snow cat demon leap through the air with its front paws extended and mouth wide open. It was going to hit Doc, and there was nothing Mason could do. He couldn't draw his weapon fast enough to fire or conjure up enough energy to blast it, either.

"Doc!" the FBI agent screamed helplessly.

Doc saw it too late and turned away, resigned to his fate.

A massive shadow swallowed the fading sunlight, casting an ominous silhouette over the battlefield. Heads snapped upward—even the charging demon paused mid-air, its glowing eyes widening in confusion.

Then, with a thunderous BOOM, the RV, known as the Beast, came hurtling down from the sky. It crashed onto the snow demon with bone-crushing force, its sheer weight driving the creature deep into the frozen ground. A sickening crunch echoed through the air, followed by the grotesque squelch of pulverized flesh beneath the steel frame.

The RV bounced once, its tires momentarily lifting before slamming down again, eliciting another wet, sickening crunch.

Then silence.

The Beast sat motionless, steam rising from its undercarriage. Nothing moved beneath it. Whatever had been there was now nothing more than a gory stain in the snow.

"Gross," Mason winced as he watched the creature splatter over the snow-covered ground.

Mason, Doc, and Brother Kiernan stared in wonder at the site of the Priest's RV, which was on top of a bloody mess.

The door popped open, and a small blond-headed kid hopped out.

"Snap, crackle, and pop, baby," Franklin roared as he flexed his small frame of muscles.

"Am I dead?" Brother Kiernan whispered. "I swear I just saw Franklin get out of my RV, which just fell from the sky."

"What's up, dumpster man?" Franklin asked Agent Mason.

"Can I shoot this kid?" Mason asked.

"I'd rather you not Agent Mason. It seems young Franklin here just saved my life," Doc replied.

"What's up, Doc?" Franklin laughed.

"I take it back, shoot him," Doc sighed.

"Franklin, where did you come from?" Agent Mason asked him, still wondering if he could shoot him.

"The RV," he replied.

The FBI agent glared at him.

"He means Franklin, where did you and the RV come from?" Doc added.

"Oh…crayon man and Jack Frost brought me. I had to stay inside the thing to steer," the blond-headed kid smiled.

"Franklin!" Agent Mason shouted, getting angry.

"He's right," I said as I slowly floated to the ground near the scene. My friends just stared at me as my feet came to rest on the snowy ground.

Doc looked at me and then up into the darkening skies. Agent Mason and Brother Kiernan looked at me with wide eyes.

"Flying now?" Brother Kiernan asked me.

"I didn't tell you I could do that?" I asked.

He shook his head.

"Uhm…did you just Jedi mind trick the RV onto this thing?" Mason asked me.

I looked at them.

"Uh…sort of," I said.

"Sort of crayon man. C'mon dude. You just dropped Brother Kiernan's beast on it's head," Franklin smiled.

"It wasn't just me," I answered him, pointing to another figure who just appeared from the tree line. Everyone turned to look at the newcomer.

"Who are you, young man?" Doc asked.

"Guys, meet Jack," I said.

"Wait a second. Our annoying little blond-haired friend called him Jack Frost a minute ago. Are you telling me this is the real Jack Frost?" Agent Mason asked.

"It is," Brother Kiernan added as he struggled to his feet.

"Like the fairy?" Mason asked.

"Like the assassin," Brother Kiernan replied, not taking his eyes off Jack.

I looked at the Priest. I was surprised he knew about Jack's past.

"What do you mean assassin?" Doc asked.

"Wherever he goes, death follows," Thomas answered. "I've been studying his work for a long time."

"You mean hunting him," I clarified.

Brother Kiernan said nothing.

"You are correct, Brother Thomas Kiernan," Jack added. "I have done some terrible things through the years."

"Because the Winter guy has his sister prisoner," Franklin blurted out before anyone else could say anything.

"What?" Mason asked. "What winter guy?"

"Chernobog," I answered.

"The God of the Dead?" Thomas asked.

More growls erupted somewhere in the distance.

"Gentlemen, I suggest we leave the area before more demon cats arrive," Doc said.

"And those ugly-looking laughing things," Mason grimaced.

"That was a Mahaha," Jack said.

"Haha, Dumpster Man," Franklin laughed, slapping Agent Mason on the back.

"I'm really going to shoot this kid," Mason said, rolling his eyes.

"Mahaha," Franklin laughed.

"That's it," Mason said, but Doc had already grabbed his hand and ushered him into the beast.

"Let's meet back at the Church. I'll tell the Squad to meet us there," I said.

Everyone nodded in agreement and got into the RV.

"Hold on. We'll have to work together to bring the RV back up," I said, looking at Jack.

"No need," the Priest replied as the beast made a loud cranking sound. I watched in amazement as the regular tires rotated one by one and were replaced by giant tires with snow chains wrapped around them.

"Look at that," Franklin laughed. "Albino Brother is playing transformer."

"I'm going to hurt. Hurt him just a little," Mason said, trying to get out of the beast, but Doc grabbed him and pulled him back in.

"Boy, Dumpster Man is sensitive, isn't he, Crayola," Franklin laughed. I slapped him on the side of the head.

"Ouch!" he cried.

"Thank you!" Mason yelled out just before the doors closed, and the beast roared through the trees and up the hillside.

9
HOG

Capron Bay High School
Capron Bay, MA
5:00 P.M.

Detective Hog Sheridan surveyed the bustling gymnasium, arms crossed over his broad chest. The high school had been transformed into a makeshift storm shelter, with volunteers setting up cots, medical stations, and supply tables. From the moment he walked in, he knew things were under control.

No surprise Anyika Tulu and Grammy Pendleton were running the show.

Both women had volunteered to come down to the school and help get things ready for all the town's residents to come in and ride out the coming storm of the century. Hog smirked as he spotted the Superintendent of Schools and Principal Hammond scrambling to follow Grammy's every command. The two men, usually so composed, now nodded like nervous recruits, eager to avoid her sharp tongue.

"Bigguh mens cya'um biggah t'ings, Mr. Sheridan," Anyika's thick Gullah accent cut through the chatter.

Hog blinked. "Uh... sorry, ma'am?"

Anyika laughed and switched to her clearer voice.

"You're a bigger man. Please pick up that big box over there and bring it over to those tables," she laughed.

Hog chuckled, grabbed the massive box without breaking a sweat, and carried it across the gym, where Superintendent Vickers and Principal Hammond were stacking supplies.

"Gentlemen," Hog nodded as he placed the big heavy box on the table.

"They put you to work, huh," Vickers said.

"Oh yeah," Hog replied. "Ms. Annie gave me orders, and I'm terrified of that woman."

"That makes three of us," Principal Hammond laughed.

Hog looked around at the people moving every which way.

"They got things moving smoothly, though," Hog said.

Principal Hammond was about to say something when some commotion came across the gym. A group of elderly men and women were being led into the gym. The first group of patients from the Lakeview Nursing Home had arrived.

"Let's go welcome our guests," Hog said, striding across the gym.

"Hank, my dear. I'm glad you can join us," Grammy said as she made her over and hugged him.

"Ma'am," he replied with a big grin. "You and Annie have this operating like a well-oiled machine."

"They listen well," she laughed, patting Hammond and Vickers on the shoulders.

"They're terrified of you and Annie," Hog laughed.

"You should be," Ms. Annie said as she joined the group laughing.

More commotion came from the entrance, this time, from a team of newcomers in blue windbreaker jackets barking orders at everyone in sight.

"Who are they?" Vickers asked as one of the women turned around, and the infamous yellow lettering appeared before them.

"Trouble," Hog sighed storming across the floor approaching the nearest agent.

"Oh no," Grammy said.

"What's wrong?" Hammond asked.

"Hog and the FBI don't play well together," she answered following the big man.

She could barely keep up with Hog as he strode across the floor and approached the first Agent he reached.

"Who is the SAC?" Hog asked.

The agent, a wiry man with slicked-back hair, narrowed his eyes. "Who are you?"

"I asked first," Hog shot back.

""Agent Goldberg," another agent interrupted. "And this must be Detective Sheridan."

95

Hog turned to face the man. "And you are?"

"Special Agent in Charge Joseph Liang." He extended his hand.

Hog didn't shake it.

Another larger man, wearing a FEMA jacket, stepped up beside Liang. His voice was thick with authority.

"We need to inspect this facility to ensure it is safe," the big man said.

"It is safe," Hog answered.

"We'll determine that," he FEMA agent countered.

Hog laughed.

"I am in charge here," the man insisted. "I'm not sure what you find funny."

"Sweeth'aat, you not in charge," Ms. Annie joined the conversation laughing.

"Excuse me Ma'am? Who are you?" Agent Liang asked.

"Someone you don't want to anger, my dear," Grammy added.

"I don't care who I anger," the FEMA agent scoffed. "The federal government is now in control."

Hog took a slow step toward him, his towering frame casting a very intentional shadow.

"No, you're not," Grammy laughed.

"Who is then?" the man asked.

"He is," Grammy nodded toward the entrance.

Chief Pendleton.

The room fell silent.

"Captain Byrd, step away from my officer," the Chief ordered.

Byrd stared at the Chief.

"That's not a request Byrd. I'd rather not clean up a mess on the floor once Hog is done with you," the Chief added.

Byrd's eyes darted between the Chief and Hog, who just smiled and winked. The FEMA agent stepped back.

"Making friends?" the Chief asked Hog.

"I learned from the best," Hog snickered.

Before the tension could settle, another group arrived, led by Senator Bradler.

"Chief Pendleton, good to see you again," the Senator said, stepping forward with a media crew trailing behind.

"The pleasure is all yours," the Chief replied cooly.

Mayor Travis pushed his way through the growing crowd.

"Robert, the President, and the Governor have declared a state of emergency," he sighed.

"I understand that" the Chief said.

"Which gives command of the situation to FEMA," the mayor began.

"Me," Byrd smiled.

"And I'm here to make sure everything moves smoothly," Senator Bradler said.

"And these toadies are your personal…scribes?" the Chief asked, referring to two people he knew very well.

"Nice to see you," Coffee smiled.

"Not really," Reed smirked. "We're here to make sure you obey the laws."

The Chief nodded.

"You mean like the ones you were convicted of breaking?" Grammy asked the disgraced reporter.

Reed ignored her.

"Ladies and gentlemen," the mayor interrupted. "The storm is beginning much sooner than expected. It is already whipping around outside, making visibility hard. We need to work together."

"Understood, sir," the Chief nodded.

"I want Mr. Sheridan to bring those boxes of water outside so they can stay cold without wasting power," Byrd said.

"Detective Sheridan," Hog said.

"Whatever, just do it," Byrd snickered.

Hog stepped towards him, but the Chief put a hand on the big man's chest.

"Not now, big man," he said. "Just do as he says."

Hog nodded. But as he turned away, he made sure Byrd saw the wink.

Byrd paled.

***

The wind howled as Hog carried a heavy box toward the supply shed. The storm had arrived.

Snowflakes slashed through the air like frozen razors, and the temperature had plummeted. He saw the shape of the shed and moved toward it—

Then he heard it.

"Hahahaha."

Hog froze.

The laughter was wrong.

It wasn't joyful.

It wasn't friendly.

It was mocking.

"Who's there?"

"Hahahaha."

A shape emerged from the swirling snow.

A tall, blue-skinned figure with clawed fingers and milky-white eyes.

The Mahaha.

Hog barely had time to react before the thing lunged.

The first punch smashed into his mouth, splitting his lip.

The second blow sent him reeling.

Hog dropped the box and squared up, wiping blood from his mouth. He'd been in plenty of fights before.

But nothing like this.

The demon grinned.

"Hahahaha."

Hog feinted left, then drove a brutal uppercut into the creature's ribs, then another to the jaw.

The Mahaha staggered—but didn't fall.

It wasn't hurt.

It laughed.

Before Hog could react, a cold fist smashed into his nose. CRACK!

Pain exploded through his skull as blood poured from his shattered nasal passage.

The demon kept hitting.

A backhand sent him spinning.

A kick to the ribs lifted him off the ground. He landed hard.

The Mahaha stood over him, smiling. Then it stomped down.

Hog rolled—just in time. He pushed himself up, gasping.
Blood poured. His vision swam. But he wasn't done.
The demon lunged again—
Hog caught its wrist.
Talons pierced his palm. He didn't scream.
Instead, he squeezed.
Bones snapped.
The Mahaha finally gasped.
"Hah,"
Hog twisted with everything he had left.
The creature's neck snapped.
It slumped.
The laughter stopped.
Hog staggered backward, collapsing.
The world spun.
He was dying.
"At least I got you first," he whispered as the darkness closed in.
A vision of Lena appeared before him.
She stood beside another figure, but he couldn't see the face.
A rainbow covered it.
"Lena…"
His voice was barely a whisper—
Then everything went black

10
DEATH IN THE SNOW

St. Paul's Church
Capron Bay, MA
5:30 P.M.

Adam's fingers flew across the keyboard, the soft clicking filling the tense air in Brother Kiernan's underground compound. When the Priest was assigned to Capron Bay, it was to investigate all the strange things around the town. The albino priest had quickly befriended the group. He was a supernatural detective, and the church's basement was a technological fortress warded everywhere on the property. No demon or evil spirit was getting onto their church's property unless they had help.

"What's wrong, Lena?" Rachel finally asked, watching her friend's restless movements.

Lena didn't answer. She just kept pacing, biting her lips, eyes distant.

"Lena?" Rachel pressed again. Dakota shot her a questioning glance, but he had no answers either.

"Something's not right," Lena muttered, finally stopping to face them. Her voice trembled slightly. "I can feel it."

"I'm sure Prentice is okay," Dakota added.

Lena shook her head.

Lena shook her head. "No. Something is wrong. I don't know how, but I know it."

Adam stopped typing. "You're just nervous with him out there with this Jack Frost character," Adam said.

"Don't forget Franklin," Dakota laughed. "He's always getting us into trouble."

"That's true," Rachel added.

"No," Lena insisted. "It's not just that. It's…"

The basement door swung open. Mollie entered, her face pale. "She's right."

100

Everyone turned to look at her. The ghost girl rarely looked shaken.

"I can feel it too," Mollie whispered. "Something's wrong. The air—it's... different."

The room fell silent. Then the alarm blared.

Adam spun back toward the monitors. The snowy footage on the screens flickered with interference, but through the thickening storm, two jeeps rumbled into the church's back parking lot. The headlights cut through the swirling white, illuminating figures climbing out. The second jeep's doors swung open, and men in white snow gear stepped into the storm.

"Who is that?" Adam asked as Mollie disappeared through the basement door to check the newcomers.

"That looks like my grandfather," Dakota said as he examined the man who exited the back door of the first jeep. The second jeep's door opened, and many men in white snow suits appeared on screen.

"What are they doing?" Rachel asked.

"I don't know," Dakota answered as they watched the white-suited men disappear in the back lot. They continued to watch as Chief Tackna said something to the driver of the first jeep, and then he walked to the back door, which was now being held open by Mollie. He gave the young blond-headed girl a big hug, and the two of them went through the door. A moment later, they came into the basement.

"Grandfather," Dakota cried out as he ran to hug the old man. He wrapped his arms around him.

"Ahh, Dakota, it is good to see you," Chief Tackna replied, embracing his grandson. He smiled, said hello to everyone else in the room, and took off his heavy winter coat.

"Dakota, there are two more boxes in the back of the jeep. Go get them please. Bring them down here," he said as Dakota quickly went outside to get the boxes.

"Where did those other men go, Chief?" Adam asked.

Chief Tackna examined the monitors on the screen and smiled.

"They have gone to their assigned spot around the Church, my young computer genius," the Chief smiled.

"They're guarding the church?" Rachel asked.

The Chief nodded.

"From what?" Mollie asked.

"Something bad," Lena said, fighting back tears.

The Chief looked at Lena and then back to Rachel.

"She just keeps saying something is wrong," Rachel replied.

"It is. I can feel it," Lena whispered.

Dakota returned through the door carrying the boxes and placed them on the table. He opened one and pulled out a heavy white camouflaged coat.

"What is this?" he asked, holding it up.

The door swung open again. A bruised and exhausted Brother Kiernan entered, followed by Prentice, Doc, Franklin, and Agent Mason. Lena's breath caught at the sight of them. Brother Kiernan wasted no time. He moved to the keyboard, punched in a few commands, and a mechanical whirring echoed through the basement.

"What was that?" Adam asked.

"I pulled a ward down," Brother Kiernan answered him just as the back door opened and Jack Frost walked through. The room became noticeably colder.

Brother Kiernan typed another set of commands in, and the whirring sound echoed again and then clicked.

"Back in place?" Adam asked.

"Yep," the Priest answered.

"Nobody is listening to me," Lena shouted, interrupting the conversation.

Everyone stopped and looked at her.

"Something is wrong!" she said and began to cry.

Capron Bay High School
Capron Bay, MA
6:00 P.M.

Anyika weaved through the packed gymnasium, her sharp eyes scanning for Chief Pendleton. The gym had become a sea of navy-blue jackets as FEMA and FBI agents took over, barking

102

orders like they owned the place. The root doctor ignored their presence, cutting through the chaos with practiced ease.

"Ms, who are you?" demanded a male's voice.

She turned to face the broad-shouldered man who had clashed with Hog earlier. His name was Byrd. He was a big man with muscles bulging under the blue windbreaker with the FEMA logo and she didn't like him.

"Have you seen Chief Pendleton?" she asked the man, ignoring his question.

He stared at her, annoyed.

Anyika stared back at him, not saying anything.

"Are you a doctor?" he asked her.

She thought for a moment and smiled.

"Yes, I am Mr. Turd?" she asked him.

"It's Byrd," he corrected her.

"Indeed, it is," she smiled. "I'm looking for Chief Pendleton."

"He is no longer in charge here," he reminded her.

"Off'uh co'se he iz," she laughed as she spoke in the Gullah language.

"I'm sorry, what did you say?" Byrd asked her.

"Oh, bless your heart," Grammy Pendleton chimed in, stepping beside Anyika. "This boy thinks he's running things."

"Ma'am, by order of the Governor, this has become a federal government operation, which means Agent Liang and myself are in command," Byrd replied.

Grammy laughed.

"I don't see what is funny," Byrd said.

"Young man, no matter where my son is, he is in charge," Grammy said.

"I don't think so, Ma'am," Byrd smiled.

"He t'inks he is still'uh in chaa'ge," Anyika smiled glancing at Grammy.

"Need I remind you what a state of emergency means?" Byrd growled.

"No need," Chief Pendleton advised, joining the group with Hammond and Vickers behind him.

"Robert," Anyika began to say.

"Mr. Vickers and Mr. Hammond, please instruct your kitchen staff to begin preparing the food for this evening," Byrd said, interrupting Annie.

Hammond and Vickers didn't move.

"I'm sorry, maybe I wasn't clear enough," Byrd said.

"We heard you, sir," Vickers smiled as he looked at Chief Pendleton.

"Go ahead, guys. We'll need to start getting everyone some food," the Chief added.

Hammond and Vickers nodded and left to get the food going.

"See Mr. Byrd," Grammy smiled as Annie laughed.

Byrd glared at the two women and stormed off without saying another word.

"What was that about?" the Chief asked.

"Nothing, dear," Grammy said.

"Robert, I haven't seen Hog since he brought the water outside. Something is wrong," Annie said.

"He's probably in the kitchen eating something," he replied.

Annie shook her head.

"No, I've got a bad feeling," Annie responded.

The Chief's stomach clenched. He'd had that same feeling ever since he walked into this gym. Without another word, he turned and made his way toward the back hall.

Chief Pendleton watched his mother and Ms. Annie wade their way through the flood of people in the gym. He checked his watch and saw his heart rate was rising. He felt it, too. Something was wrong, but he figured it was just the chaos within the school and the beginning of the storm outside. Now, though, with Annie saying something was wrong and Hog was missing, he got much more worried.

He pushed through the crowd to the hallway where Hog had taken the water earlier. The lights in the long corridor were off, and the light from the gym faded the deeper he went. He could see the doors at the end that led to the storm outside. He felt his heart rate accelerate as he closed in on the exit.

The wind echoed inside the hallway as it shook the doors, trying to get inside. The storm was growing in strength quickly, making the Chief even more nervous. He had seen a lot of bad things in his time in the Army and as a police officer, but a storm of this magnitude was not one of them. The hallway ended, and he swallowed hard, not sure what the outside world would look like, as he pushed the door open.

It didn't move.

He pushed harder on the push bar, but it didn't open. The Chief stepped back from the door to examine them.

Whoosh

They suddenly shook violently as a tremendous gust of wind hammered against the doors from the outside. It was like the storm had a mind trying to get inside the school and get to him. He pushed that thought from his mind and looked at the push bar. It was dark still, and I couldn't really see the details. He ran his hands along the bar until he found the lock. It was pushed in.

The door was locked from the inside.

Fear struck him.

Someone had locked the door from the inside, and the only reason was to keep something outside. It could have been someone locking the door to make sure the wind didn't rip it open, but all he could think was that someone locked it to keep Hog outside.

He stepped back and kicked the door as hard as he could.

Clang!

The sound roared through the hallway, and the double doors shook but didn't open. He kicked them again.

Clang!

They shook again and bulged outward, but the lock was held.

He stepped back to kick again.

"Chief!" Principal Hammond shouted from behind. "What are you doing?"

"The doors are locked, and I think Hog is still outside," he answered.

"Hold on. I have the key right here," Hammond added as he stepped up and inserted the round allen wrench key into the hole. The lock clicked, and the Chief pushed through the doors into the wintry chaos beyond.

105

***

Priscilla Reed eyed the Chief from the corner of the gym. She watched the exchange with Director Byrd from FEMA and followed him as he moved towards the gym exit. Something interesting was happening, and she wasn't going to miss it. She pulled out her phone, flipped the recording feature, and followed the Chief out of the gym.

Her career began as an investigative reporter long ago in a high-crime section of New Orleans. She spent many nights in dark alleys and creepy buildings following people to get the dirt on them. Back then, there wasn't much she wouldn't do to get the story. It had been a long time since she did any of the dirty work for a scoop, but she felt her interest returning.

The phone rested casually in front of her and recorded the Chief as he made his way down the darkened hallway. Even though it was nearly pitch black in the corridor, the phone would still record everything. Reed was careful not to get too close to the police officer. He was very good at his job, unlike many other cops she had followed earlier in her career.

She watched as he pushed on the doors, but they didn't give. Something was wrong. She could sense the tension in the Chief as he examined the doors. Suddenly, he stepped back and blasted the door with his foot, but it didn't open. The sound of the kick exploded through the hallway, and she instantly ducked behind a large pallet of boxes. It was a good thing she did because someone came running through the hall behind her. The figure passed without seeing her.

Another loud clanging burst through the hall as the Chief kicked the doors again. She refocused on the phone to zoom in on the newcomer as he approached the Chief. She tried to listen in on what was said, but the only word that could be made out was "Hog." That was enough, though.

It wasn't hard to figure out the Chief's right-hand man was locked outside in the freezing cold storm of the century. How did that happen? Did someone lock him out? Was someone trying to kill a Capron Bay police officer? Things had gotten very interesting.

Reed looked around and saw she was in a hallway that was crossed from the one the Chief and the other person were in. She noticed another doorway at the end of her hallway that had a big red "Exit" sign above it. She ran to the end of the hallway and instantly heard the whipping wind beyond. She swallowed hard and pushed her way through the door.

The world was a wash of white swirling wind as she went outside. The freezing cold temperature slammed into her like a wave of ice-cold water. Reed quickly scanned the area to see what was happening. She could only see a few feet in front of her because the storm was swirling so hard. She noticed the corner of the building and realized the Chief's door was on the other side. She had to find out what was happening, so she fought the snowy wind, shuffled her feet to the corner of the brick wall, and peered around it.

It was very tough to see and hear, but Reed could make out the shape of Chief Pendleton as he exited the school. His voice broke through the roaring wind, but she couldn't make out what he was saying. A shape lying on the ground drew her attention. A large figure lay on the ground in the snow, and she could see a pool of deep red circling the large shape on the ground. The person on the ground was clearly bleeding. The crimson red reflected clearly in the sea of white.

Her heart began to race. The body lying on the ground had to be Detective Sheridan, and he was clearly injured. She was about to put away her camera phone and help when she saw movement from the corner of her eye. She froze in place as a large dark shape appeared from the tree line. She couldn't see the details of this new man, but for some unknown reason, she was instantly scared.

The moment Chief Pendleton stepped outside, the wind hit like a wall of ice. The temperature had plummeted. Visibility was barely a few feet through the blinding snow.

"Hog!" he bellowed.

Nothing.

"Hog!" he yelled again but knew it was useless.

Then he saw it. A dark shape lying in the snow, a deep crimson stain spreading around it.

He ducked a little bit to avoid the gales of icy flakes and shuffled his feet through the building snow on the ground. He got closer to the shape and saw the crimson-red swelling around it, and for some reason, he knew it was his best friend.

"Hog! he yelled and ran to the dark shape, not caring about the snow and wind slamming into his face. He went to his knees and slid the remaining few feet to the body.

"Hog!" He yelled again turning the big man's face towards him. His eyes were closed, and his blue skin was ice cold.

"What did you do, you big fool," he whispered as he checked for a pulse.

"Chief," Hammond yelled from the door.

The Capron Bay police chief ignored him as he felt for a pulse. He rolled him over to see where the blood was coming from, and he saw the two sets of puncture wounds.

"What in the world did this?" he asked as he put his fingers on the big man's neck again, checking for a pulse.

"Hog! Don't you die on me, you big jerk," he yelled. "Hog!"

His life-long best friend didn't move.

"He is mine, mortal,"

Pendleton's head snapped up. A figure stood just beyond the swirling snow, untouched by the wind.

Dark coat. Sunken face. Black eyes that swallowed the light.

And beside him, something else—something massive, glowing with frozen blue fire.

The figure said nothing as it stepped closer. The snow cleared in front of the dark shape, and the Chief could see it was a man. He was of average height and dressed in a long black overcoat. His black hair was slicked back, ending at the collar of a white button-down shirt with a red necktie he wore underneath the black coat.

"Who are you?" the Chief asked again.

Pendleton's jaw clenched. His fingers tingled, energy crackling along his nerves.

"I am…here for him," the figure said, pointing to Hog.

"I don't think so," the Chief replied, studying the man. The pale skin was tight and sunken at his pointy cheekbones. His lips were drawn back underneath a long, narrow nose and creepy black eyes.

The man said nothing as he continued to stare at the Chief.

The Chief said nothing. His fingers pressed on Hog's neck, searching for a pulse. There was none.

"He is rightfully mine," the man said.

"I'll be bringing him inside, so you can go back to…wherever you came from," the Chief replied.

"You can take him inside. I don't about that," the thin man said.

"Who are you?" the Chief asked again.

"I am…a harvester," the man answered. His words cold and tinny.

"A harvester?" The Chief said his fingers still pressing on Hog's neck.

"He is mine," the man said again.

"You just said I can bring him inside," the Chief added. "You must be confused."

"You can take the body. I don't care about that. I want his soul," the man smiled.

"What?" the Chief asked.

"Mr. Pendleton, your friend is no longer with the living," the man said.

A massive figure appeared at the man's side. Robert Pendleton was not a person that scared easily but this figure frightened him. It stood half a foot taller than the Chief. It wore no clothes, revealing translucent skin that pulsed with ice-cold glowing blue blood that ran along its veins and arteries. The skin ran over the demon's head like a monk's cloak. A bright glowing orb rested in the middle of the chest, beating like a heart would.

The long muscular arms ended in hands with sharpened claws. They carried a long, glowing, razor-sharp sickle with icicles hanging from the blade. The other end had a long chain that disappeared somewhere beyond.

"You can't have anything," the Chief swallowed hard. "I don't care if you brought muscle."

The man glanced at the giant creature standing next to him.

"He is not my friend," the man whispered. "He is a messenger of Chernobog."

The thin man and the giant demon said something to each other in some language the Chief didn't understand. The thin man didn't seem happy about what was said.

"Chernobog has offered a deal," he said.

"Who is this Chernobog?" the Chief demanded. He was getting angry.

The thin man noticed a faint yellow glow on the man's fingers. He took a small step back.

"The winter lord will give you twenty-four hours to turn over your son," the man said.

"Did you just say my son?" Chief Pendleton replied as anger began to flow within.

The man nodded and felt the anger growing inside the police chief. He could see the man fighting to calm down.

"There is no need for violence, Chief Pendleton," the man said nervously as he watched the faint yellow glow grow stronger.

"No harm will come to your son," he told the Chief. If he comes freely, he will teach him how to use his powers. Your friend there will live, and the people of the town will live."

"And if he doesn't?" the Chief asked.

"Your son will die, as will everyone in this town," he said.

"Of course they will," the Chief nodded and looked at the giant demon and thin man.

"Look around you, Chief," the giant demon growled. His voice was thick and grainy like a snake would sound.

"The big glowy thing speaks," the Chief said.

"The storm is here. The Army of winter will follow, and you will all die," it laughed. "Give us Prentice and he and everyone else lives."

"It is true, Chief Pendleton. He is telling the truth," the thin man advised.

"No," the Chief said.

"You have twenty-four hours," the giant glowing demon said and vanished.

The Chief squeezed his eyes shut. A flurry of colors swirled in his mind like a category-five tornado. They churned and twirled, threatening to overwhelm every sense in his body. Finally, the torrent of colors settled on a combination of yellow and white glowing like burning gold.

A searing pain surged through his mind as he watched golden energy cascade from his thoughts, racing along the nerve pathways of his body. His gaze traced the electrifying current as it spiraled down to his hands. Suddenly, his eyes snapped open just as the energy leapt from his fingertips into Hog's chest. Like the jolt of defibrillator paddles, he felt the crackling surge of electricity pierce his friend's body, a desperate attempt to reignite the spark of life.

The Chief remained silent, his left hand pressed firmly against Hog's neck, searching for a sign.

Thump…...thump……….. thump…thump…thump.

A faint pulse. Weak but steady. A faint smile tugged at his lips. Hog was alive—barely, but alive.

"He's alive. So, you can't have him," the Chief growled, defiance etched in his voice.

"He's still dying, sir," the man replied coldly. "A Mahaha's blade struck him. His time is short, and I *will* return for his soul."

"Not happening," the Chief shot back, his tone unyielding.

Suddenly, the woods erupted in a cacophony of howls and screeches, a chorus of unseen creatures wailing from every direction. It sounded as though the forest itself had come alive, teeming with hundreds—perhaps thousands—of malevolent beings.

"They're coming, Chief," the man warned. "Hand over your son, and he'll keep his word. Until then, the demons will slaughter as many as they can. My night will be… busy." With that, he turned and vanished into the shadows.

The Chief hoisted Hog's limp body, struggling to his feet as the biting wind and snow battered him, nearly knocking him off balance. "Hang on, buddy," he muttered, steadying himself before trudging toward the door.

"Hammond!" he bellowed, kicking the door with all his might. It swung open, revealing Hammond and Vickers, their faces etched with alarm.

111

"What happened?" Hammond shouted, his voice barely audible over the howling wind.

"No time to explain," the Chief barked. "Get him inside—now!"

***

Priscilla Reed wasn't exactly sure what had just happened. She had been hiding behind some pallets, watching the exchange between Chief Pendleton and the thin man. He couldn't see the man's face, but she was creeped out by him the minute he appeared. She was shocked when the snow seemed to part for him as he approached the Chief.

She couldn't hear the entire conversation but understood enough that the man was there for Detective Sheridan. He wanted the man lying in the snow. He appeared to be dead, and a strange thought popped into her mind. The man was a grim reaper here to claim the dead.

"How could that be?" she laughed. "There is no such thing."

Then, the giant glowing creature appeared out of nowhere. He was massive. She couldn't see what he looked like. The snow and wind were too firm to obscure her vision, but she could see he was huge and appeared glowing with icy blue. The things' words were as clear as could be. They seemed to rise above the driving snowflakes.

Her eyes continued to watch the exchange as the giant beast demanded the Chief's son in exchange for the people of the town, including the Chief's detective. The police chief refused, though, which was not surprising. She heard the conversation and the threat of killing everyone in town, but she didn't believe the threat was legitimate. Then, the howls rose high into the storm from the surrounding tree lines, sending a chill of fear down her spine.

"What is going on here?" she whispered as she watched the big man disappear. She steadied the camera phone to record the exchange. Her hands didn't shake from the cold but fear. Whatever just happened, Priscilla Reed suddenly believed they could kill the whole town.

112

The thin man's final words told the Chief that people would die, and if he turned over his son, he could save the town. To her astonishment, he still refused. Even though it was apparent that something supernatural was occurring in the forest and would lead to the death of dozens of townsfolk, if not all, he refused. The exchange ended, and the Chief picked up the big detective and returned to the school.

She looked at her phone and stopped the recording. She quickly replayed it, making sure she got everything on video. The smile crossing her face was as big as Priscilla Reed's ever had.

"We'll see how much this town will love you now, Chief," she mumbled.

She looked around and slithered back through the school door. She squatted down in the dark shadows of the hallway and waited for the men to pass. She watched as they struggled to carry the wounded police officer back towards the gym, and she waited. A few moments later, after checking the hall to make sure it was clear, the disgraced media member shuffled out of the darkness and into the gym.

11
THE CHENOO

"Lena is not wrong. Something's off," Jack said, glancing toward Lena, who sat on the couch with Rachel's arm wrapped around her. I sat on her other side, squeezing her hand in reassurance.

"Wait, I'm still stuck on the idea that you are...the real Jack Frost?" Agent Mason asked as he sat at the table.

"C'mon, Dumpster Man, keep up with us," Franklin said as he patted Mason on the shoulder.

Mason shot him with a deadly glare.

"Why did he call you dumpster man?" Jack asked.

Mason just rubbed the scar on his cheek.

"When Prentice first met ran into him, they didn't see eye to eye and Prentice hosed him down with colors slamming him into the dumpster where a nasty fisher cat left him that scar," Franklin said patting the FBI agent on the shoulder.

"Franklin, are you twelve?" Doc Eddings said.

The blonde-haired boy nodded.

"I fear you may not reach thirteen if Agent Mason has his way," Doc advised.

"What? Franklin asked, looking at Agent Mason.

The special agent un-snapped the holster on his sidearm and winked at Franklin.

"Oh," Franklin smiled. "I'll be quiet now."

The tension in the room eased. Even Lena cracked a small smile.

"You're welcome," Franklin mouthed silently to everyone at the table.

I just shook my head, trying not to laugh.

114

"Look, Chernobog has used storms like this to eliminate his targets before. The snow provides cover for his winter demons to swoop in and kill anything he wants," Jack advised.

"When was the last time this happened?" I asked.

"1922 in northern Canada," Jack replied.

"1922…1922," Doc whispered as he stood and began to pace.

"Yes, 1922," Jack said again.

"No, no…I know what you said. I'm trying to remember what it was," Doc said.

"Anjukani Lake," Jack said.

"Of course, the Inuit Village that disappeared," Doc proclaimed.

Jack nodded.

"Wait, the entire village went missing. I remember now," Brother Kiernan added. "The fur hunter found it completely empty."

Adam pulled it up on the monitors for everyone to see. The story contained a bunch of photos of the abandoned fishing village.

"It says the trapper notified the Canadian Mounties, and they went to the village and found it completely abandoned," Adam said.

"There was nothing? Dakota asked.

"I have heard stories about this village," Chief Tackna said. "They say the Ninngappoq came to the village and took everyone."

"What does Ninngappoq mean? Dakota asked his uncle.

"Monsters," Jack asked.

Chief Tackna nodded.

"The winter demons came in and took or killed everyone?" Agent Mason asked. "The Mounties had no idea."

"They didn't take everyone," Jack said simply.

"The story says there were no survivors," Adam said. The trapper… Joe LaBelle said the village was totally empty.

"He lied," Jack said.

"Why would he lie?" Rachel asked.

"Was he a part of it? Did he lead the monsters there?" Franklin asked.

115

Jack shook his head. "LaBelle hid someone. A little girl," Jack said.

"There are no reports of a little girl in any of the stories. I just did a metadata search," Adam said.

"Yeah, no mention of any survivors, let alone a little girl," Agent Mason added as he scanned the reports.

"Because he made sure no one would ever find her," I said, realization dawning. I looked at Jack. He didn't deny it.

"I'm confused," Franklin said.

"Surprise, surprise," Mason laughed.

"Hey, don't make fun of my Frankie," Mollie said, appearing right next to Mason.

"Ahhh!" the FBI agent screamed like a baby and fell out of his seat.

We all tried not to laugh, but when Lena snorted with laughter, we all followed.

"That's not funny," Mason stammered as he sat back in his seat.

"Actually, it is," Chief Tackna laughed.

"I will have the Feds raid your reservation for weapons," Mason sneered.

"But you gave us many of those weapons," Tackna smiled.

Mason stared at his friend. "Not the tomahawks," he added.

"I don't think those are illegal for them to possess, my dear Mason," Doc added.

"Doc... shut up," Mason laughed.

"Sorry, Dumpster Man," Mollie said, hugging the FBI agent.

"It's okay, kiddo," Mason laughed, returning the hug.

"Wait, she can call you Dumpster Man, but I can't?" Franklin asked.

"I like her. I don't like you," Mason smiled.

"Not fair," Franklin pouted.

Dakota slapped him in the head.

"Ouch," he shouted.

"Okay, okay. Let's focus," Adam ordered. "Back to the fishing village."

"So, Chernobog sent the storm and the demons to get this girl. This guy LaBelle shows up finds her, and saves her," Brother Kiernan said.

"Why would Chernobog want her, and why would LaBelle save and hide her?" Mason asked.

"Because she is like me," I said.

Jack stayed silent.

"She is a rainbow warrior like me," I said. "Isn't she Jack?"

His silence said everything.

"Why didn't you tell us that?" Lena demanded.

"Because he helped save her and hide her," I added. "And he promised he would never say anything."

Jack exhaled, giving me a knowing look.

My cell phone rang simultaneously as Doc's, Brother Kiernan's, and Agent Mason's. We all looked at one another. I looked at the number. It was Dad.

"Hey, Dad," I said.

"PJ is Lena with you?" he asked. "If she is, don't look at her."

"Yep," I answered, trying to sound casual, but I understood something was wrong.

"Listen to me. You need to bring her to the school as quick as possible. There has been an incident, and Hog is in bad shape," he said.

"Yep, okay," I said.

"You need to come with her," he said. "You need to get here quickly."

"Yep, okay," I said, trying to keep the fear from showing.

"PJ, listen to me. This is not good. Understand me?" he asked.

"Yep, gotcha, Dad," I said as my hands shook.

"Get here as quick as you can," he said.

"Yep. Okay, Dad. Will do," I replied.

"Okay, see you when you get here," he said and hung up.

I slid the phone back into my pocket and looked at the group.

"Okay, new plan," I said.

"It's my Dad, isn't it?" Lena asked.

117

I didn't know what to say, so I said nothing.

"Prentice, tell me now," she demanded.

My hands shook as I glanced at Brother Kiernan and Agent Mason. They looked worried.

"Prentice!" Lena exclaimed.

The FBI agent and priest nodded at me. Their thoughts were clear. Tell her. I swallowed hard, trying to calm myself.

"Yes. The Hog has been hurt at the school," I whispered.

"I knew it," she cried as Rachel wrapped her arms around her. Mollie and Dakota went over to her, trying to reassure her.

"What condition is Henry in?" Doc Eddings asked, referring to Hog by his real name.

"How bad?" Agent Mason's thoughts pushed into my mind. He hadn't done that in a long time.

"Bad. Dad says to get there as fast as we can," I said.

"Crap," he replied. *"What happened?"*

"I don't know," I replied.

"Tell her," He said.

"Look at her," I answered.

"We need to go as fast as we can, so she should know," he added.

I nodded and told them what Dad had said.

"My father says we need to get there as fast as possible," I told everyone.

"Let's go," Franklin ordered. Everyone into The Beast".

Everyone started packing up. Chief Tackna grabbed a radio.

"Pnieses! Back to the jeeps. We are headed to the school for an emergency," he commanded.

Everyone looked at him.

"My warriors will escort us to town," he smiled.

"A reverse posse," Mason said, smiling at the Chief.

"I don't like you, Agent Man," the once Wampanoag chief said.

"I know Dumpster Man is annoying, isn't he," Franklin said, putting his arm around the sitting Chief.

"Franklin, my grandfather will scalp you," Dakota said.

"Haha—wait, what?"

Tackna reached out and ran a hand over Franklin's hair.

He quickly withdrew his arm from the Chief's shoulder.

"C'mon, he's got a lot of hair to scalp," Mason said, sounding disappointed.

"Hey," Franklin said, not sure if everyone was serious.

"Good hair," he whispered.

"Hey," Franklin cried out.

Whack!

"Move," Rachel ordered Franklin as the Chief and Mason erupted in laughter.

"Not funny," Franklin cried out.

"Move," Mollie ordered him.

Laughter filled the air, breaking some of the tension as we threw on coats and raced outside to Brother Kiernan's RV.

The storm had arrived. And the war had begun.

***

By the time we spilled out into the howling night, the Chief's men were already back, huddled by the Jeeps, their breath fogging in the frigid air. The Chief climbed into one of the vehicles with his crew, while the rest of us crammed into The Beast, our mobile command center. Brother Kiernan turned the key, and the engine roared to life. Monitors flickered awake, casting eerie blue light across our faces, when a sudden, guttural suction sound rattled the steel walls.

"What was that, Thomas?" Doc asked him.

"Warding's up," Brother Kiernan replied as he eased The Beast out from the church lot, tailing one of the Chief's Jeeps. Another followed close behind, a shadowy caravan swallowed by the storm.

The blizzard raged like a living thing, a maelstrom of white fury under a blood moon that stained the sky a deep, ominous crimson. Visibility was a cruel joke. Snow lashed at the windows, turning the world into a shaken snow globe. Swirling flakes danced on invisible torrents of wind, stinging like needles. Thunder boomed overhead, a deep growl followed by jagged streaks of lightning that split the dark.

"Lightning?" Agent Mason wondered.

"Thunder snow," Doc corrected, his voice steady. "Think category five hurricane but swap the rain for ice and chaos."

119

"Can you even see the jeep?" I asked Brother Kiernan.

"Barely," he replied.

"A storm like this hasn't been seen in over a hundred years," Doc told us all.

Mason glanced at Jack, the winter fairy perched near the back. "Can Chernobog whip up something this nasty whenever he feels like it?"

Jack shook his head, silver hair catching the monitor glow. "No. He needs the stars aligned, celestial chaos, and a world drowning in disorder."

"There has certainly been a lot of chaos going on," Mason added.

"Indeed, there has been Mr. Mason," Doc commented.

I studied Brother Kiernan. Tension carved lines into his face, his grip on the steering wheel unyielding. "You, okay?" I asked, my voice softer.

"Just trying to concentrate in front of me," he said.

"Jack, can you light the way?" Franklin piped up from the back.

"Do I look like Rudolph?" he replied.

"Well, no," Franklin grinned.

"Look out!" Rachel shouted.

A hulking shadow erupted from a front yard along Old County Road, snapping trees like brittle bones as it barreled onto the snow-choked street. The lead Jeep didn't stand a chance, the monstrous form slammed into its side with a deafening crunch. Metal screamed and shattered, shards flying through the whipping wind as the Jeep rolled violently, tumbling into the opposite yard. It flipped three times before smashing against a gnarled oak, dislodging a cascade of snow. The three tribal warriors inside scrambled out, vanishing into the blizzard's embrace.

"What just happened up there?" came the Chief's voice over the radio.

"Thomas?" Doc bellowed.

"What is that? Rachel shouted as we all looked out the windshield. It was a pure sheet of snow blanketing the night. All we saw was a massive shape in the roadway.

Jack stood, his expression hardening. "It's a Chenoo." He strode to the RV's door.

"A what? Mason asked.

"An ice giant," Jack replied as he tried the door handle.

"What is this? Game of Thrones?" Dakota shook his head.

"Jack, what are you doing?" Lena asked him.

"Going out there," he replied coolly. "Brother Kiernan, drop the warding so I can get out."

"SCREEEEEE!" the creature screamed.

"Open the door, Brother," I said as I stood up.

"Prentice, what are you doing?" Lena's eyes widened, her hand reaching for me.

"What are you doing?" Jack asked.

"Those men need help," I said, meeting Lena's gaze. "Jack and I are the only ones who can do this."

"Prentice," she snapped, her voice cracking.

"Yeah, c'mon, Crayon, man. Did you see how it threw that jeep?" Franklin asked.

I nodded.

"I can handle this," Jack added.

"Can you?" I challenged, locking eyes with him. His bravado faltered, a quiver in his voice, uncertainty clouding his icy stare.

"Yes," he mumbled, but his quivering voice and nervousness in his eyes gave him away.

"Didn't think so," I smiled. "Look, Jack and I will take care of this...what did you call it?"

"Chenoo," he muttered.

"Right. The Chenoo. We'll meet you at the school after," I said.

Agent Mason stood up.

"You need to get to the school and help there," I said.

"Kid, you don't give me orders," the FBI agent said.

Doc intervened, his tone calm but authoritative. "Agent Mason, Prentice is right. Your skills are critical there."

Mason reluctantly agreed.

"You have to melt its heart," Dakota said out of nowhere.

"What?" Rachel asked.

121

"Chenoos are ice giants," Dakota explained, shrugging. "Old legends say if you melt their heart, they die."

"I don't think it's a legend anymore," Franklin laughed.

"What is going on?" Chief Tackna's voice crackled over the radio.

Brother Kiernan grabbed the radio and keyed the mic.

"We have a...roadblock," he replied. "Your warriors just got knocked off the road."

"I have them. They just jumped in," he shouted back.

"Turn around and go the other way," Brother Kiernan said.

"Prentice, are you sure about this?" Doc asked.

"Jack and I can handle this. You guys get to the school," I told him.

"Prentice," Lena said, grabbing his hand.

"I'll make it there. I promise," I smiled.

"You better or I'll kick your...," she began.

"SCREEEEEE!" the beast roared.

A hiss of air released as the warding dropped. I shoved the door open and leaped into the storm, Jack soaring out beside me, his wings slicing through the snow. "Go!" I yelled, and the door slammed shut. The Beast lurched backward, followed by the Chief's Jeep, retreating into the white void. I didn't look back— Brother Kiernan would get them out.

"SCREEEEE!" The Chenoo loomed ahead, its massive form leaning forward, arms rearing back like a predator about to strike.

"The choochoo's ugggly," the voice said behind me.

"Franklin! What are you doing?" I screamed.

"I can't let you have all the fun, crayon man," he laughed as he stepped up to my right, holding something in his hand.

Jack landed to my left, smirking. "Looks like your buddy wants in."

"SCREEEEE!" A second Chenoo lumbered out from the yard, bigger, horned, and meaner, its bell-shaped head crowned with jagged spikes. Glowing purple eyes burned through the snow, dripping with malice.

"I don't see where this is fun," I said.

"Frosty, ready to rumble?" Franklin rocked on his heels, grinning.

"SCREEEEE!" The larger Chenoo bellowed, shaking the ground

"Jack, have you fought these before?" I asked him.

"No," he said.

"We just gonna stand here?" Franklin prodded.

The beasts began to circle us, their heavy steps crunching the snow. "I've got the right one," I said. "Jack, take the left."

"And me?" Franklin asked.

"Stay put," Jack and I barked in unison.

"FREEDOM!" Franklin yelled charging straight at them.

"Get back!" Jack shouted, but Franklin was already gone, swallowed by the swirling snow.

"Crap," I growled, sprinting after him as Jack took to the air, a streak of silver against the blood-red moon.

The smaller Chenoo roared, lumbering toward Franklin. I wouldn't reach him in time. A blast of golden energy erupted from my hands, crackling with rainbow hues—red, blue, gold— but the beast dodged with surprising agility. Then flames tore through the snow, bursting from Franklin's flare.

"What the…," I whispered.

The Chenoo shrieked, terror flashing in its purple eyes as Franklin's fire licked at its fur. It skidded, claws gouging the road, but momentum carried it forward—straight into Franklin. "Crayola, light it up!" he hollered, dropping to his knees and sliding between its legs. He lobbed the flare at its chest, and I understood.

I unleashed a bolt of searing red energy. It struck the flare midair, igniting a torrent of flame that engulfed the Chenoo. Tendrils of fire, crimson, amber, violet, danced across its body, the stench of burning fur thick in the air. Its eyes widened in agony as it dove into the snow, thrashing to douse the blaze.

Jack swooped down, unleashing a stream of icy blue energy. My next blast merged with his, the flames shifting to a blinding cerulean heat. The Chenoo's screams faded as it crumbled into ash, embers glowing briefly before the wind swept them away.

"Piece of cake," Franklin said, brushing snow off his pants.

"What…how…" I began.

BAM!

The larger Chenoo hit me like a freight train, its bulk sending me flying. I crashed into the overturned Jeep, flames licking around me, metal groaning under my impact. I tumbled into a snowbank, and my breath kicked out of me. Pain should've followed, broken ribs, burns, but nothing came. I wasn't on fire. I'd passed through the blaze unscathed.

I patted myself down, half-expecting missing limbs. Nope. Intact. *What's happening to me?*

I waited for the pain of broken bones and maybe a crushed spleen or a severed leg. I expected something to be damaged after hitting the jeep as hard as I did, but I felt okay. I ran my hands over my body just to double-check that I wasn't split in half. Whew! I wasn't.

Combat echoed—BAM, BAM, BAM—snapping me back. I staggered up, still waiting for agony that never arrived. The Chenoo had hit me hard, and I'd smashed into a burning Jeep. "Am I dead?" I whispered, glancing at the snow where I'd landed. No broken body stared back. Relief flooded me.

"Prentice, watch out!" Franklin's voice rang out.

I turned just as the Chenoo charged, its hairy foot swinging. No time to dodge—it punted me over a fence into a backyard, straight into a frozen pool. Ice cracked beneath the cover, and frigid water swallowed me, wrapping me in its green shroud. I kicked hard, muscles surging, and exploded out, landing on the deck. Icicles dangled from my hair, my hands, freezing instantly in the air. I caught my reflection in the glass door— scarred, bruised, but whole.

Anger ignited inside me. "Ahhhhh!" I roared, and the ice melted, steam rising as flames erupted around me—red, gold, blue—swirling like a rainbow storm. Pain? None. Just power.

BOOM! Metal and glass shattered ahead. "Jack, look out!" Franklin yelled.

I glanced at my reflection again. Flames danced over me, but I felt alive, invincible. *Am I dying?* No time to wonder.

"Franklin!" Jack's shout pierced the storm, followed by Franklin's scream.

"Ahhhhh!!" I screamed.

I didn't yell because I was in pain. Oh no…it was much worse. The anger raged in me for a few moments, and as a result, the ice quickly melted from my face and hands. It melted because I was suddenly on fire.

BAM, BAM, BAM!

More sounds of combat erupting from the roadway.

"Jack, look out!" I heard Franklin yell just before an explosion of glass and metal thundered from the roadway.

I took a step forward. My legs and arms seemed to move normally. My mind was clear, and I was in no pain. But I was on fire. I still couldn't understand what was happening.

"Franklin!" Jack yelled from somewhere in front of the house.

"Ahhhhh!" I heard Franklin scream.

I had to get back out there. I turned and ran to the snow-covered gate. I grabbed the black iron handle and watched it melt in my grip. What was going on?

I bolted for the gate, grabbing the iron handle, it melted in my grip. I kicked the wood, splintering it, and ran toward the chaos. The street was a warzone: flipped cars, one ablaze, illuminating the blood-red night. A broken hydrant sprayed water that froze midair, a surreal sculpture in the storm.

"That's something you don't see every day," I mumbled as the water continued flowing and turning to ice.

The Chenoo swiped at Jack, who darted through the snow, blasting icy energy. A claw caught him, sending him skidding across the pavement like a snowball gaining mass. "SCREEEE!" it roared, charging him.

"Whack, whack, whack!"

Snowballs pelted its head. Franklin knelt in the street, hurling them with deadly aim—one hit its purple eye. A wild-eyed Franklin was kneeling in the street, making snowballs as fast as he could, then launching them at the big hairy beast. I had to admit, I was impressed he found one of the eyes. It had to have hurt. Franklin threw hard. The beast staggered, then roared, lunging

125

for him. Franklin slipped, face-planting in the snow, emerging with a snowy beard and wide eyes as the Chenoo closed in.

"Hey, ugly! I'm not your football!" I yelled, flames trailing me as I charged. Its eyes widened in fear at the sight of me, a blazing figure sprinting through the storm. I flung my hands forward, unleashing cannonballs of multicolored fire. They slammed into its arms, igniting fur. It dove into the snow, but a blast tore off a horn, eliciting a piercing scream.

A claw slashed my cheek—pain flared, sharp and real. *Why this but not the fire?* I ducked its next kick, rolling aside. Franklin leaped onto a car, then onto the Chenoo's neck, gripping its horn and whacking its head with a baton.

"YAWWWWWW," Franklin screamed at the top of his lungs as he sprinted forward leaping onto a snow-covered car, propelling himself into the air and landing on the massive beast's head and neck. His short legs wrapped around the Chenoo's neck, and his left
hand grabbed hold of the remaining horn.

"Franklin! What are you doing?" I yelled at him.

"Saving your fiery butt," he shouted.

"Yee haw!" he whooped, riding it like a bronco, a small metal baton in his hand. Whack, whack, whack, whack. He was playing whack-a-mole with the Chenoo's head.

It roared in pain as the small solid metal baton found its mark with each swing. I could hear the thud of the metal slamming off thick bone each time Franklin swung the weapon. The beast began hopping around, trying to shake Franklin free, but the kid had a solid grip and wouldn't let go. It was like watching a bucking bronco trying to kick the rider off.

"There is something seriously wrong with that kid," Jack said as he appeared beside my flaming body. He made sure to stay far enough away from my human blowtorch.

"You have no idea," I answered.

"Flames?" he asked me.

"Don't ask how. I have no idea," I replied.

"Ridem cowboy!" Franklin laughed as he continued to hammer away at the beast. Dark crimson blood flowing down the Chenoo's face. The monster continued to buck and flail its big arms upward, trying to hit his rider.

"It's kind of funny," Jack said.

"He has a knack for that," I added.

I spoke too soon. A claw clipped him, knocking off it's back.

I reacted a little too late. The Chenoo spun around as fast as it could. Like a baseball bat, he clenched his hands together and swung them with tremendous force, connecting with Franklin as he fell. The new term in baseball is exit velocity which describes how fast a baseball comes off the bat when the hitter connects. Franklin's exit velocity had to be over 100 mph as he rocketed towards the house they were in front of. Franklin's body smashed through the painted glass of the front door and disappeared into the house beyond.

"Franklin," I shouted as I fired more blazing fire bolts at the hairy creature. They exploded off its head, sending orange embers shooting in all directions. Small flames began to grow and sprout in various places of the fur. He howled in pain.

Jack shot up into the air and began firing a volley of icy blue bolts that slammed into it. They didn't blow up the fire, but they had to be painful because it screeched in pain. I stopped firing as Jack swooped into the air, observing the scene. The now one-horned Chenoo growling at us.

"You want more Bumble?" I asked it.

"Did you just call it Bumble...like from Rudolph?" Jack laughed.

"Bumbles bounce," I shouted angrily.

The beast growled one more time, turned, and ran for the tree line. I fired a burst of flaming energy that struck the Chenoo right in the butt. He howled, grabbing his butt, and hopping into the woods and disappearing into the darkness. Jack landed next to me, and we stared at the darkened tree line, but it was gone.

"Should we go after it?" Jack asked.

"Let it go. We kicked its..."

Boom!

A car exploded, shooting flames high into the sky.

"Can you put the fires out?" I asked him.

He nodded and shot into the air, buzzing around, firing cloudy icy bolts at the fires, extinguishing them quickly. His feet touched down in the snow next to me a moment later.

"Good job," I said.

He fired more of the fire extinguisher energy at me, engulfing me in a cloudy haze. I was surprised, but I didn't budge. I just stood still until he was done. When the cloud cleared, I looked at him.

"Am I still cooking?" I asked him.

"No. But your face doesn't look good," he said.

I shrugged, trying not to focus on the raw, burning skin.

"That was interesting," I said.

Franklin stumbled out, bleeding from a gash on his head and his pants were burned off below the knees.

"Great teamwork, guys," he smiled.

"You, okay?" I asked him.

He nodded and took a bite of something.

"What are you eating?" I asked.

"Found some leftover Famous Pizza in the fridge. There's more in there," he said just before falling face-first into the snow.

"Franklin?" I shouted.

"I'm good," Franklin's muffled voice rose from the snow as he held up the pizza. "Still tasty."

12
BLOOD ON THE SNOW

Capron Bay High School
Capron Bay, MA
7:00 P.M.

The gym's fluorescent lights buzzed overhead, casting stark shadows across the makeshift medical bay in the corner. Dr. Taft bent over Hog Sheridan, his gloved hands trembling slightly as he examined the jagged wounds tearing through the man's stomach. Blood pooled beneath the cot, dark and thick, soaking into the hardwood floor. He paused, glancing around the curtained-off space as if the walls themselves might overhear.

"Dr. Taft, what caused this?" Chief Pendleton's voice was steady but edged with urgency.

"Claws," Taft said finally, his tone low. "Long, sharp claws ripped him open."

"Bear?" Melissa asked, her hands deftly hooking an IV bag to the stand. The moment Chief Pendleton had staggered in carrying Hog, the gym had transformed—blinds snapped up, a corner cordoned off, a battlefield triage born in minutes. No one needed to see the gore. Dr. Taft and Melissa, fresh from the nursing home, had taken charge, with Grammy's steady presence anchoring them.

Anyika slipped through the curtains, followed by Pam Sheridan—Hog's wife—and Grammy, her coat dusted with snow from her ride with Captain Lynch. Melissa threw her arms around Grammy, a lifeline in the chaos, while Pam's sobs broke the sterile silence.

"Is he okay?" she asked to nobody in particular. "Where is Lena?"

"Dr. Taft is going to take care of him," the Chief said. "Lena is on her way. Agent Mason and Brother Kiernan are bringing her.

129

Pam nodded, tears streaking her face. "Will he make it?"

Grammy draped an arm around her. "Dr. Taft's doing all he can, honey."

"Robert," Pam pressed, turning to the Chief, "don't sugarcoat it. Is he going to be, okay?"

He exchanged a glance with Taft, who shook his head slightly. "I don't know," Taft admitted. "He's lost too much blood, and the wounds… they're rotting."

"Rotting?" Pam's eyes darted between them, wide with disbelief.

"Poisoned," Melissa said, sparing her husband and the doctor the burden. "Something in the wounds is spreading."

"From what?" she asked.

"Claws," Taft repeated, hesitant. "Not like any I've seen."

"Claws? From a bear?" Pam asked, wiping her eyes.

"No bear did this," Anyika cut in, her voice firm, tinged with her Gullah cadence. "Not dem claws."

"What?" Pam asked. "What else has claws like that?"

Captain Lynch slid the curtain back and stepped in. He nodded at the Chief and Dr.Taft.

"Mountain lions sometimes make their way down here," Dr. Taft said.

"Mountain lions?" Melissa asked.

"No mo lias," Anyika stammered, shifting to her Gullah accent to stress the words.

The room stilled, the hum of the gym beyond the curtains fading to a hush. Pam's irritation flared. "What's she mean, 'lies'?"

Nobody answered.

"Chief," Anyika said. "It iz time."

He nodded, exhaling heavily. "A Mahaha stabbed him."

"A what?" Captain Lynch's brow furrowed.

"Robert? What are you talking about?" Melissa asked her husband.

"My friends, have you not seen all the strange and weird things that happen around this town?" Anyika asked.

"What is a Mahaha?" Dr. Taft asked.

130

Anyika stepped forward, her presence commanding. "A snow demon, dat's what. Y'all seen de strange t'ings in dis town—don't act like you blind."

"A snow demon?" Lynch asked. "Really?"

Commotion erupted beyond the curtains—shouts, footsteps. "Let's give Pam some space with Hog," the Chief said, ushering them out. They slipped through the fabric wall, but Melissa grabbed his arm, halting him.

"What's going on, Robert?" Her whisper was fierce, searching his face.

"Mel, I'll explain everything—I promise. But not now." He nodded toward the growing noise. "We've got company."

Melissa's eyes followed her husband as he approached the commotion. A man dressed in a thick black overcoat had arrived with a small entourage. She didn't recognize him until he took the overcoat off, and she saw he was wearing his traditional red suit with a golden cross hanging around his neck.

"Cardinal Murphy," she whispered.

"Mel?" Pam said from Hog's bedside.

Melissa ducked back inside, leaving the Chief to stride toward the newcomer.

"Cardinal Murphy," he said, extending a hand.

"Chief Pendleton," the Cardinal replied, his grip firm. "I'm here to aid Capron Bay however I can."

"I appreciate it, sir, but are you sure you want to be here?" the Chief asked him.

"We don't have much of a choice now, Chief Pendleton," Charles Dawson said as he joined the conversation. "It is too dangerous to go back now."

"Chief, you remember my assistant Charles Dawson," The Cardinal said. "It was his idea to come down."

"I do," the Chief answered, shaking his hand.

"We're just happy to help," Charles replied, removing his overcoat. He was wearing a heavy red Boston College sweatshirt.

"Eagles fan?" the Chief asked.

"Is there any other school?" Charles laughed. "Where can we help?"

"The town's lucky to have you, Chief," Murphy said, surveying the chaos—cots, nurses, frightened faces.

131

"He's not in charge, Your Grace," Agent Liang cut in, approaching with a man in a FEMA jacket. "I'm Special Agent in Charge Joseph Liang, and this is Captain Michael Byrd from FEMA."

"I'm sorry, who are you?" Charles asked.

"I'm Special Agent in Charge Joseph Liang, and this is Retired Army Captain Michael Byrd from FEMA," the Agent answered.

"Yes, we're in charge here," Byrd added. The Governor has declared a national emergency for Capron Bay, which means we are now in control."

"Oh, bless your heart," a honeyed Southern voice drawled above the din. Fiona Thompson sauntered over, her smile sharp as she hugged the Chief.

"Why does everyone here think we're not in control?" Byrd snapped, frustration boiling over.

"Young man, y'all got no idea what's comin'," Fiona laughed, patting his arm.

"Ma'am, who are you now?" Agent Liang demanded.

"Fiona Thompson," Cardinal Murphy supplied. "Special assistant to Chief Pendleton."

"Fiona, how did you get here?" the Chief asked.

"Hitched a ride with the Cardinal from New Orleans," she said with a wink. "Couldn't resist his charm."

Charles grinned. "She was on our flight. Had to bring her along."

The Chief smirked—Fiona's knack for bending people to her will was unmatched.

"Ms. Thompson, I assure you, we have authorization from the Governor himself and Senator Bradler. We are in charge here," Byrd said.

"Y'all need to act like you have some sense, my friends," Fiona laughed. "That piece of paper may say you are in charge, but look around you, sir. You are not even close to being in command here."

Before Byrd could retort, the gym doors crashed open. A man stumbled in, blood dripping down his face, his eyes wild with terror. "Something's in the storm!"

"Stan, what happened?" someone shouted.

132

"There's something in the storm," he screamed.

"Stan, what are you talking about?" someone asked him.

"There's something out there—in the snow!" Stan backed away from the doors, his voice rising to a shriek. The crowd surged, FBI agents sprinting to peer outside.

"Stan, where are you hurt?" he asked the man examining his bloody face. A nurse from the nursing home ran to help.

"It's not mine," he stammered.

"Tell me what happened," the Chief said as he placed a hand on his arm.

Stan looked at him. His eyes were wild with fear.

"It's not mine," he mumbled, wiping at the blood. "I was with Beverly Cooper. We were almost here when something—something big—hit her. Blood sprayed everywhere, and she was gone."

"Someone else is out there," a woman screamed. "It's Trevor Carson and his wife Lynn."

An FBI agent cracked the door open, stepping into the storm as another held it ajar. Screams filtered through—distant, desperate. "Come on, folks!" the agent yelled.

A woman's wail cut short with a sickening thud. "No!" the agent roared, then flew backward into the gym, slamming onto the floor. His chest was a gaping ruin—heart torn clean out.

The Chief ran over to Anyika and the dead FBI Agent.

"His heart has been torn out. In one clean blow, something hit him and ripped out his heart," Anyika said.

"Shut that door," the Chief ordered, and another FBI Agent slammed it shut.

"What just happened?" the Agent cried out.

The door banged from behind him.

"Agent Carson, you keep that door shut," Byrd ordered the young man. "Secure that door."

"Let us in. Please let us in!" Lynn Carson screamed as she pounded on the door.

"Open that door," the Chief demanded.

"Agent Carson, you keep the door shut," Byrd countered.

"Byrd, they need help," Chief Pendleton roared.

Lynn's scream shredded the air, and blood streaked the window. "She's dead!" someone wailed.

133

"The Moseleys are out there—something's chasing them!" a man yelled from the bleachers.

"It's the Moseleys. Something is chasing them in the storm," a man yelled as he stood on the bleachers looking out a small window.

"Open the door," Chief Pendleton ordered.

"Keep it shut!" Byrd snapped, FEMA agents piling against it.

"Help us!" the Moseleys cried, their pleas muffled by the storm.

"Liang, there are people out there that need help," the Chief shouted.

"We need to worry about everyone in here," Byrd yelled.

The Chief surged forward. "Byrd, open it *now!*"

"Help!" more cries echoed from beyond the doors.

"Chief Pendleton, I need to remind you who is in charge here," Byrd smirked.

Agent Liang met the Chief before he could reach Byrd.

"Chief Pendleton, I'm ordering you to stand down," the Agent in charge said.

"You tell him to open those doors right now," the Chief demanded.

"Not going to happen," Byrd said, shaking his head.

"Help us!" The Moseleys' pounding grew frantic.

"Byrd, open the door," Chief Pendleton said, stepping by Liang.

"Agent Manfredo, arrest this man immediately," Liang ordered another FBI agent.

"Help us!"

Liang grabbed hold of the Chief's right hand.

The Chief stepped back, grabbed the man's hand with his right hand, and spun him around. It caught the FBI agent by surprise, and he couldn't keep his balance. He fell backward against some classroom chairs set up in the gym. Chief Pendleton ignored the Agent and stepped towards the doors.

"Byrd, get out of my way," he demanded.

Bryd threw a wild punch. The Capron Bay police chief blocked the punch with his left hand and drove a right uppercut into Byrd's chin. The man's legs buckled, and he collapsed on the gym floor.

"Open the door!" he barked at the two agents guarding it. They hesitated, then stepped aside as something slammed the wood, a girl's scream echoing.

The Chief burst through the door into the storm beyond. The agents moved in to shut the door behind him.

Grammy's voice cut through. "Close that door, and you'll answer to me!"

The Agents backed away from the door.

When the Chief got outside, he could see the Moseleys huddled together just outside the door.

"Hurry, get in," the Chief said.

"It took Sandy," Mr. Moseley shouted.

A girl's scream rang out. "Help!"

Two troll-like creatures loomed in the blizzard—short, muscled, with glowing red eyes and gorilla snouts. One, bright blue-furred, clutched Sandy; the other, darker, hefted a club. They snarled, edging away from the trees as a guttural *"SCRAWWWW"* erupted from the shadows.

"Let her go," the Chief ordered.

The one holding Sandy growled.

The club-wielder grunted and charged, weapon raised.

Main Street
Capron Bay, MA
7:30 P.M

The RV fishtailed around a bend, snow chains clawing at Main Street's buried pavement. The storm roared, a living beast under the blood moon's crimson glare, piling snow a foot deep. Evergreens loomed, their branches bending inward like skeletal hands grasping at The Beast. Brother Kiernan's grip on the wheel was iron, fighting the slide.

"We shouldn't have left them back there," Agent Mason muttered, eyes dark.

"Prentice knows what he is doing," Dakota replied.

The FBI agent just glared at Dakota.

135

"I'm gonna strangle Franklin," Mollie hissed, rubbing the warding tattoo on her arm as the RV swerved.

"They'll be okay," Rachel said, squeezing Lena's shoulder. Her best friend sat with her head buried in her hands. She was worried about her father and now Prentice.

Whoosh

Something huge flew over the RV a few feet in front of the truck. The shadow was huge, big enough to be visible through the driving snow squalls.

"What was that?" Adam shouted as he watched the security monitors.

Whoosh. It passed again, wings cutting the snow.

"Thomas, I suggest we hurry up," Doc said.

"Thanks, Doc," Brother Kiernan replied.

"I'm just saying, that thing seems…rather large," Doc added.

"Got it, Doc," Brother Kiernan replied.

Agent Mason leaned over in the front seat, trying to get a better view through the windshield.

"Adam, see that panel with the three buttons in a row. The red, yellow, and green buttons?" Brother Kiernan asked.

"Yes, sir," Adam replied as his wheelchair was strapped into the computer panel on one side of the RV.

"Flip the yellow and green ones," the priest ordered.

"Yes, sir," Adam answered and flipped the buttons.

Three of the large monitors on the bottom suddenly combined into one large viewing area, and a targeting circle appeared in the middle of the screen. Two slots on the keyboard panel slid open, and two joysticks popped out. Each had a trigger at the top of the handle.

"Whoah. Cool," Adam declared.

"Brother K is that some kind of missile system," Dakota asked.

"Not exactly," he replied.

Adam pulled the trigger on the right one.

Adam squeezed the right trigger. Skeeew. A blast rocked the RV, a pine tree thirty feet away exploding into splinters on the screen.

"What was that?" Rachel shouted.

136

"That was an electromagnetic rail gun," Brother Kiernan added.

"How did you get your hands on one of those?" Agent Mason demanded.

"What is that?" Doc asked.

"It uses electromagnetic force to launch a projectile at a high rate of speed," Thomas explained.

"Yes, but it doesn't use an explosive or anything," Mason said.

"It's a high rate of speed that does the damage," the priest replied.

"That can kill supernatural things?" Adam asked.

"If it comes with electromagnetic power," Thomas replied.

"Of course, electromagnetic power disrupts supernatural molecular structure," Adam added.

"Seriously, kid, how do you know all this stuff," Mason asked him.

"Adam's IQ is off the charts. He is a real genius," Doc commented.

"You kids are unreal," Mason muttered, shaking his head.

BAM. The RV shook as the flying creature soared above it, striking the roof.

"Whatever that was, it's huge," Adam shouted.

"Shoot it, kid," Mason said.

"Yes, young Adam. Please shoot it," Doc added.

Adam turned the right joystick, and the image on the screen rotated in a circular motion. He moved the left controller, and the video shifted up and down, but nothing appeared on the screen.

"Whoah," Thomas shouted as he fought to turn the steering wheel. The back end of the RV slid through the snow until the snow chain-covered tires caught the pavement beneath the inches of snow.

"Sorry," he shouted to everyone.

"What's going on back there?" Chief Tackna's voice crackled over the radio.

WHAM. The flying creature slammed into the jeep, careening into the woods and down an embankment. They could hear the shouts of the men inside it.

"Grandfather!" Dakota shouted.

Brother Kiernan jammed on the brakes. The back of the RV began to slide to the right. Thomas fought to turn the wheel to the left for a moment. The tire rotated the opposite way, and then he wheeled it to the right, going with the spin. This caused the RV to calm its movement, and the Beast came to a stop.

"Flip that switch, Doc," Thomas shouted, slamming it into the park.

Doc did as told, and the locks and wards were released.

Mason, Dakota, and Mollie bolted from the RV and raced to the overturned jeep.

"Grandfather," Dakota shouted as he slid down the hill.

"Dakota, I'm okay," Chief Tackna replied. "We're all okay."

Growls rose from the trees—high-pitched, hungry. "Hurry!" Mason shouted as Mollie vanished into the dark.

"C'mon, hurry up," Mason shouted as Mollie vanished into the darkness.

The Wampanoag tribesmen clambered up, Dakota and Mason hauling them to safety. *"Argghhh!"* A beast's scream split the night.

"Move!" Doc yelled from the RV's door.

Another scream—closer. "Sounds painful," Mason quipped.

"I think we should listen to the librarian," Tackna stammered as the group moved to the Beast. One by one, they piled into the truck.

"Where is Mollie?" Rachel asked as she stood at the entrance.

"She vanished out there," Mason replied as he glanced back, trying to peer through the blinding snow.

"Here," Mollie said, materializing beside them, grinning.

"Whoah, kid!" Mason jumped.

"Sorry—dozens of monsters out there. We need to get out of here they all seem hungry."

"That screaming?" Dakota asked.

138

"My handiwork," she said. "But more are coming."

"Let's go, folks," Brother Kiernan shouted from inside just as a large, hairy beast burst from the tree line and ran straight at them.

"Come on, kid," Mason shouted, shoving Mollie into the RV. Everyone else followed and stepped in. Mason turned to get in when something sharp punctured his back. His eyes widened in pain.

"Mason!" Mollie yelled just as the FBI agent was yanked backward by a chain made of sharpened hooks. Mason slid through the snow until he reached a big, hairy beast.

Everyone watched as the FBI agent rolled to his feet, trying to run. Giant, meaty hands jerked on the chain, reeling Mason in. He rolled with the movement, trying to defend himself. The chain was whipped to the right, and Mason was lifted off the ground.

"Argh!" he yelled as the sharpened hook dug deeper into his back, and he soared through the air, slamming into a thick tree with a sickening crack.

The monster laughed and yanked on the chain. Thick hairy hands pulled one over the other, pulling Mason through the heavy snow, leaving a streak of dark crimson blood behind. He tried to dig his fingers into the ground, but he was weakening from the loss of blood. One of Chief Tackna's warriors jumped from the RV and raised his rifle, aiming for the beast.

Whoosh

Giant claws swooped down and dung into the warrior before he could pull the trigger. He screamed in agony and tried to wriggle free of the massive claws but couldn't. He was scooped up in the gigantic, clawed feet and lifted high into the air, disappearing into the whipping snow. The warrior's screams grew weaker as the beast vanished.

Mollie tried to get out and help Mason, but Dakota grabbed her, pulling her back.

"Let me go," she cried, struggling against his grip.

"G...go! Get out of here!" Mason managed to yell as he lay at the beast's feet.

Everyone inside the RV turned to look at the FBI agent struggling to get to his knees. He was bleeding everywhere. He

139

raised his hands and fired a yellow streak of lightning at the monster, but the bolt fell weakly to the snow. He tried again, but his fingers just sparked. His power was fading as he continued to lose blood.

"Hahahaha," the creature laughed deeply as he reached down and picked Mason off the ground by his shirt. Thick, muscled arms lifted him easily upwards towards a widening mouth. Sharp fangs dripped with saliva as they spread open.

"No!" Mollie shouted as tears streamed down her face.

Dakota grabbed Mollie and wrapped his arms around her to cover her eyes. He tried to look away but couldn't. His gaze stayed glued to the scene.

"I hope you choke on me," Mason said, blood bubbling from his mouth.

The demon opened wide, prepping for his dinner.

"No!" Dakota whispered. "No".

Capron Bay High School
Capron Bay, MA
7:35 P.M.

The Chief drew his sidearm and fired. two shots tore into its chest, blue blood spraying. It stumbled but kept coming.

BAM, BAM! Thigh and shoulder hits slowed it, but not enough. He holstered the gun—useless—and braced as the club swung down. He dodged right, the wind of it grazing him, then drove his knee into the beast's gut. It grunted, unfazed, and backhanded him hard, sending him sprawling into the snow.

Pain flared in his jaw as he rolled, the club smashing inches from his head. Scrambling up, he spat blood and blocked another swing with his arm, the impact jarring him to his knees. The troll laughed, yellow teeth glinting.

Pendleton scrambled to his feet, spitting blood from his mouth. He saw the club racing towards his face just in time and threw his left arm to absorb the blow. The force of the blow knocked him to his knees. Pain seared through his arm, but he didn't think it broke.

The troll smiled and laughed at the Chief as he struggled to stand.

"Laugh it up, Smurf," the Chief muttered as he studied the monster. It stood a few inches shorter than him and was covered in dark blue fur, but that did nothing to hide the thick and powerful muscles that bulged all over the body. It reminded the Chief of a gorilla, the only one that carried a massive war club and seemed to want to eat him.

The beast stared back at him and grinned. The lips spread from the fangs, revealing yellow rotting teeth inside the gaping mouth. The creature's yellow eyes looked diseased and bloodshot. They glared at the Chief with evil intentions.

It lunged at the Chief, trying to swing the club at the same time, but it was too close. Pendleton stepped towards the monster and slammed a fist into the face. The Chief expected it to be hard as a rock, but it wasn't. He felt the soft tissue of the mouth give way under his punch, and thin bones shattered.

The troll stumbled backward in pain, crying in agony, blue blood flowing from its face. The Chief didn't hesitate. He followed the first blow with a flurry of punches. His fists were fast, and the monster couldn't block them fast enough. Each punch landed on the soft face, pummeling the ugly-looking mug into a bleeding mess. Blue blood shot everywhere, including the Chief's uniform. The thick war club fell to the snowy ground.

He stopped and examined his victim. The troll stood on weary legs and tried to look at the Chief, but its eyes were swollen shut.

"You done?" the Chief asked it.

It growled and ran on weak legs towards the Chief. Robert picked up the club and swung it caving its skull with a wet crunch.

The second troll roared in anger. The Chief looked towards it just in time to see him throw the little girl to the side and charge him. He pounded through the snow with powerful legs and arms.

The Chief drew his sidearm firing two quick rounds. The bullets slammed home into the soft face spraying blood. It fell to the snow-covered ground sliding to stop at the Chief's feet.

141

The Chief scooped Sandy up, her terrified sobs muffled against his chest and ran for the doors. "Open up!"

The set of double doors swung open. Anyika and Fiona stood bracing each door against the swirling winds. The Chief sprinted through the doors into the warm gym. The doors slamming shut behind them.

"Chain 'em!" Grammy barked at the agents.

He handed Sandy to Mr. Moseley. Sandy clung to her father, Anyika soothing her as nurses swarmed. Mrs. Moseley crushed the Chief in a tearful hug. "Thank you," she choked out.

"Thank you," she uttered through sobs.

"Make sure she's okay," he told her pulling away.

Agent Liang approached, jaw tight. "Chief Pendleton—"

A fist to Liang's face sent him sprawling, out cold. The gym fell silent, all eyes on the Chief—blood-streaked, fierce, unyielding.

"Every door locked and chained except the front two," he commanded. "Four FBI agents at each, ready to open for survivors. Four lookouts on the bleachers. Now!"

"Chief Pendleton, you will be arrested," Byrd advised.

"When this is over, do what you want," the Chief shot back. "Until then, you're relieved."

"You can't—"

"Argue, and I'll toss you out myself," the Chief growled. "I'm in charge.

142

13
EIGHT SECONDS OF GLORY

Hobomack Rd
Capron Bay, MA
7:40 P.M.

Agent Mason dangled in the beast's grip, its jagged claws digging into his flesh. The gaping maw loomed closer, fangs dripping with saliva, and he wondered—would it swallow him whole or chew him to bits? The thought faded as blood gushed from the hooked wounds in his back, his vision blurring into shadow. He didn't care anymore; death was close.

BLAM!

A thunderous blast ripped through the storm, shaking the snow beneath Dakota's feet. His ears rang, a high-pitched whine drowning out the wind. He blinked, focusing on Mason—still limp in the creature's grasp. Then the beast's head vanished, torn off in a spray of dark gore, leaving a ragged stump. Mason dropped, crunching into the thick snow, a faint yellow spark flickering in the blood pooling from his back—weak but stubborn, like a candle refusing to die.

"Wow!" Adam screamed from inside the beast.

"Nice shot, young man," Doc yelled.

"What was that?" Dakota asked with his ears still ringing.

"Our young friend blew the beast's head off with the rail gun," Doc answered.

Before Dakota could say anything, Mollie pulled him by his arm.

"Come on," she cried as she bolted to Mason's side. Everything cleared for Dakota at that moment. Adam blasted the beast with the gun atop the RV. He blew its head clean off. The rest of the creatures backed off, fearing more rockets from the rail gun.

"Dak!" Mollie yelled again, trying to pull Mason into the snow.

Dakota snapped out of it and ran to help.

Mollie yanked Dakota's arm before he could respond. "Come on!" she cried, bolting to Mason's side. Clarity snapped into place—Adam's blast had saved him, and the other creatures were retreating, wary of the RV's firepower. "Grab an arm!" Mollie ordered. Dakota obeyed, hauling Mason up as Doc and Chief Tackna joined them. The two remaining Wampanoag warriors pitched in, and together they dragged the FBI agent into the RV, leaving the headless corpse behind.

A massive shadow soared overhead, wings slicing through the blizzard's crimson-tinged haze. SKRAAA! A primal screech echoed for miles, rattling Dakota's bones. Doc slammed the door shut. "Thomas, get us out of here!"

The screeching primal screech pierced the blizzard for miles.

"Thomas, get us out of here!" he yelled, slamming the door.

Brother Kiernan floored the gas. The RV fishtailed right, chains clawing at the snow until they caught, launching the vehicle forward through the storm. *SKRAAA!* The cry came again, directly above.

"Thomas!" Doc shouted.

"I heard it, Doc!" Brother Kiernan replied.

"Uh, guys," Adam said. "We have company coming behind us."

The monitors flared to life, revealing blue ape-like creatures sprinting through the snow, their ice-blue fur shimmering with a sickly glow under the blood moon's eerie light—frozen flames against the white.

"What are those?" Mollie asked, peering over Adam's shoulder.

"They look like trolls," Dakota added.

"They are Vulzal," Chief Tackna told them all. "Winter snow trolls."

WHACK!

A blow rocked the RV from above, jolting everyone inside. Dakota grabbed the wall, Mollie clung to a seat, and Adam's wheelchair slid, crashing against the locked door.

"Adam, get back on the rail gun and take that out!" Brother Kiernan shouted from the driver's seat. "Chief hit the purple button on the panel. There are murder holes in the RV. Take them out."

Tackna pressed the glowing button, and a drawer slid out, revealing a cache of weapons, rifles, blades, a tube-like launcher. He handed rifles to his warriors as Adam strapped himself back into the control console. Small, warded slots, murder holes, snapped open along the RV's sides and rear.

"Murder hole?" Mollie asked.

"They are openings where defenders can shoot or throw things at their attackers," Doc added just as small windows slid open in the back and sides of the RV.

BAM!

The truck rocked as Adam fired a blast of the rail gun.

Adam pulled the trigger again. Nothing.

"Brother K, this is empty," he yelled.

"It takes a minute to recharge Adam," the priest replied.

Bang! Bang! Bang! Bang!

Shots rang out from the warriors at the rear, rifles blazing through the holes. The RV slowed as it neared a bend, a sheer hundred-foot drop to the rocky shore looming on the left. Kiernan gripped the wheel tighter.

"The Vulzal are everywhere," one of the warriors said.

"They are fast," yelled the other.

"Breath, aim, and hit your target," Chief Tackna encouraged them.

"Let me out. I can take some out," Mollie shouted.

"Absolutely not, young lady," Doc answered.

"Why? I can help," she replied.

"Not with that beast above," Tackna said.

"Agreed," Doc said.

SKRAAA!

The creature screeched above, right on cue.

"They're right," Dakota added.

145

"Then give me a gun!" Mollie grabbed the tube-like weapon from the drawer, unnoticed by the others. *Crack, crack, crack!* The trolls slammed jagged, frost-rimed clubs—glinting with eerie green veins—against the RV's side. She slid the tube through a murder hole, aimed at a Vulzal, and pressed what she hoped was the trigger.

BOOM!

The blast lit up the stormy night, a fireball of orange and gold swallowing four trolls. Charred bits rained down, spooking the others into retreat. "Well, that worked," Mollie laughed, brushing soot from her hair.

"Well, that worked," Mollie laughed.

Doc couldn't say anything as he shook his head, trying to clear the ringing from his ears.

"I am just happy you pointed it the right way," Brother Kiernan laughed.

"What do you mean? Of course, it was the right way," Mollie said, examining the weapon. She noticed a similar opening on both ends.

"Oh," she said, realizing she could have had it backward and would have blown up the inside of the RV. She looked at everyone inside.

"Huh," she giggled.

"Just make sure you keep pointing it in the right direction, bazooka girl," Doc laughed.

Mollie nodded and slid another small projectile into the tube.

"I think I just soiled my pants," Dakota said.

Laughter erupted, cutting through the tension. "Hold on!" Kiernan yelled, yanking the wheel right. Thuds clanged off the left side, followed by guttural screams as trolls tumbled over the cliff.

"What was that? Doc asked.

"Uhm…some of our snow Smurfs just went for a swim," Thomas answered.

"It's a hundred-foot drop onto the rocks, Thomas. That's not swimming," Doc added.

"That's the point, Doc," Dakota shouted.

"Ohhh," Doc replied, realizing some trolls just fell to their death.

SKRAAA!

BAM!

Adam fired again.

"Missed," he yelled.

Screeeeecccchh!

Claws streaked across the roof and Adam glimpsed the creature on the monitor.

"It's huge," he shouted. "But it looks like a giant winged version of Big Bird."

"Great. A giant killer big bird," Dakota said.

"That yellow bird always gave me the creeps. It looks like a deranged turkey," Chief Tackna said.

"Is that a Thanksgiving thing?" A weak voice gurgled. They turned. Mason's eyes fluttered open, a dim yellow glow pulsing in his irises, fading as he spoke.

They all turned to look at the FBI agent, who was now conscious.

"Glad your insults are intact, imperialist," Tackna replied.

Mason gurgled a laugh. "Don't make me laugh."

Bang, Bang, Bang, Bang!

More rounds were fired from the back at the pursuing trolls.

"What happened? The last thing I remember was me about to become something's dinner?" Mason rasped.

"Young Adam pulverized the monster's head with the rail gun," Doc informed him.

Mason struggled to turn towards Adam.

"Thanks, kid," he grimaced.

Adam flashed a thumbs-up, eyes on the targeting screen. "Getting a Millennium Falcon vibe," Mason coughed, blood bubbling up. He passed out again.

Doc's gaze met Tackna's, worry etched deep. "Thomas, hurry. He's fading."

Brother Kiernan looked in the rearview mirror and saw Doc's eyes. The librarian shook his head.

Kiernan glanced in the rearview mirror, meeting Doc's eyes. Doc shook his head. "Crap," Kiernan whispered, flooring it.

Bang! Bang! Bang! Bang!

Shots mingled with troll shrieks. *Boom!* Mollie fired again, blasting a cluster of Vulzal. "Nine for me, Dakota, how many you got?"

"What?" Dakota replied.

"I've got nine of these things. How many did you whack?" Mollie smiled.

"Whack?" he asked

"Yeah, you know, whack, gank, smoke, hose, make them sleep with the fishes," she smiled.

"Huh?" Dak replied.

"She means kills," Doc declared.

"Oh," Dakota declared as it dawned on him. "Wait...you've been watching movies with Franklin, haven't you?"

Mollie laughed and pulled the trigger again. *Boom!*

"That's twelve," she shouted.

Bang! Bang! Bang! Bang!

"Fourteen!" shouted one of Tackna's Wampanoag warriors.

Mollie looked at him. He winked back.

"Oh no, you don't," she said, jamming a round into the tube, and pulled the trigger.

Boom!

Longcove Rd
Capron Bay, MA
7:45 P.M.

A distant *boom* rolled through the storm, faint but sharp, like thunder with teeth. I glanced up, wondering if the RV was still out there fighting. "It's cold out here," Franklin said, his teeth chattering over the wind.

"That's because your pants are burned off," I told him. He nodded.

"Wait until Mollie hears I went bucking bronco on that Chenoo," he replied with a big smile from ear to ear. "I'm going to get a nice big kiss."

"Is he always like this?" Jack asked.

"You have no idea," I said. "You have no idea," I said, scanning the dark houses lining Longcove Rd. After the Chenoo fight, we'd trekked there, guessing Brother Kiernan might take this route to the school. Hobomack Rd was the only other option, and that *boom* made me think they'd hit trouble. "No idea."

Franklin hugged himself, his face paling to a faint blue. The houses stood silent, windows black, power out, families likely at the school. "They're warmer inside than out here," I said, catching Jack's eye.

He nodded. 'We should get him in one. Warm up."

Franklin shook his head, stubborn as ever. "We need to get to the school."

I looked at Franklin. He was trying to be tough, but I could tell he was freezing. His face was turning blue, and his body shivered in the falling snow. I glanced toward the houses on both sides of the road. They all looked dark and closed.

"They are all probably at the high school," Jack said, noticing I was looking at the houses.

"They all lost power," I added. "But inside, they'll still be warmer than here."

He could tell I was getting concerned about Franklin.

"We should go inside one and get warm for a few minutes," I said.

Franklin shook his head.

"We should get to the school," he said, trying to be tough.

"That's over two miles away," I replied. "We need to get warm."

"I'm good, Crayon Man. We're like the three amigos: Crayon Man, Frosty, and...wait, I need a name," he shuttered as his body shivered.

'What?" Jack asked.

"I n...n...n...need a n...n...n...name," he shivered.

149

Jack looked at him and was about to say something, but I held up a finger and thought for a moment. I know Franklin, and he wasn't going to stop. Once he got a thought in his head, he wouldn't give it up.

It dawned on me.

"How about 8 seconds," I said.

"Huh?" Franklin asked.

"What are you two talking about?" Jack asked. "We need to get shorty here inside."

"I...d...don't like s...shorty," Franklin said, shivering from the freezing temperatures.

"8 second was a cowboy named Lane Frost," I said glancing at Jack.

"Frost?" Jack looked at me.

I nodded and shrugged my shoulders.

"R...r...right, Franklin said. "Th...the mmmovie...8 Seconds," he stammered.

I nodded. As I talked about this, I made my way to a large colonial house on Long Cove Rd. Franklin and Jack followed me.

"Let's get inside, and we'll finish talking about your name, okay?" I asked him.

He nodded, finally realizing he had to get warm.

I looked around to ensure nobody was watching as I smashed the corner of the glass. I laughed as I did it.

"What's funny?" Jack asked.

"We just fought a monster called a Chenoo. I'm a rainbow warrior, and you are the living and breathing Jack Frost," I laughed.

Jack looked at me.

"And I'm worried about breaking and entering?" I shrugged.

Jack nodded.

"...your d...d...dad is the Ch...chief," Franklin shivered.

"Yeah," I said.

"Yeah. I've seen him. You're screwed," Jack laughed.

"R...right," Franklin said, shaking as he turned blue.

I unlocked the door, and we slipped in. The house was cold, power dead, but warmer than the storm. I sparked a fire in the brick fireplace, the orange glow chasing shadows across the room. Jack pushed Franklin into a chair by the flames, stepping back—he didn't like the heat.

A few moments later, I had a fire in the brick fireplace, and Jack made Franklin sit in a chair right in front of it. I noticed Jack take a few steps away from the fire. He didn't like being near flames. I made some hot cocoa I found in the pantry, and within a few minutes, Franklin seemed to be warming up.

"He needs some new clothes," Jack said.

I nodded and ran upstairs, trying to find some clothes. I went from room to room, searching for clothes that fit him. I saw something in the last room. I opened the closet and smiled from ear to ear. I grabbed what I thought would look best on him and ran downstairs. The living room was dark except for the fire.

"Feeling warmer?" I asked him.

He nodded, sipping the hot cocoa.

"He's much better," Jack said.

I nodded and handed him the pile of clothes I had.

"There is a bathroom down the hall. Go put them on," I told him.

Franklin returned, the firelight revealing his new outfit: a sweatshirt with Elsa from *Frozen*, proclaiming, "This Princess is a big sister, and we like warm hugs." Jack burst into laughter.

"What?" Franklin asked.

"Looks good on you," I said, trying not to laugh.

Franklin looked at his new sweatshirt. It had a big picture of Elsa from Frozen and the words, "This Princess is a big sister, and we like warm hugs."

Jack and I lost it, laughing hysterically. "Very funny," Franklin said, smirking.

"Very funny," Franklin smiled.

We continued laughing for a few minutes.

"You guys done?" he asked us.

"Are you warmer?" I asked.

He nodded.

"There was nothing else in the house, dude," I told him. "Besides, it looks good on you."

"Now, what about this 8 minute?" he asked me.

"Lane Frost rode the bull K Walsh or Taking Care of Business for eight full seconds," I told him.

151

Franklin nodded.

"I like it," he laughed.

We all laughed.

"We could be Jack squared," he said.

Jack stopped laughing. "Uh…no,"

"Okay, how about the 8-second Frosty Crayon?" he said, looking at us. He clearly wanted a nickname.

We shook our heads. "Come on," he whined. "You've got Crayon Man and Frost, the freaking winter fairy—a fairy's cooler than Franklin!"

"What does that mean…a fairy?" Jack asked.

"What about COB?" I spoke.

"COB?" he asked.

"Yeah, you know…Care of Business. The bull he rode," I told him.

He shook his head.

"How about TCob?" Jack asked.

Franklin shook his head.

"Well, you rode a Chenoo," I said, trying to help him. I could see he really wanted a nickname, and he…kind of earned it.

"I would say pain in the…." Jack began.

"How about Chinook?" I said, interrupting Jack.

"Chinook?" Franklin asked.

"Well, you rode the Chenoo. Lane Frost rode K Walsh," I said.

"Thought you said it was Taking care of business?" Jack inquired.

"The bull went by K Walsh and Taking Care of Business," I told him.

"How do you guys know so much about bull riding?" Jack laughed.

"Crayola lived as a redneck for all his life until he moved here," Franklin said, sipping his hot cocoa.

I looked at him in surprise.

"Well, you did live in North Carolina," he laughed.

"So?" I spoke.

"That's the South," he smiled. "That means you're a redneck."

"What are you, a Yankee boy?" I asked him.

152

Franklin looked at me quietly for a moment.

"What?" I asked.

"Yankee Boy!" he said.

"I like it," Jack added.

"I don't," he answered. "I hate the Yankees."

I nodded, agreeing with him.

"What's another name for bull?" Jack asked.

"Ox!" Franklin declared. "Crayon man, Frosty, and Ox."

I glanced at Jack, and we started laughing.

"Yeah, boy. I am Ox," he shouted.

"Hahahahahaha," I couldn't start laughing. "Yeah. Ox in an Elsa shirt."

"You know what they say," he said.

I looked at Jack and shook my head, trying to tell him not to ask. He didn't listen.

"No, what?" he said.

"You got to let it go, Jack," Franklin sang.

A flicker of color—red, blue, gold—danced behind my eyes, unbidden, sharp as a blade. Then pain lanced through my skull, a hot, jagged spike. "Argghhhhhh!" I screamed, clutching my head as the room spun. Something dark pulsed beyond the storm—a shadow laughing in my mind.

14
SILVER AND SCREAMS

Capron Bay High School
Capron Bay, MA
8:00 P.M.

"Chief, what's going on out there?" Walt Gates demanded, his voice cutting through the gym's hum. The crowd pivoted, eyes on Chief Pendleton, waiting.

He glanced at Melissa and Grammy. They nodded. "Robert, the cat's out of the bag," Fiona said, her smile sharp.

Anyika wiped blue troll blood from his cheek, nodding agreement. "How's Hog?" he asked Melissa.

"He's the same. He's lost a lot of blood, and we don't have any to give him," his wife replied as she went back into the makeshift room.

The Chief sighed.

"Chief?" Walt pressed, as more townsfolk gathered, tense and expectant.

"Chief?" Walt asked again as more people gathered around, waiting for him to explain what was happening.

"They've been through enough, sweetheart," Grammy said. "Your dad, me, Chief Tackna—we've kept secrets too long. Time's up."

He nodded, stepping onto the creaking bleachers. "Okay—"

"I'll tell you what's happening," a woman's voice sliced through the murmurs. Priscilla Reed perched on a silver folding chair, chin high.

"You again?" someone shouted from the audience.

"Go home, liar," yelled another.

The Chief shook his head, exasperated. "Monsters are out there," Reed declared.

"No kidding," Walt Gates laughed.

"Yeah, kind of obvious," another woman said.

Reed swallowed hard, faltering. "He could've struck a deal with them," she shouted, jabbing a finger at the Chief. "I overheard it in the storm—skulking near your dying detective."

"He could have struck a deal with them," she shouted, pointing towards the Chief.

His eyes narrowed. She'd caught his talk with Hog's attacker. "What?" a man asked.

"What deal?" another pressed.

"What are you talking about?" another man asked.

"The monsters want his boy," Reed said, voice rising. "I heard it clear as day—some man offered to spare us all if the Chief handed him over."

Silence fell. "He refused," she laughed. "He'd rather we die."

Grammy edged closer to Reed, glaring. The Chief raised a hand, stopping her. "Is that true?" someone whispered.

He met their stares, spotting Agent Liang icing his jaw, glaring back. Byrd was nowhere in sight. "Chief?" Walt asked.

"it's true," Robert said.

Gasps rippled through the room. "There are monsters," he added, pointing at Reed. "One's right there."

Laughter erupted. "He just roasted her," Fiona whispered to Anyika.

"Grammy might still rip her apart," Anyika murmured.

Reed froze, silent. "We saw you outside," a man shouted. "Something's in the snow."

The Chief nodded, hands up to calm the rising tension. "You deserve the truth."

"Gonna tell them your son's got magic powers, and you've lied about it?" Reed snapped.

"Lady, shut up," Walt barked, not even glancing her way.

The crowd hushed, waiting. "Headlights incoming—fast!" someone yelled. They surged to the windows.

The Chief bolted to the doors, ready to help. Bright beams cut through the snow, racing toward the school. "Brother Kiernan's truck," he whispered.

"What's that in the sky?" Anyika gasped, pointing at a massive shadow slicing the blizzard.

The Beast
Capron Bay, MA
8:10 P.M.

Bam!

"Dang it," Adam shouted from his seat. "Missed it again."

Wham! The Crimson Skreaver slammed the RV, its crimson-streaked wings battering the roof. Brother Kiernan swerved right, tires screeching.

Bang, Bang, Bang, Bang! Twenty-two, young warrior," a Wampanoag fighter grinned.

"Twenty-two young warrior," one of Tackna's men smiled.

Mollie glared at him momentarily before turning back and concentrating on her shooting.

Wham! The beast slammed the RV again.

"Someone shoot that thing," Brother Kiernan shouted from the driver's seat.

"I'm trying," Adam replied.

"Do or do not. There is no try," Doc yelled above the chaos inside the RV.

Adam paused, staring. "Did you just quote Yoda?" Dakota asked.

"I am not completely culturally ignorant," Doc smiled.

Bang, Bang, Bang, Bang! "Twenty-five," Mollie shouted as she continued to fire on the army of trolls chasing them.

SKRAAA! The Crimson Skreaver screeched, its shadow swallowing the RV as it looped back. Kiernan squinted through the snow, spotting a faint glow. "I see the school!"

WHAM! The beast hit again. Kiernan braked hard, chains biting snow as the RV skidded.

"Adam!" Thomas barked.

"Do or do not. There is no try," Adam whispered to himself. He closed his eyes and pictured the Skreaver's arc.

BAM!

He pulled the trigger.

Longcove Rd.
Capron Bay
8:15 P.M.

"Jeez, Crayola, my singing isn't that bad," Franklin laughed Elsa sweatshirt glowing by the fire.

I shook my head.

"Prentice, are you okay?" Jack asked.

I raised a finger, silencing them, focusing inward. "Who's this?" I thought.

"Doesn't matter. You need to get to the school," the voice said.

Why?" I asked.

"Get to the school," it urged.

I looked at Jack and Franklin.

"We need to get to the school," I said. "Now".

"Let's go," Franklin said, no questions, hopping up and heading for the doo

He stood up, dressed in his Frozen clothes, and approached the front door.

I watched as Jack lunged and shoved Franklin. He slammed into the couch and flipped over it, leading to a loud crack when his body hit the floor.

Jack lunged, shoving Franklin into the couch. He flipped over it, crashing with a crack. "Jack?!" I shouted as the door exploded inward, glass and wood shrapnel flying. A splinter stabbed my cheek, blood trickling.

A massive figure barreled in, slamming into Jack. The entangled bodies slammed into an old grandfather clock, smashing it to pieces. The gong echoed throughout the room with an echo of metal vibrating through the cold room. Glass and wood littered the floor from their impact into the family heirloom.

Jack's arms and legs were entangled with the beast. The thick scaled tail with a sharp talon at the end whipped back and forth. I heard grunts and thuds watching Jack fight the creature with every ounce of energy he had,

"It's one of those cat dragons," I whispered, recalling Doc's earlier fight. "Arghhhhh!" Jack screamed as its teeth sank into his shoulder, shaking him like a rag doll. Blue blood oozed.

Franklin grabbed a fire poker and swung wide, joining the fray. A shadow loomed in the doorway, crunching glass. Ice-cold wind howled behind it, a death knell. Pure evil radiated from the figure.

Everything disappeared around me. Jack and Franklin engaged the demon cat to my right, but I heard none of it. My eyes focused solely on the hovering creature that now stood in the house.

The walking corpse took up the entire doorway before the shattered door frame. The thing's head was clear bone with small antlers on top of the head. There was no hair or fur. Its dark red eyes sunk deep into thick sockets. A long snout extended from the bony face with two razor-sharp fangs protruding from the mouth. It looked like an animal's head but sat on a human form.

The body was covered in an ancient-looking leather jerkin like one a Native American would have worn centuries ago. Powerful skeletal arms hung from the body and were much longer than they should have been. Sharpened claws took the place of what should have been fingered.

Long legs covered in leather stood atop thick booted feet. Even though I could not see the legs because they were covered, I knew they were also skeletal. I could see a faint red light pulsing at the chest.

"I can see it's heart," I whispered.

I didn't move. The creature's sunken eyes stared at me. Its gaze pierced me—death, decay, insatiable hunger. Franklin soared past, slamming a wall, but it felt distant. It was a Wendigo, and it wanted my flesh.

158

I felt the evil. It was wreaked of death, decay, and pure evil. This creature didn't care what it killed. It would destroy everything.

In the corner of my eye, I noticed Franklin soaring across the room, slamming into the wall. Even though it was just a few feet from me, their battle seemed like an ocean away. All I could do was focus on this thing standing there before me.

"Prentice," Jack screamed again. This time, the voice drew my attention. I turned towards him. He was pinned against the wall by the cat demon. The monster's front claws were embedded in Jack's shoulder. A bright blue liquid flowed from the wound.

"Crayola man, you gonna just stand there?" Franklin yelled.

I blinked my eyes as I stared at my friends. I knew they needed me, but everything moved in slow motion.

"Prentice," the voice inside my head said. *"Prentice. Focus. The beast is clouding your mind."*

The cat demon swung sharpened claws at Jack, who ducked and rolled. I saw his eyes wince in pain as he avoided the massive claws.

"Prentice," the voice inside my head said. *"Prentice. Focus. Calm your breathing."*

WHACK!

My head rocketed to my right as the open-handed slap cracked against my face.

"That will work, too," the voice laughed.

"Dude!" I shouted.

"Get in the fight, Crayon man," Franklin yelled after slapping me as hard as he could.

Clarity snapped back. "Arghhhh!" Jack cried as the beast bit his leg, blue ichor spilling. *Bam, bam, bam, bam, bam, bam!* Red flaming spheres erupted from my hands, slamming the cat dragon with sparks. Burns seared its scales.

Bam, bam, bam, bam, bam, bam! I fired again. It squealed, torso exploding in a shower of scaly flesh. "Yeah, deranged Tigger!" Franklin whooped as chunks splattered him. "Ewww, gross."

159

Jack struggled to his feet, but I grabbed him. My hands touched his ice-cold flesh just as a massive boot slammed into my back. I rocketed through the wall into the kitchen, hitting the counter, air bursting from my lungs. I rolled over, crashing to the floor, gasping.

"That'll take some spackle," I muttered, hopping back through the hole. The Wendigo faced Franklin and Jack, both bleeding, Jack's arm limp.

The beast stood opposite Franklin and Jack, who were in severe pain. Jack was holding his limp arm by his side, and he was bleeding from multiple wounds.

The beast turned its hollow eyes towards me.

"Hey, dead Bambi," I taunted.

"It's a Wendigo," Jack rasped, wincing.

Franklin's eyes widened with fear—a Native legend, half-dead, all terror. *Bam, bam, bam, bam, bam, bam!* My fiery blasts bounced off it. "Color power won't hurt it," Jack whispered.

"Bam, Bam, bam, bam, bam, bam!" I fired.

The sparking balls of fire just bounced off the beast with little effect.

"Color power won't hurt it," Jack whispered.

"Maybe good old-fashioned strength will," Franklin said as he lunged at the beast with another fire poker.

The creature's bony hands slapped him into the TV stand, screen shattering. "Dang, Wendy's strong," he laughed, spitting blood.

The beast looked at Franklin and tilted his head.

"Yeah, that's right. I called you…Wendy," he smiled, making sure to emphasize the girl's name. You look like Wendy."

I smiled at his wise crack.

The beast stepped towards Franklin, but he shot to the right just as Jack fired some icy blue bolts of winter magic at it. Each bold shattered like icicles, striking like hard cement when they hit it. They had no effect either.

The Wendigo flashed out a thick booted foot kicking Franklin right in the shin as he tried to scurry out of the way. He tripped and rolled into a side table with a big heavy lamp on it. The lamp hit the floor, breaking into a hundred shards.

Franklin got back to his feet. His eyes raged with anger.

160

"You don't trip in a fight, Wendy! Everyone knows that," he shouted.

"Wendy," the beast replied, sounding just like Franklin.

The blond-haired boy glanced at me.

"Did he just...use my voice?" he asked me.

I nodded.

"Okay, that is the creepiest thing I've ever heard," Franklin said.

"Yeah, you should hear your own voice," Jack laughed spitting blood out.

The Wendigo flashed, smashing Franklin into a figurine cabinet. I kicked its midsection, hard. It grunted, unmoved, swiping claws I dodged. My punch hit plated skin, another grunt, no stagger

Its hand seized my throat, claws piercing. "Prentice!" Jack yelled. *WHAM!* It wailed, dropping me.

I fell to the floor and rolled away from the demonic creature.

Franklin stood there holding something shiny in his hand.

"What is that?" I asked.

Franklin glanced at it.

"I'm not sure. I was on the floor, so I just grabbed it," he said.

The beast shook his arm, trying to get rid of the pain.

"You like that, Wendy," Franklin said.

Jack fired more icicles, but they shattered against the monster's body.

I grabbed hold of Franklin's hand, examining his weapon.

"It's a candlestick," I said.

"What? Like...like Mr. Mustard did it in the library with the candlestick?" Franklin asked, looking at his weapon.

I nodded.

"So, candlesticks hurt this thing. Jack, go find more candlesticks...wait, maybe some candles will work too," Franklin said.

"Really?" I asked him.

"What?" he answered.

"It's the silver dummy," The silver in the candlestick hurt it," I said.

"Like a werewolf?" Franklin asked.

I nodded, closing my eyes and focusing on the candlestick.

I turned, and a silver bullet of sparking energy arced from my fingers. The energy crackled through the room as it slammed into the Wendigo with static bursts of energy. The beast stumbled backward, howling in pain, but didn't fall.

"Your color is true silver," Jack said. "But it does hurt it."

Franklin didn't hesitate. He ran at the beast, hitting the ground on his knees and sliding toward the monster. He swung the silver candlestick and everything he had. The makeshift weapon cracked the Wendigo just below the knee. The sound echoed throughout the room, and the beat screamed in pain.

Franklin was up on his feet quickly with another furious attack. He brought the weapon high, striking the animal skull underneath like an uppercut. The beast's head rocked backward but grabbed hold of Franklin with those bony hands.

"Oh boy," my friend said as the Wendigo threw him through the window, and he disappeared into the snowy darkness beyond.

"Bam, Bam, bam, bam, bam, bam!" I fired more silvery bullet rounds from my fingers, but I felt each one growing weaker and weaker as they shot from my hand.

Each one struck the beast, and he grunted in some pain but not much.

"I don't see anything else that is silver," Jack said, looking around the room.

I shook my head.

A blood-curdling scream roared from behind the beast, and Franklin ran through the smashed doorway, took a baseball crow hop, and threw the candlestick as hard as he could. The monster reacted but was too slow. The silver piece of furniture whipped around and slammed into the beast's head with a sickening thud.

The Wendigo collapsed backward, landing on its back. The house shook when it hit the floor.

"Take that, Wendy!" he yelled as he flew by the fallen Wendigo, Jack, and I.

"C'mon," he yelled.

Jack and I didn't hesitate. We followed him into the kitchen.

He didn't stop. He burst through the back door. As we followed him, we could hear the Wendigo stirring. The blow had knocked it out for a moment but didn't kill it.

"Franklin," I whispered.

He didn't turn around. He pushed through a side door of the garage.

We followed.

Two tarps were covering large shapes in the garage.

"WENDY!" we heard the beast roar inside the house in Franklin's voice.

"Yeah, that's still creepy Franklin said, grabbing something off the wall. He tossed one to me.

I caught the jangling shape and looked at a set of keys.

"What..." I was going to ask, but I realized what he was doing when he ripped off the tarps. Two snowmobiles sat quietly in the garage.

"WENDY!" the beast yelled. We could hear it pounding through the house.

"Jack, get on," I said, hopping before him. Jack got on behind me.

Franklin got on his.

"Uhmm...Prentice," Jack said. "The door".

Franklin turned him on.

"Vrmmmm," it roared to life. Mine followed, and I felt the hum of energy beneath me as the vehicle came to life.

"Crayola! Franklin yelled, but I was already ahead of him. I fired several red balls of energy at the doors. The old New England style garage doors exploded into a thousand pieces as Franklin's bike shot through the debris and hit the snow running.

My snow bike followed Jack, squeezing to hold on. Ahead, the Wendigo burst through the kitchen door and ran full speed at us. It was fast. The driveway was long, and there was no other way to get out.

Franklin wasn't going to make it. The dead corpse was going to grab him.

"The keys," I said. "Jack hold the handlebar."

He didn't hesitate.

163

I grabbed the set of keys in the ignition. I ripped a silver key that was dangling off the keyring and reared back. My arm shot forward as hard as it could. The key released from my fingers and tumbled end-to-end through the whipping snow.

I watched it in slow motion. The beast was about to grab Franklin with those long, skeletal arms. He leaned as far to his left as he could. I thought I saw a smile creep across the skeletal face as his talons reached for Franklin. The key pierced the glowing red eye in the sunken socket.

The beast's hands immediately went to protect his eyes from further attacks. Franklin kicked out as his snowmobile raced by the ancient evil. His foot landed hard in the Wendigo's crotch, and it keeled over in pain.

My snowmobile hummed by, and I followed with another kick, which cracked against the monster's bony knee. A vicious crack echoed in the storm, and the beast roared in anger and pain just before falling to the snow-covered driveway.

I followed Franklin's glowing taillights as he turned right on LongCove Road and headed towards the school.

The vehicles glided over the snow-packed road.

"WENDY!"

We all heard the monster behind us roar the word, sending a chill to everyone's spine because it sounded just like Franklin.

The Beast
Capron Bay, MA
8:20 P.M.

The massive, winged creature swiped a giant claw at the moving truck below, but the vehicle swerved at the last moment, avoiding the enormous claw. The creature roared in frustration and began to circle back around.

The rail gun projectile slammed into the ancient winged demon at the base of the long neck. The devil's eyes widened in momentary pain as the huge bullet penetrated scale, skin, muscle, tissue, and bone alike. The round burst out of the other side of

164

the creature, flew for a hundred more yards, and fell harmlessly into a thick wooded area on Capron Bay.

The beast's pain was momentary as it flew on. Its grotesque, diseased eyes widened for a brief second and then fell out of the sky. The neck was severed from the beast's massive torso. The neck fell, landing on top of the bug R with a thud. The massive body fell to the ground, crushing two blue trolls as it landed right in front of the truck.

Thomas spun the steering wheel to the right, causing the RV to lurch and begin spinning. The beast's neck slid forward enough for the face to hang loosely over the windshield. Its lifeless eyes stared into the RV.

"Nice job, Adam!" Brother Kiernan yelled, fighting the steering wheel to keep the truck upright.

"Indeed, nice shooting," Doc said.

Chief Tackna patted Adam on the shoulder.

"They've backed off," Mollie shouted.

"Lucky for you, young lady," the warrior smiled as he winked at her.

"Why," Dakota asked.

"Maybe Big Bird was their leader," Adam added.

"I don't know, but look, Chief Pendleton opened a small garage door," Doc said.

Brother Kiernan wheeled the big RV, and it stopped parallel to the door the Chief had just opened.

"Let's go everyone out," Doc shouted.

"Keep the weapons," Brother Kiernan shouted.

Tackna's men jumped out and covered the RV's side to ensure no more beasts were coming. Lena jumped out and ran into the school. She found A and wrapped her arms around her as tightly as possible.

"Come, child, I'll bring you to your mom and Dad," Anyika answered, escorting Lena to the makeshift hospital room.

Adam lowered himself on the platform and pushed his way into the school. Mollie and Dakota followed, followed by the Chief, Doc, and Brother Kiernan.

"Let's go," Chief Tackna ordered. The two warriors followed everyone in, and Chief Pendleton slammed the bay door shut and locked it behind them.

Beep! The RV's alarm kicked in.

Everyone looked at Thomas because he clicked the alarm button.

"What? That's my home," he said.

Everyone laughed.

"Everyone okay?" Chief Pendleton asked as they all walked into the school.

"Mason needs medical attention," Chief Tackna cried out as his two men carried the FBI agent into the gym.

"He's lost quite a bit of blood," Doc added.

Several nurses and doctors ran over. Doctor Taft followed.

"Can we get him set up next to Detective Sheridan?" Dad asked Taft.

"Of course," he answered, and they ushered the wounded agent off to the makeshift hospital room.

"Where is Prentice and Franklin?" the Chief asked.

Thomas glanced at Doc.

"Doc? the Chief asked.

"They got out along the way to fight...something," Doc replied.

"They were with Jack Frost," Dakota added.

The police chief looked at him.

"It is true, Chief," Thomas said. "Jack Frost."

"Nothing surprises me at this point," the Chief said.

"Jonathan Eddings," Fiona cried as she pushed past Thomas and the Chief. She went to hug the thin librarian, glanced to her left for a brief moment, and stopped.

Mollie tried to slide behind Dakota and Chief Tackna before her mom could see her, but it was too late. Fiona stopped moving and looked at the curly blonde-haired girl.

Mollie stopped trying to hide and just waved to her mother.

Fiona's confused and shocked eyes stared back.

"Fiona," the Chief whispered.

Doc stepped over and placed his hand on her shoulder. Fiona looked at him.

"Do...do you...do you all see her?" she stuttered, looking at everyone.

Everyone glanced at one another, not sure what to say.

"Go ahead," Chief Tackna whispered, tapping Mollie on her shoulder.

"Hi, Mommy," Mollie said, tears streaming down her face.

Fiona collapsed.

"Fiona," Doc cried out.

Chief Pendleton looked at her and felt her neck.

"She's fine, just passed out. Let's get her to the curtained room," Chief Pendleton said.

Doc swept Fiona up in her arms and carried her away.

Mollie stood crying. Chief Tackna's warrior looked at his fellow soldier and leaned down.

"That doesn't count, young lady," he smiled, squeezing her shoulder.

Mollie laughed as tears continued flowing.

"Someone else is coming!" came a shout inside the gym.

Everyone ran to the windows again. The familiar hum of snowmobiles broke through the wind and snow.

"Two snowmobiles," someone cried out.

"It's Prentice," Brother Kiernan said

Dakota and Rachel ran to the door. Two FBI agents tried to stop them.

"You can't open those doors," one of the Agents said, holding his hand up, blocking Rachel and Dak.

BAM!

A hulking figure slammed into both agents, driving them onto the floor.

"Dad?" Rachel proclaimed.

Hall of Fame linebacker D'ontae Gainey stood up from his double tackle.

"Got to clear the way for my baby girl and her boyfriend," his deep voice echoed.

The two FBI agents rolled on the floor, groaning in pain.

"Wait, what?" Dakota asked, looking at Rachel's Dad.

"You better treat her right, son."

"Yes, sir," Dakota stuttered.

"Help me with the door," Rachel told Dak and her dad.

The three of them struggled to push the door open. The wind beyond tried to slam it back on their face. Mr. Gainey's powerful legs dug in and pushed. The door swung open in time to see the snowmobiles skid to a stop right in front of them. Prentice, Jack, and Franklin hopped off and hurried inside the gym.

15
WORLD BETWEEN WORLDS

Capron Bay High School
Capron Bay, MA
8:30 PM

"Where is Lena?" I asked Dakota and Rachel, who surrounded me. Druss bound up on his hind legs, his tail wagging furiously.

"Hey, buddy," I whispered, scratching behind his ears.

"She's with Hog and her mom," Dad said.

"How is he?" I asked.

"Stable for now," Dad replied. "We'll see her soon."

Mollie ran to Franklin, sobbing, her arms wrapping around him tight. He hugged back, silent, glancing at me. I shrugged—sometimes even Franklin knew words weren't needed.

Brother Kiernan stood there looking at me. At first, I thought he was mad at me, but his stare turned into a smile.

"About time, young man," he said.

"Franklin drove a little slow," I laughed.

"No way, Crayon man. I was Dale Earnhart out there," he said.

"Who is this?" Dad asked, pointing to Jack.

"Uh, Chief," Brother Kiernan interrupted. "We have a story to tell you."

"I'm Jack," the winter fairy answered, offering his hand.

Dad shook it, brow furrowing. "Hand's cold, Jack."

"You should feel his heart," Franklin laughed as he wiped a tear from Mollie's face.

He asked her nothing and said nothing to her. I was amazed at how my sarcastic friend knew when he just needed to give her a hug.

"What I want to know right now is something from Franklin," Dad said.

169

"Me?" Franklin tensed.

"Did you let it go?" Dad grinned.

Mollie laughed. We all did.

Franklin was confused as he looked at me.

I pointed to his shirt.

He looked down at his clothes.

"Ohhh," he laughed. "You bet I did, Chief."

"Brother Kiernan, can you find a classroom for us to meet in?" the Chief smiled.

The Priest nodded and walked away. Franklin held onto Mollie's hand and followed.

"She's pretty upset, huh?" I asked Dakota.

He exchanged a look with Rachel. "What is it?" I pressed.

"Ms. Fiona saw Mollie," Rachel whispered.

The words hit like a freight train. Silver sparks flared in my chest—too hot, too fast—from the Wendigo fight. The world spun, bile rising, darkness creeping into my vision. "Prentice!" Dakota shouted as my legs buckled. I heard my body hit the floor before I felt it.

"He's seizing," was the last thing I heard Dad yell before the darkness swept over me.

I blinked awake under a crystal-clear blue sky, sprawled on a beach. Soft sand cushioned me, just like my first seizure. I scrambled up, scanning for Poppa. A figure stood ankle-deep in the water near the tree line, gazing at the horizon.

"Poppa!" I yelled, running down the beach. My feet sank in the soft sand as I ran. The man didn't look at me. He just stared straight ahead toward the horizon.

"Poppa," I shouted again as I got to him.

He turned towards me.

It wasn't Poppa.

"Who are you? I asked.

His face shimmered—black scales gleamed, then faded, features blurring. Red eyes glowed faintly through the haze. "Hello, Prentice," he said, voice low and raspy...

"Do I know you?" I asked.

"We've met once before," he said, shaking his arm.

"You…were in the rainbow," I said. "I shot you."

He nodded.

"You deserved it," I sneered.

"Well…I deserve a lot, but I don't think I did right then," he laughed.

His smile shifted. At first, it was like a person's smile, but then it became like a…lizard's mouth.

"Yeah, you deserved it," I laughed.

"If you say so," he shrugged.

"Who are you, blurry man?"

"Some call me the dark God. Others call me the black God," he said.

"Chernobog," I added.

"That too," he snickered, bending over to pick up a rock. He glanced at me and fired the rock into the water. It skipped and skipped and skipped until it disappeared into the horizon.

"You throw like a girl," I chuckled.

He laughed.

"I've been told you are tough," he said. His words were a little angry, and suddenly, he came into focus for a moment. I saw a long, jagged scar on his right arm.

"Funny, I've heard you're not that tough," I said.

His angry eyes glared at me.

"Nice scar. I hope I gave you that," I smiled.

He laughed.

"What do you want?"

"You," he answered quickly.

I nodded and looked out over the water. I bent down, picked up a rock, and tossed it in my hand. I glanced at him.

He stared back.

I turned and skipped it. It kept going just like his.

"Look at that," I said.

"Huh. Nice arm."

"Better than yours."

He laughed.

"Why do you want me?" I asked.

"I like you," he replied.

"That's a lie."

"You…remind me of…well…me," he smiled.

171

"I'm better looking…and smarter," I winked.

"You are sarcastic," he shook his head.

He was growing angry. The angrier he got, the more I could see his face.

He turned and walked out of the water.

"I don't think you understand, my young friend," he said.

"I'm not your friend," I fired back, trying to make him angry.

"Right now, you are going all…. shake and bake in a school gymnasium," he said mimicking a seizure.

I froze. I was seizing back in the school.

"You are helpless to your friends," he said.

"It won't last long."

"No. But you will be tired. You will be weak."

"So."

"I have the school surrounded. My army can take it anytime. Even with you at full strength, you can't win."

I stared at the ocean, it's calm mocking the storm I'd left. Jack, Franklin, and I had fought all night to reach the school. I didn't know the full chaos there, but his words rang true. "The whole town's there, like ants huddling. I'll kill them—unless you surrender."

"That simple?" I asked, skeptically.

"You are smart for your age," he laughed, throwing another rock.

"You've been around for…how many years?" I asked the dark God.

He thought for a moment.

"Forever," he laughed, holding his arms wide as if to say the world was his.

"All those years, you're still so stupid," I laughed.

He took a step towards me.

"I'll never surrender to you," I growled, ready to fight.

"Then they will all die," he snickered.

"We'll fight. The whole town will fight."

"You only have a few hundred. I have thousands," he smiled. "Once I'm done with the school, I'll find everyone who stayed in their homes."

"Your army is weak, just like you," I laughed.

He got angry.

His face came into complete focus. His black skin shined in the sunlight. He had a beard that was perfectly groomed. His red eyes glowed a deep red, and he appeared very angry.

172

I slid my feet into a fighting stance, ready to take on the Dark God.

"You can't fight me," he said.

"Your arm says I can," I smiled.

He growled at me and began to grow. His eyes grew a deeper red, and I saw him getting angrier.

"You are ugly when you get mad," I laughed.

"You little...."

He grunted, and his body soared backward through the fresh air. He hit a palm tree with a crack, but it wasn't his body. The tree cracked in half.

"You're not welcome here," Poppa said, appearing beside me.

I glanced at him.

"Hey, PJ," he said.

"About time you appeared. I felt you as soon as I started talking to Mister Creepy," I said.

"I wanted to see what he had to say," he answered.

"Argghhhh," the dark God roared as he got to his feet. Thick black wings extended from his back, and his body broke out in thick scales. Sharp talons protruded from his hands and feet.

He took a step towards Poppa and me but never made it. He was lifted off his feet and dangled in the air.

A man appeared standing in front of the Dark God. His massive hand wrapped around Chernobog's neck, holding him high above the ground.

The Mountain of Massachusetts had joined the fight.

"You're not welcome in this world," the big man proclaimed, his voice echoing over the crystal-clear water.

Chernobog fought and struggled in the Mountain's grip but couldn't shake loose.

Poppa moved forward.

"This is not your world. You have little power here," Poppa told him.

The Dark God stared back.

The Mountain squeezed.

The God of death struggled and gagged.

"I can rip your head clean off right now," the Mountain declared, squeezing a little harder.

"We can't do that," Poppa said.

The Mountain released his grip, letting the evil beast fall to the ground.

173

He grabbed his throat, rubbing the pain away. He glared at me.

"Remember what I said. Surrender, or they all die," he uttered, then vanished.

I looked around for a moment, expecting some kind of sneak attack, but it didn't come.

"What was that?" I asked.

"In this world, he wields no power," Poppa said.

"What is this place? Is it heaven?"

"No, it's not Iowa either," Poppa said, referencing Field of Dreams, one of his favorite movies.

"I know…there are no corn fields," I smiled and hugged my grandfather.

I stepped back and turned to the Mountain.

"What's up, big man?" I smiled.

"Huh?" he asked, looking upward toward the sky. "Nothing is up there."

I laughed.

"This is a world between worlds. The Gods…they have no power here. It is a place above them."

"Gods? There is more than one?" I asked.

He laughed.

"Kid has a lot to learn," the Mountain said.

"Hey, I didn't just look up to the sky, did I?"

He looked up again.

Both Poppa and I laughed this time.

"What?" he asked.

"Never mind, big man," Poppa patted him on the shoulder.

"Can he kill them all?" I asked my relatives.

They glanced at one another.

"What do you think, PJ?"

"I think he was telling me the truth."

"So, what are you going to do, kid?" the Mountain asked me.

I looked out at the water, thinking of my family and friends and the innocent people of Capron Bay. Then, an image of Lena appeared in my mind. I smiled.

"Sucks to be him," I grinned.

The Mountain nodded and smiled.

"He's strong, though. I could feel it in him."

"He is a God," the Mountain said.

"What about you, PJ?"

"I don't know. I don't know if I'm strong enough yet."

Poppa nodded.

"And your dad?

"No way he surrenders," I laughed. "He's way too stubborn."

"No kidding, he gets that from Grammy," Poppa chuckled.

"What about your friend, kid? What about them?"

I shook my head.

"Nope. They won't give up. I bet Franklin is trying to provoke a fight right now."

"I like that kid," the Mountain added. "He's tiny, though."

"The townsfolk?" Poppa asked.

"I don't know. They might turn on Dad."

"Don't give up on them. There are some good people there. Don't give up on yourself or your family and friends," Poppa told me.

"We've been fighting his army all night. One at a time. They might be too strong if they came together, and both Hog and Mason are down."

He nodded. The Mountain said nothing.

"And I got myself in a mess with Mollie and her mom."

"Prentice!" the voice echoed in my head. It was Dad. They were trying to wake me.

"Time is almost up, PJ," he smiled.

"Prentice, easy son," Dad's voice was stronger now.

"Mollie can come here," Poppa said.

I glanced at him with sorrowful eyes.

"Whatever happens, PJ, remember I love you. Your friends love you. You are a Pendleton.

"I love you too, Poppa." I hugged him. "Will I see you again?"

"When the wind hits you, the big guy and I will be in it. Until then, remember everything you've been taught. Your power comes from your desire to help people. There is true strength in helping people. Remember that because it will come back to you. What you give freely can return to you."

"I don't understand," I told him.

"A warrior must believe in his strength of will, purpose, heart, and soul."

I smiled at his David Gemmell reference.

"Prentice, come on. Breathe nice and slow. That's it." Anyika's voice was talking now. "Say goodbye and come back to us."

175

"She can see?" I asked.

"She can. She will. Trust Anyika. I love you, PJ," Poppa said, and he faded away.

I looked at the Mountain. He was starting to shimmer and fade.

"Hey, kid," he said.

"Not today!" we said together before he disappeared.

My eyes blinked rapidly, and my vision came into focus.

Dakota and Rachel stared at me while Dad held me from behind. Ms. Annie was kneeling next to me, holding my hand.

I looked at Rachel.

"Hi," I said.

She smiled as tears streamed down her face.

"What, you don't say hi to me?" Dak asked.

"Dude…she's so much better looking than you!" I smiled.

Druss' long tongue slobbered all over my face.

"Yep, he's back", dad laughed.

My legs were weak. Rachel wrapped her arms around me tight, trying not to cry, but I felt the soft weeping. Dakota noticed and took hold of my arm to steady me.

"Thanks," I whispered.

He nodded and smiled back.

I looked around the gym and saw a group of people wearing blue windbreakers hovering together.

"Feds," Dakota nodded.

"I can see that," I said.

"I can smell them," Chief Tackna said. His men nodded next to him.

"One look might be angry," Dakota pointed to the agent I recognized.

"Dad, is that the guy from the Bahamas?"

He nodded.

"He looks…angry,"

"Your Dad put him in his place several times," Anyika smiled.

I nodded, figuring as much. I took it all in. There were only a few hundred people, but Chernobog told me he had thousands. There was no way we could hold them off.

"The storm is worsening out there," Tackna said.
"We're okay in here. The generators will hold," Dad said.
"The generators aren't going to matter," I grimaced.
"Why not?" Anyika inquired.
"Chernobog and his army are coming."

16
ALPHA

Capron Bay High School
Capron Bay, MA
9:00 PM

The gymnasium buzzed with an eerie hum as we threaded toward the office Brother Kiernan had secured. Blue-jacketed FBI and FEMA agents, yellow letters stark on their backs, shot icy glares at Dad, leading our ragtag crew through the huddled crowd.

"They don't like your Dad," Jack uttered.

"They're Feds," Dakota replied. "Nobody likes them."

"I thought everybody liked the FBI," the winter fairy asked.

"Maybe, at one time," I answered as I noticed the medical curtains in the corner. "We've had some issues with them."

"Wait, isn't Agent Mason with the FBI?" Jack muttered.

"He's different," I replied.

Jack nodded.

"Dad?" I asked, pointing to the curtains. "Is Hog in there?"

He nodded.

"Jack, I'll be back in a few," I said.

He didn't answer.

"Jack?" I turned to look at him. He didn't answer, his eyes locked on an older woman on a cot against the far wall, her smile faint but knowing.

"Jack?" I asked him.

He stopped walking but didn't answer.

"Jack?" I tried again.

"Crayon Man, go see Lena, we've got Frosty," Franklin said, nudging me forward.

"Go," Rachel ordered.

178

I glanced back—Jack still stared, the woman smiling softly. "Yo, Frosty the Snowman, move it," Franklin said, tugging his arm toward the group.

I turned away, heading for the curtains. Grammy and Anyika's voices murmured beyond. I took a deep breath and stepped in.

Lena launched from her chair, arms wrapping around me tight. I hugged back, silent, expecting tears—but she held steady. After a moment, she stepped back.

Hog's hulking frame lay still on a cot, an IV dripping into his thick arm. Mrs. Sheridan gripped his hand, her face etched with worry. Beside him, Dumpster Man, Mason, rested under a blood-stained blanket, another IV above. Fiona lay on a third cot, chest rising slowly, no tubes or wires.

"I gave her some medicine to help her sleep," Mom said. "She was hysterical. She kept saying Mollie was outside."

Anyika and Grammy glanced at me.

I shrugged my shoulders. I didn't know what else to do.

"I need air," Lena whispered.

"Come on. Let's go get some water," Grammy said, taking hold of my hand as Lena grabbed my other hand.

"I'll go get you guys some water," Ms. Annie told Mom and Mrs. Sheridan.

The four of us exited the small room and crossed the hall so they couldn't hear us.

"Are they okay?" I asked bluntly, looking at Lena.

"I don't know," Ms. Annie replied. "They've both lost a lot of blood."

Silence hung. I squeezed Lena's hand. "Fiona?" I braced for Grammy's wrath.

It didn't come. "We knew this'd happen eventually," Anyika whispered.

"That's the least of our problems right now," Grammy said.

"Crayola!" Franklin yelled, waving his arm across the gym. "Come on."

"We're all meeting in an office," I said.

"Lena, go ahead, honey. Go sit with your mom," Grammy said.

"No. I'm coming. I'm going to find whatever did this to Dad," Lena stammered storming after Franklin.

I looked at Ms. Annie and Grammy. "You guys should come too," I said. "You're going to want to hear this."

"This town is never dull," Ms. Annie said following me through the crowd.

As I navigated my way through the crowd, I noticed Jack. He was sitting in a chair next to the little older woman, and they were whispering.

"Go ahead. I'll be there in a moment," I said.

"It's Prentice, isn't it?" a voice boomed behind me.

I turned—a tall, pale man in a black robe with red fringes, a golden cross dangling. Cardinal Murphy. Beside him, a plain figure in tweed, Charles Dawson. His brown eyes chilled me, like that basement long ago when Alpha's pain seared through me.

"Your Eminence," I said, echoing Kiernan's formality. "Apologies."

"Nonsense, son," the Cardinal said, grasping my hand—ice-cold, his ring sharp. "We met briefly at a funeral. Brother Kiernan speaks highly of you and your friends."

"He has?" I asked, glancing at Charles. That stare—calculated, familiar—prickled my neck.

"He certainly has," he assured me.

"Where is Brother Kiernan?" the other man said.

"With my dad," I said, studying him—tweed jacket, grey turtleneck, pressed pants, duck boots. Too plain, like he meant it. "He's always wearing red," Charles noted, nodding at the Cardinal's fringes.

He was tall and plain. He was wearing a brown tweed jacket with a black pocket square. His light brown pants were pressed perfectly and tucked into dark brown duck boots. Underneath the tweed coat was a heavy grey turtleneck sweater. His face was clean-shaven and square, with neatly trimmed black hair. His brown eyes were cold and calculating. I marveled at how plain he was. Nobody is that plain except Charles Dawson.

"He's with my dad," I smiled.

"Your Eminence," someone said from the corner of the room.

The Cardinal waved and smiled.

"Excuse me, Prentice. Everyone is asking me to pray with them during this storm. Can you tell Brother Kiernan to come see me when he can?"

"I'll let him know, sir," I smiled.

"He's always wearing red," his assistant commented.

"Yeah," I nodded. "I don't like red. People who wear red are real jerks."

"Young man, are you calling the Cardinal a jerk?" Charles Dawson asked me.

"Nope," I shook my head.

"But you just said people who wear red are dumb."

"I'm not talking about him," I said, locking eyes. That cold stare—it hit me, a memory of Alpha's sneer.

"Huh," he whispered.

"I don't like dumb people," I added.

"Young man, Cardinal Murphy is one of the highest-ranking members of the Catholic Church?"

"I've told you I'm not talking about him," I nodded.

He stared at me.

"Nobody dresses that plain unless they try to be plain," I laughed. "Like you."

I felt his angry eyes staring at me.

"I have to go attend to the Cardinal," he said.

"Oh, Alpha, Alpha, Alpha," I taunted, testing.

He froze, then spun, rage blazing. A red glint flickered in his brown eyes—Chernobog's mark. My hands sparked red.

"I knew sooner or later, I would come across your stench...Chuckie," I snickered.

He swung around to face me. His eyes raged with anger.

"Go ahead. Make my day," I smiled.

He glanced at my hands and relaxed.

"Your time is running out, Prentice," he smiled. You're already down two. By the way, how are Detective Sheridan and Agent Mason?"

I took a step towards him.

"If anything happens to either of them, I'm coming for you," I whispered.

"Why wait?" he replied.

He froze, then spun, rage blazing. A red glint flickered in his brown eyes—Chernobog's mark. My hands sparked red.

"Ahh, you're Chernobog's little toadie. I should have figured that," I laughed.

"What's so funny?" Alpha stared at me.

"You are nothing but a worker bee," I laughed.

More anger in his eyes.

"You'll never be the boss. You'll always be a sidekick."

"I'm no sidekick," he shouted louder than he anticipated.

People turned to look at us.

"Charles," Senator Bradley said, appearing at our side with the reporter Priscilla Reed. "Is everything okay here?"

The two men quickly looked at one another. It was easy to see they were friends.

"So, you have a greasy politician in your pocket, too," I added.

I know what you're thinking. I'm a foul-mouthed kid who insults everyone, and you're not wrong. I can do that a lot, but after everything we've been through, I don't like these guys, and I will let them know it.

"You are talking to a sitting Senator, young man," Bradley said.

"And you are talking to a rainbow warrior," I fired back.

"P-man. Everyone is waiting for you," Franklin said, appearing by my side. "Uh… everything okay here?"

Silence.

"Uh…crayon man?" Franklin asked. "Who are your pals?"

"Franklin, this is Senator Bradler and Ms. Reed," I said. "And my boring-looking friend is none other than…Alpha."

"No way!" Franklin laughed. "The robe-hiding jerk?"

"Disrespectful brats," Reed hissed.

Franklin laughed.

"Did I say something funny, young man?" she asked.

"Didn't you just get out of prison? He grinned.

"Point," I smirked.

"You've got a smart mouth," Agent Byrd said, striding up, jaw swollen.

"Been told that," I shrugged.

182

"Someone should shut it," he growled, eyes darting nervously—something unseen spooked him

"Looks like someone already shut yours," I said, referring to his swollen jaw.

He lunged, grabbing my shirt, lifting me. I itched to blast him but held back. "Problem?" Brother Kiernan asked, joining us.

Byrd dropped me, glaring. "This guy's an ugly turd," Franklin laughed, pointing.

Byrd reached for him, but Brother Kiernan's knee slammed his gut, then rocketed up, cracking his jaw. Teeth clacked as Byrd crumpled. Kiernan eased him to a cot, tucking him in. "Good night, friend," he whispered, turning back.

"Thomas!" Charles barked.

"Sorry, Mr. Darwin," Brother Kiernan said.

"No need to be sorry, Brother K," Franklin grinned.

"Yep, this guy is Alpha," I said.

"What?" the Priest asked.

"I don't know what these kids are talking about," Charles answered.

Brother Kiernan glanced at me.

I nodded.

"I was starting to think it was the Cardinal," Brother Kiernan said.

I glared at Alpha, memories of that factory basement flooding back. Lena's screams, my pain. Anger swelled, legs glowing red, burning hotter. "Crayon Man," Franklin whispered, nodding down.

"Prentice, let's go," Brother Kiernan told me. It was more of an order than a request.

I nodded, trying to calm down and doing my best not to look like a fiery candle.

"Thomas, you need to think about who your friends are," Alpha sneered.

Brother Kiernan paused. "Prentice…"

I froze. Since the seizure, my eyes caught flickers, spirits swarmed the gym. White and blue figures, some human, some skeletal, darted among the crowd, hungry and angry. Worse, pure

183

black shadows slinked along floors and walls, limbless, faceless, watching us.

"You guys coming?" Franklin asked, oblivious.

Only Kiernan and I saw them. "Harbingers of death," Alpha smiled, glancing back.

I stepped forward, ready to blast him and the shadows screamed, unheard by all but me. Kiernan grabbed my arm. "Not now, let's go."

Alpha's grin widened. "Your time's coming, Prentice and your father's too."

Bradley smirked, Reed laughed. Rage flared—red heat surged. "Lena's waiting," Franklin said, snapping me out.

"Crayon man, Lena is waiting," Franklin said. His words snapped me out of my anger.

I followed them, silent. The shadows squealed, scattering as I passed, they feared me. I stopped, turning to Alpha.

"Your little demon army is afraid of me," I said.

Our eyes locked—he swallowed faintly. "Not surprising," I grinned.

"Why is that?" he asked.

"You're scared too," I said, walking away before he could reply.

17
FROST AND FIRE

Capron Bay High School
Capron Bay, MA
9:30 PM

Everyone squeezed into the small office, the wind howling outside like a distant scream. I edged toward Lena, perched in a chair against the far wall. Dad leaned on a table up front, his face set. I paused beside him.

"We got some problems out there," I whispered.

"Hold that thought," he said. "We're coming clean—right now, right here. No more secrets."

I nodded, sliding next to Lena. She glanced up, forcing a faint smile. I squeezed her shoulder lightly.

Dad scanned the room, then turned to Brother Kiernan. "Thomas, everyone who needs to be here is here. Lock that door."

Brother Kiernan nodded and stood in front of the door.

"Mom, how are they?" Dad asked Grammy.

"They've both lost a lot of blood, but they are both…," she started.

"Thick-headed?" Anyika muttered.

"Well, yes." Grammy chuckled. "But they are also big, strong, healthy guys."

"Especially Hog," I added, squeezing Lena's shoulder again.

"Toughest guy I've ever known," Dad laughed.

"They need better care," Grammy grimaced.

"They'll make it through the night," Doc said. "Storm clears tomorrow—we'll get them to a hospital."

Everyone nodded in agreement, trying to reassure Lena.

"Before we tackle what's out there, we've got Fiona and Mollie to deal with," Dad frowned

185

Nobody said anything for a moment.

I took a deep breath.

"I'll tell her," Franklin said, standing up and puffing his chest out.

Dad raised his eyebrows, looking at the small blond-haired boy.

"This is my fault. I must tell Ms. Fiona the truth," I interrupted, winking at Mollie.

"Yep, Prentice should do it," Franklin agreed, plopping back down fast.

Laughter broke the tension.

"The whole truth," Anyika said, accent gone. "No holding back."

"I know," I sighed. "I know."

"Okay, we'll be here for you both," Dad said, smiling at Mollie, who was trying not to cry.

"What is going on here?" Grammy asked, trying to change the subject. "With this storm?"

"They want Prentice," Dad said.

"Who does?" Grammy inquired.

"Chernobog," I mumbled.

"What?" Doc asked.

"His name is Chernobog," I bellowed. "He's the God of Winter."

"And the dead," Chief Tackna added.

"There's that, too," I grimaced.

"You mean...like the devil?" Rachel inquired.

I nodded my head slightly.

"You've pissed off the Devil now too?" Franklin laughed. "Dude... I'm good at detention and irritating teachers. But the devil? Wow."

"What does this God of Winter want Prentice for?" Grammy asked.

"He wants me to join forces with him," I told them. "Work with him."

Knock, knock

We all turned to see Jack knocking on the door.

"Who is that?" Grammy asked.

Brother Kiernan opened the door, letting Jack into the room.

"Everyone, this is Jack," I said, introducing him to everyone. "Jack Frost."

"Like...the Jack Frost?" Dad asked.

I nodded.

"Assassin," Anyika muttered, Gullah accent thick.

"What? Grammy asked. "Assassin?"

"Jack was sent here to kill me," I told them all.

"It is what he does," Anyika glaring. "He kills."

All eyes turned to Jack.

"It is true. I kill for the Dark God," he nodded.

"There is more to the story, though," Dad added, studying Jack. "Isn't there?"

Jack nodded, eyes darting nervously. "Chernobog's held my sister captive for years.

"Forcing his hand," Dad said.

Jack nodded again. "I am not proud of the things I have done. I have tried to do the right thing when I could, but there have been times when I have...," he said.

"Killed," Lena interrupted.

He dropped his gaze, shame clear. "If he doesn't join, I'm to kill him," Jack corrected Grammy.

"He's already told me the whole town will die if I don't give Prentice to him," Dad added.

"There is an army out there in the storm," Doc told them.

"Army?" Grammy asked.

"An army of Demons and Goblins," Tackna said.

"The usual bad guys," Doc shrugged.

"Oh, is that all? Grammy looked at Doc.

"Wendigos," Jack added.

"That thing is called the Chenoo, too," I said.

"And the Mahaha with giant claws," Franklin chimed in.

"Oh...anything else?" she asked, shaking her head. "Is that what got Henry?" Grammy asked, using Hog's real name.

Dad nodded.

"And Agent Mason," Doc mentioned.

"Maybe I should just give myself up," I blurted.

187

Whack! Lena's fist slammed my gut.

"No way, Crayola," Franklin shouted.

"Absolutely not," Rachel stammered.

"We go down fighting," Dakota declared.

"Not happening, Prentice," Adam backed his chair up to the door blocking it.

"PJ, that's simply not going to happen," Dad said, ending the conversation. Everyone made it clear that giving myself up was not an option.

"He will send his minions. We've fought only a handful tonight, but he will send hundreds." Jack said loud enough for them all to hear.

Franklin started laughing.

"Young master Franklin, what is so funny about that?" Doc inquired.

"Jack said hundreds," Franklin smiled.

Jack nodded.

"That's it? That's not enough. We can take them," he laughed.

Everyone laughed.

"Okay, let's figure this out," Dad said, quieting everyone down. "Jack, what can you tell us about him?"

"What is there to tell," Jack said.

"How old is he?" Adam asked.

"From what I know, he's as old as time. They call him Primordial," Jack answered.

"He a transformer?" Dakota cried out. "Great."

"It means he has been an original since time began," Adam laughed. Not Optimus Prime."

"Yeah, yeah. I knew that. I was just testing you all," Dakota said, glancing at Rachel.

"You're cute," she smiled and winked at him.

"Chernobog is the God of darkness," Brother Kiernan interrupted.

Everyone turned towards him as he wandered around the room.

"Isn't that Satan?" Lena asked.

"Not quite a young lady," Cardinal Murphy commented. "But close."

188

"Chernobog or Chernobog hated God for creating humans just as much as Satan did. He became jealous, and he has tried to destroy the human race ever since," the Priest said.

"Wait a second," Adam mumbled. "So there is another evil God besides Satan?"

"No, son," Cardinal Murphy shook his head. "There are many figures throughout history who had divine-like powers."

"Like Greek gods," Dakota blurted out.

"In a manner of speaking," the Cardinal replied.

"That's what he needs Prentice for," Jack said.

"Me? I'm not going to help him destroy the world?"

"It's your power he needs," Adam interrupted. "He must have a way to take your power."

Everyone looked at Jack.

"I don't know for sure, but I think so," he answered.

"How do we destroy him?" Dad asked.

Jack shook his head and shrugged his shoulders.

"There has to be a way to kill him," Rachel sneered.

"People have tried. Lesser Gods have tried. Nobody knows how. That's why I came to Prentice. I was hoping his power might be strong enough," Jack sighed.

"Me?" I said again.

"When I first saw you, I felt the energy and strength inside of you. I've never felt that before," Jack said. "But, after tonight. I don't know."

"Ancient Catholic lore says the grace of an angel can destroy a god," Brother Kiernan told everyone.

"I have heard Angel blood can kill the most powerful beings," Jack added.

"Angel blood?" Mollie asked, sitting quietly and listening to everyone until now.

"It contains all of the energy from the soul of an Angel," Doc told her.

"Legends say when an Angel dies, his blood becomes a powerful energy that can be used to defeat evil. It is commonly called Angel Grace," Brother Kiernan said.

"Angel grace is a potent energy source," Chief Tackna told us. "It can be hazardous to use it in this way. The legends say a weapon of immense power must be covered in blood."

"Does anyone know an Angel?" Franklin asked. "I mean, besides Mollie here."

Mollie blushed.

"Smooth," Dakota high-fived his shorter friend.

Everyone looked at the kid. He just has a way about him. "What?" I asked.

"We're talking about Angels. Does anyone know one? Alive or dead?" he shrugged.

"I'm confused. Angels are real?" Rachel looked at all of us.

We all turned to Brother Kiernan, looking for an answer. After all, he was a spiritual warrior for the Catholic Church.

"They are very real," Cardinal Murphy interrupted. "Everyone knows of the war between God and Satan. The Archangel Michael led God's army against Satan, otherwise known as Chernobog," he explained.

"Wait…Chernobog is Satan?" Lena cried out. The name took on a whole new meaning.

Both Cardinal Murphy and Brother Kiernan nodded.

"It was a brutal conflict," Doc added. "Much worse than the Bible describes."

"Are any angels still alive?" Dad asked the Priest.

"Nobody has seen one in thousands of years," Brother Kiernan added. They either died out a long time ago or want nothing to do with mankind."

"I might know of one," Grammy spoke up.

Everyone looked at her.

"Mom?" Dad asked. It was the first time I had ever seen my father flustered.

"There was a file your father kept locked up and hidden away from the rest of his files. I never thought anything of it until right now," she said.

"I don't remember any of Dad's files mentioning Angels or Angel blood," Dad said.

"He had a secret cabinet in his office at the station and home," Grammy said.

"We've been through both," I answered.

"He also had one in the garage," Grammy said.

"He did?" Dad questioned.

190

Grammy nodded.

"It is in the floorboard underneath the tool cabinet," she smiled.

"Why didn't you tell me about this?" Dad was irritated.

"I never really thought about it until now," Grammy shrugged.

"Doesn't matter, Dad," I said. "We just have to go get it."

Dad nodded in agreement.

"Okay, Brother Kiernan, we're going to take the RV," Dad began to say.

"You need to stay here," I said.

He looked at me.

"He's right, Robert," Grammy said. "You need to stay here."

"If you leave, Agent Byrd and Agent Liang will take over," Anyika said.

"How are we going to get the files then?" Dad asked.

"We can go get them," I volunteered.

Dad shook his head.

"Come on, Dad."

"Absolutely not, Prentice," he replied.

"Why not?"

"Because I said so."

"That's stupid," I declared.

Nobody said a word. They were just watching.

"No," he said again. "That's final. I'll have some of the patrolmen go get it."

"They are out rescuing all the folks stuck in the storm, Robert," Doc reminded him.

"That's really stupid," I shouted.

"Why is it stupid?" Dad hollered back.

"Because he's the only one who can do it," Lena interrupted. Her words were calm and confident.

Dad stopped and looked at her and then at me. He closed his eyes and sighed. He knew she was right.

"I know," he whispered.

"Prentice is right," Grammy added. "He is the only one who can do it."

Dad looked at Doc and then at Chief Tackna.

191

They both nodded in return.

"He's not the only one," Franklin interrupted.

"Young Franklin, who else can do it?" Doc asked him.

"The supernatural squad can do it with him," Franklin declared as he puffed his chest out again.

"We're in," Lena and Rachel declared.

"Me too," Dakota said.

"I'm in," Adam smiled.

"You need your friendly neighborhood ghost," Mollie said.

"No. I'm not letting a bunch of kids go into this storm with all kinds of things trying to kill you," Dad bellowed.

Nobody said a word.

Dad paced back and forth, looking at everyone.

"I've seen what they can do, Robert," Doc said, looking at me.

"It is true, Chief Pendleton," Chief Tackna added. "These young warriors are indeed strong and resourceful."

"Dad, nobody else can go. You know that. You need to be here. Grammy and Ms. Anyika need to stay to help with Hog and Agent Mason," I said.

"I shall accompany them," Doc stood.

"I'm in," Jack said.

I shook my head.

"We need you to stay here and help defend this place if Chernobog attacks," I told him.

"That leaves me," Brother Kiernan said, looking at Dad. "I'll make sure they are okay."

"Wait," I began to say.

"Nonnegotiable, Prentice," Dad commanded. "He goes with you."

"Besides, who is going to drive," the Priest added.

"I can drive," Franklin shouted. "If I can drive Doc's car, the Beast is easy."

"He's right. Driving my car is harder than the...wait...what do you mean if you can drive   my car?" Doc asked Franklin.

"Uh... never mind," Franklin laughed, sitting back down.

"I can drive!" Franklin shouted. "If I can handle Doc's car, the Beast's easy."

"He's right—my car's harder—wait, what?" Doc blinked.

"Never mind," Franklin laughed, sitting.

Syracuse, NY
9:45 P.M.

The wind's howl faded as the portal snapped shut, a distant echo from Capron Bay. Chernobog stretched his neck, sand spilling from his hair. The gateway was gone, only an ancient stone wall staring back.

"Argh!!!!!" he bellowed, slamming his massive fist into the stone block. The wall shook but didn't crack. He opened his fist and turned it over, examining the knuckles. There wasn't a mark on them at all. Anger swelled within, and he wanted to punch the wall again but didn't. He wasn't sure the wall would hold.

He wished he had struck the kid. He thought the mighty punch he had just hammered the wall with would have crushed Pendleton's head like a grape. A small smile crept across his face as the anger faded, imagining the irritating boy bursting into a bloody mist from his divine power.

Chernobog turned and strode down the hall. His giant steps echoed throughout the dark dank halls of the castle. He shoved open the massive wooden door leading to his office beyond. He took off his thick coat and tossed it onto an old Roman couch.

The monitors on the walls were alive with activity. One screen showed a weatherman standing on a street corner, explaining how this was the storm of the century. Another monitor showed a man, whose face was full of make-up, sitting in a studio from one of the broadcast networks declaring the storm resulted from global warming. Another showed angry college students blaming the previous President for the storm.

Chernobog scanned all the screens, and the anger he was feeling moments ago had vanished. His storm was wreaking

193

havoc on each broadcast, and seeing all the anger and arguing made him warm and fuzzy inside.

His eyes settled on another monitor, which had an image of a young girl on it. Her face was twisted with rage as she shouted into the camera. She was demanding world leaders listen to her complaints about the environment. The God of the Dead shivered as he watched her fury spew for all the world to see.

"She cracks me up," he smiled. "And to think, I had nothing to do with her hatred of the world."

The phone on his desk beeped.

"What is it?" he spoke into the speaker after pushing the button.

"Sir, we have a call from Frost," the voice replied.

"It's about time, Frost," he said, sitting in a giant chair.

There was no reply.

"Frost?" he said, growing impatient.

Again, I am still waiting for a reply.

"Are we having second thoughts, Frost? I'm growing tired of your act. I'm just going to rip your sister apart now."

He heard a deep sigh from the other end.

"They're heading home. They may have information on something that can kill you," Frost said. He could tell it hurt the fairy of the winter to betray Pendleton.

"They are looking for Angel Grace then," he said. "I wonder who told them about that. You're playing with fire, Frost."

Silence.

"You've been looking for Angel Grace for how long now? This is your chance to get both."

Chernobog sat back in his chair and momentarily thought about the words. He looked at the wall across the room. It was adorned with Angel trophies. Each of the items on display was a trophy he had taken from the various angels he had killed throughout the centuries.

"Any idea where they will find our prize?"

"They don't know. At least not until they read the folder Pendleton's grandfather kept hidden. I've heard...," the voice trailed off.

"Frost?"

Another sigh.

"I have heard the prize is somewhere close," he whispered.

Chernobog took a deep breath, trying to calm himself.

"You've done well, Frost," he said. "Perhaps, when this is over, I will let your sister go."

Silence.

"Can I see her?" Frost asked.

Chernobog thought for a long moment. He ran the idea through his mind to see if it had any negative aspects.

"You may," he said and hung up the phone.

He thought seeing his sister would remind him of what was at stake here. He also realized he would not need the winter fairy when Pendleton was gone.

"When this is over, Frost, I'm going to feed you and your sister to my hell hounds," he smiled.

18
BURNING THE BREACH

Storm-lashed High School
Capron Bay, MA
10:00 PM

Getting to our house and Poppa's garage files in the storm of the century was just half of the problem. We had to leave the school gymnasium and pass Chernobog's army first. We ran through many different plans before settling on a very simple one. We would walk out, get in the Beast, and drive away into the blizzard.

Dad led us out of the small office and back into the Gym. There were many people in the Gym, and the noise level was very high, but silence took over when the Chief strode into the large room.

It took a little while for people to realize where he was headed—or rather who he was heading to. The townsfolk of Capron Bay parted for him along the way. They could tell he was on a mission. Even though he had only briefly been the Chief, people knew not to get in his way.

If you weren't from the town, you didn't know how to get out of his way. Agent Byrd was about to find out the hard way as I watched him step in front of Dad.

"He just doesn't get it, does he?" Franklin laughed.

"This is going to be funny," I said, smiling.

Byrd stood in a fighting stance.

"Pendleton, when this is all said and done, you will be...." Bryd began to say.

He never finished. Dad slammed a left into his midsection. The FEMA Agent gasped and keeled over at the waist. He never saw or felt the right hand that followed connecting with his jaw. The big man collapsed to the floor. He was out cold once again.

Agent Liang watched but didn't move.

"Chief Pendleton!" Senator Bradler yelled. "Your actions disgrace this state, and you will be held accountable when the storm passes."

"I can't wait to see that. I'll be there with a camera when he's dragged out in cuffs," Priscilla Reid declared.

"Mayor Travis! I demand you relieve the Chief of his duties immediately," the Senator stammered.

Mayor Travis, who had been talking with the Cardinal, looked at Dad.

"You're asking me to fire Chief Pendleton?" he asked the fat politician. Members of the Town Council stood behind the mayor.

"I'm not asking, Mayor. I'm telling you. If you do not fire him, I will ensure this town never gets any Federal or State money again. That includes cleaning up this storm."

"Prentice," Dakota said.

I ignored him. This was very entertaining.

"Now, now, Senator Bradler. I think this should wait for the coming days," Cardinal Murphy said, trying to intervene.

"I'll also make sure you don't win re-election, Mayor," Bradler added.

"Are you blackmailing me, Senator?" the mayor asked.

"Prentice," Dak said again.

"Shhh," I answered.

The Senator's eyes flashed to the mayor and then at the crowd.

"You're going to regret this," he said, pointing a finger at my dad.

He grabbed the finger, bending it as far back as he could.

"Owwwww," the greasy fat man howled.

Before he could finish crying, Dad spun him around and slapped a set of handcuffs on the esteemed Senator from Massachusetts.

"What...what are you doing?" he demanded to know.

"You're under arrest for attempting to bribe a public official," Dad informed him.

"You can't. Agent Liang!" he yelled.

Liang didn't move.

197

"I'm turning you over to my two newest deputies," Dad smiled as he handed the handcuffed prisoner to Brother Kiernan...uh, I guess it was now Deputy Brother Kiernan.

The smiling priest grabbed Bradler's hand and ushered him towards the doors. Doc was right behind him.

"Prentice!" Dak nearly shouted this time.

"What, Dakota?" I houghed.

"Where is Alpha?"

I looked around. Charles Dawson was nowhere to be found.

"Alpha man ghosted," Franklin added.

"He's as greasy as the Senator," Adam chuckled.

"We'll see him again," I said. "Right now, we have to go," I told them.

We all followed Brother Kiernan and Doc to the Gym's front door.

"What are you doing?" Bradler shouted.

"We're going for a sleigh ride," Doc said to him, trying not to laugh.

"What? We're going outside?" he cried out. His eyes flashed with fear.

"Yes sir," Brother Kiernan told him, dragging him to the door.

Our plan was simple. We figured Senator Bradler was Chernobog's toadie, and the God of the Dead wouldn't want to kill us if his prized spy was with us. Getting a man that high up in the Federal government was not easy, and we figured he wouldn't want to hurt him.

"You sure this is going to work, Robert?" I heard Grammy ask my father.

"No. Not really. But it's our best shot," he said, winking at me.

"Uhmm...crayon man?" Franklin asked.

I looked at him and my friends.

"I guess we'll find out," I tried to force a smile.

The door burst open, revealing the storm's wrath beyond. Everyone thought the door opened by itself, but Jack and Mollie had gone into invisible mode and forced it open.

Doc and Brother Kiernan disappeared with a crying Senator Bradler in tow. His cries instantly vanished as the wind and snow engulfed the three men.

I turned towards my friends.

"You guys ready?" I asked them.

They all looked at each other and then back at me. Lena winked at me. Rachel nodded. Dak and Franklin grabbed Adam's chair and lifted it. They were going to carry Adam out to the RV. A moment later, they disappeared into the storm.

I stopped for a moment and glanced back at Dad and Grammy.

"What about Mom?" I asked him.

"Yeah, that's going to be a problem," he smiled.

"I got her," Grammy smiled and kissed me. Go find Poppa's angel."

I fist-bumped Dad and took off after my friends.

"Wait, where are they going?" Mrs. Gainey asked, standing behind Dad with Mrs. Wells beside her.

I hesitated and watched Dad look at my friend's parents.

"My friends. Please come with me. We have a lot to discuss," Chief Tackna said as they stepped up next to Dad. His words seemed to calm everyone down. A pang of guilt washed over me. All of my friends were risking their lives for me. We had kept a big secret from our parents for a couple of years, but it was all coming out now because of me. The whole storm was because of me.

My eyes drifted to voices calling for me from the snow and then back to the people in the Gym. If I just give myself up now, this all ends. Nobody has to go out into the storm and fight a demonic army. Nobody else has to get hurt.

The busy Gym stopped. Everyone inside the place seemed to stop in place. Nothing moved. My breathing grew heavy as I glanced toward the ceiling. The bright generator-powered lights filled my eyes, and I couldn't focus on anything. Beads of hot sweat boiled up on my forehead. I tried to focus on the school banner, but I couldn't. Whispery gasps edged from my mouth as my lungs pumped in and out, crying for air. Blood erupted through my body like a freight train, thundering and pounding down the track toward my head. Inky darkness crawled

199

from the corners of my eyes as rancid smoke forced its way into my nose. My stomach began to churn with a roiling sea of bile, ready to erupt into my throat.

"Not now," I whispered. The words echoed over and over, waiting for the seizure to hit.

"Young man. Are you okay?"

I knew the question was spoken softly, but somehow, it sounded as if it exploded inside my head. The words' melodious tone rolled through my ears, gliding toward my mind. The peaceful sound flowed over my mind and into my body. The mighty torrent of calmness pushed everything back into the depths of my being.

The inky blackness slunk back into the shadows, and I blinked my eyes until my vision came into crystal-clear focus. A cold hand touched mine, and I looked down. The kind eyes of a little old woman looked up at me from her wheelchair.

"I'm… I'm sorry, Ma'am?" I asked her.

"You looked a little…shaky," she said. Her cold skin was suddenly warm, radiating heat from my hand and swarming over the rest of my body.

"Uhm," I stumbled to say anything.

She removed her hand but continued to stare at me.

"I…I think so," I smiled. "Do…do I know you?"

She laughed.

I waited for a response, but nothing came. She smiled and rolled her wheelchair back into the Gym.

I stared for a long moment as she disappeared into the crowd.

"What just happened?" I whispered to myself.

"Prentice!"

The words were distant and muffled.

"Lena!" I whispered, realizing my friends were outside in the maelstrom. I turned and plunged into the snowy darkness.

Gymnasium Shadows, 10:05 P.M.

"Why do you people let this man do whatever he wants to do in this town," Priscilla Reed asked a woman sitting on a cot in the middle of the Gym. The woman was wearing a Capron Bay High School sweatshirt.

"You live here, don't you?" the reporter asked, holding out her cell phone to record any response.

The woman ignored her and lay on the cot, closing her eyes.

Reed stormed away, looking for another person to ask. Everyone she went up to didn't give her any answers. Most didn't even acknowledge her with any answer at all. Those who did speak to her gave her nothing of substance.

She saw the mayor speaking with Cardinal Murphy and stalked toward the duo.

"Mayor Travis, what will you do with Chief Pendleton?" she demanded.

The mayor laughed.

"I don't see what is so funny. You Chief of Police just kidnapped a Senator, for God's sake," he growled.

"He just kidnapped a United States Senator," she rambled. "Not to mention assaulted a FEMA agent."

The mayor glanced to the side and saw Agent Byrd sitting in a chair with an ice pack on his face. His smile grew larger.

"Ms. Reed, perhaps this isn't the best time for this matter," Cardinal Murphy said, trying to intervene.

"And you, you complicit in this travesty. One of your Priests is nothing but a thug for the police," she cried.

Cardinal Murphy winced hearing the words. He knew Brother Kiernan's talents often led to physical confrontation, and he seemed to have become close friends with the Chief and his team.

"What will the Church say when I bring the story to them?" she snickered.

"Ms. Reed," the mayor interrupted. "If you have an issue against Chief Pendleton or anyone in the department, please file a formal written complaint with the Town Council."

"I intend to do more than that."

Mayor Travis turned to see Penny Sorenson standing with her assistant, Theresa Morgan. Penny was wearing an expensive Helly Hansen winter parka and one of those thick Russian wool hats.

"You look surprised to see me, Mayor," Penny smiled, removing a thick winter mitten from her hand and holding it out for the mayor to shake.

"Well, there are Capron Bay citizens here who need help, so it is a little surprising to see you here," the mayor smiled, keeping his hands in his pockets.

Penny's eyes flared with anger at the insult.

"I intend to hold an emergency meeting of the Town Council, and you will be removed as Mayor," she smirked.

Chief Pendleton joined the group but said nothing.

"And I'll have you removed as well, Mr. Pendleton," she said, staring at the Chief.

Chief Pendleton stood still, not saying a word.

"Finally, someone in this town who isn't afraid of this man," Reed laughed. "I'll be there the day they take you away in handcuffs."

The Chief said nothing, which made Reed even angrier.

"My, I sense some tension in this little meeting of the minds," Grammy said as she joined the small group.

The women glanced at Grammy but said nothing.

"Ms. Reed," Grammy said, nodding in the reporter's direction, but the angry newswoman didn't reply.

"Why, Penny. It is good to see you came to the emergency shelter," Grammy smiled.

"Of course, I would be here," she replied.

"I'm surprised you knew where it was," Grammy giggled and turned to Robert and the Mayor. "The town's leadership team is in the office waiting for you, Robert," Grammy told him, nodding to the Mayor and Cardinal Murphy.

"Mr. Mayor, shall we?" the Chief said, looking at Travis.

The mayor nodded and moved past the Chief towards the office in the back of the Gym. The Chief followed.

Penny Sorenson took a step to follow but was stopped by Grammy.

"I said town leadership,"

"I am Town Council President," she laughed.

"In name only," Grammy replied. "You are not going back there."

Penny was going to challenge the Chief of Police's mother but decided not to when their eyes met.

"Cardinal Murphy, would you be kind enough to join us?" Grammy added, not taking her eyes off the other two women.

Penny scoffed and stormed away. Reed followed.

"It seems you and Ms. Sorenson are not fond of one another," the Cardinal said.

Grammy laughed, looping her arm into the Cardinal's.

"You can say we have a...history."

"One, I'm not sure I want to hear about," he smiled as they walked towards the offices in the back.

Fires of the Parking Lot, 10:10 P.M.

It was pitch black outside. The only lights came from the temporary lights installed on the high school roof, which were powered by the emergency generators. The snow was falling as hard as I'd ever seen it. A school bus to the right of the parking lot was buried in one huge snow pile as high as the bus. All you could see was the school bus sign on its roof. Blankets of white swirled in every direction, making it hard to see further than a few inches before my face.

"Prentice!" someone called me nearby. Even though I knew they were close, the yell sounded like a mile away. I moved off to my left, trudging through the thick snow. I could barely lift my leg higher than the building flakes.

Lights suddenly flared in front of me, and the sound of an engine rumbling to life broke through the raging wind. It was the RV. They got to it and turned it on. The headlight beams fought to break through the falling blanket of white, but it was enough for me to see. I followed their path, struggling through the snow. I shielded my eyes and focused on the engine's rumbling when a massive shadow appeared before the beams. The enormous shape covered most of the headlight's glow, but I could make enough details of what stood before me, which was terrifying.

The one-horned Chenoo I had fought earlier in the night howled in anger and blocked my path to the RV. His fur scorched off its right side from our last fight. Its hateful eyes met mine.

I grinned.

It roared, charging, snow spraying as its feet pounded. "Prentice!" Lena's cry rang from the RV.

I heard Lena's voice cry out again from the RV. I snapped. Enough was enough. Images of the night flew through my mind. What had my friends done to be the victim of monster attacks tonight? What had the town done? Nothing. They were all innocent victims of Chernobog and his demons. Fury consumed me, and my body exploded with anger.

BAM, BAM, BAM

Blazing rockets of rage flew from my hands. The power bursting from me surprised me, and I stumbled backward momentarily. I maintained my feet as I watched the energy I had just released bare down on the ice demon. It had no chance. The projectiles exploded one right after the other as they found their mark. The last one left a small mushroom cloud in its wake. The rising smoke and flame lighting the blizzard covered the darkened sky in its brightness. Monsters and demons scurried everywhere, trying to escape the violent blast.

Rage swelled—I became a .50-cal turret. *THUMP, THUMP, THUMP!* Fireballs sprayed as I spun, uncontrolled. "Whoa, Crayola!" Franklin yelled, lifting Adam, awe in his voice. Snow glowed orange—tracer fire in a warzone. Screams and burning fur stench filled the air, my anger shredding Chernobog's ranks.

THUMP, THUMP, THUMP, THUMP, THUMP, THUMP.

"Yeeeeaaaahhhhh!" I roared, carpet-bombing the lot.

A hand grabbed me—I spun it hard, too late seeing Lena. She flew into a snow pile.

"Lena!" I shouted, rushing over. The drift was thick—she struggled.

Shrieks echoed as fires blazed, casting an eerie glow. I pulled her free—she shoved me off, furious. "I'm sorry," I said. "Didn't see you."

"You gotta be kidding me." "You were doing this," she said, pointing toward the schoolyard.

I turned—devastation. A van burned, monsters scrambling. A dumpster smoldered, green plastic melting. A cruiser's frame glowed, cracking in flames.

A snow-covered school van burned brightly, illuminating monsters running around, scrambling to put out burning fur. A dumpster smoldered as pieces of green plastic and metal mixed with falling snow. The metal frame of a Capron Bay police cruiser glowed and cracked as flames consumed it.

I couldn't meet her eyes, staring at the snow, ashamed. I'd protected us, but could've hit Dad, burned it all—Lena, the squad, everything. "Come on," Lena said, grabbing my hand, pulling me to the RV. I followed, too guilty to look back, fearing Dad saw my shame.

19
FLAMES OF MAYDAY

Streets of Capron Bay
Capron Bay, MA
11:00 PM

The wind roared outside the Beast, snow slamming the windshield as we trudged through drifts piled high on the streets. I couldn't tell the road from sidewalk—everything was a blinding white wall. Brother Kiernan gripped the wheel, squinting into the void. Ground, trees, landmarks—all swallowed by the storm. I pressed my face to the window, searching for a sign of where we were, but it was useless, just endless white.

Rustling echoed beyond the glass, something followed, faint but persistent. I shook it off, lost in silence with the squad. After my carpet-bombing in the schoolyard, had I shaken them? My rage had exploded, Lena couldn't pull me back. Were they scared of me now? Or was it everything—Chernobog, the attacks, the night's weight? Either way, it was my fault. He came for me, hurt Hog and Mason for me, threatened the town for me.

"Prentice?" Lena whispered, squeezing my hand.

I continued to stare out the window.

"Prentice?" she whispered again. "What's wrong?"

"I'm fine," I mumbled, shaking my head.

"Uhm...I don't think so," Dakota added.

"I'm fine," I said again.

"Crayola, dude, you can't lie to us," Franklin laughed.

"I'm fine," I mumbled again.

"You're a human Christmas decoration."

"You're glowing," Rachel added, voice tight.

I glanced down—purple shimmered over me, a nightlight haze. After the fire in the lot, exhaustion turned purple in my veins—guilt bleeding out.

"Great," I sighed.

"Kind of looks like radiation glow," Adam said as he typed away at his keyboard.

"Wait…. you're not going to go all nuclear on us, right?" Franklin laughed, taking a step back.

"If I did, taking one step away from me isn't going to help you. I'd take out the whole town," I said as I gazed over my purple shine.

"He is correct," Adam replied. "Both Nagasaki and Hiroshima explosions would have wiped out all of Capron Bay."

I sighed.

"Adam, I really don't think that is helping," Rachel added.

Adam looked up at me.

"Uh, sorry, Prentice," he offered, forcing a smile.

I shrugged.

"I don't think our colorful friend will explode," Doc laughed. "Purple is just the color of sadness; I believe that is what you feel right now. Is it not Prentice?

The Beast bumped and fishtailed momentarily, forcing us all to grab onto something.

"Sorry," Brother Kiernan shouted from the driver's seat.

"It's also the color of the Epilepsy Foundation," I said, trying to change the subject. Months of seizures had taught me that—purple was my shadow now.

They all stared.

"Well, you all know I can go funky chicken," I smiled.

"Don't say that" Rachel said, frowning.

"I prefer floppy fish," Franklin smiled, fist-bumping me.

Whack! Mollie's hand caught his gut. "Ughh," he doubled over.

"Not nice," she snapped.

"It's okay, guys," I laughed. "I have to be able to smile and laugh at it."

I wasn't lying about that. The seizures terrified me in every way possible, so I often turned to laughing and joking about it as a coping mechanism. People didn't like it, but they didn't understand. Seizures terrified me—joking was my shield. They didn't get it, but I needed it.

I forced a grin. They stared—Franklin wheezing, catching his breath.

"What?" I asked.

207

"Look," Dakota pointed at me.

"Yeah, Crayola. You're not going to go all mushroom cloud on us anymore. The glowing is gone."

The purple faded I was normal again. Their chatter had pulled me from the dark. "Thank you," I said, squeezing Lena's hand. She kissed my cheek.

I blushed.

Franklin stepped in to sit next to me.

Franklin edged closer. "If you kiss me, I'll blast you into the blizzard for Chenoo chow," I warned, stifling a laugh.

"Okay, okay," Franklin giggled, ducking behind Mollie for protection.

"Go ahead, throw him out in the snow," Mollie giggled.

Laughter erupted.

"Mayday, mayday," the Beast's two-way radio crackled to life.

We all froze momentarily as we listened to the international saying for help.

"Mayday, mayday," the radio roared again through the static.

Brother Kiernan scooped up the radio mic from its cradle and keyed it.

"Acknowledged. Over?" he spoke into the radio.

"We need help," came a woman's voice from the other end.

"Who is this, and what is the situation?" the Priest asked.

"It's Beverly Mancini," she replied. *We're at the Marina. Giant waves just washed over the docks and the pier. It's all flooded. Boats and water cover the entire place."*

Brother Kiernan glanced at us. We all listened intently.

"Are you hurt?" he asked.

"I'm not, but Ralph is, and there are other people down here. We're trying to stay out of the water. We need help," she said again. *"There is nowhere to go."*

Adam tapped a button on the Beast's console keyboard, and a GPS map of the town appeared.

"The Marina is a mile south," Doc added, tapping the screen where the Marina was.

"Grammy's house is about a mile the other way," I added.

A scream erupted from the radio.

"Beverly?" Thomas shouted.

"There's something in the water," she shouted. *"It looks like a giant...giant...snake."*

Adam typed away.

Brother Kiernan handed the mic to Doc so he could focus on driving.

"Beverly, this is Doc Eddings. Can you evacuate? Can you get inside somewhere?" Doc asked.

"The water has flooded the streets. We're standing on a truck," she replied. *"The water is rising."*

"We have to go help," I said.

"But we have to get to Poppa's files," Lena countered.

We locked eyes. Guilt choked me—but their screams cut deeper. I had to act.

"Ahhhh," the scream roared from the mic. *It just grabbed Jessica Irving! It took her right off the second-floor balcony of the bait and tackle shop!"*

"Guys, we got to help them," I said.

"It's a Palraiyuk," Adam said, pulling an image on the monitor.

"Eewww," Rachel hissed. "A water dragon."

The creature on the screen looked like a mix of a giant snake and a crocodile. Like a water dragon. It had the long, sleek body of a snake with thick fur and six stubby legs with razor-sharp talons on each toe. That wasn't the worst part about it. The worst part was that it had two massive crocodile heads with sharp teeth.

"What is that?" Mollie gasped, looking at the image.

"It's a sea serpent from the Alaska islands. Lore says it can snatch its victims right off docks, jetties, and boats in mere seconds," Adam added as he scanned another monitor.

"Jets?" Dakota asked. "How does it get that high?"

"Jetties Dak. Jetties," Adam answered him.

"You know, the structures that extend into a body of water to influence the way current moves," Franklin explained. "It can be a formation of rocks or a man-made pier."

"Well, National Geographic has spoken," I said.

"Good one, Crayola," Franklin laughed.

209

"How do you know it's that? Rachel asked.

"Look, we've encountered every winter demon tonight. This is the last of the top 10 demons. Besides, do you know of another water monster?"

"The Loch Ness monster," Franklin blurted out.

Everyone looked at him.

"What?" he held his hands out. "You asked about a water monster."

"In Scotland?" Lena shot back.

"You didn't ask where?" he smiled.

"It's coming around again," Beverly shouted. "No, there are two of them!"

"Hold on," our driver yelled as the Beast swerved to the right, sending the back-end spiraling through the thick snow.

"Thomas?" Doc asked, holding on for dear life.

"We have to go help them," Brother Kiernan shouted over the roar of the wind outside.

"Yes. We do," I added. "Squad up, boys and girls."

"Why did it have to be snakes?" Dakota asked. "I hate snakes."

"It's technically not a snake, Indy," Adam answered him, smiling. Dakota just looked at him.

"Indy?" Dakota smirked.

"Crikey," Franklin shouted. "Let's go wrangle up some Crocs…or is it wrestle a snake?" Franklin asked.

"Both," Lena added, grabbing an electro staff from the armory cabinets.

"Whatever it is, we're going to kill it," I said, snapping my arms outward and igniting my hands. The flames danced and rolled around my fists, but I didn't feel any heat or burning sensation—just glowing orange and red flame.

"That's cool," Rachel smiled.

I stared at my hands and felt the power flow from them.

"Amazing," Rachel whispered.

"Isn't it?" I said, staring at the bouncing flames.

"How are you doing that Crayola?" Franklin asked.

"I have no idea," I answered, staring at my hands. This is the first time I've done this."

I rolled my hands, and the flame vanished.

"Can you do it again?" Adam asked.

I snapped my arms out, and the flames popped to life once again. I rolled them over, and they stopped burning.

"Cool," Adam whispered.

"Young Master Adam," Doc interrupted. "What does your computer say about killing this gator snake creature."

"Gator snake. I like it, Doc," Mollie fist-bumped the Librarian. She still had the warding on her, making her feel solid to the touch.

"Let me see," he mumbled as he scanned the information. "What?"

We all waited for him to explain.

"You got to be kidding me?" he added.

"What is it?" Lena asked.

"Says it can swim through the Earth, including sand and snow," he explained.

"This thing can swim on land?" Dakota shouted. "Great!"

"Great, now it's like a gator-snake-worm," Franklin proclaimed.

"How do we kill it?" Lena asked again.

Adam didn't say anything.

"Adam? How do we kill it?" Rachel asked him.

He turned slowly towards us. "We have to cut both its heads off," he swallowed hard.

We all looked at each other, realizing this had just gotten a lot harder. We would have to fight a giant gator-snake-worm creature, and she said there were two.

"Maybe we should just head to Poppa's house," Dakota forced a thin grin.

"Help!" Beverly's voice boomed on the radio.

"No. We have to help them," I said. "It's the right thing to do."

"Help!"

"We're on our way, Beverly," Doc keyed the mic. "We're coming!"

"Let's go get some Palraiyuk souvenirs," Lena said.

"Crikey!" Franklin laughed.

Flooded Marina
11:30 PM

The Beast crested the hill and came to a sliding stop on the thick, snow-covered road right in front of the Capron Bay Marina Visitors Center. Brother Kiernan shoved the big RV into the park and squinted through the windshield, trying to see through the whipping snow.

"The water reaches all the way past the general store," Doc shuddered. "The storm surge must have been terrible."

"We have to park here by the visitor's center," Brother Kiernan added, annoyed. "We'll have to make our way down the hill on foot."

We all looked at Adam.

"Don't even think about it," he argued before we said anything.

"Dude," Dakota began to say.

Whirr.

Adam pushed a button, and the tires on his wheelchair hissed as thick tracks slid from a compartment. He slowly rolled over the rubber tires, encasing them all. We all looked on in amazement.

"Dad upgraded my chair to make it driveable in the snow," he smiled.

"Wait, we picked you up and carried you back to the school," Franklin proclaimed.

"I didn't see a need to pull this out yet," our wheelchair-bound friend quipped.

Rachel laughed.

"What's so funny?" Dakota asked her.

"Adam is a transformer for real," she laughed.

"I am Optimus Adam," he proclaimed, sitting taller in his seat.

We all laughed.

"Let's hope Optimus Adam doesn't become snake food," Franklin replied.

"Are you sure," I began to say.

Adam cut me off.

"Don't even think about leaving me behind. I'm not letting you all go down there fighting Capron's own Frozen Nessie without me," he declared.

I looked around at them all. My eyes settled on Brother Kiernan, who was always the voice of reason for us at times like this. He shrugged his shoulders.

"If there is one thing I've learned about all of you since I first met you, it is that you are the most stubborn group of kids I've ever known, and you are all fiercely loyal to one another," he added.

"All for one," Dakota smiled.

"And all for one," we all said together.

"Alright," I said, opening the door and stepping into the storm of the century.

Music erupted from the RV's speakers, cutting through the hissing of wind. It was Peyton Parrish, Franklin's favorite new singer. He was a Viking-themed singer who also banged out Disney tunes like Let it Go. But now what was blaring over the Beast's speaker was his favorite song called "We Are Vikings".

I stepped into the storm, pride swelling as each friend followed. Snow slowed them, like an action-hero montage. Lena swung her staff, loosening up her muscles as she took her place next to me. I looked at her and smiled ear to ear. Whatever was going to happen, she would be by my side. Franklin and Mollie stepped up, followed by Dakota and Rachel. Dak looked down at the flooded and half-frozen Marina and swallowed hard. I admired him the most. He was more scared than anyone, yet here he was, standing by our side, ready for supernatural war.

Brother Kiernan looked like an albino ninja stepping behind us. I was still amazed at how we became friends with a monster-fighting man of the Church who wasn't much older than us. Doc Eddings' tall, thin frame fought the gusting wind and looked down at us all. Here he was, the town's aging Librarian, ready to go into a supernatural battle with many kids.

We all glanced back at the last member of our team and his new nickname, Optimus Adam. He was the last one in the big RV, and we watched him in amazement as his new snowmobile wheelchair exited the Beast's door. We all gaped in awe at him as he fell forward flat on his face with a thud into the thick snow.

"Adam!" Lena, Mollie, and Rachel shouted, racing towards our fallen friend.

"Optimus! Are you okay?" Franklin yelled through the snow.

Adam's hand shot up in the snow with a mighty thumbs up.

"I am Optimus Adam, and I send this message. I am...OTAY!" he shouted, but his face, covered in heavy snow muffled his words.

Everyone laughed, including Doc, who usually didn't find our sense of humor funny.

"Oh my God! Did you see him face plant?" Franklin cackled.

"Man Down! Man Down," Dakota shouted as he bent over, laughing so hard.

"Optimus snowman," I gasped, trying not to choke from laughing.

"Come on, you guys," Lena glared at us. "Stop laughing and come help."

None of us moved. We were still laughing too hard.

"Doc?" Rachel pleaded for the one guy who wasn't supposed to be laughing.

Doc tried to stifle the laughter until he glanced at us all.

"Sniper!" he howled, doubling over.

"Oh my God," Brother Kiernan roared as he slipped and fell backward into the snow.

The girls had gotten Adam up and sitting upright now. He spit out some snow as he watched us all laughing at him.

"See, even the Catholic Ninja falls in the snow," he giggled, pointing to Thomas lying on his back in the snow.

"The Priest yelled. Oh My God," Doc added through more laughter, which caused us all to laugh as hard as we had in a long time.

The laughter went on for another minute. Even the girls started laughing, although not as hard as we were. They knew they shouldn't laugh at the expense of our handicapped friend, but it was too funny not to.

"Remember when he hit the stop sign?" Dak laughed, referring to the last time we did the hero assemble montage. We all laughed for another minute.

"WENDY!" the word shrieked through the lashing snow and wind.

Franklin and I froze, all laughter disappearing.

"Did you guys just hear someone yell, Wendy?" Rachel asked.

"WENDY!" The word cut through the storm, and we all felt the evil within the voice. To make it even worse, the wind and snow suddenly stopped, and the eerie silence of a cold winter's night settled on us all.

Something stalked towards us somewhere in the trees, hidden by the big thick branches and inky blackness. It was loud. It was big. We could hear the gasping breath as it snapped everything approaching us.

"Get ready," I shouted to everyone.

"What is it?" Rachel cried out.

"Get Adam back," Franklin thundered, grabbing Adam's chair. There was no sarcasm in his voice, which made everyone else uneasy.

"Everyone behind me," I tensed, snapping my hands out in front of me, igniting the powerful flames.

"Dude, remember, the colors won't bother this thing," Franklin croaked.

"WENDY!" the voice slithered louder and closer this time.

"Wait. It sounds like Franklin," Mollie added.

"Yeah, I kind of busted its chops earlier tonight," Franklin laughed nervously.

"It wants you, buddy," I said, glancing at Franklin.

"Get in line," he quipped, referencing that he irritates most people.

"What is it? What have you made angry now, young Franklin," Doc asked.

"A Wendigo," Dakota whispered.

I stared at the creature standing at the edge of the tree line. It was studying us intently. The head moved slowly, looking at each one of us for a moment. The moonlight cast a bright glow

215

reflecting off the snow, illuminating the beast. It stood unmoving and unbothered by the hammering wind. It was tall and sickly thin. It had to be almost seven feet tall, with ash-grey skin stretched tight over a gaunt and bony frame. The bones of the chest and torso were visible underneath the sickly skin, but lean, powerful muscles ran along each arm and leg. The freakishly long arms ended in razor-sharp claws. I couldn't see the monster's feet, but I imagined they, too, had deathly sharp talons attached.

"What is a Wendigo?" Lena shouted.

The beast turned towards her, drawn by her voice. The glowing red eyes were set deep into lifeless sockets rimmed by a skeletal face resembling a dead deer or elk. Large gruesome antlers rose from the bony skull face.

I stepped in front of her, and it looked at me. I could have sworn it smiled just before screeching "Wendy" again.

"It is the evil spirit of the forest with an unbelievable hunger for flesh. It will eat anything it can get its hands on," Dakota cautioned.

"WENDY!" it shrieked again, spreading its muscled arm outward as if daring them all to run.

"Okay, is anyone else getting a Predator vibe from this thing?" Franklin scoffed, trying to sound funny, but his words were full of fear.

"This is the Apex Predator of Native American lore," Dakota added.

"How do we kill it?" I asked.

"I don't know," Dakota replied.

"You said silver hurts it?" Brother Kiernan asked as we all stood ready for the Wendigo to charge.

"It did earlier tonight. Franklin, Jack, and I came across it," I explained.

The beast moved to its left, slowly shuffling through the snow, but the eyes never left us.

I took steps to follow it, making sure I stayed between it and my friends.

"Legends says it wants to eat everything it comes in contact with," Dakota shivered.

A scream erupted from behind us down the snow road to the Marina. I didn't take my eyes off the Wendigo.

"Prentice," Brother Kiernan said. "Franklin and I will take care of…Wendy here. You take the rest and go take on the sea beast."

"Yeah, Crayola, you go and…wait…what?" Franklin

"What?" I glanced at him.

He pulled a long steel blade from a sheath strapped over his back. The sharpened steel sliding from its covering echoed through the thundering wind and snow. The Priest stepped up next to Prentice, instantly moving into a fighting stance that looked like an ancient Samurai warrior.

I noticed the beast stopped moving. It had caught a glimpse of the blade in Thomas' hands. I looked at it. It was impressive and old. The blade was long and shiny and razor sharp. It glistened in the blowing snow down to a thick silver handle carved into a dragon's head. I noticed some symbols and writing on the cross guard. I made a mental note to ask him about it later. If there was a later.

"I told you. Ninja Priest," Franklin declared, gaining a little confidence as he stood beside our sword-wielding friend.

"Is that Excalibur?" Rachel asked.

"It is Ascalon," Doc replied. It is the blade St. George used to kill the dragon."

"What dragon?" Lena asked.

"I don't care if it killed Smog or Pete the Magic Dragon," Franklin laughed. "As long as it cuts Wendy here in two."

"WENDY!" it screeched again, taking two steps closer to us.

"Help!" came more screams from behind us.

"Prentice. Go," Brother Kiernan added. "We got this."

Mollie stepped up next to me.

"Wipe this off of my arm," she said, lifting her sleeve and revealing the warding on her arm.

"Mollie?" I whispered.

"Do it. Please. I can be more helpful in my other form than this one," she pleaded.

I glanced at Lena and at Franklin.

"She's right," Lena added. "We can always put it back on her."

"I don't think it's…" Franklin began.

"I don't care what you think. I'm helping," she shot back.

Franklin said nothing. He knew it was an argument he wasn't going to win.

"Okay," I said. I reached down and grabbed a bunch of snow and wiped all the ink from her arm. As it faded, so did she until she was gone entirely from everyone's view except mine. She took a step towards the beast but kept my grip tight. She looked at her arm and then at me.

"Be careful," I said. "Promise me."

Our eyes locked for a moment. She nodded, and I let go. She vanished in front of me. I could always see her in her spectral form except when she didn't want me to.

"Go!" Thomas ordered.

I nodded and turned towards the Marina. Lena, Rachel, Dakota, Doc, and Adam followed. Adam's chair, reinforced by the tracks, sliced through the thick snow with ease and was able to push to the front.

"See. I can't get out of an RV, but I can move through the snow, boys and girls," he laughed.

"Hey, what do we do with Adam when we get to the water?" Dakota asked.

Adam skidded to a halt in front of us, looking at me.

"We'll figure that out when we get down there," I said, moving down the hill.

20
MUTINY

Capron Bay High School
Capron Bay,
11:30 PM

Chief Pendleton stood underneath the basketball net cranked up to the gym rafters. He glanced down at the floor, remembering his playing days. He had watched Hog post up on smaller opponents many times right in this spot. Each time, the big man would be shouting for the ball so he could get an easy layup or the occasional rim-shattering dunk if he could get a lot of momentum going.

Voices snapped him back. Some yelling at him, others defending, most just scared, shouting into the void. Council whispers grew as Priscilla Reed's accusations echoed, a low hum of dissent made their way through the crowd.

His eyes shifted to the rafters where the school's state championship banners hung. There hadn't been any since he and Tank graduated. It had been a couple of decades since the school was competitive at the state level. He knew many of the coaches, and they were all excited because this group of young middle school kids, of which Prentice and his friends were a part, were supposed to be good. They hoped they would bring a banner or two back to the school.

His gaze moved to the makeshift emergency room they had set up, which was nothing, but a couple of hospital sheets squared off to prevent people from seeing behind them. Sadness overtook him at that moment as he knew his best friend was fighting for his life, along with an FBI agent who had become a trusted colleague and loyal friend.

"Robert," his mother's words brought him back to the people shouting in front of him.

He forced a smile, meeting her steady gaze.

"Folks," Mayor Travis spoke. "The Chief is doing everything he can to keep us safe."

"He is. He is," Cardinal Murphy nodded, trying to add another authoritative voice to the situation.

"All he has done is bring an unknown threat to this town and put his fame and glory before everyone's safety," Priscilla Reed shouted back. The Chief looked at her. She was good. She had managed to gather some support for her argument that he should be replaced, including the head of the town council, Theresa Morgan, who had now appeared with a small group of people behind her.

"Ms. Morgan," Mayor Travis greeted her. "Have you Come back to voice more displeasure at our situation? Have you finally met the townsfolk?"

The Chief smiled again at the mayor's sarcasm. Everyone knew the knock-on Theresa Morgan was that most people in the town didn't even know who she was because she didn't care to meet them. He also knew she got appointed because of some influential people in the town and the state.

"Joke all you want, Mayor," she snickered. "We've got most of the council here for an emergency hearing."

The mayor said nothing.

FEMA Agent Byrd and FBI Agent Liang, along with Senator Bradley, appeared behind her. "The Governor has authorized an emergency removal of all leadership at this time," the Senator advised.

"My dear chubby and greasy Senator Bradler, we both know that can't occur," said a sweet southern belle.

Chief Pendleton smiled as Fiona Thompson parted the crowd before him. She didn't look at all like she had been unconscious for the past two hours. Her proper and sweet southern accent always calmed everyone, and her stunning beauty shocked most men when they first looked at her.

"Who is this that just insulted me," the Senator demanded.

"I am, Senator Chicklet, Chief Pendleton's legal counsel, sir," Fiona answered with a wink and smile at Robert as she strode through the crowd and took her place next to the Chief and the Mayor.

"She is actually the town's legal advisor," Mayor Travis added.

"Wait, I thought I was," a balding man standing behind Theresa Morgan piped up.

"You're fired, Francis," the mayor replied. "Ms. Thompson is your replacement."

"Wait…you can't do that," Francis shouted.

"Lighten up, Francis," the Chief informed him. "Or my men will escort you from the building into the snow beyond." Two Capron PD officers quickly stepped into view to make the threat clear.

Francis hushed.

"I don't think the mayor has that authority," Theresa claimed.

"Oh, contrare mon friaire," Fiona smiled. "The esteemed Senator has already informed everyone the Governor declared a state of emergency here in Capron Bay."

"He did," Theresa agreed.

"I do declare that gives the mayor the ultimate power to make unilateral personnel decisions for the safety of everyone in town, including you," Fiona kindly informed her.

"Is that a threat?" Theresa replied.

"She sure is feisty Mayor Travis. Where did you find her?" Fiona asked the mayor.

"He didn't find me anywhere. I earned my position," Theresa fired back. "Why don't you take your fake southern belle accent and go home to whatever back-water town you came from."

The crowd, slightly amused with the banter a moment ago, now tensed. Theresa Morgan had thrown the gauntlet down. The Chief considered stepping in and ending the conversation but decided to play it out and see if Fiona's words got them to reveal their next play against him.

Off to the side, Agent Byrd stepped up and whispered something into the Senator's ear. A smile slowly creased the fat man's slimy cheeks as he turned and walked away, gesturing for Byrd, Liang, and Reed to follow him.

"Bless your heart," Fiona sighed. A true Southern lady knows rudeness, arrogance, and ignorance go hand in hand. Never be any of them, dear. It is unladylike."

"I am not a lady," Theresa chided.

The crowd went silent.

"Ms. Morgan, I don't care what pronoun you use. This is about us, Southern Belles. We don't start fights, we finish them." Fiona responded. Her final words were said loudly and clearly with no accent.

The Town Council President scoffed, said nothing and turned from the group, following the Senator and his toadies across the room.

"Well, Robert. That was…unpleasant," she said to her friend.

"Oh, I'm not so sure," the Chief replied. "I got a kick out of it."

"As did I, Ms. Thompson," the mayor grinned.

"It was pretty amusing," Cardinal Murphy added, introducing himself to Fiona.

"What do you suppose Byrd whispered into Chicklet's ear," the Chief said, using the name Fiona had for the Senator.

"I'm not certain," she answered.

"I'm guessing, based on how he confidently strode off, he figured out the one power the town council does have at the moment," the mayor advised.

"And what would that be?" the Chief asked.

He told them, "The Governor can't fire me, but he can move to impeach me, which requires a two-thirds vote from the town council."

"That two-thirds," the Chief said, nodding to the group that just walked away.

The mayor nodded.

"Which would then install the acting Town Council President as Mayor," Fiona lamented.

Mayor Travis nodded.

"Any chance the council won't vote for it?" Cardinal Murphy asked.

"If the whole council were gathered here, they would never side with her. But only two-thirds of the council must be present, especially during a state of emergency," he informed them.

"And that group will do just that," the Chief sighed.

The mayor nodded.

Pendleton sighed, eyeing Bradler's clique on the bleachers. Reed caught his gaze, her sly smile lingering too long.

The Chief just studied the group as they talked. Priscilla Reed stood just behind Theresa Morgan, talking to the other town council members. They were all nodding in response. Senator Bradler spoke a few words as well. Then, one by one, each council member raised their hands.

"What are they doing?" Grammy asked, standing next to her son.

"Looks like the Mayor just got replaced," he replied.

"What?" she gasped.

"I believe the Senator and Ms. Morgan are leading a mutiny against the mayor," the Chief concluded as he watched the group.

"That's not good, Robert," Grammy griped. "Not good at all."

The Chief nodded.

"I'm guessing they just voted to replace me," Mayor Travis wondered.

Theresa Morgan glanced towards them at that moment as if she heard the mayor. She smiled at them.

"What now?" Grammy asked. "You know she will remove you immediately."

"I know."

"And here comes her messenger," the mayor said, nodding towards Priscilla Reed, who was heading their way with a smile from ear to ear.

The Chief spoke before she could say a word.

"Mr. Travis," she smiled, using a generic name, not his title. "The Town Council would like to see you."

The mayor nodded and looked at the Chief.

"Coming?" he asked.

"Yes, sir," Robert replied.

"He wasn't asked for," Ms. Reed snickered.

They both walked towards the group, ignoring Reed's words. Theresa Morgan smiled from ear to ear as the two men approached.

She was about to speak when the Chief cut her off.

223

"You've all voted to remove Mayor Travis under Article XI, section 18, subsection 28a of the town charter, which reads that if the governor declares a state of emergency, a majority of the town council can act to remove the mayor to preserve the well-being and safety of the citizens of Capron Bay," he smiled.

Theresa Morgan said nothing, appearing deflated as the Chief recited the words stealing her thunder.

"That is correct," Senator Bradler interrupted. "The mayor is relieved by the majority vote of the present council members."

Both the Mayor and the Chief scanned the members, but all of them looked away, clearly ashamed of their actions.

"And I assume Theresa is now the acting Mayor," the Chief said.

"I am," she boasted.

Neither man said anything.

"And my first act is to remove you from your position, Mr. Pendleton," she smirked, trying to insult him by not using his title.

He stared, her eyes flicked away, unnerved.

"And I appoint Agent Byrd as interim Chief of Police until the town can find a suitable replacement," she murmured with her back to the Chief. "And the FEMA agents are hereby deputized as official law enforcement officers in Capron Bay and Massachusetts."

"Unbelievable," Mayor Travis laughed. "You don't care about this town at all."

"It's okay," Pendleton said, hand on Travis's shoulder. "Let's leave them to it."

"Robert Pendleton," Byrd said, stepping into the Chief's path with several of his FEMA agents behind him.

Robert said nothing meeting his gaze. He noticed none of the FBI agents stood by Byrd's side.

"You are under arrest for assaulting a Federal Agent on multiple accounts," Byrd declared, raising his voice for anyone watching.

Robert said nothing.

Mayor Travis said nothing.

Theresa Morgan said nothing.

224

The crowded gym was silent as the citizens of Capron Bay stopped what they were doing to watch the standoff.

"Place him under arrest," Byrd ordered several of his agents. None of them moved. They were either unsure of what to do next or simply afraid of the Chief.

Byrd glanced at the agents to either side.

"Take him into custody he ordered again.

Nobody moved.

"Do it yourself, Byrd," the Chief smiled.

"Agent Byrd, we can surely hold off on taking Mr. Pendleton into custody until an official inquiry can be held that can review his actions," Senator Bradler interrupted, trying to relieve the tension within the gym.

"Very well," Byrd added as quickly as he could.

The Chief smiled, knowing the man was relieved he didn't have to try to place handcuffs on him. It irritated the FEMA agent.

"The smile will be wiped off soon," he scoffed.

"Why wait," the Chief replied, blinking rapidly for a second. A wave of energy exploded within his body, running from his feet all the way up until it sparked in his eyes.

Now acting Chief, the FEMA agent stepped back and saw the Chief's eyes briefly blaze yellow.

"Robert", Grammy said, grabbing hold of her son's arm. "Chief Tackna and Fiona wish to speak with you back in the coach's office."

The Chief nodded and walked past Byrd without saying another word. Grammy smiled at Byrd and began to follow her son when Priscilla Reed stepped into her path.

She looked at Grammy and smiled.

"Seems your son's time has run out," Ms. Reed declared.

Grammy didn't say anything.

"I can't wait to do my first story on my new show about the corrupt Pendleton family in Massachusetts and how they used their power to get what they wanted," she laughed.

Grammy laughed.

"Maybe I'll interview you first from prison," Ms. Reed giggled.

Grammy cackled hysterically.

"What is so funny?" Reed asked.

"You. You are funny," Grammy chuckled.

"I don't see why," Reed retorted.

"Cause you actually think you're going to have your own show," Grammy laughed.

"I've already gotten offers," she snickered.

"I'm sure you have. Cockroaches tend to stick together," Grammy smiled. "But that isn't it."

Reed said nothing, clearly irritated at being called a cockroach.

"It's just that it will be hard to do a show from prison or from a hospital," Grammy grinned.

"Did you just threaten me?" she gasped.

"Yes, dear," Grammy nodded. "I absolutely did."

"I'll see to it you are held accountable," Reed stammered.

"If you hurt my family, and that extends to everyone in this town, there won't be enough left of you to do any kind of show," Grammy whispered to Reed with a smile from ear to ear.

Reed stepped back and glared at Grammy.

"How dare you," Reed snorted.

Grammy held up her right index finger, silencing the reporter. "Shh," she whispered as a flame erupted from her finger.

Reed stumbled, eyes wide with terror.

Grammy smiled, snapping her fingers, and as quickly as the flame appeared, it vanished without a trace.

"What...what are you?" Reed quivered.

"I'm a Grammy, and you would be wise to remember what I said," she growled before turning and leaving Reed shaking in her boots.

Grammy entered the coach's office to find Robert pacing back and forth, Chief Tackna, Cardinal Murphy, and Anyika sitting in the chairs in front of the whiteboard.

"Robert?" she asked.

"I'm okay, Mom. They are just trying to think about their next move

The Mayor and Fiona walked in and closed the door behind them.

"Annie, how are they?" Grammy asked, referring to Hog and Agent Mason.

"They need more help than I or the doctors can give them here," Anyika grumbled.   The Chief nodded, glancing at everyone until his eyes settled on Fiona.

"How are you?" he asked her.

"I am wrapping my head around everything around this town. I even thought I saw my baby girl earlier this evening," she added.

The Chief glanced at Anyika, who shrugged her shoulders.

"Can they legally remove the mayor and chief Ms. Fiona?" Cardinal Murphy wondered.

"They can, at least for now. I believe the law will side with you, Robert, once this awful storm clears and the state of emergency gets lifted," she clarified.

Jack opened the door and stepped into the room.

"Who is this young man?" Fiona asked. "And where is Jonathan and our young Priest?"

"This is Jack," Grammy told her. "He's a friend of the kids."

"Chief," Jack said. "We have a problem."

"We got lots of them," Anyika added.

"I overheard them saying they need to give Prentice to the guy in the snow," Jack informed them.

"Morgan and the Senator?" the mayor asked.

Jack nodded.

"It isn't an option," the Chief growled.

"Chernobog will attack in the morning," Jack countered. "With everything he has."

"We will be ready," Grammy snapped.

"We're outnumbered," the winter fairy added.

"We're not giving Prentice up," Grammy shot back.

Jack nodded again.

"We will fight," Chief Tackna announced. "We are not in the business of giving in to demands."

"Is it terrorists out there?" asked Fiona.

"Nusso," Anyika shook her head.

"What do you mean not so?" Fiona looked puzzled.

227

"You know Gullah?" Anyika asked her.

"My dear Charleston sister, of course I do. What kind of southern belle would I be if I didn't know all the dialects of our people."

"I knew I liked you," Anyika smiled.

"If it isn't terrorists out there, then who is it?" she asked.

"The God of winter," Cardinal Murphy informed her.

"Who it is doesn't matter right now," Chief Pendleton told them. "What matters is that Prentice and the team find the angel's grace so we can fight the darkness outside."

21
DIVIDED WE FALL

"Franklin, get behind me," Brother Kiernan ordered.

"No can do, Padre," he replied, shaking a thick silver chain behind his back.

"What? Where did you...?"

"Adam still had it in his chair compartment. When I heard Wendy here, I grabbed it, remembering Jack said silver hurts it. I didn't want deer boy to see it."

"You're a surprising kid," Thomas replied.

"WENDY!" the beast screeched again and charged. It moved with incredible speed and agility. The mighty snow gusts didn't slow it down at all.

"Spread out," Thomas barked. They stepped apart, forcing a choice—but the Wendigo halted mid-field, red eyes glowing, studying them. It flexed sinewy muscles, sniffing with a wet, guttural huff.

"What's it doing?" the boy shouted.

"It's... it's studying us," the Priest answered.
The Wendigo's huge eyes glowed red as it stared at them. The thing flexed its muscles and sniffed the air. The huffing sound it made while gathering in the scent was disgusting.

"Dude, you might want to blow the snotty nose," Franklin chuckled. "I heard that from here."

"Howwwwllllll," the beast bellowed and pounded its chest as it settled the demon eyes on Franklin.

He took a step back.

"Franklin," Brother Kiernan whispered. "Run"

He didn't listen. He pulled out this thick chain and dangled it from his right hand. The monster's eyes glanced toward the silver chain and then back at him.

229

"I'm tired of running and being bullied," the blond-haired boy sneered. "Come get some, Wendy."

"Hahahaha," the deep, sandy laugh erupted from the creature's mouth.

"Okay, now you sound like you've been playing in the litter box and swallowed a bunch of dirty litter, Wendy."

"Hungry," it belched and pointed at Franklin. "Eat!"

He readied himself.

"Come on then," Franklin challenged. "You're not going to like me for dinner."

The beast roared and was about to charge him when it screamed in agony. Brother Kiernan moved with lightning speed as the boy taunted the demon. It didn't see him until the silver blade sliced through the back of the knee, tearing muscles and tendons, causing the left leg to crumble to the snow.

The Wendigo's scream rose above the torrent of snow and wind as it struggled to stand. Thomas swung the blade again, but the beast recovered quickly, swiping a massive hand across its body, striking the Priest, and lifting him off the ground. Thomas flew into the snowy night, disappearing into

Franklin launched into a frenzied charge, swinging the chain as he ran at it. He looked like a Viking Berserker, with his scruffy blond hair blowing in the wind and whipping the silver chain around with ease and

Franklin veered to the side that the beast was wobbling on, knowing if it lunged for him, the leg would have to support his body weight. Thomas' Ascalon blade had cut deep, and a dark blackish goo flowed down the leg, staining the snow.

The beast did just what Franklin thought it would, and it nearly fell to the ground in pain, giving him an opening to strike. Using all his strength, he swung the silver-plated chain with every ounce of power, and the beast caught it with both hands and wrapped the razor-sharp talons around the links. It held firm to the silver as it burned into its palm.

Franklin's eyes met the Wendigo's.

It smiled.

"Oh, crud," Franklin shuddered.

The beast yanked as hard as it could before Franklin's brain could process the move and tell his hand to let go. It felt

230

like his arm was being pulled from his body as his body rocketed off the ground. He finally let go and flew through the snow-filled air.

"Argghhh," he grunted as his body slammed into the side of the RV with a bang.

The blizzard swirled around him as he tried to stand. He trembled as he tried to focus on the Wendigo, who laughed at him.

"Happy Birthday!" Franklin exclaimed before falling face-first into the snow.

The monster threw the chain into the snow and limped towards Franklin.

"Eat," it gurgled and reached for the boy.

"Not so fast, dear boy!"

Brother Kiernan swung the Ascalon blade in a mighty arc as the beast turned. The creature tried to block the attack, but the blade sliced through his wrist quickly, severing his hand.

A blood-curdling cry of pain ripped through the snowy sky, and the beast fell backward, staring at its own arm. Taking a step back, Brother Kiernan raised his blade to eye level and prepared to strike again.

The Wendigo glared at him with eyes full of rage and pain.

"WENDY!" it screamed.

Whack!

The snowball smacked off its head with a thud.

"Arghh," it whined as ice and snow blasted the eye. It brought the arm with the missing hand up to wipe the snow away, but it smeared black goo along its face.

"Do you need a hand?" Franklin laughed, steadying himself on weak legs and woozy from slamming into the RV.

Capron Bay Marina
11:45 PM

"Spread out," Prentice whispered to everyone as they slowly made their way down to the marina. Everything was silent except for the wind and the sloshing of the water, which had

231

receded and crested at the base of the hill leading out of the marina. Cars and boats were strewn about everywhere. The storefronts and buildings had their front windows smashed out from either the water shattering the glass or something worse.

"Where is everyone?" Dakota whispered. "Two minutes ago, they were screaming for help on the radio.

"They must be hiding," Doc added.

"Or they're dead," Adam said as he moved his chair up onto the walkway of the coffee shop where there was no water. He clicked a button on his chair, and the monitor on his chair came to life.

Blip...blip...blip.

The quiet sound of radar scanning the area.

"You have radar on that thing? Lena asked.

"Doesn't every wheelchair?" Adam laughed.

Blip...blip...blip.

It scanned the marina again.

Lena and I moved to the left, where the water washed up against a pick-up truck. As the wave shrank away, a logo for Famous Pizza was visible on the door.

"Oh, no way," Dakota griped. "Taking out the marina is one thing, but doing this to Famous Pizza's delivery truck makes me angry."

"Always thinking with your stomach," Rachel joked as she and Dakota hopped up onto a beached boat.

"I believe I see your father's boat out there, young Rachel," Doc said, pointing to the "Six Rings." "It is still floating unharmed in the harbor."

Adam started laughing.

"What is so funny, Master Adam?" Doc asked.

"The Six Rings is unharmed while that boat is wrecked," he said, pointing to the boat Rachel and Dakota stood on.

"It's the Dolphin," he chuckled.

Everyone laughed at the upside-down Miami Dolphins logo on the side of the boat.

"Shouldn't laugh with this year's record," Lena countered.

"They'll get a good draft pick," Rachel argued.

Blip, blip, beep,

Everyone stopped.

232

Blip, blip, beep

"Adam, where is that coming from?" I asked.

"It's moving towards you, Lena," he replied.

Blip, blip, beep.

"Another one to your right, Rachel," Adam added.

Blip, beep, beep

"It's closing on you, Rachel."

"I don't see it," she answered.

Blip, beep, beep.

"The other one is getting closer to Lena too."

Prentice pulled Lena closer as Doc jumped in front of her.

"Doc! What are you doing?" Prentice shouted.

Beep, beep, beep.

"Closing," Adam yelled.

Beep, beep, beep.

"I don't see it," Dakota asked, pushing Rachel further onto the overturned boat.

Beeeeeeep.

Silence.

"Adam, where did they go?" Lena demanded to know.

"I...I don't know. There is nothing on the scan," he answered.

Beeeeeeep.

The night went silent.

Everybody froze.

The only thing moving was the gentle waves of water and the cold breath coming from our mouths.

I scanned the waters for the creatures but saw nothing.

"Adam," I whispered.

"I got nothing," he answered.

"Maybe they're gone," Dakota hesitated.

The clouds drifted through the night sky, covering the moon and casting the marina into darkness.

"I can't see anything now," Rachel shuddered.

"Neither can I," Lena added.

"Prentice, can you use x-ray vision or something?" Dakota asked.

"I'm not Superman," I scoffed, looking at him. A ray of moonlight broke through the cloudy night sky and illuminated the Dolphins logo.

"Dolphins," I whispered.

The memory of swimming with the dolphins in the Bahamas came to me. I remember the intelligence, grace, and power the animals had. I also remember communicating with them in the water.

No. It was through the water. I was using the water to communicate with them.

"There are no dolphins this time of year in Capron Bay," Doc advised.

"Except for the upside-down boat," Dakota laughed.

"I still don't see anything on sonar," Adam informed us as he stared at his monitor.

"I don't need it," I said as I lay down, casting my hand into the water.

"What are you doing?" Lena asked.

"I'm searching," I whispered, closing my eyes and reaching out with my mind.

The energy within my mind grew stronger, and my senses searched the water but found nothing. These things seemed to be hidden. The question is, where.

I stood shaking my freezing hand.

"Maybe they're gone like Dakota said," Rachel piped up.

I shook my head.

"They're here," I said.

Dakota edged along the boat. I glanced at it, eyes widened

"Under the boat!" I shouted

It exploded upward—water and debris sprayed. Dakota and Rachel flew, splashing into the harbor.

"Rachel!" Lena shrieked.

"Adam, can you see them?" I blurted.

"No. I can't see where they went," he shouted back.

"Prentice, where are they?" Lena boomed, hauling herself up onto the Famous Pizza truck.

I looked around, but there was no sign. It had been about ten seconds.

"Adam, start a clock right now," I ordered.

He didn't answer. He just started clicking buttons on his laptop.

"Been about 12 seconds," I shouted.

"Yep...I got it," he answered.

Doc ran onto the bookstore's outdoor patio, which was usually six steps up from the road but was now level with the water.

"Doc, anything?" I asked.

"Nothing," he replied, scanning the water.

"20 seconds," Adam shouted.

Time was ticking, and I felt panic starting to overtake me. I looked at my hands, and they radiated a sickly green and yellow glow, reminding me of vomit.

"30 seconds," Adam shouted, moving his chair to get a better look at the water.

I felt the vomit energy creeping further up my arms and down my legs.

"I got nothing," Doc shouted.

"40 seconds," Adam added.

I jumped on the truck where Lena was trying to find her friends, but I didn't stop. I took two giant steps past her and dove into the ice-cold water of Capron Bay Marina.

Visitors Center
Capron Bay
11:50 PM

Brother Kiernan moved with sword held high. Even without a hand, the Wendigo charged the Priest at lightning speed. Thomas brought the Ascalon sword up to meet the blow, but with one mighty swipe of the creature's uninjured arm, he was knocked off his feet, and the sword vanished into a thick snowbank.

He knelt, shaking his head as he tried to clear the fog caused by the decisive strike. Suddenly, the monster launched a powerful kick. When he saw the kick coming, he rolled away, feeling the air whooshing past his face. After scrambling to his

235

feet, the Wendigo hit him again, knocking him back to the ground. The nightmare creature moved in to finish him.

Whack, whack, whack!

Franklin was known for throwing hard on the little league pitcher's mound. He was also known for not knowing where he was throwing half the time and for drilling batters often. Somehow, in this fight, each snowball found the mark, pelting the Wendigo off the side of the head. They didn't hurt the beast, but they did make it angry.

It turned towards Franklin.

"Come on, Wendy. Pick on someone your size," he taunted before letting three more snowballs fly. The first smacked it right off the face. The following two buzzed by its head, landing somewhere in the snow.

"Argghhh," the beast roared and barreled towards Franklin, forgetting about Brother Kiernan.

"Oh boy," Franklin whispered as he took off into the tree line, trying to trudge through the thick snow. Like a mad snowman, he ducked under branches weakened by the snow and burst through others.

Behind him, he heard the monster's growl. The Wendigo could not duck under anything. The demon was so big and fast that it tore through thick branches and snow-covered bushes after its prey.

"Wendy!" the thing shrieked.

Franklin stopped behind some thick pine trees. He remembered Dakota saying the legendary Wendigo tracked its prey with an incredible sense of smell.

"I really wish there was some mud here," he whispered, thinking he could cover himself with mud to mask his scent, but he knew if there was, it was frozen.

He heard it, getting it closer. He took off running again. The snow was getting heavier in the air and thicker on the ground, tiring his legs and burning his lungs. Franklin turned to look back, and he fell.

Under the water
11:50 PM

236

As I plunged deep into the marina, I felt the water chill me to the bone. I glowed a brighter yellow now instead of the vomit color I had been wearing a few moments before. My internal clock said Rachel and Dakota had been underwater for over a minute, but I couldn't hear Adam. The average person could hold their breath for 60 to 90 seconds, and since both were good swimmers, they might be able to hold their breath for closer to 90 seconds. However, there were also two monsters in the water with them. There was no way to know if they had pulled them deeper or even further out.

I felt like Aquaman barreling through ice-cold water as fear and cold filled my muscles with endorphins. In case you didn't know, endorphins are the body's natural painkillers. They are released by your brain during moments of shock, freeze, fight or flight, trauma, stress, or physical pain. In this case, it was all of the above.

They also turned me into a glowing yellow torpedo. I don't mean an actual torpedo, but I do mean yellow. In the blink of an eye, the vomit color had turned to a blazing yellow that illuminated my path deeper into the water. I wondered if they could see me from the surface.

Suddenly, I turned around to see a mouthful of razor-sharp teeth bearing down on me. Two dozen serrated teeth angled backward were about to have me for a midnight snack. Everything slowed down, and I realized there was nothing I could do. This thing was too fast. It would take me a second too long to move out of the way, no matter which way I went.

At that moment, I knew I had failed. My friends were somewhere in this water, losing air or even worse. I wouldn't be able to help Mom, Dad, and Carolyn. Anger and sadness took over, and I closed my eyes, waiting for the end.

I was yanked from below.

Something wrapped around my feet and pulled me deeper into the depths. The surprise and force of being pulled deeper caused my arms to shoot upward into the monster's path. I waited for the pain to tear into my hands and arms, but the beast's mouth barely missed ripping my fingers off. I felt the rush of its muscled form tear through the water above me, and I

237

thought I heard what sounded like an angry roar reverberating in the water. I got angry.

I quickly looked down, ready to fight whatever had pulled me deeper, and felt my body rage with a fiery red burst of glowing energy. That energy faded when I saw what had saved me from being torn about those teeth.

Rachel and Dakota each held a foot.

They let go and floated up to me. I wrapped my arms around both for a moment. I realized their eyes were growing weary and beginning to sink. My internal clock had lost track, but it had to be over two minutes now—maybe even three.

Capron Bay Marina
11:52 PM

"Doc!" Lena screamed.

"I can't see them," he answered, sounding panicked for the first time Lena could ever remember.

Blip, blip, blip.

Adam's sonar rang out.

"Where are they, Adam?" Lena shouted.

Adam paused, looking at his screen.

"Adam?" she shouted again.

"That's not them," he whispered, confused at what he saw. It wasn't coming from the water.

"How is that possible?" he said.

"Adam!" Doc roared. "What do we have for time?"

Adam still needs to answer. He was trying to figure out what we were seeing on this screen. The blipping was coming from behind Lena.

Then, he remembered the stories of the Paiyaruk. It could burrow through mud, dirt, and...

"Snow," he whispered. "Lena! Behind you!"

Lena was too busy searching the water to hear him. She was taking her shoes off, getting ready to dive in.

"Lena!" Adam screamed as loud as he could. "Behind you!"

Doc heard him and saw a pile of snow barreling towards the truck Lena stood on. She was completely unaware of the threat coming her way. He glanced at Adam, who was yelling at Lena, but she was too busy searching the depths and looking for her friends.

He had to act fast. He ran as fast as his lean frame could move in the snow.

Adam saw Doc move. His long, gangly legs loping in and out of the thick snow. He looked like a high jumper as they approached the bar.

"What is he doing?" he wondered. His eyes traced the path from Doc to the burrowing threat approaching Lena and then back at Doc. He watched as Doc took one last loping stride, and he jumped. Seeing the nerdy librarian leap from knee-deep snow into the air was a sight. Adam clicked a button on his chair and snapped a photo just in time to get Doc to land on the wooden railing of the patio.

His long, lean legs didn't stop. He propelled himself off the railing, which now collapsed as he pushed off. The monster emerged from its snow tunnel as Doc pushed himself off the collapsing deck.

The head broke through the snow first. It was a long, flat head with a rounded snout that was beginning to open, and even from his position, he could see the rows of razor-sharp serrated teeth. As the body emerged, he could see the gray skin covered with scales, and even through those scales, he could see powerful muscles ripple with the jump toward Lena.

Tiny, disproportionate legs with sharp talons ran along the bottom of its body. As it burst from the snow without making a sound, it looked like a longer and bigger Komodo dragon.

"Lena!" Adam shouted again.

Adam watched in terror and amazement as Doc soared like Superman through the snowy night alongside a terrifying snow demon version of a Komodo Dragon. He judged the distance and did the math. Doc wasn't going to get there before the beast.

Doc saw the beast emerge from the corner of his eye but kept his focus on Lena. He stretched out his lean frame, reaching with his arms as far as he could.

"Lena!" he yelled.

Lena finally heard something and turned around. She froze.

"Doc! Lena!" Adam cried out.

Doc's fingers reached for Lena, and he won the race. His hands shoved Lena an inch before the beast's mouth could tear into her flesh. The teeth barely missed her face, but the muscled beast's body slammed into both at the mesh point.

Adam heard the impact through the snowy wind. It reminded Adam of a linebacker hitting the quarterback and running back at the exact same time as the handoff and explosion of shoulder pads and helmets slamming into each other.

Lena's head rocketed backward as she flew off the truck, splashing into the icy depths of Capron Bay Marina. Doc spun to his left from the blow, and his head crunched off the pizza delivery sign, shattering the cold plastic into tiny shards that sprayed everywhere. The blow knocked him unconscious, and Adam watched in horror as he rolled off the truck into the ice-cold water.

The monster slowed from the heavy blow and landed on the truck. Its long, forked tongue shot from its mouth, and it turned glowing red eyes towards Adam. It smiled, half slithered, half walked off the truck and disappeared into the water.

"No!" Adam screamed.

He glanced backward towards the visitor's center, hoping to see Brother Kiernan or Franklin, but they were gone.

"What am I going to do? What am I going to do?" he asked himself.

He had to act fast.

After unbuckling his safety restraint, he pushed himself off the chair. Suddenly, he collapsed in a thick blanket of snow. He knew what he had to do, no matter how cold. Using his fingers, Adam clawed along the walkway through the snow. His hand reached up to the deck railing, and he pulled. The occupational therapist had tried to teach him how to do pull-ups for a long time, but he had never succeeded.

240

"Argghhhh," he screamed willing his muscles to pull.

A burning sensation spreading throughout his straining muscles. Slowly, his frail body rose even though his arms were trembling. His mind racing with thoughts of falling.

"They...need...me," he roared, pulling with all his might. Tears streaming down his cold cheeks. That's when he felt it. There was a movement in his right foot. Adam felt his toes curling into his shoes which dug into the snow for the first time, easing a bit of the weight from his arms. A surge of energy shot through him, fueling his movements as his arms tensed with power. With one final push from his toes, he propelled himself upward, swinging his body over the wooden railing before plunging into the icy water below.

22
UNITED WE STAND

Somewhere in the woods
Capron Bay, 11:53

Franklin tumbled down the snow-covered ravine. "Oof... ugh... arghh," he grunted, rolling through thick drifts, back slamming a rock—air fled his lungs. Gravity didn't relent—he thudded into more stones, crashing through snow-laden branches.

Crack! His head clipped a rock—warm blood seeped as he rolled on, red streaks dotting the snow. He tucked his shoulders, a human snowball, softening blows—until a ramp launched him into void

His head caught the edge of another rock, and he felt the warm flow of more blood as it seeped from the wound as he continued his journey down the hill. His eyes tried to focus on everything through the snow and trees.

He rolled, trying to get his feet under him, but the fall was too fast. He continued to roll, realizing he had to go with it. He tucked his shoulders, trying to make himself into a human snowball to absorb some of the blows he was taking. He rolled a few feet without hitting anything and thought it was working until he rolled onto a small ramp of snow. When his body crested the ramp, he fell away into nothing.

Panic flared—three seconds airborne. He puffed into deep snow, impact softened. Lying there, he coughed, copper in his mouth. "That sucked," he rasped. "Great, collapsed lung or something."

"Wendy!" the scream came from the top of the hill he had just avalanched down.

He rolled to his feet, trying to stand. His whole body ached, and his left ankle roared with pain as he tried to stand. He glanced down, expecting to see the bone sticking out, but it wasn't, and his foot still pointed the right way.

"Wendy!" came the scream again. This time, it sounded closer. Then he heard the beast crashing and sliding. It was coming down the hill.

"This thing doesn't quit," he spat, getting more blood out and turning to see where he was.

His heart sank.

He was in some kind of gulley. Steep walls of dirt and roots covered in snow rose on all sides of him. He would have to climb out, and he had to do it fast.

"They have to be fifteen feet high," he stammered. "Crap".

"Wendyyyyy!" the scream hung in the cold air for a moment, and he felt the thudding of massive feet landing hard on the snow-covered ground behind him.

He turned to see the Wendigo. It bent at its knees to absorb the blow from the fifteen-foot jump, and its head looked down to the ground.

Franklin hobbled a few steps away until his back struck the dirt wall. There was nowhere else for him to go.

The beast rose on muscled legs and turned its entire seven-foot-tall body toward Franklin. The hateful, glowing, sunken red eyes settled on him. Its arm dripped with black goo, making the monster look more terrifying.

"You are one ugly dude," Franklin quipped, locating a broken branch about the size of a bat lying near him.

The beast tilted the antler-covered head back slightly and roared in anger. The mouth widened, revealing fanged teeth on the top and bottom. It crouched in a fighting stance, raising both arms out wide. Taloned fingers on one hand and a bloody stump on the other.

It took a step forward.

"Wait. Wait just one second," Franklin shouted. "Let me get ready."

It stopped and stared at its prey.

"Eat," it croaked.

"Whoah," Franklin said, holding his hands out wide.

"Eat," it laughed again, taunting Franklin.

243

He sighed.

"Hey, why did the one-armed man try to cross the road," he asked the creature.

The demon stopped and stared at him. Franklin could see his eyes trying to understand what he was saying.

"To try and get to the second-hand store," Franklin laughed, pointing to the bloody stump.

The beast stared back.

"Get it? Second-hand store? See, you don't have a second…"

"Wendy!" the beast roared again.

"Oh, come on then," Franklin shouted back, shuffling to his left.

The beast moved right, and they circled one another for a moment.

The demon moved in.

Franklin grabbed the thick branch and swung it with everything he had. The beast blocked it with his stumpy hand, shattering the dead tree limb.

Franklin looked at the smashed limb and then at the Wendigo.

"Okay, that was a bad idea," he laughed and tried to grab some snow-covered roots to climb out of the gulley.

It was on him before he could even climb one step. It grabbed onto his jacket and flung him across the gulley. He crashed into the opposite wall. He felt a rib crack as his head smashed into a thick root.

He slumped to the ground, trying to focus on the monster, but his vision blurred, and he saw several approaching him.

"Eat," it bellowed again, grabbing Franklin and hauling him to his feet. The glowing red eyes looked him over.

"Eat hand first," it screeched.

"I hope you choke on it, you ugly-looking deer boy," Franklin shot back as the monster grabbed his right hand and pulled it towards its pointy fangs. He fought to pull it away, but the beast was too strong.

He felt hot breath on his fingers as he turned his eyes away and waited for the pain. He didn't want to see his fingers become an appetizer.

Whoosh!

A gust of wind shot past Franklin's face, and the monster released its grip. Franklin opened his eyes to see the Wendigo fly across the gulley and slam into the opposite side.

It cried out in pain and anger. Before it could recover, an invisible force lifted it above the deep gulley and drove it straight into the ground. Whatever it had for bones or skeletal structure gave way with a sickening crack.

"Eeehhh," it groaned in agony on the snow-covered ground.

Franklin watched in stunned silence as it fought to stand. He looked around, trying to figure out what had happened.

Another woosh of air blew past and slammed into the Wendigo's head, spinning it off its feet, and it crumbled back to the ground.

A small blue spectral figure appeared on the gully's edge, and Franklin smiled.

"That will teach you to pick on my boyfriend!" Mollie shouted.

"That's right, Wendy...wait, did you call me your boyfriend?" he asked the ghostly Mollie.

"Duh," she smiled back, and he could see the bluish form turning red.

The beast stirred and roared with anger.

He grabbed another thick branch and brought it down on the creature, smashing it down on its head. The branch shattered like before, but the beast buckled to the ground this time.

"That's my girlfriend that just whipped your butt, Wendy," Franklin laughed.

It lashed out with a big foot and kicked Franklin in the legs. His knee gave way with a crunch, and he collapsed beside the monster.

"No!" Mollie's cry pierced the wintry night, and she swooped in.

The Wendigo was ready this time, and he caught her by the throat with his good hand. Franklin watched from the ground

245

and made a mental note that demons can touch ghosts. He scrambled to his feet, but the stumpy arm cracked him, the side of his head spraying black goo all over his face.

He stumbled back but didn't go down. He shook his head and watched as the Wendigo's bony fingers squeezed Mollie's neck.

"Franklin," she wheezed.

"Let her go," he yelled.

"Kill ghost," it gurgled.

A bright, silvery glint flashed in Franklin's eye.

Whoosh, whoosh, whoosh.

The beast turned.

Franklin cried out in pain as he hobbled and leaped into the air.

Something sliced through the air, heading towards him.

Whoosh, whoosh, whoosh.

He caught the hilt and spun around in mid-air, bringing the Ascalon blade down with his last bit of strength. The blade sliced through the Wendigo's remaining hand, severing it from the wrist.

The hand fell helplessly to the ground as the monster's grip on Mollie was gone. She shot up into the night, gasping for breath as the demon unleashed an unearthly scream into the night. The second stumpy arm flowed with black ooze.

"I was hoping you caught that," a battered and bruised Brother Kiernan gasped as he appeared at the edge of the gully looking down.

"I made sure to follow my coach's instructions," he smiled and tapped the Wendigo on the head with the Ascalon blade.

Its raging red eyes looked up at him.

"With both hands," he quipped, bursting out in laughter.

"That's not right," Brother Kiernan whispered as Mollie appeared by his side.

"You good kiddo?" he asked.

She nodded, stretching her neck.

The beast lunged at Franklin with a massive foot. Franklin didn't even think about it. He reacted, bringing the blade down on the monster's leg. The blade's sharpness was true again, and it cut clean through the ankle, severing the Wendigo's foot.

"Come on, man," Franklin stammered. "Why did you make me do that?"

The beast didn't even scream this time. It just mewled in agony and pain.

"What do we do with this thing?" he asked.

Thomas shrugged.

"Leave it," Mollie said.

Franklin glanced at the Priest and then at Mollie.

"It has killed how many people over the years. I doubt it will anymore. Besides, didn't Dakota say they need to eat all the time, or they will starve? It won't last long," she said.

"Either we leave it, or you execute it," Brother Kiernan explained.

Franklin shuttered at that thought.

"I'm no executioner," he whispered. "But I'm going to make sure of something first."

They looked at him as he grabbed the Wendigo by the antlers and tilted its head back. He quickly used the blade to slice the fangs out of its mouth.

"Wow," Thomas cringed.

"That's probably for some little kid you ate years ago," Franklin explained to it and turned away.

"A little help here," Franklin said as he tossed the blade up to Brother Kiernan, who caught it with ease. A few moments later, they were all standing above the gulley.

Mollie quickly turned her head back up the hill.

"What is it?" Thomas asked.

"They need our help," she said.

"You go," Thomas commanded. "We'll be right behind."

Mollie vanished.

Franklin turned back, looking at the hapless Wendigo.

"See ya," he said, waving at his crippled attacker. "Please, no need to wave back or stand on my behalf."

Depths of Capron Bay Marina
11:53 PM

Everything went black. Usually, I feel the color swelling, building, flowing through my body, and spreading over it. This time, the change was instant. I flipped from a bright, blazing yellow to a wicked, powerful black, and I instantly knew what to do.

I grabbed Dakota and Rachel in one swift movement and rocketed through the freezing water, exploding from the depths and soaring into the air above the marina. Ice-cold water sprayed and dripped from us as I carried them away from the demon.

"Adam," I heard Rachel gasp as we landed on the roadway where the flood stopped.

Dakota collapsed, gasping for breath and spitting out some freezing Capron Bay salt water. Even though she was breathing heavily, Rachel whipped her head around, scanning the bay. I assumed she was searching for any signs of the new Massachusetts version of the Loch Ness Monster.

I heard her say something but ignored her, focusing on my hands. They were black. When I say black, I mean entirely black. The only thing I can describe it as was a deep space black and darkness where light dies. They should have been cold and freezing, but I felt nothing but strength and energy.

"We got to destroy that thing," I declared.

"Adam," Rachel responded wearily, dropping to a knee and drawing my attention. The time underwater had sapped her strength.

"Adam," I called out. "How long were we under?"

No answer.

"Adam?" I called out again.

No reply.

Rachel sucked in quick breaths as Dakota stood on trembling legs. "He fell...into...the water."

"What?" I gasped, seeking his empty wheelchair on the deck.

"I saw him fall," she blurted out. "From the railing."

"Where is Doc and Lena?" Dakota wheezed, still trying to catch his breath.

I glanced at where they last were. They were gone. Panic set in as I thought about what I was seeing or instead wasn't seeing. Adam's chair was empty, but she said he had fallen.

"Did the thing get him and pull him in?" I asked.

She shook her head.

"I saw him fall over the railing as if he climbed it," she panted.

"He must have tried to go in after us," I whispered.

"Or Lena and Doc," Dakota coughed.

I looked at where the chair was and then at where Doc and Lena were last. They would be in two different places. I looked at Rachel and Dakota, gasping for air still and shivering as the snow and wind picked up. Neither were in any condition to return to the water to look for them.

"I'll g..g..go…get…Adam," Rachel shivered.

"No, stay here. I'll get them," I cursed, knowing I had to choose between Lena, Doc, and Adam. I hoped they would be able to handle themselves wherever Lena and Doc were. I knew Adam could swim, but in this cold, his arms would only be able to push his body along for so long. I ran towards Adam's empty chair.

I ran as fast as I had ever run. The night flashed with a variety of colors. As I passed, I quickly saw my reflection in a storefront window. The black was now a variety of colors. I was a pulsing, glowing kaleidoscope of every color imaginable. A human multicolored glow stick sprinting and sloshing through knee-deep snow and ice-cold water.

Leaping onto the deck, I saw the snow trail from his chair to the railing. He dragged himself over the railing, only to plunge into the water, which meant he was going after all of us, not just Rachel but Dakota and me as well. He should have waited for me to surface for that. It meant Doc and Lena were pulled under by the beast, or maybe the second beast we thought was here.

I leaped over the railing, landing a perfect rainbow-colored dive and plunging into the water again. The multicolored glow from my emotions illuminated the murky water more than the yellow did earlier. But I couldn't see my friend anywhere.

Wham!

Something slammed into my side, forcing a bubbled grunt. I felt my glow weaken with the blow as I searched for what hit me. There was just murky water.

Movement.

Fast.

Wham!

Another strike. This hit harder and got me in my stomach more than the ribs.

I bubbled another grunt and swallowed some freezing water with it, but I managed not to cough, which would have opened my mouth even more.

As I twisted and turned, the rainbow glow gave way to a glowing red. I floated in the water, searching for my attacker. It had to be the Paiyaruk, but I saw no sign.

I felt the movement behind me and the rush of displaced water, but I turned too late. It hit me square in the chest. I waited for the pain of sharpened teeth ripping into my skin, but the pain never came. Instead, I was being driven through the water by the strange-looking creature. Water sped past me as it hit like a tackling dummy driving the sled backward.

I grabbed hold of what I thought were its ears. It was slimy and scaled, and I could feel the evil pulsing through the body. I dug my fingers in, trying to hurt it, but I did not affect it. I tried to push off the monster, but I couldn't. We were moving too fast.

My shoulder slammed into something, spinning it away from us. I glanced down and saw Adam's wide, panicked eyes staring back at me. We had hit him, and now, he was sinking.

On the surface, meanwhile, Rachel limped toward the truck.

"Where are you going?" Dakota gasped as Rachel took one last deep breath and hopped onto the truck.

"I'm looking for Doc and Lena," she shot back, scanning where she had last seen her friends.

Dakota stood up and joined her a moment later, shivering as their wet clothes drained the warmth their bodies had left.

"I don't see them," she feared.

"Me neither," he shook, glancing down towards his feet. "Is that blood?"

Rachel looked down and saw a streak of blood on the truck.

"Dak," she groaned.

"We don't know that it belongs to them. It could have been there before," he hoped.

The air erupted with an ear-piercing cry, disorienting both kids as the beast burst from the water toward Dakota.

He was too slow. Its head barreled into Dakota, driving him off the truck and into the water. Rachel could barely turn her head in time to see her friend disappear into the water with the creature. She didn't see the spiked tail at all as it whipped across her face, slicing her skin and spinning her around on the truck, but she managed to stay on her feet. The blood flowing from a gash on her cheek warmed her skin as she struggled to stay upright.

BAM!

The demon hit the truck. It shook, wobbled, and groaned before leaning over to one side. She tried to balance herself by spreading her legs out and using her weight to steady the vehicle, but the exhausted girl's muscles gave out, and she crumpled to one side. Her weight forced the truck to roll even more, and she slid, falling into the frigid water. Her arms flailed, trying to get back to the surface. She rose slowly as her lungs screamed for air. She was nearing the surface when something grabbed her feet and dragged her deeper.

Dakota tumbled head-over-heels into the water with a splash, and he realized it wasn't as cold as he had thought since he was already shivering. He twisted and rolled under the water, trying not to swallow any. He kicked for the surface, gasping for breath as he breached the cold water. He searched for Rachel and the thing that knocked her into the bay, but he saw neither.

He watched as the truck slowly rolled away from him and panicked, knowing Rachel was still on it when he saw her last. He feared she was now in the water, so he swam around to the other side, turning his head to breathe before plunging deeper. That's

251

when he saw a figure floating in the water and immediately changed direction to swim to them.

"Doc," he gurgled when he recognized the gangly librarian floating face down. He quickly rolled him over so his face was clear of the water. He saw the blood flowing from a deep laceration on his forehead.

"Come on, Doc," he cried, seeing he wasn't breathing. The boy immediately wrapped his arms around the older man and kicked as hard as possible, trying to push himself to shore.

"Doc, wake up," he kept urging his friend, but he got no response. He glanced toward shore. It was still at least thirty feet to go. He groaned, wondering if he could make it.

"Doc, wake up. Please!" he cried out. Still no response. He kicked harder, causing his head to sink beneath the surface. He barely closed his mouth in time but couldn't get a good deep breath. His lungs begged for more air as he forced his burning arms up to hold Doc above the water, making sure he didn't sink with him.

He kicked again, but his legs cried out for energy as the muscles burned every ounce away. The thought of him drowning scared him, but the idea of letting Doc drown too because he was tired terrified him, and his fight or flight mechanism kicked in. A burst of energy flowed through his body, and he kicked as hard as he could. His head broke the surface, and he turned with one arm holding Doc and the other driving through the water as his legs kicked.

"Come on," he gasped, moving faster. However, he knew the sudden burst of energy was fading, and he still had twenty feet to go. His breath fumed before his eyes, and he strained his lean frame.

Something grabbed onto him.

"No!" Dakota screamed, expecting to be pulled under and fighting desperately, trying to break free until he realized he wasn't being pulled under. He was being pulled towards land and fast.

"Dakota, it's me," Mollie appeared before him, dragging him and Doc into the thick snow.

"Mollie," he cried, tears streaming down his frozen cheeks. "Doc's not breathing."

The spectral girl dragged her two friends far away from the water. Dakota fought hard to stand on shaking legs but summoned the strength to steady himself.

"Dak!" Franklin yelled as he tumbled down the snow-covered hill. Brother Kiernan is right behind him.

"He's not breathing," Dak shuddered.

Franklin dropped to his knees, listening to Doc's breathing. He tilted his head and pinched his nose and mouth-to-mouth resuscitation, trying to blow air into Doc's lungs. Dakota and Brother Kiernan looked on in desperation and surprise, realizing the kid knew CPR.

Franklin knelt higher and clasped his hands together, pushing down on Doc's chest while counting out loud. He switched to breathing again and then chest compressions again. He did this for an eternity, alternating between breaths and compressions.

"Come on, Doc!" he grunted with each compression.

"Dakota, where's the others?" Mollie asked.

He ignored her, watching Franklin try to save Doc's life.

"Dak," she shouted.

He blinked and looked at her.

"The others?" she asked again.

"They're somewhere in the water, even Adam," he said, pointing to the abandoned wheelchair.

Mollie didn't hesitate. She vanished instantly, followed by a small splash about ten feet into the water.

"Come, Doc," Franklin shouted, pressing down on his chest.

"Doc," Dakota whispered, watching helplessly. "Come on, Doc!"

Brother Kiernan said nothing. He watched emotionless as the boy fought death. He knew they had been fighting death all night, but this was different. This was the power that destroyed life. It happens to everyone naturally, but this is the result of evil. A tear rolled down his bleached skin, and he wanted to turn away, but he forced himself to watch. He looked on as Franklin tried to save what he realized was his best friend.

He grew up without friends because of his skin pigmentation. He was the freak and always kept away from

253

everyone. He was abandoned by his parents and taken in by the Church, but even they were just caretakers. There wasn't much in the way of love or friendship. When he arrived in Capron Bay, he finally knew what that meant. When he became friends with this fiercely loyal group of kids and the adults in their lives. Then there was this kind and surprisingly enjoyable librarian, everyone called Doc, who was now dying before his eyes, and he couldn't do anything to save him.

Except pray.

He turned tear-filled eyes up to the snowy sky.

"Come on, Lord," he whispered. "I'll give anything. Please don't take Doc. Please."

Adam's arms stretched out for me, and his eyes pleaded for help. It wasn't hard to figure out what happened. He went to help his friends, but his arms grew too tired to support his body in the water, especially when it was cold. I remember Dad making all the officers take winter swim training to learn how fast the cold water drained the energy away from the body.

It was happening to Adam right now, making me...angry.

"You wouldn't like me when I was angry," I thought. I closed my eyes, picturing the Hulk and his green muscles bulging and bursting through his clothes.

The sea monster continued to drive me through the water away from the drowning Adam. The water spread wide as our excelling bodies displaced the water we were going through.

Until I stopped.

The brightness of the rainbow exploded within me, and I stopped our movement instantly. My hands clamped down on the slimy sides of the Paiyaruk head and lifted. The force and violence of the sudden stop, combined with my lifting motion, caused the beast's tail to tumble over its body like the back end of a car coming to an utterly sudden stop, lifting off the ground and swinging over the front end.

I looked at its thirty-plus-foot length as it rose toward the surface. I heaved. It moved with massive force, and the tail rose toward the surface as the head swung below, following the same direction. It could not stop its movement. I watched from below as it breached the surface, tail first, followed by the body and then the head.

Once it disappeared above the water, I took off after Adam, who was sinking deeper and deeper with his arms extended upwards. I could tell he was unconscious, and water was flowing into his lungs.

"Adam!"

Tears flowed down Brother Kiernan's cheeks as he watched Franklin.

Dakota sobbed as Franklin breathed into his mouth again and then more compressions.

Doc didn't move.

"Franklin," Brother Kiernan whispered, placing his hand on the boy's shoulder, but it didn't stop him.

More breaths followed by more compressions.

"Franklin," he whispered again, kneeling next to him.

"Doc," Dakota moaned.

Franklin finally stopped and knelt back, looking up at Thomas.

"Doc?" he said.

Brother Kiernan wrapped his arms around the boy, but he pushed the Priest away.

A splash broke the surface, drawing their attention.

One of the sea serpents breached the marina tail first, followed by the rest. They looked on in amazement as it tumbled end over end, tumbling through the snow-filled air. It continued spinning until it slammed into the side of the boat rental shop with a deafening crash.

Watching one of the monsters get tossed like a rag doll gave Franklin one last burst of energy, and he balled up a fist and raised it high into the air.

"Come on, Doc," he screamed, swinging his fist down onto Doc's chest. When the boy's fist came into met Doc's chest, a spark of bright white light flashed for a moment, and Doc's body convulsed as if struck with emergency heart paddles. Brother Kiernan was the only one to notice the small burst of energy.

255

They looked on.

Nothing. Doc didn't move.

Franklin turned and buried his head into the Priest's chest. Thomas looked on fighting back tears. Dakota wrapped his arms around Franklin, sobbing.

Thomas turned his eyes upward one last time, wondering.

"Wh…why…does my chest hurt?" the words were whispered but still sounded like a bullhorn exploding through the blizzard to the three of them as they turned.

Doc was blinking, rubbing his chest, and spitting out water.

"Doc!" Dakota and Franklin cried out, hugging him tight.

Brother Kiernan cried, turning his eyes to the heavens again. A shooting star soared through the night, clearly visible through the twisting and rolling snow gusts, and Thomas smiled.

"Easy, boys," Doc grumbled. I have a pounding headache, and my chest feels it was like I was kicked by a mule."

"Nah, that was just Franklin using you as a human punching bag," Dakota laughed.

Doc looked at the blond-haired boy and nodded.

Franklin nodded back.

"Why does my mouth feel like I've been kissed?" Doc asked, wiping his lips.

"Franklin kissed you a bunch for CPR," Dakota giggled.

Doc looked at him again.

"Well, Doc…I won't tell Ms. Fiona. I promise," Franklin grinned.

"I'm going to have to tell Mollie," Doc smiled in return.

"Ms. Fiona…wait…what?" Franklin asked.

"Hey, that thing looks like it's stuck on the side of the shop," Dakota said studying the serpent. It had remained upside down after it hit the shop, just hanging there.

The four of them trudged over to it. As they got closer, they could see why it hung there. The boat rental shop was called Trident Rentals, and a sign attached to a thick trident extending from the side of the building hung there. The slimy beast had been impaled by the trident and just hung there.

Mollie rocketed through the murky, cold water, searching for her friends. She swung herself to the right and left but saw nothing. There was no creature, no Lena, and no Rachel. She wondered where they were as panic swelled inside her ghostly form.

A flash to her right.

Pain ripped into her legs, and she solidified in the water.

She looked at her leg in amazement. She was bleeding.

Another flash.

Something slashed her arm, and more blood dripped.

She looked around, eyes widening as a monster hovered in the water before her. The form was terrifying. A dragon-like head with a mouthful of razor-sharp teeth with a body stretching almost thirty feet, with alligator-like limbs every six feet and serrated talons on each toe. Her eyes examined the body, which ended with a tail resembling a stegosaurus, she thought. It was a round shell-looking appendage with spiny, sharp spikes attached.

She looked at it floating there before her. As terrifying as it looked, what made her fearful was its face. It had glowing red eyes full of hate and smiled at her. It was a pure evil grin straight from the underworld.

Mollie stuck her tongue out at it.

The beast's eyes narrowed and shot towards her. It moved with lightning speed, driving through the water.

She braced herself for impact.

Whoosh!

It soared past her as she was yanked under its path. In an instant, her eyes went from terror to surprise and then happiness when she saw Lena holding her ankles. Her friend had pulled her out of the monster's way at the last second.

Then, panic set in as she realized she was struggling to breathe. How could that be? She was a spirit, but her leg and arm pain returned. The demon's cuts made her go back into physical form, and she remembered that the Wendigo was able to see her after her surprise attack and nearly choked her out. Realization dawned. They can see me in ghost form, and they can hurt me.

Her lungs ached, and she struggled to rise.

Lena grabbed her jamming something into her mouth. She pulled back at first, but then she felt the air flowing into her mouth. She took a deep breath.

Lena held up an object for Mollie to see. It was a mini tactical scuba diving cylinder. It had the words "Minute Man Tech" engraved on it. Adam's Dad's company.

She pointed to the one in her mouth and to Lena's asking where they came from. Lena pointed to a small bag wrapped around her waist. One of those fanny packs. The words "Six Rings" were embroidered into the bag. Mollie nodded, realizing they had come from the boat belonging to Rachel's Dad.

They turned towards the beast, now circling back around.

Lena tapped Mollie and held up her hands.

Mollie, breathing through her tank, shook her head, pointing to the gashes and the blood.

Lena nodded, understanding that Mollie was in physical form and couldn't use any supernatural powers to fight this thing. She looked around and then up. They were too far away from the surface, and there was nowhere else to go. They would have to make their stand here.

She tilted her head to the side meeting Mollie's gaze. They nodded, smiling at each other through the breathing cylinder, and turned towards the Paiyaruk.

Evil hate-filled eyes stared back. This time, they could see a glowing green slime dripping from the fangs. Lena took a deep breath as a science class memory came rushing back.

The Komodo Dragon's bite is terrible, but the saliva does the most damage. The bacteria-filled saliva poisoned its victims and was supposed to be excruciatingly painful. This thing had a head resembling that of an apex predator, and it was coming for them.

The dragon-looking, underwater-breathing monster barreled towards them, and they had nowhere to go.

It got closer.

They readied themselves.

Closer.

They would go down fighting.

Closer.

They clenched their fists, ready to hit it as hard as possible.

Its mouth gaped open, a sinister glow radiating from within as thick, green saliva dripped in slow, viscous strands.

Whump!

The beast let out a deafening scream as a sharpened spear tore into its face just below the eye. The screech was so piercing it echoed even beneath the water. Thrashing wildly, the monster surged past them, desperate to dislodge the embedded weapon.

Mollie and Lena spun around to find Rachel hovering nearby, her breathing ragged but her eyes burning with fury. A larger tactical rebreather covered her face and chest, and in her grip was a speargun, its barrel marked with the familiar "Six Rings" logo.

Without hesitation, the girls moved. Rachel was visibly drained, even with the rebreather. Each grabbing an arm, they propelled her toward the surface.

I reached Adam, wrapping my arms tightly around him as the swirling colors intensified, casting a brilliant glow over everything around me. With a powerful surge, I shot toward the surface. Just before breaking through, I caught a glimpse of Mollie, Lena, and Rachel clinging to one another as they ascended. They were equipped with some kind of scuba gear, their figures illuminated in the shifting light.

I made a mental note to figure out how they managed to get scuba gear *underwater* in Capron Bay. But that would have to wait.

With a sudden burst of power, I rocketed from the water like a missile launching from a submarine, soaring through the air toward solid, well, *snow-covered*, ground. As I gained altitude, my eyes locked onto Franklin, Brother Kiernan, Doc, and Dakota standing near a shop, their attention fixed on something.

At first, I couldn't tell what captivated them. Then it hit me, it was one of Capron Bay's very own Loch Ness monsters. The same one I had hurled to the surface.

"I threw that thing this far?" I mumbled landing in the snow and placing Adam down.

259

I shook him.

"Adam," Dakota yelled, collapsing to his knees in the snow.

Franklin quickly followed with Doc and Brother Kiernan "He's not breathing," I shouted.

"Move," Franklin commanded me. "I'm an expert at this."

He leaned over and pinched Adam's nose.

"If you kiss me, I'm going to throw up in your mouth," Adam gurgled, spitting water out.

"You're alive!" Franklin screamed.

"Geez," Adam coughed and wheezed. "I'm not Frankenstein."

"What?" Dakota asked him, puzzled at his words.

"Come on. Tell me you've seen Young Frankenstein," Adam laughed and choked on some quality H2O.

"Perfect movie, Master Adam," Doc added.

"Well, we know Doc is better," Brother Kiernan laughed, slapping his friend.

"Ouch!"

"Sorry."

"I thought you were drowning," I told him.

"I was, but I have severe asthma, and when I hit the water, I panicked, and an attack set in, closing my airways. It made it harder for all that water to get in," he replied.

"Dude, you're a bad man," I said. "You hauled yourself over that railing after them."

He nodded. "And…believe it or not, I felt my feet. They pushed me over the edge,"

We were shocked and didn't know what to say.

Our moment of surprise shattered as Lena, Rachel, and Mollie emerged from the water, trudging through the icy mix of snow and slush. Each had a breathing apparatus clamped between their teeth, their bodies weary and movements sluggish with exhaustion.

We rushed toward them. Dakota sprinted to Rachel, while Franklin caught a bloodied Mollie as she stumbled forward.

I was just about to reach Lena when a long, spiked tail lashed out, yanking her feet from under her and sending her crashing face-first into the water.

I was the only one who didn't scream for her.

"I've had enough," I roared, launching into the night, propelled by a shimmering wintery rainbow that arced high into the dark sky. The magic coursed through me, surging along the smooth, radiant bands of energy, saturating every fiber of my being.

With effortless precision, I lifted off the rainbow, soaring higher until my body naturally shifted into the perfect vertical form of an Olympic diver.

Power pulsed through my muscles as I extended my arms forward, locking my elbows and aligning them with my ears. My core tightened, every movement controlled, and I plunged into the water with a seamless entry—barely disturbing the surface with a whisper of a splash.

As energy surged through me, my glow ignited the water beneath the surface, flooding the depths with brilliant light. The serpent recoiled, desperate to escape the blinding radiance, but there were no shadows left to hide in. I was a living torch, and there was no escape from me.

The glow illuminated everything, the world above the surface and the depths below. The creature's tail coiled tightly around Lena, dragging her backward as she thrashed, kicking furiously with her free foot. She landed a solid strike, but it wasn't enough. The beast yanked her deeper into the bay.

I tensed, ready to intervene, but before I could move, a new force spilled into the icy water. A power not my own.

It came from above.

"Where do you think you're going?" Franklin shouted, grabbing onto one of the creature's spiked tail barbs and yanking with all his strength.

Dakota splashed back into the water and seizing another spike.

Rachel followed, griping tight.

Mollie grabbed hold as well.

Adam clawed his way to the edge, wrapping one hand around the creature's heavy tail ball while his other dug into the thick snow behind him, anchoring himself down.

Doc sank his hands into the slimy tail, gripping for leverage.

Brother Kiernan stepped into the water, wrapped his arms around the beast's tail, and grabbed onto its reptilian hind legs.

"Argh," he yelled and pulled as hard as he could.

Together, they all heaved, refusing to let go. I simply floated in the water, watching. The demon's eyes widened in surprise as it suddenly stopped moving forward. Then, that surprise turned to panic. It wasn't dragging them into the depths, they were pulling it toward shore.

Above, I saw the tail release Lena. She scrambled to her feet and, with a sharp glare, delivered a final kick before grabbing onto one of the last remaining spikes.

I grinned

A split second later, a long, forked tongue shot toward my face, a glistening spike at its tip, dripping with glowing green venom. Instinct took over. I caught the tongue mid-air with my bare hands, narrowly avoiding the deadly barb. A searing burn spread across my skin as the venom ate away at my flesh, but the pain didn't faze me.

The demon thrashed violently, trying to retract its tongue. I held firm.

With all my strength, I drove my fist straight into its snout. A sickening crunch echoed through the night as bone shattered beneath my knuckles. The beast let out a piercing screech, writhing in agony, but my friends never let up. Inch by inch, they dragged it out of the water. Together, they were stronger than this demon and it knew it.

Its glowing red eyes darted around frantically before finally squeezing shut. The struggle ceased.

"It's surrendering," Franklin declared as we neared the surface.

Then, a low hum vibrated through the water. My hand tingled.

Electricity.

The realization hit me just as an explosion of energy erupted from the demon's body.

"Let go!" I shouted, leaping from the water and blasting a swirling storm of wind, ice, and snow at my friends. The force knocked them backward, hurling them clear of the creature—except Franklin.

The beast's tail snapped around his leg, locking him in place.

ZAP!

A blinding bolt of electricity shot out, sending Franklin flying twenty feet into the air before crashing into a smoking pile of snow.

I barely had time to register the sight before pain screamed through my body. My arm yanked forward, nearly ripping from its socket. I clenched my teeth, refusing to let go. A gut-wrenching rip tore through the air, followed by the sickening sensation of flesh being torn apar

A high-pitched ringing filled my ears. I braced myself for the worst.

My arm is gone.

But when I forced my eyes open, I was shocked to see it still attached. Equally shocking, I was still holding onto the tongue. Only now, it dangled lifelessly from my grasp, still connected to the mangled remains of the Paiyaruk's head.

"Yuck," I muttered, dropping the severed mass into the dark waters below.

"Franklin!" The others shouted, rushing to the crater of snow where he had landed.

I followed.

Franklin slowly emerged from the snow, a thin trail of smoke rising from his scorched blond hair.

"Wow," he coughed, blinking. "What a rush."

Dakota grabbed his hand to pull him out.

"Ouch," he cried as a tiny bolt of electricity zapped him when he touched his friend.

"Are you okay, man?" I asked.

"I think so," he smiled, shaking his head and causing tiny electrical sparks to crackle from his body.

I grabbed his arm and pulled him to his feet. The electricity dancing across his body didn't faze me.

"Careful, Prentice," Doc warned. "Seems young Franklin is charged up."

Franklin smirked. "Does this make me electrifying?"

"You just got electrocuted," Adam groaned from where he lay in the snow. "It'll wear off."

"Aww man, I was hoping we could be Crayon Man and The Charger," he coughed.

"What am I going to do with you?" Mollie teased.

"His hair is as white as mine," Brother Kiernan chuckled.

"Is it over?" a voice cried out from the upper windows of one of the buildings.

We all turned to see a woman peering through an open window.

"Mrs. Mancini. Is everyone okay?" Doc asked.

"Some people are hurt up here, but I think we're all okay. What was that?"

"YEEEEEEOOOWWWW!" the scream came from behind us.

We spun around just in time to see the second Paiyaruk hurtling toward us, its gaping mouth lined with dagger-like teeth, dripping glowing green saliva.

Moonlight glinted off steel.

SHLUNK!

A single, fluid strike.

Brother Kiernan swung the Ascalon blade with terrifying speed, slicing deep into the beast's flesh.

The monstrous body crashed into the snow, skidding to a stop as thick, black ichor pooled from the wound. Its severed head tumbled forward, rolling to a halt just inches from Adam.

Lifeless eyes stared straight at him.

"Yuck!" Adam shouted, shoving it away.

Franklin grinned, running up and kicking the head. It soared through the air, landing with a splash as it sank into the depths of Capron Bay.

"It's good!" he cheered, throwing his arms up like a victorious kicker. Tiny sparks flickered from his fingertips.

264

Doc chuckled. "That was quite the kick, Franklin. Maybe you can play for the Patriots."

Franklin smirked. "Nah, the Chargers."

A tiny bolt of electricity crackled from his fingers.

Doc sighed. "I walked right into that one, didn't I?"

23
IJIRAQ

Capron Bay Marina
Capron Bay, MA
12:30 AM

"We have to get them all to the school," Brother Kiernan spoke softly as Rachel bandaged Doc's bleeding head.

I scanned the gathering crowd—familiar faces from town, clustering near an untouched nursing home bus. "Brother Kiernan, can that hold them all?" I asked, nodding at it.

He eyed the bus, then the group. "I think so," he nodded.

"Someone is going to go with them," I said.

He nodded looking around.

He glanced around. "Doc should, his wound's bad," Lena cut in.

I met her eyes, she glared. "Don't even think it, I'm with you."

"Someone has to go with Doc," Brother Kiernan said.

"Dakota and Rachel are pretty banged up," Lena observed.

"Adam too," I added, studying my friends—wounded, exhausted from the night's fights. Moonlight hung over the bay—I wanted them all safe at school, but they'd fight me.

"Doc's bleeding bad—he goes. Adam's hurt, but we need his tech at Poppa's. He stays. Lena's not leaving you," Kiernan said beside me. "Rachel and Dakota are more use at school than Franklin and Mollie."

I looked at him and nodded. He was right. Dakota and Rachel weren't going to like it but it made sense. Besides, Franklin would somehow get himself in trouble back at the school.

I called them all together and told them of the plan to split up.

266

"I don't like it guys," Rachel argued. "We should come with you."

"I agree," Dakota added.

Surprisingly Doc didn't argue.

"I will drive the van," Doc pointed out to everyone. I think he knew his wound needed some medical attention.

"No, I think Mr. Williams can drive the transport van," Thomas nodded towards the nursing home driver who was standing nearby.

The guy nodded back.

"I still say we come with you," Dakota said. "Let Franklin and Mollie head back to the school.

Franklin shook his head.

"I don't think that is such a good idea," I commented.

"Why not?" Rachel asked.

"No, Franklin'd start a riot at school," I said.

"He's right," Lena smirked.

"I wouldn't get in trouble," Franklin laughed, "but I'm not going."

"What were those things?" Mrs. Mancini asked running up to the group. She was wearing a thick heavy coat that was completely dry and a woolen beanie on her head with a donkey symbol representing Democrat on the front and a Penny Sorenson for Mayor pin on it.

"What things?" Franklin answered.

"Those," she pointed to the headless carcass.

"Oh those. Adam here flushed his pet sea monkeys down the toilet, and they grew huge in the sewers," Franklin replied. "Right Adam?"

"Uh, yeah," Adam coughed, hiding a smile.

"Sea monkeys?" she scoffed.

"Yes, Ma'am," Franklin smiled. "Very popular in Japan. It is one of the only things Adam has from his homeland."

Adam coughed looking away to cover a smile.

We stifled laughs, Doc too. "They're gone now," I said

"Sea monkeys you say?" another man repeated what Franklin said. "I remember having them."

"Me too," came another voice.

267

"What were their names?" Mrs. Mancini asked, getting annoyed

Adam hesitated.

"Joe and Taylor. He's a big Swiftie. You should hear him scream 'Anti-Hero' in the shower," Franklin quipped tapping Adam on the shoulder. "Ain't that right?"

Adam coughed into his fist. "Please stop talking."

"You liked them so much that you cut one's head off?" she inquired staring at Adam. "Are you mocking me young man?"

We all watched the interaction trying not to laugh.

"No M'am," he muttered.

"He's very distraught," Franklin grinned. "In fact, he refused to do it."

"It is true," Brother Kiernan interrupted. "I had to help young Adam out."

"He had to use a very special blade," Franklin smirked pointing to the sword at Brother Kiernan's side.

"A sword," she said.

"My father used to collect swords," another man proclaimed. "He named them all. Does that have a name?"

"It is called the...," Thomas began to answer.

"The Swift Saber, named it after Taylor. Adam's idea."

"Young man," Mrs. Mancini scoffed.

"Okay, Franklin, RV time," I said grabbing his arm and leading him away.

"Did you see her face?" he chuckled.

"Yeah, I did and you're lucky she didn't throw a snowball at you," I told him.

"Ahh...I was just having some fun triggering her," he giggled.

"Okay, Dakota and I will head back with Doc," Rachel said." You're right. Franklin might start a riot on the bus before they get back."

"Go, get Doc on board and get them to the school," Dakota said.

I ushered Franklin into the RV—Mollie pushed a soaked Adam after. Kiernan lifted him in. "Adam, hit the heat blowers by the shower—dry off," he said.

Lena came running up.

"They're all good," she said.

"I painted some runes around the bus. They should be protected long enough to get there," Thomas said.

"Runes? What did you use?" Lena asked him.

"Uhmm…you don't want to know," he shook his head.

Lena and I both looked at him for a moment not sure what he was talking about.

"The…the blood of the monsters," he grimaced.

"Gross," Lena gagged.

He shrugged—I laughed as the bus vanished into the snow.

"They'll be fine," Lena reassured me.

"Come on—Poppa's files," she tugged my coat.

I nodded, hopping aboard.

Pendleton House
Capron Bay
1:00 A.M.

It was a slow trip but we didn't encounter any more snow demons on the way to my house. The RV trudged through the snowy embankment at the edge of our driveway and slid to a stop at the edge of the garage.

Brother Kiernan grabbed the mic and keyed it.

"Transport 1 over."

"Go ahead," Rachel replied from the van's microphone.

"You, okay?" Thomas asked.

"Roger that. We're pulling up to the school now," she answered. "The lot is empty and everything is still smoking."

I hung my head remembering setting the parking lot and everything in it on fire. It was not one of my finer moments.

"Everything clear?" the priest asked into the radio.

"The door is opening," she cackled back.

We all held our breath expecting monsters to come running out of the school.

"It's the Chief and Ms. Annie," Rachel said. We could hear the relief in her voice. "We're pulling up and emptying the bus."

269

"Roget that. Let us know when you're all in," he told her.
"10-4"

"Well, they made it back unscathed," he smiled. "That's good."

"Why were they not attacked," I wondered.

Everyone looked at me.

"I mean, it's a bus full of civilians with an injured Doc and only Rachel and Dakota to help fight anything off."

"The school could have come to their defense," Lena pointed out.

"Yeah, but not before taking out some people on the bus," I reiterated. "Something doesn't seem right."

"Transport 1, keep your head on a swivel. The fish stink," Thomas spoke into the mic.

"Roger that. Wondering the same thing," Rachel replied, and the line went silent.

"Let's hope it's just us looking into things because we've been attacked all night long," Adam noted.

"Maybe," I muttered. "I just don't think so."

"Well, whatever is going on back at the school, we have to hope they can handle it because we have some files to dig through," Lena announced to us all.

She was right. We had to focus on what was in front of us and find the grace so we could help everyone back at school.

"Adam, scan the area," I ordered him.

He clicked on some keys on his laptop and the console of the RV. The screen blipped as a clear yellow line circled the monitor.

Nothing blipped.

He did it three more times and each time, the line completed the circle with no interruptions.

"Doesn't appear to be anything in the area. At least nothing giving off heat."

"Which doesn't mean much since these are all snow demons with ice for blood and snow for flesh," Franklin growled.

We all nodded.

"Either way, we have to go in and find the Angel Grace," I said as I opened the door and stepped into the blizzard beyond.

The biting snow slapped me in the face like a hundred stinging bees as I stepped from the RV. The storm had picked up over the last few minutes. The wind was stronger and blew the snow around faster and harder.

"Adam, you stay inside and monitor our location and do any research we need," I ordered. For once, he didn't argue but handed each of us an earpiece to stay in contact. He was beaten up and exhausted from the fight at the marina and he knew he would be more help inside the Beast.

We looked shredded. Franklin bled from cuts, Mollie's white hair crimson-matted, Lena's clothes torn, face bruised. Brother Kiernan limped, dragging his foot, "Broken ankle," he grimaced.

"You good?" I asked him.

He nodded.

He nodded. Pride swelled, these warriors would fight to the end.

"Grammy said the garage, right?" Franklin asked yelling over the wind and snow.

I held up my thumb.

He nodded and pushed open the garage door.

"Ahhhh," he jumped back from the door.

"What is it," I shouted rushing over, the squad followed.

Franklin bent, laughing. "My shadow—spooked me."

"Jeez," I muttered, heart slowing.

"We all thought it," Brother Kiernan said, sheathing Ascalon.

"C'mon, let's get inside. It's cold out here," Lena said as she stepped by us and into the garage. She clicked on the light, but nothing happened.

No house lights either, just faint moonlight through trees. "Something's off," I muttered, shadows flickered.

"Shadows!" Adam shouted over the radio. "Watch out for the...."

I saw a flash of movement from the corner of my eye. Two glowing eyes moved towards Franklin.

I turned towards the eyes, and they vanished.

"What the?"

271

In a flash, Franklin was flung across the garage slamming into a pile of old Christmas decorations. His body disappeared in a mess of ornaments and plastic snowmen.

"Franklin," Lena shouted as a pair of red eyes appeared next to her. She turned quickly but was cracked on the head by an invisible force spinning her into a wall full of rakes and shovels clanging to the ground.

"Ijiraq," Adam shouted in the earpieces. "Invisible creatures that exist in between the living and dead. You can only see their glowing red eyes from the corner of yours."

Thomas drew the sword and whipped it around through the air hoping to cut down an invisible foe but hit nothing.

I turned towards Mollie.

Crack

A fist slammed into my face just to the side of my nose. I spun and staggered but stayed on my feet. Before I could recover, a thick-clawed foot slammed into my gut nearly dropping me to my knees, but I stood fighting to keep my breath.

Crack

An arm thundered into the back of my neck and this time, I fell to a knee. Stars circling my vision, but I stayed conscious.

"Don't let them grab hold of you," Adam shouted. "They can drag you back into their world."

I glanced to my left and saw Brother Kiernan lose his sword. He got hit with something knocking it from his hands. The ancient blade clanging to the ground disappearing under a shelf of boxes.

Crack

Another punch cracking my cheek spraying blood from my lips. The blow nearly knocked me to the ground, but I braced myself against the cold concrete floor.

I searched for my assailant but only saw a shelf of boxes exploding from an invisible force slamming into it.

Mollie grabbed my hand, pulling me to my feet and then she vanished.

"Mollie," I gasped.

"These creatures are in my world," her voice echoed.

"We can't help you," I said. "We can't see them."

272

"Catch," Franklin shouted as he stepped over plastic snowmen and crushed ornaments.

I caught the bag and examined it.

"Fake snow?" I mumbled.

"Yeah, dump it all over," he shouted spraying open a bag he had in his hands.

The fake snow flew all over the garage. Some of it floated harmlessly to the ground while some of it stuck to invisible shapes throughout the room revealing several sets of red eyes.

I sprayed the bag of snow I had around in a wide circle and dusting several shapes showing three sets of eyes closing in on me.

I saw the outline of one of the demons swiping at Franklin, but my small friend ducked the clawed hand and slammed a fist right into the no-no squares of the red-eyed monster. I cringed watching the ghoulish eyes widen in pain as a high-pitched squeal erupted from its mouth.

"Well, this one is a guy," Franklin shouted thundering a knee into the bottom of his snow-covered head. The Ijaraq collapsed to the ground in a mix of snow and red eyes.

A flash to my right and I turned in time to see sharp claws heading for my eyes. I brought both of my hands sweeping across my body slamming into the creature's wrist with a crunch. The claws never reached my face. They hung uselessly attached to a wrist that was now pointing in the wrong direction. I didn't hesitate. I flung both of my hands backward and connected with an invisible face with a double-handed smash. I felt the bones give way as the monster's legs gave out collapsing to the ground.

A baseball bat held by invisible hands sliced through the air crunching flash and bone when it found its target.

"SCREECH," the Ijiraq screamed as Mollie appeared with the bat in hand. The monster appeared now to all of us. It looked like a fur-covered human with a set of small antlers on their heads. Glowing red eyes with no actual eyeballs sat atop a fur face with sharp fangs protruding from their mouths.

Thomas wrestled with an invisible creature that only had a small amount of snow on it but it was just enough to make it out. The beast headbutted him with those antlers and Thomas fell backwards into a pile of boxes. The monster kicked quickly, and this thick foot cracked against his chin, sending him tumbling to the floor. The monster grabbed a garden hoe swinging it down towards his face.

"Thomas," Franklin shouted sliding the sword over to him.

In one swift movement, he grabbed the ancient handle and swung it high. The blade sliced through fur, flesh, and bone severing the Ijiraq's arm just above the wrist. The sharpened garden hoe lost speed but still slammed into the ground an inch from Thomas' cheek.

The beast howled in pain, running through the open garage door into the blizzard.

"All of you stop right there," hissed a ghoulish voice from behind.

We all turned to see one of the Ijiraq in full hairy form with one thick arm wrapped around Lena's neck and a sharp terrifying blade held to her throat with the other hand.

"You, rainbow boy," it hissed.

"Who me?" Franklin interrupted.

The beast flashed an irritated look at Franklin which allowed me to turn slightly so I was standing square with Lena and her hostage taker.

"Not you mutt," it hissed.

"Did you just call me a mutt? If I'm a mutt what does that make you?" Franklin retorted.

"I'd say he looks like a demented, red-eyed Ewok," Lena choked out.

"Come with me or she dies," it screeched pushing on the blade that pinched Lena's neck drawing a trickle of blood.

"If you hurt her," I growled.

"Just shoot him," Lena winced as the blade pushed deeper into her skin.

Lena mouthed something to me, winked, and moved her head a fraction of an inch to the right.

"I will kill her...."

Bam

A burst of red and silver shot from my hand. The red was full of power and energy while the silver refined it making it more delicate and pinpoint forming an icicle. It zipped through the air piercing the beast's head between the glowing red eyes and exiting the ghoulish skull from behind.

The Ijiraq fell backward slamming onto the cold concrete floor and the ancient knife clanged to the ground next to it. The other injured creatures squealed in unison and ran from the garage into the snowy night.

"Rudolph the red nose Ijiraq, got a third hole in his furry head," Franklin began to sing as he walked over the dead beast scooping up the knife.

"He must have been their leader," Thomas said.

Mollie rushed to Lena grabbing her. She was wobbly but stayed standing.

"You, okay?" I asked her, taking her hand in mind and squeezing. "Don't be mad at me."

She wrapped her arms around me squeezing me tight.

I did the same.

"Thank you," she whispered into my ear.

I said nothing. I just held her.

"Is this a group hug?" Franklin asked.

Mollie whacked him in the gut.

"Ughh," he gasped. "Guess not."

"Is everyone okay in there?" Adam shouted in the earpieces.

"Yes, Adam. We are okay. The Ijiraq are gone," Brother Kiernan told him.

"Check out this cool-looking blade the red-eyed Grinch dropped. It's ours now. He has no more use for it," Franklin said.

"I'll take that," Thomas said grabbing the blade from Franklin and sliding it into his belt.

"I can never have anything nice," he muttered.

"What about me?" Mollie asked.

He coughed and for one of the very few times since I knew him, Franklin had nothing to say.

"Hug her," Adam whispered in the mics.

We all laughed as Franklin's face turned beat red when Mollie hugged him.

"Hey, look," Lena said pointing to a corner of the wrecked garage. Boxes, decorations, and lawn equipment were strewn everywhere but the chaos cleared one section of the floor.

275

Sitting there embedded into the concrete was a large safe door with an electronic keypad attached.

"It's Poppa's safe," Lena cried out kissing me on the cheek.

24
RED EYED RIDDLE

Pendleton House Garage
Capron Bay
1:00 A.M.

It was Poppa's secret safe, hidden in the garage floor,
only Grammy knew. "Franklin and I'll ditch these furry
Grinches," Brother Kiernan said. "You and Lena, crack it open—
see what's inside."

I nodded.

"What do I do?" Mollie asked.

"Stay by the front door. Make sure we have no more
surprises headed our way," he smiled.

Mollie nodded and took up her spot by the garage door.

"Why do I have to help with cleanup?" Franklin griped.

"Because I said so," Thomas shot back.

"Well, if you put it that way," Franklin laughed, dragging
one of the Ijiraq out of the garage.

Lena and I cleared the debris from the safe to get a better
look at it. It was a steel plate about the size of a ceramic tile,
about one square foot. It had nothing on it, no writing, no label,
and no keypad or dial.

"Adam, I think I'm going to need your help here," I
spoke into the mic.

"Mollie, can you come grab a camera?"

A minute later, Mollie returned with a hard hat and a
small GoPro camera attached. I strapped it on my head. Franklin
and Brother Kiernan had finished removing the Ijiraq, too, and
huddled with us, looking at the safe.

"Can you see?" asked Adam.

"Roger that," he replied. "Okay, that's just a steel plate
cover. Run your fingers around the edge and see if there is a lip
or anything you can grab."

277

I did what Adam said. I could feel the tiny space between the cover plate and the rest of the safe, but I couldn't get my fingers in there to pull it off.

"How about a knife?" Lena said. "Franklin, bring that blade over here. The one you took off the evil Grinch."

"Baldy took it from me," Franklin complained.

A smiling Thomas handed me the blade.

I took the blade but thought it would be too thick to open the lid. I tried to slide it in between, but I was right, it was too thick to get in there. We looked around for something thinner to use.

"Adam, is there anything on the RV that you, see?"

"Nada Chief," he answered.

"Hey, Prentice, do you guys have horses?" Franklin asked.

"What?"

"There's a horseshoe on the wall there," he said, pointing to an old beat-up horseshoe hanging on the wall.

"We've never had horses that I know of," I said, grabbing it and feeling its weight. I didn't know much about horses, but I knew this was too heavy for a horse's hoof.

"That's a magnet," Adam spoke into the mic.

"I think so," I replied, kneeling beside the safe.

I placed the ends in the center of the steel plate, and there was a click. The plate rose just enough to attach to the magnet so I could pull it off.

"There we go," Adam said.

Our excitement disappeared when the cover revealed a thick, heavy steel door with an antique bronze handle about four inches long, a circular biometric ten-number keypad on the other, and a digital message board on the top.

"Well, that looks hard," Lena griped.

"What does it say on the top?" Adam asked.

"Riddle me this and riddle me that, you have ten seconds to solve each, or the contents inside will be out of reach...press 1 when ready."

"Poppa loved his riddles," I grimaced.

"How hard can they be?" Adam asked.

"Let's find out," I swallowed and pressed 1.

Beep…beep

I read the message out loud as it scrolled across the screen.

"The Founding Fathers Signed the Declaration of Independence on which day?"

"That's easy, July 4th," Franklin said moving his finger toward the keypad.

1…2…3,

The clock ticked on the screen.

I slapped his hand away from the pad.

"Why did you do that?" he yelped.

"Because it's not true. It's August 2nd," I said, typing the answer. "July 4th is a myth."

"No way,"

"Beep, beep. One down," the message read.

"Well, what do you know," Franklin marveled. "I've been lied to my whole life."

"Hiroshima and which city were chosen as targets for the Atomic bomb?"

"Nagasaki," Lena blurted out.

I shook my head.

"Kokura," Adam spoke into the mic.

I typed Adam's answer into the pad. It was true. Kokura was the chosen city, but it was bypassed for Nagasaki instead because of the weather.

Beep, beep. Two down," the message read.

"The British defeated the colonists at Bunker Hill," the next one scrolled across.

"I even know this one," Franklin said. "The answer is yes."

"Nope," Mollie interjected.

"They won the battle," he argued.

"Yes, they did, but it wasn't Bunker Hill. It was Breed's Hill," she told him as I typed in the answer.

Beep, beep. Three down.

"Who was the first black player to play professional baseball?" Lena read the next question.

"Jackie Robinson," Franklin declared.

"Wrong," Brother Kiernan informed him.

279

"Moses Fleetwood Walker," I typed.

Beep, beep, four down, and one to go! You have three chances on this one.

"Oh boy," Lena whispered.

"Who is my hero?"

"That's it?" Adam sputtered.

"He loved Teddy Roosevelt," I said, typing it in.

A big red "X" blasted across the screen.

10...9...

"Oh man," Mollie gasped as the clock ticked.

8...7...

"Quick...Lena, you spend a lot of time with him," I said.

"Uhm...he loved Ted Williams. He called him the greatest hitter who ever lived," she blurted out.

I typed it in.

Another big red "X" buzzed the screen, and the clock ticked away.

6...

"We only got one more try," I muttered.

"Think, it's not Roosevelt or Ted Williams," Lena exclaimed. "Who else did he talk about in history or sports?"

I shook my head.

5...

"I didn't know him very well," Brother Kiernan said. "But he seemed to be a God-fearing man. Could it be God?"

"I don't think so," I shook my head. "He used to say God can't even determine your destiny. Only you could."

4...

"Grammy," Franklin cried out.

I looked at him.

3...2...

I typed it in

1...

"*My Love of a Lifetime*," the message read, followed by a hiss of air and a click.

I twisted the handle and opened the door, revealing several folders wrapped with an elastic band.

"How did you know that?" I asked him.

"Did you ever see Poppa with Grammy? He worshipped her," Franklin grinned.

"He did," I nodded tear rolling down my face. Lena grabbed my hand and squeezed.

"He's so romantic, isn't he?" Mollie purred, kissing Franklin on the cheek.

"I don't know how he does it," Adam wondered.

"Grab the folders, and let's get into the RV," Brother Kiernan ordered. "Before an evil Olaf appears."

"Don't," Lena rasped, pointing to Franklin.

"What?" he retorted.

"You know what," she cringed.

"Man, Lena, you just got to…Let it Go!" he sang.

I could tell Lena wanted to hit him but started laughing instead.

I pulled all the files out and double-checked that nothing was left. Two minutes later, we sat at the table inside the Beast.

Lena and Mollie took a folder titled "Angel Grace." I grabbed one without a title.

"Does that say the Vatican on it?" Brother Kiernan inquired, pointing at a blue folder. I nodded and handed it to him. He took it and sat down at the far end of the table. I could feel his anger mixed with intrigue as he opened it.

"What does that one say?" Franklin asked, grabbing a pink folder.

"Anjukani?" Adam read it out loud. "What Jack was talking about earlier."

"What does that mean?" Franklin wondered as Adam tapped away at his keyboard.

I opened my folder, and on the first page was an old black-and-white photo of a man dressed in an old winter parka, wearing heavy woolen gloves and furred boots. He was standing next to a cluster of teepees on thick snow and ice.

"Anjukani is known as the Village of the Dead," Adam exclaimed reading his laptop. We all paused in our reading to listen to him.

"Like Jack said, in November of 1922, a fur trapper named Joe LaBelle went to an Inuit village in Canada's northwest territory that he had traded with many times on Anjukani Lake.

281

According to this, he had been there many times and was good friends with the villagers. However, that night, the village was empty. Not a single soul was there. No sled dogs and no people," he read. "But Jack talked about the girl surviving and joe rescuing her."

"Inuit people are Eskimos, right? Mollie asked.

"They are the Eskimo people. Like Native Americans, they comprise many tribes," Thomas told her.

"They're a mix of Asian people, too," Adam added. "Not like Japanese or Korean but more like Russians and the different cultures that live way out in eastern Russia and Siberia."

"In that cold and barren land," I said. "They're tough people."

"How many people were in the village?" Franklin inquired.

"Two thousand," Adam answered.

"That's a lot of people to go missing," Lena added.

"This must be Joe LaBelle," I said, pointing to the picture in my folder. He was a tall white guy with a thick beard and dressed in a long fur coat. He was probably in his late twenties or early thirties but looked fifteen years older from his time in harsh conditions.

"Yep, that's him," Franklin said, showing us another photo of Joe from his folder. In his picture, a young Inuit girl and a team of sled dogs were standing with him.

"According to LaBelle, the village still had hot food burning on the stoves, and the huts were full of clothes, which meant they didn't abandon the place because they needed those clothes to survive the cold weather," Adam added.

"The Vatican sent investigators to the village along with Canadien Mounties and Mr. LaBelle," Brother Kiernan said as he read his information.

"Why would the Vatican get involved?" Lena asked.

"They must have thought there was some connection to the Church," Thomas answered.

"And they were trying to link it to Angel Grace," Lena said.

"It seemed they all believed there was a connection between the villagers disappearing and Angel Grace," Mollie added, holding up some photocopies of official Vatican notes. Angel and Grace were scribbled on the pages several times.

"What is Angel Grace? Franklin asked.

"We all have blood coursing through our bodies, right?" Brother Kiernan asked us.

We all nodded.

"Angel grace is angel blood, but according to the legends and Biblical lore, it's not fluid like blood. It's an energy that flows through their bodies and gives them Heavenly power," he added.

"It's their lifeblood," I said.

"Not just their lifeblood. It is believed when Angels bleed, grace brings everything around it to life or enriches it. If the grass is dead, it will suddenly come to life," he told us.

"Can it bring life back to life?" Adam asked.

"What do you mean?" Lena asked.

"If an…animal is dead and Grace comes in contact with the animal, will it come back to life?" he explained.

"Some ancient stories say it can while others say it can't. Some say it depends on the Angel. If it's an Archangel, it is believed to be powerful enough to conquer death," Thomas continued.

"If Chernobog is God of the Dead, that makes him like Satan. An Archangel," I added.

"Well, there are seven Archangels," Thomas advised.

"Wait, I thought there were only three. Michael, Gabriel, and Raphael," Adam replied.

"They are the ones talked about the most. There is also Uriel, Sariel, Ramiel, and Raguel," Thomas told us.

"Lucifer is, too," I added.

"Yes, he is. But he lost the title when he was cast from heaven," Brother Kiernan added.

"Right, so Chernobog must be one, too," Franklin smiled, knowing where I was going with this.

"Many in the Church believe there are many more Archangels than talked about in the Bible because they don't want to admit there is a lot of evil walking the Earth," Thomas shivered.

"It makes sense. His army is made of demons resurrected from the underworld or hell, right? Lena asked.

"Makes sense," Thomas nodded

"We know Archangels have a lot of power," I said.

"We know Angels have a lot of power," Lena smiled.

"Some even say angels can shoot energy blasts," Adam added as everyone looked at me.

"Prentice, are you an Angel?" Franklin laughed.

"No, I'm not," I shook my head.

"Oh yes, you are," he retorted.

"What?" I challenged him.

"You're Lena's Angel," he giggled.

Everyone laughed.

"I walked right into that one," I grimaced.

"You are my Angel snookum's," Lena played along, pinching my cheek.

Everyone laughed as I blushed.

"How is Angel Grace linked to a vanishing Eskimo village?" Mollie asked, bringing us all back.

"That's a good question. It seems something bad happened to the villagers, and Angel Grace is a benevolent power," Brother Kiernan spoke more to himself than to us.

"What if it's a bad Angel? Can their Angel grace destroy things?" Mollie asked.

Nobody said anything, but it made sense.

"I mean, there are bad Angels, right?" she asked.

"Lucifer was an Angel," he answered.

"I don't think this has anything to with a bad Angel. This is Chernobog," I said.

"How do you know?" Lena wondered.

"I don't know, but Poppa did. That's why he kept all this hidden."

I flipped another page, and it was Joe LaBelle again with the same Inuit girl petting the sled dogs.

"Adam, what can you find out about Joe LaBelle?"

He went to work on his laptop, tapping away on the keys and then swiping the touch screen in every direction.

"Doesn't seem to be much about him. He declined all interviews from the newspapers. Several books were written about the mysterious disappearing villagers, but he always declined to be a part of them," he said.

284

I flipped through some more pages in the folder as I listened. It was full of old newspaper clippings about the village and a few photos of LaBelle and the girl. I studied her. She was about ten or twelve, maybe, with long black hair. She had dark skin and a wide flat face with a long nose and crystal-blue almond-shaped eyes. She looked familiar to me, but I didn't know any Inuit people.

"There were even some documentaries about the village, but he never appeared on camera. The stories say Aliens abducted all the villagers or a murderous pack of big foot creatures killed them all," he read.

"We know it was Chernobog's demons, and he was after the girl," Lena added.

"There was nothing else in the safe? We didn't miss anything, did we?" Adam asked.

"Like a bottle of Angel Grace?" Franklin asked.

"Well…yeah," Adam muttered

"There was nothing else inside. It was empty," Thomas replied.

"We're missing something," I huffed, slapping the table with my palm.

Lene placed her hand on mine. Her touch was soft and smooth, calming me. I stared at our hands for a moment. Lena's freckled hand rested on mine next to a picture of Joe LaBelle and the Inuit girl.

"Where would Poppa keep a bottle of Angel Grace?" Adam asked.

I stared at the photo some more. I felt the warmth of Lena's touch.

"Maybe inside his bathroom?" Franklin laughed.

"What? Why would he do that?" Mollie asked.

"I don't know. Like a bottle of shaving cream or something," he shrugged.

"Angel Grace in a Barbasol can?" Adam laughed.

"Yeah, like Jurassic Park. The dinosaur DNA was in a Barbasol can, wasn't it?" Franklin snickered.

"It's not Angel Grace," I said, rising from my chair. Everyone looked at me.

"It's Angel Grace," I declared.

"Uh…crayon man, you feeling, okay?" Franklin asked me. "Did you hit your head fighting the Ijiraq?"

"Angel Grace isn't a thing. It's a she," I declared, tapping the photo of the Inuit girl. "And I know where she is."

"You think the Rainbow Warrior girl's name is Grace?" Adam interrupted.

"But she escaped," Lena chimed in.

"With Joe LaBelle," Mollie added. "He rescued her."

"And Jack," Franklin said.

"And Poppa knew it," Adam barked.

"I'm willing to bet Joe kept her hidden for as long as he could, and then your grandfather took over," Thomas claimed.

"Back to school—now," I insisted.

25
FANGS OF LOYALTY

Capron Bay High School
Capron Bay,
1:30 A.M.

Chief Robert Pendleton entered the makeshift hospital room, eyes on his best friend Hog and Agent Mason. Pam Sheridan slept in a chair, clutching Hog's unconscious hand. He crossed to his wife, Melissa, cradling a tired Carolyn on her lap, Druss sprawled beside them.

"Daddy," Carolyn whispered

"Hey, peanut," he said, scooping her up, squeezing tight.

"Where's PJ?" she yawned.

He glanced at his wife. "He's out with Doc and Brother Kiernan helping some people stuck in the snow," he told her.

"I want to help people, too," she told him. "Druss and I can."

"I'll tell you what, we need some more blankets here. There is a pile of fresh blankets over by the scoreboard. Why don't you and Druss go grab some for Mommy and Auntie Pam," he tickled her, putting her down.

"Okay, come on, Druss," she said, and the dog hopped up and obeyed his girl.

The Chief watched his little girl and the golden retriever squeeze through the white screens into the gym.

"Robert, will you tell me what is going on?" Melissa asked him.

He leaned over, kissed her forehead, and sat in the chair beside his wife.

"Well, Mayor Travis has been removed by the town council, and then they fired me," he confessed.

She figured out "Theresa Morgan."

He nodded.

"Can she do that?"

"At least for now. Whether or not it holds up after the storm, I don't know," he admitted.

"Who's in charge then?"

"Agent Byrd."

"That idiot FEMA guy?"

He nodded again.

"What about the FBI agent Liang?"

"He does what the Senator tells him, and Bradler put Byrd in charge."

She shook her head.

"Don't worry, the guys won't listen to them. They'll come to me first," he smiled.

"That's because they love you just like I do, but you must tell me what's happening?"

"I will, but right now, I just want to rest for a few minutes," he yawned, resting his head on his wife's shoulder.

Melissa said nothing, knowing her husband was exhausted.

"This way, Druss," Carolyn giggled, moving between cots and people. She knew precisely where the blankets were, having helped Ms. Annie and Ms. Fiona fold them earlier. The young girl dodged a couple of guys wearing those blue jackets with the FEMA lettering on the back. Druss brushed through them, making sure he kept up with her.

"Hey," one of them said.

"Watch it," another muttered.

She glanced at them, laughing, knowing Dad didn't like them very much, but she didn't slow down.

"Young lady, you stop right now," commanded a woman's voice. She looked up, saw the woman the mayor was arguing with earlier, and tried to go around her. The woman grabbed Carolyn by the hand, stopping her instantly.

"Ouch," Carolyn cried out. "Let me go."

"No running in the gym," the woman ordered.

Druss' fur rose on his back, and he growled at Theresa Morgan.

"Whose dog is this, and why is it here?" the new Mayor hissed.

"That's Pendleton's mutt," Agent Byrd told her.

Druss growled again.

"He's not a mutt," Carolyn shot back.

"This must be his daughter, then," Theresa scowled.

"You're a genius," the young girls laughed.

"You're a brat, just like your brother," Byrd glared at her.

"Druss growled again, taking a step closer.

Druss sensed danger—Theresa's grip wasn't friendly, he watched the woman grab Carolyn by the hand. He could tell it wasn't a friendly grab, and he heard his girl cry out in pain. It made him angry. He warned her to let the girl go, and the other man stepped closer. He smelled sweaty and grimy.

"Grrrr, stay away from her," Druss growled.

Morgan ordered, "Leash that animal and place it in a confined room." A couple of the FEMA agents stepped up with a thin rope.

"Leave him alone," Carolyn gasped.

"And please ensure this young girl isn't wandering around here unattended," the new Mayor sneered.

Druss growled again, baring his teeth this time.

"She's not unattended."

Theresa and Byrd turned to see an elderly woman shuffle through the group of FEMA agents.

"She looks it to me," Byrd snarked.

"Nonsense," the old woman laughed. "Can't you see this beautiful dog is with her?"

"He needs to be leashed. We don't need loose dogs running around here. They're dangerous," Theresa protested.

"You don't like dogs, do you?" the old woman smiled and held her hand out to Druss.

When the old woman intervened, his senses calmed. She had kind eyes and a warm smile. Druss wagged his tail in greeting and sniffed her hand. The scent of flowers sifted into his nose, and he felt at ease with her. She would help Carolyn.

"No, I don't like dogs. They're dirty and dangerous," Theresa replied.

Druss growled at her in reply.

"Seems he doesn't care for you much either," she smiled.

"We've done nothing to him," Byrd answered.

"You grabbed his child," she mocked the new Chief of police. "And threatened to lock him up."

"He doesn't understand that" one of the agents grunted. She laughed.

"He most certainly does," she proclaimed.

"Well, we're going to bring her back to her father and make sure he's not wandering around," Byrd hissed.

Druss growled again.

"I don't trust you," the old woman glared at him.

He stared back.

"I don't trust a person who doesn't like dogs, but I trust a dog who doesn't like a person," she grinned.

"Fine, you take her and the mutt back," Byrd stammered. "But if I see either of them wandering around again. I will put the dog into the pound."

Druss growled again, but the old woman patted him on the head, soothing his anger.

"Come on, little one. Let's head back to Mom and Dad," the old woman said, holding her hand out to Carolyn, who took it with a smile.

"What's your name?" Carolyn asked her.

"What do you think my name is?"

"You smell like a Rose, is that your name?"

"You're exactly right," they smiled.

Druss yipped as he trotted along next to them. A minute later, they came to the small medical area.

"Come meet my mom and dad," Carolyn told Rose.

"They're resting, little one. Maybe later, okay?"

Carolyn nodded.

"You be careful around here. Some of these people aren't very nice," the old woman said.

"I will. Oh wait, I must get some blankets," Carolyn cried out and took off before the old woman could say anything.

Druss bolted after her.

"Oh dear," the woman sighed.

"I see headlights," an agent shouted, looking out the window.

"What is it?" Agent Liang yelled out.

"Doesn't matter what it is, don't open the door," Byrd ordered.

"Emergency shelter, this is Professor Eddings. We are pulling up to the gymnasium now," the radio cackled.

"It looks like a transport van," a woman proclaimed.

"I don't care what it is. Nobody opens that door," Byrd commanded.

"Open that door right now," Chief Pendleton demanded, striding across the gym floor.

Several Capron Bay police officers bolted for the bay door.

"All Capron Bay officers need to stand down," Byrd fumed.

"We have some injured folks on board," the radio squawked.

Chief Tackna and several men joined the Capron Bay officers at the bay door, pulling the emergency chain to raise the door.

The bus came to a skidding stop in the snow a few inches from the bay door. Although the headlights were covered in snow, they still blinded anyone who looked at them.

His eyes were fixed on Carolyn as he weaved through the sudden chaos. People were shouting and running to the back of the building by the big door, but she was headed in the opposite direction to get blankets. His nose tingled with danger as he picked up a scent that did not belong there. A smell of death and decay hung in the air, but it wasn't there a few minutes ago. Something evil was in the building.

"I got you now, you mangy mutt," a man scowled and grabbed his collar. "You're getting locked up."

Meaty hands tried to tie a rope around his neck, but Druss spun away, catching the man's fingers in the collar. He saw a tall, thin man talking to Carolyn and then taking her by the hand.

He was yanked back when he tried to bark and warn Carolyn to get away from the man but Druss struggled to focus on his girl while the man dragged him along.

"Sir, let that dog go immediately," Fiona advised.

"He needs to be secured, Ma'am," the agent replied.

"Young man, I can go from being a proper lady to redneck crazy before you can say bless your heart," Fiona replied.

Druss snarled, trying to escape, but the man held on.

"If you don't let that dog, go, you'll be stationed in the coldest part of Alaska for the rest of your career," Fiona added.

"That's if Chief Pendleton doesn't shoot you first," Anyika laughed.

The FBI Agent held onto the leash and glanced at Fiona and Anyika.

"Now, young man," Fiona ordered.

The young man took a deep breath and released Druss.

He twisted and took off, flying through the gym, staying low to the ground so he could pick up her scent. It was there, but it was mixed with something vile and sinister. Druss reached the blankets and sniffed the air. He smelled her skin, her hair, and her clothes. It came from a darkened hallway off to the left.

"What is he doing?" Fiona wondered. She remained with Anyika and the FBI agent, watching the golden retriever disappear down the darkened hallway.

"Wait a second, where is Carolyn?" Anyika asked.

"Oh dear," Fiona gasped. "Someone has taken her."

"Or some thing," Anyika added.

"Taken who?" the FBI agent asked them.

"Son, you better hope Chief Pendleton just shoots you," Fiona warned him as she and Anyika took off following Druss.

He kept to the shadows moving down the hall. His heart thundered in his chest as he tried to move on quiet paws. Carolyn's smell grew stronger, and so did the smell of death.

Growls flanked right and left. A door groaned open at the end of the hall.

"Druss!" Carolyn screams but is cut off.

More growls to the left and right.

He smells the creatures. They aren't dogs. They are evil, and he must fight to get to his girl.

Chief Tackna's men flanked the incoming van, scanning the tree line for any creature or demon. The wind-driven snow made it hard to see, but they stayed vigilant, waiting to take on any threat that appeared. The fires from Prentice's explosion earlier were replaced by a faint trail of dying smoke.

Doc, bloodied and bruised, stepped from the transport van with the help of Rachel and Dakota. Both kids tried to usher him into the gym, but the librarian refused to go in before any of the other folks exited the vehicle.

"Dakota, are you and Rachel hurt?" Tackna asked his grandson.

"We are okay, Grandfather, but Doc needs medical attention," Dakota answered.

"Some others to do," Rachel added.

The Chief nodded and gave a few commands. A second later, a mix of medical staff and Chief Tackna's people helped everyone from the bus and into the gym.

"Guys, where's the rest of the team?" Chief Pendleton asked as he examined Doc's wounds.

"They went on to your house," Rachel told him.

"They are okay, Robert," Doc advised. "Thomas is still with them."

"What happened then?" he asked.

"We got an SOS about sea monsters attacking the marina," Doc said. "We went to help."

"Paiyaruk?" Tackna asked.

"Yes, Grandfather," Dakota filled him in.

"They're dead now," Rachel added.

Mrs. Mancini walked up to the group.

"Chief and Chief," she nodded. "Professor Eddings, the kids and the Priest saved us from those things."

"Mrs. Mancini, what happened out there?" Theresa Morgan asked, approaching the group.

"Theresa, you're not going to believe this. A pair of sea monkeys that grew huge in the sewers attacked us at the marina," the woman began.

"Sea monkeys?" the new Mayor restated with a look of disgust on her face.

The Chief glanced at Rachel and Dakota. Both looked away.

"It's true. Where is that blond-haired boy? He said their names were Joe and Kamala," she insisted.

Theresa gave the Chief a dirty look, huffed, turned, and walked away. Mrs. Mancini followed her, trying to explain how sea monkeys could get so big.

"Franklin?" the Chief wondered.

"Franklin," Doc confirmed.

"Did he really say their names were Joe and Taylor?" Chief Tackna smiled.

Doc nodded.

"And he told her the sword Brother Kiernan used to cut their heads off was named Swift Saber," Rachel laughed.

"No, he didn't," Chief Tackna keeled over laughing. "God, I love that kid."

The first attack came from the right. The beast was on four legs and moved fast. Sharp teeth dripped with saliva as they roared towards his face. Druss shot low, getting underneath the creature, barely avoiding the gnashing teeth.

The second monster attacked before he could get to his feet. It landed on top of Druss. It was bigger and heavier than the golden and used its weight to pin him to the floor.

He rolled, trying to break free, but razor-sharp teeth sunk into his shoulder. He roared in pain and jerked his lean body as hard as he could. The force of the movement surprised the demon hound, and he was able to buck it off his back.

294

Druss saw the hound raise its head, giving him an opening, and he moved fast. Despite the pain flaring from his shoulder, he twisted violently and bit into its exposed throat.

The creature yelped in pain and tried to wriggle free.

He held on, refusing to let go.

The first creature attacked again. Its massive body slamming into Druss, forcing him to let go of his prey, which scrambled away, whining in pain. He stayed on his feet, growling at his foe.

Druss studied his enemy. Like him, it had four legs. It was grey skinned, with patches of hair on its back and feet. A jagged scar ran down the side of its body, and bright red eyes glared back at him.

It growled.

Druss growled.

It attacked.

Druss tried to move, but he wasn't quick enough. The hound's teeth latched onto his ear and tore flesh and fur from his head. He swung his head away from the attack, but the devil dog lunged again. Sharp claws sliced into his belly, opening a wide gash in the skin.

"Yelp!" he cried out.

The second attacker returned and bit into Druss's paw. He felt the teeth push into the flesh and bone. The golden realized this dog made a fatal error and made him pay for it.

In a classic canine attack move, Druss bit down on the back of the demon's neck. Teeth squeezed hard, and he shook his head violently back and forth. His enemy mewled in agony and went limp.

The scarred hound lashed out again with the sharp claws and swiped across Druss' face. He couldn't move quickly because he held the other dog in his mouth. The claws tore into the snout, opening several wounds. Druss let go of the other. It dropped to the floor unmoving.

Scar didn't let up. He sank his teeth into Druss' face, but the golden didn't panic. He rolled with the attack as hard as he could. His foe's teeth were still embedded, and the roll carried him over Druss and slammed his body into the concrete wall, causing him to release Druss.

The golden scrambled to his paws and slammed his head into the bottom of the dog's jaw with a crunch.

Scar squealed in pain from the headbutt. He didn't waste any time. He clamped down on the paw and pulled as hard as he could. The other dog slid along the floor, and Druss spun fast. Scar spun with him, crashing into the wall again, and slumping to the floor.

Adrenaline still pumped through him, and he grabbed onto Scar's neck, whipping his head back and forth, determined to end this fight and get to Carolyn. The demon hound whined in agony, and Druss let it go.

He took a step back, growling as he did. Blood flowed from multiple gashes all over his body. Both dogs lay low to the ground. Blood is flowing from their wounds. Scar slinked forward on its belly giving Druss a cry of submission.

The golden allowed the two to stand both tucking their heads and their tails. Druss growled allowing them to leave. The two demon dogs turned and hobbled out of the open door into the storm beyond.

He stood watching for them to disappear before staggering on all fours and collapsing to the floor. His eyes drifting to the open door, knowing his girl is somewhere. He tried to summon enough energy in his wounded body to crawl towards the open door.

"Druss," Anyika cried out, kneeling next to him and stroking his bloodied body.

"Look at the streak of blood," Fiona gasped.

"He's trying to crawl to the door," Anyika noticed.

"Carolyn must have been taken out through the door," Fiona shrieked, running to the door. She stepped into the blizzard, trying to see anything she could but the snow was too thick.

Fiona shut the door, shaking her head. "I can't see anything," she shuddered. "Look at all the blood. Druss fought something off".

" This is demon blood," Anyika pointed out, scooping Druss up.

"What?" What do you mean demon blood?"

"We must get him help. He's losing a lot of blood," Anyika said.

"What about Carolyn?" Fiona asked.

"We have to tell Robert," Anyika told her hobbling back to the gym carrying a bloody Druss.

Druss whined, looking back at the door.

"It's okay, my fur baby. We'll get her back," Anyika promised.

Druss whined weakly wagging his tail.

26
SURRENDER

Capron Bay High School
Capron Bay,
2:00 A.M.

"Doc, sit—I'll get Melissa to check your head," Chief Pendleton ordered.

Grammy pressed a cloth to the egg on Dakota's head while Rachel's mom iced her daughter's bruised face. Her dad handed out warm blankets.

"I'm okay, Mom. It's just some bruises," Rachel protested, but her mother ignored her.

Chief Tackna and his men stood watch, keeping FBI and FEMA agents at bay. Capron Bay officers hovered near their leader—title gone, command intact. The Capron Bay police officers in the gym also made sure not to stray too far away from their leader and his family. Even though he was no longer the Chief of Police, he was still in charge to them.

Robert and Melissa came out of the Hog's room, and Melissa lifted her eyebrows at the sight of a bleeding Doc and bruised and battered Dakota and Rachel.

"Let me take a look at that, Doc," she said, giving her husband a nasty look.

He was about to say something when a commotion from behind caught everyone's attention. Fiona and Anyika were walking through the parting crowd on the gym floor.

"Robert," Fiona shouted. "Druss needs some help!"

"What happened?" he asked, taking the bleeding dog from Anyika.

"He's been attacked," Fiona answered.

"We found him like this in the back hallway," Anyika added. "He's lost a lot of blood."

"Oh my God, Druss," Mellissa cried out. "We need a doctor. Someone get the Doctor."

297

"No," Chief Tackna interrupted, turning to one of his men. He said something to the man, who took off towards the bay door where the transport van was.

"Mahkai will come," he said.

"Who?" Melissa asked. "We don't need a medicine man."

"Mahkai is a medicine man, Melissa," he smiled. "But, he is also a United States Army-trained veterinarian."

"Let's get him inside," Chief Pendleton told them, and he slipped into the small room. Grammy and Fiona pushed in another medical table, and he laid Druss down on it. The dog whined and tried to lift his head. Pam Sheridan stood from her seat. A look of concern etched on her face.

"What happened?" she asked.

"We're not sure," Melissa replied, hugging her friend.

"Easy boy," the Chief said, running his hand along his head.

A minute later, one of Chief Tackna's men came running in. He had short-cropped black hair and was wearing an 82nd Airborne sweatshirt. Several nurses and a doctor also came over to offer their help.

"I'm Mahkai," he said to Chief Pendleton and Melissa. "Please let me take a look."

"We can help," one of the nurses said.

"I don't have much in equipment or medicine, but whatever you need," the Doctor offered.

The veterinarian nodded and got to work examining Druss.

"Robert, let them do their job," Grammy said as the Chief, Melissa, and Pam stepped from the room.

"Can I help?" Cardinal Murphy asked, joining the group.

"We can use some prayers, your grace," Doc rasped.

"I can do that," the Cardinal replied.

A small crowd had gathered now, and there was a growing murmur of concern about what was happening. Everyone was asking what was happening.

"Wait, wait, wait a minute," the Chief snapped.

Nobody listened. The chatter continued.

"Shut up," he scoffed.

The crowd went silent.

"Where is Carolyn?" he pleaded.

Fiona and Anyika glanced at one another.

"What? What do you mean?" Melissa asked.

"Robert...," Fiona began to say.

"Your daughter is unharmed," a voice declared.

Everyone turned to see a tall, thin man striding across the gym floor. He had been dressed casually in a brown suit earlier, but now, he was garbed in a red ceremonial robe and wore an upside-down cross necklace inlaid with a man with ram's horns on his head and serpents slithering around him.

"Charles?" Cardinal Murphy inquired. "Why do you look like that?"

"He is the one they call Alpha," Dakota interrupted.

"The one who attacked Prentice and Lena back in the chemical factory, the one who tried to bring the demon back to life at Minute Man Cemetery," Rachel added.

"And the one who brought in the Boo Hags," Anyika huffed.

"What...what are you talking about?" the Cardinal asked.

Chief Pendleton didn't wait for an answer. He moved across the floor in two long strides and grabbed Alpha by the neck, squeezing as hard as he could.

"Where is my daughter?" he raged.

"Let him go, or I'll be forced to shoot you," Agent Liang ordered appearing with his gun drawn. Byrd and several more agents appeared at his side. All had firearms pointed at the Chief.

Capron Bay officers joined the group, drawing their sidearms in return and ordering the FBI agents to drop their weapons. The standoff between federal agents and the Capron Bay Police Department had been brewing all night and the gym was erupting into a modern-day version of the OK Corral.

**Main St
Capron Bay,
2:05 A.M.**

"Two minutes out," Brother Kiernan shouted steering the big RV through the thick snow and blinding conditions.

Adam's chair started to roll sideways, but Mollie grabbed it, pulling him back.

"Can you even see out there?" Adam shouted.

"Not really. I'm letting the force guide me," Brother Kiernan yelled back.

"I actually believe him," Franklin snickered.

"We must be ready for an attack once we get into the lot."

"One minute," he yelled.

We all got ready to fight. I glanced at Lena and couldn't help but feel something was wrong.

Capron Bay High School
Capron Bay,
2:06 A.M.

The Chief ignored the FBI agent's commands, squeezing Alpha's neck harder.

"Woah…woah…," Anyika uttered as she stepped between the Chief and Agent Liang.

"Ma'am, please get out of the way," Liang demanded.

"No suh," Anyika replied.

Dakota stepped up next to her.

"You'll have to shoot us too," Rachel added, joining them.

"What is going on here?" Melissa cried out.

"She…she…is…unharmed," Alpha coughed out, trying to breathe as the Chief threatened to crush his windpipe.

A faint yellow glow began to spread over the Chief's boots.

"I think you need to hear my friend out, Chief Pendleton," Senator Bradler pointed out as he joined the conversation.

The Chief's eyes darted to the Senator.

"It would be in your daughter's best interest," the Senator affirmed.

He released Alpha, who fell gasping for air.

300

The Chief turned to all his men and women and raised his hands, letting them all know not to fire, but every one of them also noted he didn't tell them to lower their guns.

"Where is she?" he demanded.

Alpha held his hand up, trying to catch his breath. '

"She is safe," gurgling.

"Where is she?" the Chief demanded again, stepping closer to Alpha.

"She will remain safe and unharmed," he reiterated. "You have my word."

Capron Bay High School Parking lot
Capron Bay,
2:09 A.M.

The RV's tires cut through the thick snow and bit into the pavement below, coming to a jolting stop in the parking lot. I bolted through the door without caring about what was waiting for me outside. The bad feeling was overwhelming, and I knew I had to get inside.

"Prentice," Lena shouted and followed me. Franklin and Mollier were right behind her. Brother Kiernan grabbed Adam's chair and lifted him through the door as he stepped down. He was not waiting for the ramp to unfold.

As I stepped into the schoolyard, I expected to be attacked by some other winter demon, but no attack came. The snow still fell, and the wind blew everywhere, making visibility challenging. Even though I couldn't see very well, I didn't sense any creatures lurking in the blizzard, which concerned me even more.

"Something's wrong," I said

"What?" Lena asked.

"Let's find out," I replied opening the door to the gym and stepping in.

"Your word means nothing," Anyika fumed as we entered the school. We weren't expecting to see Capron Bay officers and federal agents pointing guns at one another.

"Prentice, that's Alpha," Lena whispered.

"I see him," I answered.

"Carolyn will not be harmed," I heard Alpha tell Dad.

Did he just say Carolyn wouldn't be harmed? I scanned the area for my little sister but didn't see her anywhere.

"Where is Carolyn?" Lena asked, but I don't think she asked me. I think she was talking to herself.

I ran through the scenario as Franklin, Adam, and Brother Kiernan joined us. Alpha was telling Dad Carolyn wouldn't be harmed. I can't see my sister anywhere. Did they have her? I felt blood boiling through my body as panic set in.

"What did you do to the dog?" Dad asked.

"That was unfortunate, but the animal wouldn't let the girl go without a fight," Alpha replied. Did he mean Druss? Of course, he meant Druss. He wouldn't leave her alone without a fight.

"What did you do?" I shouted, stalking toward Alpha.

"Prentice," Lena grabbed my arm, but I broke free, feeling the rage and hate to exploding within.

"Crayon man, don't," Franklin warned.

I fired an energy blast, not waiting for him to answer me.

Alpha's eyes widened at the flaming cannonball heading for him.

Everything slowed down within the gym. All the people, including Dad and Alpha, stopped moving. The world suddenly stopped. The rocket I fired at my enemy sparked, fizzled, and disappeared into thin air.

I turned to see a shadowy figure gliding across the room. I gazed at the spectral form until he came into focus, and the hairs on the back of my neck prickled all over. He was enormous, standing close to seven feet tall with massive shoulders bulging with bulky muscles and a thick neck.

He had a chiseled face with ice-blue eyes and snow-white teeth set against a thick grey beard hanging in two tightly wrapped braids stretching to his waist. He wore a thick black fur robe with a dark tunic underneath. On top of his head was a scarred helmet with razor-sharp horns angled upwards. He moved smoothly across the room. I could see his heavy boots touching the hardwood as he strode towards me, but it seemed like he floated above the floor.

"Chernobog?" I whispered as he stopped about six feet from me.

"In my human form, young warrior," he answered. I heard his voice, but his lips didn't move.

"You didn't look like this in the in-between," I noted.

"That is true. There, my power is limited. Here, not so much," he smiled.

"You have my sister?" I demanded.

He nodded.

"What do you want?"

He laughed.

I said nothing.

"You and your friends," he said, turning to the gang, who all stood frozen in time. "Have all fought valiantly."

I said nothing.

"I am impressed. You're all stronger than I thought you were."

"Give us Carolyn," I sneered.

He laughed.

I swallowed, and for the first time, I felt nervous, with a tinge of fear setting in.

"I can tell you're scared young warrior. There is no shame in fear," he crooned.

I said nothing.

"Like I said, you and your friends have proven to be worthy adversaries, but you can't win this fight," he boasted.

"Why is that? I asked.

"The demons you fought tonight are just a taste of what is out there. There are dozens more Prentice," he promised.

I knew an entire army was just waiting to pounce on us.

"It is time to negotiate a surrender," he gloated.

I looked around at my family and friends and felt the sadness set in. He was right. We couldn't win, and now he had Carolyn. I felt hopeless.

"What are you offering?" I asked him.

"I will give you your sister back, of course," he began.

I felt a moment of anger spark inside me. He felt it, too.

"Easy there, young man. I can imprison her with Frost's sister, or I can just eliminate her from the equation," he warned.

The anger faded, replaced by hopelessness.

"You won't hurt anyone else?" I asked.

"I will not," he shook his massive head.

"What do I have to do?"

"It's quite simple. Give me your power," he grinned.

"How do I do that?"

"At sunrise, there is a pagan yule ritual and an incantation requiring a blood oath that will drain your power and grant it to me," he said. "Once we have completed the solstice blood oath ritual, you will have your sister back and your town."

"If I don't?"

"Your sister will experience an eternity of suffering, and I will destroy this town and everyone in it," he threatened.

"Like you did with the Inuit at Anjukani village?" I asked.

The mention of the village caught him off guard. I felt him hesitate for a moment and wondered why.

"That was unfortunate, but you can see what happens," he shrugged.

"What happens when you fail?" I goaded him.

His eyes shot towards me, and he was going to say something, but he stopped himself.

"You have my terms, young man," he sneered.

"I don't trust you," I shook my head.

"You don't have much of a choice," he said. "You can say no."

"I'm thinking about it," I told him.

"I'll just take your powers anyway, and everyone you care about will be dead," he laughed.

I studied his face. His eyes never wavered.

"Part of me would prefer you to do that," he smiled. "It is your choice."

"I want Jack's sister, too," I informed him.

"Frost's sister?" he laughed.

I nodded.

His continued laughter was annoying.

I said nothing.

"You're serious?" he asked.

I nodded.

"You know he has been playing you the whole time?" he asked.

I nodded again.

"You knew?"

"I did. I've known all along. From the moment I met him," I confirmed.

"Interesting," he mumbled.

"And he has been playing you, too," I winked.

"Frost has always been trying to play me," he laughed.

"Yeah, but he has hidden the one thing you have been searching for," I prodded. "For a very long time."

Chernobog laughed for a long moment.

"And what would that be?" he asked me. "There have been many things I have been looking for."

"That secret will be mine until you carry through on your end of the deal," I chirped.

The God of Winter studied me for a long moment. Neither of us said anything.

"Do we have a deal?" I asked. I give you my powers, you give me Carolyn, Jack's sister, and you leave the town unharmed."

"And you will give me whatever else Jack has hidden?" he asked me.

"One more thing," I added.

"You're pushing your luck, kid," he sneered.

"Can you bring someone back from the dead?" I inquired.

"Hah," he bellowed. "You're asking for some heavy God-like magic now."

"You are a God, are you not?"

"The power of resurrection requires the ultimate sacrifice," he smiled.

"You mean a life for a life?" I sputtered.

"Indeed, it does. A life for a life. It is the most powerful magic there is. Some call it black magic, but it's not an evil process. It is merely a power of life over death," he told me.

"And you have that power?" I asked him. "Someone as powerful as you must."

"I see your game. It doesn't matter. The power over death can only come with great cost, Prentice. Great cost," he smiled.

"Understood. Will you grant it if I ask for it?" I asked.

He looked at me for a long time.

"I will," he nodded. "A life for a life."

"A life for a life," I echoed.

"Then we have a deal," he cackled.

"Explain it to me first," I told him.

"It's quite simple, really," he smiled. "There will be a stone altar in place. It's called Shepard's Stone. I draw a ward on your hand that matches the one on the altar. You place it on the altar at sunrise as I recite an ancient enchantment, and your power leaves your body."

"Into you?" I asked.

He laughed.

"No, boy. Your power will flow into an urn where it will be kept safe," he assured me.

"Why do you want my power?" I asked him.

He laughed again.

"You're wondering what evil and nefarious deed I have in mind?" he smiled.

"Uhm…yeah. After all, you don't have the best reputation," I told him.

"Fair enough. I am the God of winter," he said.

"And the dead," I added.

He ignored me.

"My lands are growing warmer and warmer, and with your powers, I will be able to stop it," he grinned.

It was my time to laugh.

"You find that amusing?"

"You're telling me I can stop global warming?" I giggled.

He shook his head.

"No, dear boy, this world goes through cycles, weather, and temperatures. Your politicians, scientists, and activists can believe whatever they want. There is nothing you irritating humans can do to change that for better or worse," he sneered.

"I'm confused," I admitted.

"When the Earth cycles into a hotter time, I must...hibernate, for lack of a better term. Your power will help avoid that problem when the time comes."

"Ahh...so I'm some kind of medicine for you?" I nodded.

He shrugged.

"For some reason, I don't believe you," I snickered.

"Whatever, kid. This conversation is beginning to anger me."

"Ooh," I waved my hands around.

I could tell he was losing his cool.

"The Quantratid meteor shower peaks at 6:30 A.M. and ends at sunrise, which is 7 A.M. Be outside the school on the eastern side by 6:30. I doubt you want to come alone, so your father can come with you," he noted.

"Okay," I acknowledged.

"We have a deal then?" he inquired.

"We do," I nodded.

"Very well," he bowed and vanished.

The school erupted in activity again.

Alpha dove to the ground to avoid the blast of energy I had fired a moment ago, but it vanished when Chernobog appeared.

Orders and commands were being shouted once again by both sides.

"Prentice?" Dad asked me.

"Have your men lower their weapons," I told him.

He glanced at me, and I nodded quietly. A moment later, all the Capron officers holstered their sidearms.

Alpha told Byrd to do the same and relayed the order to the federal agents. They listened and lowered theirs. I watched the FBI and FEMA agents for a moment. I noticed a shadowy, inky color slither over their faces. It was there for just a brief second, but it was there. It was as if a shadowy evil tattoo flowed across their faces. I hadn't noticed it until this moment. They all had it except for Alpha, Byrd, and the Senator. I suddenly wondered if they were being controlled by some unseen force.

"Prentice, what is happening?" Dad asked.

307

"I'll tell you in a few minutes," I said, looking at Alpha.

"You made the deal with him, didn't you?" he smiled.

I said nothing.

"Be on time," he laughed, telling me he knew exactly what was coming.

"I will be," I retorted. "Make sure you are too."

"I'm not part of the deal," he smiled.

"I know. That is why I'm going to kill you," I threatened.

The smile left his face, and fear flashed across his eyes.

"Get out," I ordered him.

We all watched Alpha slink away disappearing down the back hallway.

"You mind telling us what is going on?" Lena demanded.

"Everyone head into the office, and I'll tell you," I said, looking at Dad.

"Melissa, can you grab Pam? Rachel, bring your parents. I want everyone in there," Dad ordered. "Prentice, you wait ten minutes and then come in."

I nodded and watched everyone follow him across the gym. I took a deep breath and stepped into the medical area. Hog lay on one cot with blood-stained bandages covering his large frame. Agent Mason lay on the cot next to him. He looked to be in pain from his battered and bruised face, even though he was unconscious. Now, Druss' blood-covered body lay there. His chest was moving up and down slightly, but the canine didn't look good.

I sat in an empty chair, watching my friends and feeling sorry for myself.

"This is all my fault," I whispered as the well opened and tears flowed. I buried my head in my hands and sobbed for a long time. When the tears finally faded, I felt the presence behind me.

"Did you ever experience anything like this?" I sniffled.

"No," she replied, placing her hand on my shoulder, trying to soothe my sadness.

It didn't work this time.

"I never had the friends or the family that you have," she lamented.

"But you had Joe and then Jack," I sobbed. "Didn't you, Angel? Or is it Grace?"

308

I turned to see the little old woman who had taken hold of my hands calming me down earlier in the evening.

"It is Angel. That is the name my parents gave me. Grace was the last name Joe gave me," she smiled.

"How long have you been in Capron Bay?" I asked her.

"Jack brought me here twenty years ago," she smiled. "He said I could trust your Poppa."

I nodded.

"Did Poppa know who you were?" I asked.

"He did. Jack and I told him everything," she admitted.

"What happened all those years ago at the village?" I asked.

"Chernobog sent his legions after me and demanded the villagers turn me over to him. They refused, and he killed everyone in the village. He would have killed me too if it wasn't for Joe," she told me.

Her eyes stared at the floor as memories flowed into her mind.

I listened without saying anything.

"Joe stumbled into the mass murder of all those people, and he barely escaped the village himself when he found me standing outside with his dogs. Joe knew there was no way he could outrun the monsters chasing him. He made a stand against the attacking monsters. I was terrified as they closed in from all sides. I didn't know what my powers were until that moment. My hands began glowing, and the power grew within. Somehow, I knew what to do, and I released blazing energy from my hands," she lamented.

"You are a rainbow warrior, and you used the power of the colors to fight the demons?" I asked her.

"I know that now, but at the time, I didn't. All I knew was I destroyed hundreds of them as they stormed from the village gates," she sighed. "I was scared to death and didn't know what was happening. I just knew I could kill them all."

I watched her struggle with the memories.

"When I was done, the survivors fled into the village, and I collapsed. I woke up hours later, deep in the woods. Joe and his dogs took me deep into the northern territory to a place he said demons feared to go," she said.

"You don't know where?" I asked.

"Inukshuk Valley. A place where evil spirits fear," she said.

"That's where you met Jack," I nodded.

"Yes. He appeared there the next morning. He told us he was sent to find me and kill me," she said. "Chernobog used him as an assassin."

"But he hid you instead?"

"For decades, he and Joe kept me on the move never staying in one place for very long," she shrugged.

"My powers were able to keep Joe alive for a couple of decades longer than he should have lived, but finally, he succumbed to his age," she sobbed.

"I'm sorry," I said. It must have been painful. She had lived with Joe for almost a century and had no living family or friends to turn to except for a double-agent snow fairy.

"Jack told me about your grandfather and that he had worked with him before. He said I could trust him," she smiled.

"So, you came here," I whispered.

Grace nodded tears welling.

"And Chernobog never found you?"

"No. Jack was able to keep me hidden from him."

"Until I showed up. I've even ruined that for you," I shook my head.

She laughed.

"He still doesn't know about me—not yet anyway, and I knew about you long before you arrived here in town," she laughed.

Her words surprised me.

"I felt you when you were born, Prentice. Poppa and I had long discussions about what to do with you and how to protect you."

"How is that possible?"

"I am one hundred and thirteen years old," she said. I have lived for over a century, and you have been the only person to be born in my lifetime who is like me.

"Nobody else is like us?"

"Nobody," she reiterated. "Jack would tell me of others who had some power with the colors, but you and I are the only two people on the planet who can control all of them."

"I can't control them. Not yet, anyway," I told her.

"Prentice, you have been able to control them since the second you were born. You must learn how to use them. There is a difference between control and use. The colors are easy to control, but using them relies completely on your emotions," she laughed.

"I'm not doing a great job of that," I shrugged.

"You are still young," she added.

"Agent Mason has some power," I told her, pointing to him.

"I know. He also bears the mark of Chernobog," she said, standing and rolling Mason's wrist over, showing a small horned-shaped scar.

"What is that?"

"It means he was once possessed by Chernobog," she informed me.

"Ahh…that makes sense now. The first time I came across him, we had a…disagreement," I smiled.

"You give him that scar on his face?" she asked.

"Well, not directly. A fisher cat did, but I helped it along," I smiled.

She nodded.

"I saw some inky shadow move across the FBI and FEMA agents out there," I said. "Does that mean they are possessed?"

"It can, but there are different levels of possession. Some people choose to let the demons take over, while others have no choice. If they have a scar like Agent Mason here, then that means they have been forced into being a demon's slave," she told me.

"Why would anyone volunteer to wear a demon meat suit?" I asked, stealing Dean Winchester's words.

"In exchange for money, for power for many different reasons," she shook her head.

"Like Jack," I nodded my head.

311

"He did Chernobog's dirty work to protect his sister. But Jack's been playing a dangerous game for a long time by playing both sides."

"I think Jack plays a lot of different sides," I smiled. "Where is he anyway?"

"He said he had something to do and would be back as soon as possible," she told me.

"You think he'll be back?" I asked her.

"I do. Jack has done many things throughout the centuries, but he has never abandoned me, and I don't think he would do that to you either," she replied.

I didn't say anything. I wondered if she was right or if he was out there waiting to join the bad guys.

"Chernobog has given me until sunrise to give myself up and turn my powers over to him," I said.

She didn't say anything.

"I agreed to," I told her.

"Prentice, you can't," she insisted.

"I agreed if he left the town alone, gave me my sister back, and gave Jack his sister back," I told her.

"You can't trust him," she urged.

"I know, but I don't have much choice," I said. "Everyone I love and care for has suffered enough. This town has suffered enough."

She sat back down. I could see her lost in her own thoughts pondering my words.

"Are you sure?" she finally asked.

"Would you have given your powers up to save your village?" I asked her.

"I…they never…," she couldn't finish.

"You were too young. You didn't know what you were, and you didn't know he would kill them all," I told her. "All I'm saying is, if you knew then what you know now, would you make the exchange?"

She looked at me with tear-filled eyes.

"I lost my whole family," she whispered.

I squeezed her hand.

"I would give all of my powers to bring them back," she sobbed.

"We can't, can we?" I wondered.

"No. We can't," she lamented.

"Well, one of my friends is a ghost," I told her.

"The little blond-haired girl?"

"That's Mollie," I said, and I told her the story of how we found her and how we managed to keep her in this world.

She nodded.

"You've seen her?" I asked.

"I have. Remember, I'm like you. I can see things normal people can't," she grinned.

"Right," I nodded.

"You haven't brought her back from the dead," she told me. "You've just allowed her spirit to become physical."

"I know," I muttered. "That's also a problem I have created. I wish I could bring her back."

"No," she shook her head. "That is not a power that anyone has."

"He does," I said. "His army outside. I think they're all brought back from the dead."

"That is a comforting thought," she smiled.

We sat in silence for a moment, staring at my friends lying there fighting for their lives.

"Can we heal them?" I asked, suddenly getting excited.

"I have tried. I snuck in here earlier thinking I might be able to, but I was unsuccessful," she lamented.

Sadness crept over me once again.

"I'm sorry," she whispered

"Will you help me pray over them?" I asked Angel.

She nodded. I took her hand and helped her to her feet. I closed my eyes and held her hand tightly. It was reassuring to know someone else understood what I was going through as I prayed silently for Hog, Mason, Druss, the rest of my family, and the town. I placed my hand on each of them to say goodbye.

"Thank you, Angel," I quivered, trying not to let the tears fall again.

"I have to go and face the music now," I told her. "Will you be okay?"

"I will. Now go. Be with your family and friends," she said.

313

I waved goodbye.

"Goodbye, Prentice," she smiled.

27
THE WHOLE TRUTH

I found Mollie leaning against the wall just outside the coach's office, where all my family and friends had gathered to hear the truth. Sometimes, I found it hard to tell if I was seeing her in her spectral form or her temporary human form from Ms. Annie's ward. This time was no different, but she didn't look happy.

"That bad?" I asked.

She didn't answer, but the sad look in her eyes told me enough.

"Did they bring you up yet?"

She shook her head, wiping away tears.

I leaned against the wall beside her but didn't say anything. We stayed that way for a long couple of minutes. I was wondering if Dad or Ms. Annie would bring Mollie up. I mean, how do you even begin talking about that. I had no idea, and the truth is, I didn't want to bring her up.

I knew we couldn't always keep her in this in-between state. Franklin couldn't deal with losing her, but she was a ghost. The real Mollie Thompson had passed away several years ago, but she couldn't let her grieving mother go. We can't let go now, but how is it fair to keep her in this in-between state? How was it fair to keep her alive and dead? It wasn't fair, and it was all my fault.

I slid down the wall until I was sitting on the floor. Mollie did the same. I wanted to bury my head in my arms and cry, but I fought the urge. Mollie put her hand on my arm but didn't say anything. We just sat there in silence.

A few minutes later, the door opened, and Dad popped his head out.

"C'mon in," he said. "Both of you."

"Dad?" I asked.

He stepped into the hall and closed the door behind him.

"It's time PJ. We've kept too many secrets, and this may be the worst one of them all," he said, putting his hand on my shoulder and winking at Mollie.

"Sir?" Mollie said.

He knelt and looked at her.

"You are one of the bravest girls I've met. I know the full story of what happened that morning. I've read the police reports. It's time your mom knows, too," he smiled, fighting the tears back.

"Mollie, what is he talking about?" I asked her.

She hung her head and sobbed.

"A Wendigo, along with his human thugs, went after her father that morning in the gas station parking lot out of revenge," Dad began to tell me.

I knew the story but didn't know it was a Wendigo.

"A Wendigo?" I repeated. "But he was human."

"Some can be in human form. Powerful ones. Mollie could see him coming and put herself between the Wendigo and her father, trying to stop it."

"And you were shot?" I whispered.

"Mollie, are you ready?" Dad asked.

She nodded.

"PJ, when you step in, take Mollie's hand, then grab Anyika's, okay?" he asked.

I nodded, not understanding what was happening.

He opened the door and stepped in. Ms. Annie stood to the left of the open door. I could see a warding symbol on the wall.

I met her gaze, and she tried to smile before turning to everyone in the room.

"Now, please do as I ask," he told them.

I watched as everyone grasped someone's hand individually until Doc took Ms. Fiona's hand tightly and held her tight.

"Prentice, come on in," he said.

I looked at Mollie.

She nodded, and her body shimmered in the faint light of the hallway for a second. When it faded, she had blood all over her.

"What the," I began. She held up a finger to her mouth to shush me. Then she placed her hand in mine and winked at me.

I stepped into the room holding a bloodied Mollie's hand.

The gasps were loud, but Fiona's scream was deafening.

"Hold on to the hands of the ones you love, and do not let go," Anyika's voice echoed through my mind.

I tightened my grip on Mollie's hand.

The world around us erupted into a swirling storm of color, a dizzying cascade that felt like hyperspace travel straight out of *Star Wars*. My body rocketed forward, weightless and untethered. It only lasted a few seconds before everything came to an abrupt stop.

A wave of nausea hit me, but I forced it down. I had ridden the rainbow before, but this, this was something else entirely. And this time, I wasn't alone. Everyone in the room had been pulled into it with me.

As my vision cleared, I found myself standing in the middle of a sunlit day at a gas station. A large overhead read, Marcel's Service Station.

"No." The word trembled through the air, but I didn't just hear Fiona say it, I *felt* it. A moment later, she began to cry.

Cars pulled in and out of the gas pumps, ordinary in every way. But then, a red pickup truck with an American flag decal rolled in, and a man in a green police uniform stepped out. He punched the pump's buttons, grabbed the nozzle, and began filling up.

Movement to our right caught my attention.

Five men, weapons drawn, approached the truck. The leader was massive—bald, with an ominous symbol tattooed on his head. The others weren't as large, but dark ink snaked across their necks, marking them as his followers. I didn't know how I knew it, but I did. They were branded. Servants.

"Daddy!" I heard a familiar scream.

Mollie.

She appeared from nowhere, running around the back of the truck, throwing herself between the men and her father.

"No!" Mollie's Dad shouted, yanking his sidearm and reaching for Mollie.

I wanted to stop it. I knew what was coming. But I couldn't change what had already happened.

The bright morning exploded into chaos.

Gunfire. Smoke. Screams.

Then, silence.

When the haze cleared, Mollie and her father lay on the pavement, riddled with bullets. Four of the attackers were also motionless, their bodies twisted where they had fallen.

The bald man stood over them, still holding his weapon. Only one of his men remained standing, his gun trained on Mollie.

The pain in the air was suffocating. I could *feel* it radiating from both Mollie and Fiona, raw and unbearable.

Then…*bang*.

The lone gunman stumbled backward, his body hitting the ground, unmoving.

Mollie's dad had fired one last shot.

Bang. Bang.

The bald man fired two more rounds into him, ensuring he never got up again.

Satisfied, he turned to leave.

Bang!

He dropped to one knee, cursing in pain.

He spun around and locked eyes with Mollie.

She had somehow forced herself up, blood pooling beneath her, her father's gun still clutched in her shaking hands.

She had shot him in the back of the knee.

The man smiled. Slowly, he raised his gun and pulled the trigger.

The scream inside my head was deafening.

Fiona's wail of grief shattered through me, more painful than any physical wound I had ever felt.

The others were still staring at the devastation—the lifeless bodies of Mollie, her father, the fallen attackers. But my eyes followed the bald man as he limped toward a dark sedan parked nearby.

The tinted rear window slid down.

A strange, eerie calm settled over me, laced with cold fury.

Inside the car sat Alpha. And beside him—the Senator.

They exchanged a few words with the wounded man before the vehicle sped away.

Then, light.

The world spun once more, dragging us through a stream of past events.

We saw Ms. Annie and another officer storm an abandoned home deep in the swamps, taking down the bald man. We saw Boo Hags lurking in the shadows, watched as Ms. Annie captured one.

Years passed in an instant.

Mollie, following Fiona.

Time folding over itself.

And then, me. Walking through my driveway. Finding Mollie for the first time.

The visions kept coming. Battles with the Boo Hags. Mollie and Franklin flirting. Annie and me debating what to do with her. The fight at Minuteman Cemetery. The battle in the woods with the Wendigo.

Everything that led us to here.

Everyone saw it.

And then, stillness.

The hyperspace light flickered away, and we were back. Back in the coach's office.

I turned to Mollie. She looked like she always did, whole again, her bloodstained form gone. Franklin was by her side in an instant, grabbing her hand as soon as I let go.

"I'm here," he whispered.

The only other sound was Fiona's sobbing as Doc held her close.

Everyone instinctively stepped back, giving Fiona and Mollie space.

"Mollie," Fiona choked out.

Mollie didn't hesitate. She threw herself into her mother's arms.

Lena squeezed my hand, her silent way of telling me she was there. There wasn't a dry eye in the room.

Fiona lifted her gaze to mine, still holding her daughter.

319

Every ounce of me wanted to look away, but I forced myself to meet her gaze. I had forced her to relive this nightmare. I deserved whatever anger she had for me, but she motioned for me to come closer.

Lena squeezed my hand again before letting go. She knew I had to do this alone.

I squared my shoulders and approached.

Fiona gently released Mollie.

"Sweetheart, go hug your boyfriend. It looks like he needs some southern loving," Fiona choked out.

Mollie didn't need to be told twice. She ran straight into Franklin's arms, nearly knocking him over.

I turned to Fiona, unsure of what to say.

"Ma'am, I wouldn't change a thing," I blurted out, surprising myself with the words. "We love..."

Fiona pulled me into a tight embrace before I could finish.

I hesitated, then whispered, "Ms. Fiona, I don't know how to keep her here."

She held me tighter. "Honey, we're southern. If something's broken, we fix it. We don't throw it away," she sobbed. "We'll figure it out. I'm not letting her go again."

I was overwhelmed by Fiona's embrace and sobbed uncontrollably. A moment later, I felt Lena's arms around me and then Mollie's.

"We got you, crayon man," Franklin sniffled, joining the embrace.

"You got that right," Rachel added.

"Forever," Dak choked up.

A moment later, the adults stepped in, wrapping all of us in one massive hug. A surge of energy flowed through me.

This was my family. This was my town.

And no one was ever going to take that from me.

28
LIVE TO FIGHT ANOTHER DAY

Capron Bay High School
Capron Bay,
2:30 A.M.

Everyone took a step back, wiping their eyes dry. I looked at them all. Franklin's Mom and Dad had gotten stuck in Florida on an anniversary trip. Dakota's parents were stuck in Washington, D.C., on tribal business. Flights were canceled up and down the East Coast.

"Sorry your parents aren't here," I told them.

"Ahh...my dad would have just given me a hard time that I have a ghost for a girlfriend.

"It does give a whole new meaning to an invisible friend," Dakota laughed.

"I'm working on that," I tried to force a smile.

"We'll do it together," Lena added.

I smiled at her.

"Besides, I'm pretty sure my dad knows something is going on, but he hasn't had the time to dig into it yet. I'm sure he'll be putting me through an interrogation when he gets a chance," Dakota shrugged.

"Can I have everyone's attention, please," I spoke loudly.

Everyone stopped talking and turned to me.

"I'm giving myself up to Chernobog," I informed them.

"No, you're not!" Mom and Dad chided me.

"Prentice," Lena fumed.

Everyone in the room looked angry and defiant.

"There isn't much of a choice. He has too many demons out there to attack us all. We know he wiped out an entire village in 1922, killing thousands of innocent Inuits to find the last rainbow warrior," I told them.

"What? Mom demanded to know.

"Anjukani village?" Chief Tackna mumbled. "So, that's what happened."

"What are you talking about?" Mom asked me.

Adam told them all about Anjukani. I added some details Angel had told me, but I didn't tell them about her being here.

"That was a village that wasn't ready," Lena answered.

"I'm not going to let that happen here," I said.

"No," Dad growled. "We'll fight."

"Dad, we don't have enough people to fight," I replied. "And he has Carolyn."

"We'll get her back," he scoffed.

"I have already made a deal with him," I confessed.

"No way," Dad shot back. Mom shook her head, glaring at me.

"Prentice!" Lena cried out, stepping back and staring at me with angry eyes.

"Crayon, man!" Franklin scolded me.

"You can't make a deal with the devil," Brother Kiernan interrupted.

"I have, and it's final," I said.

"What are the conditions of this agreement, Master Prentice?" Doc asked.

"I will give him my powers, and he will leave the town alone and give Carolyn back to us," I confirmed.

"And he'll leave everyone alone. Just like that?" Dad asked.

I nodded.

"And you believe him? After everything we've seen him do. He's just going to let everyone live and walk away," Lena glared at me.

"He said he'll heal Hog, Agent Mason, and Druss too," I added.

"Don't you dare use my dad as an excuse? He would never want you to do this," Lena shouted, looking at her mom. Ms. Sheridan nodded in agreement through tear-stained eyes.

322

"She's right," Dad argued. "Hog would be the first to say you're crazy and that we'll fight."

"I may be new to this whole…magic…color thing," Rachel's Dad said, waving his hand like a magic wand.

"Abracadabra," Franklin interrupted.

The former linebacker looked at him.

"Y… you…were waving your hand around…like you had a…you know, a magic wand," he stuttered.

"Franklin," Mollie scolded him.

"Sorry," he groveled.

"As I said, I'm new to this abracadabra stuff, but I know a liar when I see one, and these folks lie. They're not going to just let everyone walk away."

Everyone nodded in agreement.

"Look," I said. "All of this is my fault. I've got a lot of blood on my hands, and I don't want to see anyone else I care about get hurt."

"How is it your fault?" Lena demanded to know.

"He wants me, he wants my powers. If I wasn't here, he wouldn't be either," I answered.

"So, it's your fault you have these powers?" Grammy sighed.

I looked at her, and the pain in her eyes was unmistakable. My words had cut deep. She had always been there for me—for as long as I could remember. Whenever she was around, every choice she made, every action she took, had been for Carolyn and me.

"If anything, this is my fault," Dad whispered. "You're my son, and I…"

"Yeah, but you don't have any powers, Dad. So how could it be your fault?" I interrupted.

He didn't answer.

A sudden thought struck me. "Do you?"

Still, silence.

"Rob?" Mom pressed gently. She was the only one who ever called him that.

"Dad?" I pushed my voice firmer now.

He hesitated, then muttered, "I don't know… I think so."

Every eye in the room turned to him.

He swallowed hard. "There are times when... things just turn yellow."

We all stared, stunned.

"But yellow is the only color I've ever...felt or seen," he admitted. "Nothing else."

"We did notice some signs growing up that you had certain abilities," Grammy admitted. "But if anyone is to blame, it's me."

My fingers clenched the chair so tightly I nearly splintered the wood. A surge of frustration burned through me—I wanted to hurl it straight through the wall.

I knew Grammy had powers. She had revealed them during the battle against the ghost pirates. We all knew. And we had all agreed to keep it a secret—*even Doc.*

But now, because of me, she was exposing it all.

"Mom?" Dad asked.

"Both of you, get your powers from my side of the family," she shrugged.

"None of that matters," I shouted, pushing the chair away. I've made my decision. I'm giving Chernobog my powers."

The room went quiet.

"What does that even mean?" Rachel asked, breaking the silence. "How does that work?"

"It has to be some ritual," Dakota added, looking at his grandfather to chime in.

"Don't look at me. I'm not an expert in this kind of thing," he huffed.

"Does he draw it out with magic?" Rachel asked.

"Or maybe...like a beheading," Franklin wondered.

"I don't...wait...what?" I sputtered.

"Franklin!" Mollie gasped.

"Dude!" Dakota exclaimed.

"Kind of makes sense. You know, there can be only one," he muttered to himself, turning back towards everyone.

We all stared in shock.

"But...I'm sure...that isn't how it will happen," he forced a smile, realizing what he was saying.

"I can't let anyone else get hurt because of me," I reiterated.

324

"You blame yourself," Dad replied.

"Prentice, it's been Chernobog the whole time," Lena assured me.

"Master Prentice, we're all in this together," Doc added.

Everyone was talking at once, their voices overlapping in a rush of reassurance, each one trying to convince me that this wasn't all my fault.

"Stop! Everyone just stop!" I shouted.

Mom wrapped an arm around me as the room went still.

"These powers cost us, Poppa. Carolyn has been taken. Hog and Mason are in there, lying in their own blood. They got you guys kidnapped and nearly killed, and it cost Officer Donegan his life," I cried.

"Prentice, that's all on me," Dad interrupted.

"I don't want these powers anymore!" I snapped, finally revealing what I was feeling.

All eyes were on me, but nobody said a word.

"I don't want them," I muttered, my voice cracking as the emotional dam I had desperately tried to hold back finally shattered. Tears spilled freely down my face.
Mom pulled me into a tight embrace, wrapping both arms around me. I couldn't bring myself to look at anyone—I just buried my head against her and sobbed.

Dad's hand rested on my shoulder—light, yet powerful. There was strength in his touch, a quiet reassurance that spoke louder than words. I knew they were all willing to fight for me, but I couldn't bear the thought of anyone else getting hurt.

After a few long minutes, Dad asked. "Are you sure, PJ? Is this what you really want?"

"Yes," I sobbed, looking up at him.

"Okay," he whispered. "Okay. We do this now, and we live to fight another day."

The room was silent again.

"What do we do?" Lena asked, squeezing my hand.

I told them everything Chernobog told me.

"The meteor shower has been sacred for many northern tribes," Chief Tackna added.

Adam was furiously typing away, trying to get online.

"Crud…I can't get online, and the laptop just died," he scoffed and slammed the laptop shut.

"Are you sure this is what you want, honey?" Mom asked me one more time.

"Yes," I nodded.

29
COLORS OF DEFEAT

Capron Bay High School
Capron Bay,
6:15 A.M.

We sat on the bleachers. Lena held my hand, but we said nothing. I knew they weren't happy about my decision, but it was final. I wouldn't let any more blood spill.

The adults huddled around the makeshift medical room hoping Hog, Mason and Druss showed some signs of improvement. Mom, Ms. Annie and Ms. Fiona all tended to medical needs while Cardinal Murphy and Brother Kiernan silently prayed for their recovery.

The Capron Bay police officers had quietly taken up position all around the medical room keeping all the federal agents away. Even though Dad was no longer the official Chief of Police, his officers would follow his orders and his alone. Agent Byrd realized this and didn't push the issue.

"Look, the fake Mayor is about to say something," Franklin sneered.

We all turned to see Theresa Morgan climb the opposite bleachers. Byrd, Liang, and Priscilla Reed flanking her.

"Where's the Senator?" Rachel asked.

Dakota glared, "Slithered back to his hole."

I glanced at my watch. Time was ticking closer.

"Can I have everyone's attention?" Mayor elect Morgan shouted throughout the gym. Despite the time, most of the people didn't sleep at all. They stayed awake worrying about the storm and whatever was inside it. The idea of monsters and demons was a lot for people to truly buy. Instead, the story of terrorists attacking the town began to circulate. It was much more believable.

People slowly turned their attention to the new Mayor. Some stayed sitting at their cots while others meandered their way over to her, forming a small crowd around her.

"I have good news everyone. The storm is slowly fading away," she told them.

"Still seems pretty bad out there to me," someone shouted back.

"Yeah, snow is still heavy," yelled another woman.

"Those things are still out there too," a guy growled.

"Can you believe this lady?" Adam ranted. "We can't let her stay Mayor."

I felt Lena's anger growing.

"Folks, the Mayor is right. The storm will be subsiding, and the enemy outside has agreed to leave and there will be no more violence," Agent Byrd informed them as he stepped up beside Mayor Morgan.

"It's true. They will leave us alone from now on," Priscilla Reed proclaimed. "Your new Mayor and Police Chief have negotiated a truce with them."

The crowd remained silent at the news.

"Chief is this true?" an old man asked.

"It is…" Byrd began to answer.

"I'm not talking to you. I'm asking Chief Pendleton," the old man taunted as the crowd turned to my dad. He didn't even look at them. He remained seated with his head bowed.

"See, your great police chief won't respond to his people. So much for serving and protecting," Reed quipped to the crowd.

"That's it," Lena raged leaping up.

"Yeah, that's right. They made a deal with the devil. The monsters and demons outside want Prentice and they gave him to them in exchange for their own hide," she yelled.

"Lena!" I whispered but she ignored me.

"Young lady," Theresa blustered.

"Is this true?" a voice in the crowd asked.

Multiple people began asking the same question.

Morgan held up her hand to quiet everyone down.

"Folks, Prentice has agreed to go with them of his own free will. Nobody is forcing him to go," she informed them.

Nobody said a word.

Quiet fell. "Why him?" a woman asked.

"Is it true, Prentice?" another pressed.

"Yes," I stood, hands shaking. "It's true. I'll go if they leave you alone."

I felt Lena's eyes on me.

"I will go with them if it means they leave everyone alone," I assured them.

"We've all seen things tonight," Reed shouted. "They will destroy us all if he doesn't give himself up."

"It's not right!" Franklin shouted.

I glanced at my watch. 6:24 AM.

"Those monsters will kill us all," another woman cried out.

"Yeah," came more shouts.

Mom and Dad stood from their chairs making their way to me. The crowd quieted down expecting him to say something, but he didn't. He just stood next to me looking me in the eye.

I looked at Lena and smiled. She jumped from the bleachers wrapping her arms around me tears streaming down her face. I squeezed her tight. A second later all my friends embraced.

"Don't do this Crayon man," Franklin sobbed.

"It'll be okay," I said. "I'll be okay".

Nobody said a word.

My eyes met Lena's and took her hand.

"You better come back," she sniffled.

I kissed her hands.

She moved in and kissed me on the lips. A rush of energy surged through my body, but I forced it away.

"I promise," I mouthed to her. "I promise."

I turned to Dad, who gripped my shoulder. I nodded and together, we made our way down the back hallway toward the back parking lot. I fought the urge to turn around, but I could hear sobbing behind me as we disappeared into the darkness.

We got to the door and looked out.

The wind was swirling, and the snowfall was as heavy as it had been throughout the last day.

"Looks fun," I said.

He stayed silent. Mom's tears fell as I hugged her. "I'll be okay, Mom. It's better for everyone," I assured but her sobs didn't stop.

I had made two promises in less than two minutes, and I wasn't sure if I could keep either of them.

"It's time," Dad whispered placing his hand on my shoulder.

I glanced at my watch. 6:28.

He opened the door, and we stepped outside.

Capron Bay High School
Capron Bay,
6:30 A.M.

"C'mon," Lena cried out and the whole gang got up trying to head toward the back hallway. The federal agents stepped in blocking their path. Some of Theresa Morgan's people stood next to them.

"Let us through!" Rachel demanded.

"No Ma'am," an agent replied.

"Ladies and gentlemen let's just head back to our seats and the Pendletons will be back shortly," Agent Byrd smirked.

"Yes, folks please sit down," Mayor Morgan added. "We don't want anyone else getting hurt."

"Threatening them, Theresa?" Mayor Travis pushed through.

"Certainly not. I'm just saying we should let the deal play out and everyone will be back safely," she reiterated.

"Then let us go," Franklin demanded.

"Young man, I'm going to put you in handcuffs," Byrd threatened.

Two Capron Bay officers flanked Franklin. They didn't say a word, but the threat was clear. Go ahead and try.

"Mrs. Pendelton!" Lena shouted as she appeared from the dark hallway.

Lena rushed to her and hugged her.

A couple of agents stepped up next to them.

Melissa's glare burned with raw anger and hatred.

"Melissa," Doc whispered placing his hands on hers. "Let's head back and wait for them to return. Come Lena. Trust Prentice and Robert."

She glanced at Doc and then back at the agents. "If anything happens to my son, I'm holding you personally responsible," she hissed.

Neither said a word.

Mellissa, Lena and Doc eased their way into the crowd. Lena went to the kids while Doc and Melissa moved to Pam Sheridan and the other adults were gathered.

"Do you see their faces?" Annie murmured to Brother Kiernan.

"Some form of possession?" he asked.

She nodded. "I have not seen that before," she said.

"Me either," he answered.

"Thomas, Annie, please join us," Doc said.

The adults huddled together.

"We have to do something," Mellissa urged.

"I agree," Annie said, "but the agents seem to be possessed."

A wave of shock rippled through the group as startled glances darted between them.

"If they're possessed, that means they aren't acting of their own free will," Cardinal Murphy added grimly. "And we don't have the resources to attempt an exorcism."

The crowd slowly shuffled back to their cots and bleachers. The federal agents followed, ensuring all the people knew who was in charge and they should just sit by and wait until the storm passed to get back to their lives.

Lena and the gang returned to their bleachers.

Jack appeared beside them.

"Where have you been blondie?" Franklin sneered.

He didn't say anything.

"Yeah, you've been a great help," Dakota chided him.

"I...," he began.

"You what?" Rachel asked. "You could've been helping here but you boogied".

Lena glaring in silence.

331

"I'm sorry," he whispered. I went to see my sister. He let me see her."

"Why would he do that?" Mollie asked him.

"In exchange for telling him where you guys went," he admitted.

"You rat," Lena shouted lunging at him. Dakota grabbed her but not before she punched him in the face.

Jack didn't move. He made no attempt to defend himself staggering from the punch but staying on his feet.

"I'm sorry," he uttered, blood forming around the corner of his mouth.

"You almost got us killed," Adam fumed.

"I know," he mumbled. "I know."

"And you're okay with that?" Rachel cursed.

He shook his head.

"Then why did you do it?" Mollie huffed.

Everybody waited as Jack slumped to the wooden bleacher.

"I haven't seen Jannie in over three hundred years," he lamented.

"What?" Rachel asked.

"She's been imprisoned for five centuries," he mumbled.

"You mean like five hundred years?" Franklin asked.

"Thats what five centuries is knucklehead," Rachel laughed.

"I'm just saying…that's…a…long," he began.

"Time," Jack finished.

"A long time," Franklin echoed.

"I'm sorry. I just couldn't turn down the chance to see her," Jack whispered.

"I couldn't imagine not seeing my sister for five hundred years," Dakota added.

"Look at Prentice, Carolyn has been gone for a few hours, and he is giving himself up to get her back," Mollie sighed.

"What?" Jack shrieked.

"Chernobog kidnapped Carolyn and Prentice made a deal with him to give himself up and give his powers to him in exchange for sister's return and they will leave the town alone," Lena griped.

332

"When?" he shivered.

"He just left. He was going to meet him outside at 6:30," Rachel added.

"No, no, no," Jack moaned panic setting in.

"Why? What's wrong?" Mollie asked.

"It's the Dziady," he panted.

"I couldn't find anything on it because there is no internet signal," Adam told him. "He told Prentice, it will be a simple process, and his power will be transferred."

"That part is true, but it requires a human bloodletting and sacrifice," Jack gasped.

"What?" they all shout.

"The Dziady is a moment where the world of the dead and the living come together. Chernobog needs immense power to keep it open long enough for his army of the dead to come through the portal," he stated.

"That power will come from the flow of blood into the Sacred Well of Orkneyjar," he said.

"Isn't that in Norway?" Adam asked.

"It is but he has the power to blend places. He can bring it here through a portal itself. Sacred waters flow between worlds and when the sacrificial blood of a powerful human hits the water, its energy tears open the barrier between worlds," he stammered.

"How can he do that?" Adam wondered.

"It doesn't matter. We must stop it," Lena ordered and before anyone could say anything, she took off.

Capron Bay High School
Parking Lot
6:30 A.M.

We stepped through the door and into a whirlwind of snow and wind, swirling in every direction. Fresh flakes tumbled from the sky, adding to the thick, foot-and-a-half layer already blanketing the parking lot. I raised a hand to shield my eyes, both

333

from the biting sting of the blizzard and to give them a moment to adjust to the storm's fury.

"What is that?" I shouted to Dad over the deafening wind.

He didn't answer, his eyes locked on the shadowy figure across the lot, trying to make sense of its shape.

And then, the snow stopped.

It didn't gradually come to an end. It just stopped.

The blizzard vanished, replaced by an eerie stillness. Above us, the night sky stretched clear and vast, stars gleaming like scattered diamonds. Where chaos had raged just moments ago, a strange, haunting beauty now lingered, snow-covered pines and oaks standing silently under the moonlight.

Opposite us, in the school's parking lot, a hooded rider sat astride a massive horse.

I glanced at Dad, then back at the figure. He remained motionless. His face was hidden beneath the hood, his features obscured. The only thing certain was his size, which was big and the horse beneath him was even bigger.

Slowly, he raised a gloved hand and beckoned us forward.

"What's he doing?" I whispered.

"He wants to us to move toward him," Dad answered.

"Yeah, that's not creepy," I whispered.

Dad turned to me. "You still sure about this?"

I swallowed hard, then nodded. "Yes, sir."

And with that, I stepped forward, walking across the snow-covered lot toward the mysterious rider, Dad, right beside me.

My gaze stayed locked on the rider, and I was certain Dad's did too. I half-expected him to disappear, charge at us, or make some sudden move—but he didn't. He simply sat there, motionless atop his massive horse, watching.
Halfway across the lot, an unnatural silence settled over the night, deeper than before, as if the world itself was holding its breath.

Then, the ground began to tremble.

"You feel that?" I asked Dad.

"I do," he confirmed.

The tremors intensified, vibrating through my boots and up into my legs. Dad and I exchanged a quick glance before looking down—the snow beneath us was beginning to blur, its crisp edges fading like an image being erased.

"What's going on?" Dad asked, his voice tense.

I snapped my gaze back to the rider. His arms were raised, palms turned toward the sky.

Then, a piercing screech tore through the air behind us.

We spun around just as the pavement erupted.

Thick, serpentine vines, covered in dagger-like thorns, exploded from the ground, writhing and twisting as they spread across the parking lot. They surged upward and outward, weaving into a towering wall—an impenetrable barrier that now separated us from the school.

A deep red glow flickered at the base of the thorned vines, faint at first but steadily intensifying. The eerie light pulsed upward, climbing the twisting trunks until it reached the top, bathing the entire barrier in an ominous crimson hue.

"A wall of razor-sharp thorns and red energy," I muttered. "This just got interesting."

"I'm not sure if the word I'd use is interesting," Dad countered.

Before I could respond, a blinding light erupted where the rider and his horse had stood.

We turned back—and the world had changed.

The school, the parking lot, the thorned barrier, all gone.

We now stood at a bend in a flowing river, its banks blanketed in untouched snow. In the distance, a towering mountain range stretched across the horizon, its jagged peaks glistening under a pale sky. But what drew my attention wasn't the mountains, it was the massive, foreboding castle nestled within them. Its dark stone walls loomed over the landscape, exuding an unmistakable air of menace.

And in the valley below?

Hundreds, if not *thousands*, of black tents stretched as far as the eye could see.

Dad exhaled sharply. "I don't think we're in Kansas anymore, Dorothy."

"Not unless Kansas suddenly got castles," I muttered.

A deep, booming voice shattered the eerie silence.

"Welcome."

335

We spun around.

There, standing just beyond the river, was Chernobog.

He loomed before a massive white tent, its fabric billowing ever so slightly in the icy air. Beside him, a roaring campfire blazed within a large ring of stone, its flames casting wild shadows against the snow.

And just beyond the fire, standing alone in the frost-covered clearing, was a heavy stone altar with nothing on it. No markings. No offerings. No tools of sacrifice. Just cold, unyielding stone, shaped with purpose.

On the side of that was another perfectly formed stone circle about three feet high. It had to be fifty to sixty yards away from me, but I could feel the energy and the power emanating from the well.

Screech!

The sound pulled my gaze upward.

Dozens of winged demons hovered high above, their dark silhouettes cutting through the sky. Just below them, a faint glowing field shimmered, an invisible barrier separating them from whatever lay beneath.

Boom. Boom. Boom!

A thunderous rhythm shook the air as war drums erupted from the rows of black tents.

Then, the horde emerged.

Demonic figures poured out, their monstrous forms bristling with weapons, eyes burning with a hunger for battle.

"Uhm…Dad?" I said.

"What?"

"That… doesn't look good."

"What doesn't look good?" he asked frowning.

I pointed to the sky. **"Those."**

He followed my gaze, scanning the sky. "I don't see anything."

"What? You don't see all the flying demons?"

He shook his head.

"How about the demon hordes by the tents? You don't see *them* either?

His expression darkened. "I see the tents… but that's it."

"Dad! Look out!" I screamed.

336

A massive figure loomed behind him.

Dad spun, reaching for his sidearm, but he wasn't fast enough. The towering creature struck him with a brutal backhand, its clawed hand connecting with the side of his head.

"Dad!" I roared, fury igniting inside me. A surge of red-hot rage coursed through my veins, and I whipped around, ready to unleash chaos.

I clenched my fists, summoning the power within me—

And nothing happened.

No energy. No cannonball of force. No crackling lightning.

Nothing.

I spun around facing Chernobog.

"Why did you do that?" I demanded.

"Silence."

Chernobog's voice bellowed across the battlefield, crashing into me like a shockwave through shattered glass.

He lifted his hands, and the earth trembled beneath me. The violent tremor sent me sprawling, my body hitting the frozen ground with bone-jarring force.

I struggled to roll and push myself up, but before I could regain my footing, a sudden blast of wind slammed into me.

It drove me face-first into the dirt.

I fought against it, muscles straining, but the sheer force pinned me down, crushing me beneath its relentless power.

Something coiled around me, squeezing tight, constricting my entire body.

I looked down, expecting to see a massive anaconda wrapping itself around me, but there was nothing there.

I thrashed, struggling to break free, but the invisible force only tightened its grip, crushing the breath from my lungs. Without warning, I was lifted off the ground, rising five... six feet into the air.

I turned my head toward Chernobog.

He was smiling.

A chill ran down my spine.

"Whaaat... are you doing?" I croaked, my voice strained.

My body began to drift toward him.

I fought harder, twisting, straining, but it was useless.

337

"Come hither," the King of the Dead laughed, his voice laced with cruel amusement.

Helpless, I floated over the icy river, gliding toward the heavy stone well, until I came to a stop right beside it.

30
LINE IN THE SAND

Capron Bay High School
Capron Bay,
6:45 A.M.

Lena weaved through the crowded gym, dodging between people as she fought to push forward. A cluster of FBI agents blocked her path, forcing her to veer left. She slipped past a group of medical personnel, leapt over a cot.

Whack!

Agent Byrd blindsided her.

His shoulder slammed into her mid-air, cutting her momentum short and sending her crashing to the gym floor.

She hit hard, her head bouncing off the polished hardwood with a sickening thud.

Pain exploded behind her eyes as the room spun. She struggled to get up, but her vision blurred, the world around her tilting as she fought to stay conscious.

"Where are you going, young lady?" he fumed, hauling her to her feet.

"Let her go!" Dakota growled, lunging forward to help his friend.

Before he could reach her, a second agent tackled him, slamming him to the ground. The man was bigger, stronger—Dakota struggled, but he couldn't break free.

Wham!

Out of nowhere, Franklin appeared, driving his fist into the agent's cheek. The agent's head snapped to the side from the impact, but he barely reacted. He didn't let Dakota go. He didn't even flinch at the hit from the smaller kid.

Before Franklin could strike again, a swarm of federal agents descended on them.

339

Hands grabbed at him.

Rachel fought to intervene, but she was seized too.

In seconds, they were all restrained.

"Let them all go!" Adam's wheelchair slammed into an agent's shins as he yelled.

"Taze him," Byrd ordered, and the agent drew a taser.

"*Ping!*"

The basketball pinged off his face, knocking the taser out of his hand. Mollie sprang for it immediately after throwing the basketball. Agent Liang grabbed her before she could get to the free taser.

"I want them all arrested!" Byrd declared, struggling to hold on to the raging Lena.

The entire gym fell silent as all eyes turned toward the commotion.

Parents, Capron Bay officers, and civilians froze, tension thick in the air. The officers instinctively reached for their sidearms, ready to draw again if necessary.

Around them, the crowd shifted, instinctively pulling back. Within moments, the gym was divided, officers on one side, federal agents and their captives on the other.

Another standoff had begun.

"Capron PD, stand down. Stand down now," ordered the new Mayor, Theresa Morgan.

"Please, gentlemen. Bloodshed is unnecessary!" Doc yelled, trying to calm everyone down preventing a gunfight.

Both sides waited impatiently for the other to act. Amid the standoff, Cardinal Murphy pushed his way through the crowd.

"Surely you can release the children, Agent Byrd?" he pleaded.

Senator Bradler stepped up beside the Cardinal, his expression firm as he addressed Agent Byrd.

"Surely, we can release the children," he agreed.

Byrd hesitated, glancing at his men, uncertainty flickering across his face.

Meanwhile, Lena thrashed against his grip, refusing to go down without a fight.

"Prentice is in deep trouble! This guy is lying!" she screamed as Byrd lifted her off the ground, stumbling backward toward the makeshift medical room.

"Stop struggling, kid," Byrd ordered, tightening his grip.

"You better not hurt her," Pam Sheridan snapped, her voice sharp with warning.

Byrd scoffed. "She's caused enough trouble already. *All* of them have. We're not letting any of them go." His tone hardened. "I want them all locked up."

A heavy silence settled over the gym.

"Liang, we're going to put them in…"

"Let. Her. Go."

The raspy command cut through the air, coming from directly behind Byrd.

Before he could react, a massive arm coiled around his throat, thick muscles flexing as they crushed his airway.

His instincts kicked in. He gasped, releasing Lena as his hands clawed at the vice-like grip around his neck.

But it was useless.

The hold was too strong.

Lena hit the ground hard, dazed, her vision swimming as she focused on Byrd's feet.

They were rising.

Her eyes followed upward, widening in shock as she realized what was happening, Byrd wasn't standing. He was being lifted.

Higher and higher, until—

Boom!

He was hurled through the air, crashing into a pile of chairs with a thunderous clatter.

An FBI agent reacted instantly, yanking out a taser and aiming it at the massive figure now standing before them. His finger tightened on the trigger.

Whack!

A long metal pole slammed down onto his wrist, sending the prongs firing harmlessly off target.

"I wouldn't do that if I were you," a second voice chuckled.

The agent whirled toward his attacker, scrambling to reset the taser. But before he could reel the prongs back in, something *huge* crashed into his chest.

A massive, hairy form drove him to the gym floor, pinning him down.

Saliva dripped onto his uniform as bared fangs gleamed inches from his face.

"Help!" the agent screamed as he turned away from the angry golden retriever.

"Do we have a problem here?" roared the bloody and bruised figure.

Detective Hog Sheridan stood tall, battered but unbroken, alongside Agent Shane Mason and Druss, all awake, all furious.

"Dad!" Lena cried, rushing forward and throwing her arms around him. It wasn't long before her mother joined, wrapping him in a fierce embrace.

"Arrest them!" Byrd shrieked, scrambling to his feet amidst the overturned chairs. "Arrest them now!"

Nearly two dozen FBI and deputized FEMA agents moved in, forming a tightening circle, ready to take them into custody.

Until half a dozen Capron Bay officers stepped forward, positioning themselves between the agents and their targets.

Tension crackled in the air.

"We outnumber them! I said arrest them!" Byrd barked, his face red with fury.

A ripple of movement cut through the crowd.

Chief Tackna and members of his Wampanoag Nation stepped forward, standing beside the officers.

Then came Doc Eddings.

Brother Kiernan.

Rachel's parents.

Fiona Thompson.

Anyika.

And finally, Cardinal Murphy.

Each one stepping into place, ready to fight.

"That's enough!" Lena's voice cut through the chaos, rising over the shouts and frantic orders.

342

She stepped forward, placing herself between the officers and her family. Within seconds, her friends moved to stand beside her.

"All of you should be ashamed for letting Prentice and Chief Pendleton go out there alone," she cried, her voice filled with raw emotion. "They're our friends!"

A ripple of unease spread through the room. People shifted their eyes, shuffled their feet, but no one spoke.

"They're the heart and soul of this town, and they need us. Prentice is giving himself up for you!"

The silence that followed was deafening.

Then...

"I said arrest them...NOW!" Byrd roared.

A quiet but firm voice spoke up behind him.

"Excuse me, sir."

Byrd spun around, face twisted in irritation. "What?"

Whack!

Grammy's right cross connected hard, snapping his head to the side. The larger federal agent crumpled to the ground, clutching his new bloody nose.

She knelt beside him, leaning in close, her voice so low only he could hear.

"If I hear another word from you," Grammy whispered, her voice sharp as steel, "I will use every ounce of my power to rip you apart. Do you understand?"

Byrd's breath hitched. His eyes flicked to hers—fiery red and glowing like embers. Slowly, he nodded.

A cold, satisfied smile crossed Grammy's face. "Good. I'm glad." She rose to her feet, turning toward Lena and the others.

She met Lena's gaze and gave her a small nod.

"Go ahead, sweetie," she encouraged with a warm smile.

Lena didn't back down. "Yes, there are demons and monsters out there," she said firmly, scanning the crowd. Her eyes landed on an elderly couple standing near the front, their hands intertwined.

"They've been there for us when we needed them most," she declared, her voice ringing through the gym.

343

A hesitant voice called out from the crowd. "Monsters are out there."

Murmurs of agreement rippled through the gathering before settling into uneasy silence.

"Yes. There are demons and monsters out there," Lena agreed, looking at everyone. Her eyes searched the crowd and settled on an old couple holding hands.

"Monsters are nothing new to you, Mr. and Mrs. Levinson, are they?" she asked the elderly couple.

The old couple exchanged a knowing glance, then looked down at their wrists—the faded numbers tattooed into their skin telling a story of horrors far worse than any demon.

Mrs. Levinson's eyes welled with tears, but she lifted her chin and looked to the crowd.

"She's right!" the older woman bellowed.

The room stirred.

"What do you want us to do?" a woman called out. "We have children!"

From the front, a fierce voice growled in response. "And mine are out there right now," Melissa Pendleton snapped.

"They chose to be out there," a man objected.

"Yes, they did!" Rachel shot back, joining Lena. "But they did it for you."

"They surrendered for all of us," Lena added, her voice shaking with emotion.

"And they will be returned to us once they have what they want," Mayor Morgan advised everyone.

Lena turned to her, fire in her eyes. "They're going to die!"

The mayor opened her mouth to argue, but before she could, a frail yet commanding voice cut through the noise.

"The young lady is right."

The crowd parted as a tiny, gray-haired woman stepped forward. Her movements were slow but deliberate, her presence impossible to ignore.

Jack, standing near the back on the bleachers, wiped a tear from his cheek and shook his head.

The old woman just smiled and nodded at him.

"Young Lena is right. They will die," she said again.

"I'm sorry, Ma'am. You are?" the new Mayor asked.

"My name is Angel," she said. "Angel Grace."

A ripple of recognition passed between Lena and her friends, but none of them spoke.

"How do you know they will die?" a man asked.

Angel exhaled deeply. "Because I've seen it before," she said softly. "I was young then, too young to do anything about it. But now I am old, and I have spent my life hiding, afraid of what lurks in the shadows. And now..." She looked down at her trembling hands. "Now, I fear I may not have the strength to stop it."

Lena stepped forward and gently took Angel's hand.

A woman in the crowd broke the silence. "Then what do we do?"

Lena didn't hesitate. "We stand together. We fight them."

The gym erupted into nervous laughter and murmurs of disbelief. Angry shouts followed.

Lena turned helplessly to Angel.

"I got this, dear," Angel whispered.

Lena stepped back as the old woman closed her eyes, bowing her head. She brought her hands to her chest, holding them close as a faint silver glow shimmered around her fragile frame.

The glow deepened, silver turning gold, then red, then shifting into a brilliant spectrum of swirling colors.

The crowd fell silent, instinctively stepping away.

Mayor Morgan retreated even farther, slipping behind a line of FBI agents.

The kaleidoscope of energy pulsed brighter, until it exploded.

A shockwave of misty, rainbow-colored energy surged outward, rushing through the entire crowd before vanishing into the gym walls.

A heavy silence followed.

Lena held her breath. What just happened?

"What was that?" she whispered to Angel.

The old woman simply raised a finger.

"Arghhhh," a man screamed to the right.

All eyes snapped toward him—an FBI agent clutching his head, collapsing to his knees in agony.

"Stop it!" someone shouted at Angel.

Then another FBI agent roared in pain, and then a third, and then a FEMA agent collapsed to his knees.

Lena turned to Angel, ready to plead for her to stop.

Until she saw it.

A dark, shadowy mass *oozing* out of the first agent's body, slithering over his skin before peeling away and dropping onto the gym floor.

The crowd recoiled in horror.

Another shadow wrenched free from a second agent.

Then another.

One by one, the dark entities were *forced out,* leaving behind pale, trembling agents in their wake.

The shadows pooled together, merging into a writhing, black mass—before suddenly shooting upward into the gym rafters and vanishing through a vent leading outside.

The room stood frozen.

"What just happened?" a woman cried out as the FBI and FEMA agents struggled to stand.

Brother Kiernan stepped forward. "These men and women were possessed—by the *Yukionna.* Winter demons that take control of a person's body and spirit, bending them to their will."

"Are you saying these men and woman were possessed?" someone asked in shock.

"They were," Angel nodded.

"And she just expelled them!" added Lena. "See, we can fight back."

Murmurs spread through the crowd, some hopeful, some still fearful.

"Folks!" she yelled.

The crowd quieted to listen to the young girl.

Rachel stepped up beside her, gripping her hand. "We're not all soldiers. We're not all trained police officers."

Dakota spoke next, nodding to the Levinsons. "But some of you are. Some of you fought in the jungles of Vietnam, the deserts of the Middle East… the concentration camps of Europe."

"I'm a lawyer," a man called out.

"And you fought your way through law school," Adam shot back. "Look at me, I can't even walk, and I'm still here, ready to fight."

"It's true, I watched that kid fall into the Marina to save his friends even though he can't use his legs," someone shouted.

"We've all been fighting our whole lives," Mollie added, her eyes shining with emotion. "And I, for one, have had enough."

Franklin stepped forward. "What are you willing to fight for? Your family? Your friends? Your town?"

"Wouldn't you fight for your family, Mrs. Porter?" Lena asked a woman standing in the front holding a baby.

"Of course," the woman replied.

"Wouldn't you, Mr. Jameson?" she asked the man beside her.

"You bet I would," he confirmed.

Lena's voice steadied. "Then why aren't we fighting for each other?"

The crowd stirred.

"This is our home," she declared. "We care for each other. We *protect* each other. And we will fight for each other!"

The gym erupted.

"LET'S GO!" someone roared.

"THIS IS CAPRON BAY!" Franklin shouted, his voice booming through the gym.

He turned to Dakota with a wide grin. "I've always wanted to say that."

Dakota sighed, shaking his head. "Of course you have, Leonidas."

Lena raised her hands, silencing the chaos.

Then she turned, walked to the center of the gym, and pointed to the floor.

"Those willing to fight—step forward."

For a moment, no one moved.

Then…

Mrs. Levinson stepped over the line.

347

"We don't need a line," the old woman declared. "Because we're all in this fight together!"

The gym erupted as the people of Capron Bay rose as one.

Shouts of "We're with you, Lena!" erupted from every corner of the gym.

"Let's go!" chants broke out, voices rising in unison.

Lena glanced at her friends, then at her parents.

Hog gave her a proud nod. "You lead them out, kiddo."

A fire lit in her chest as she turned toward the crowd.

"LET'S GO!" she roared, sprinting toward the rear doors.

The people of Capron Bay surged after her, a roaring, unstoppable force. Some ran, some walked, some even rolled forward in wheelchairs, but all of them charged into the night with unwavering determination.

As Lena burst through the doors into the back parking lot, her citizen army poured out behind her.

Leaving the gym completely empty.

Even Theresa Morgan and the once-possessed federal agents followed, swept up in the march toward battle.

31
THE END OF THE RAINBOW

The Void
6:55 A.M.

Panic clawed at my chest as fear consumed me.

I struggled against the invisible chains constricting my body, muscles straining, but the grip was unrelenting—I *couldn't* break free.

My eyes darted to Dad. He was still down, motionless.

Then, I looked past him.

Beyond us, in the distance, the army of darkness loomed vast, unholy force waiting at the edge of my world, ready to break through.

"What have I done?" I whispered to myself.

"You have made an honorable decision, Prentice," Chernobog gloated.

I locked eyes with him, fury igniting in my chest as I fought to summon the strength to break free.

"You can stop trying. You won't be able to break free. Once you willingly crossed into the void between worlds, you became powerless. You can do nothing here," he chuckled.

"You gave me your word," I grunted.

"I did, and I shall keep it," he said, his voice calm yet unwavering. "I will not harm the good people of Capron Bay, and I will release your sister."

He extended a hand, gesturing toward the side of the tent.

I hadn't noticed her before, but now my eyes locked onto Carolyn.

She was bound and gagged, trapped inside a small cage beside the tent. Her wide, fearful eyes met mine, silently pleading.

Rage ignited deep within me, a flicker of power sparking to life.

But just as quickly, it faded.

349

I clenched my fists. "Let her go," I demanded.

"I will. I gave you, my word. As soon as the ceremony is complete, she will be allowed to return," he assured me.

"And Dad? " I asked.

"He is fine. He will take her back," he smiled.

"And your army of demons?" I asked, my voice sharp. "What are they going to do?"

He chuckled, a cruel glint in his eyes. "Well, they're going to destroy the world, of course."

My fists tightened. "You said the town would be unharmed!" I snarled.

"And it will be," he snickered. "My forces will leave Capron Bay untouched. The people can go on with their lives."

I glared at him. "In a dead world?"

His smirk widened. "Well, we never agreed not to destroy the world, did we?"

Fury erupted inside me.

"I'm going to stop you!" I roared.

A lightning bolt tore from his hand, striking me in the shoulder. White-hot agony seared through my body, but I refused to scream. I clenched my teeth, forcing the pain down, burying it deep.

"Time is ticking, Rainbow Warrior," he sneered, drifting toward me. "Let's begin."

With a flick of his wrist, an invisible force yanked me into the air and hurled me over the well.

I braced for the plunge, expecting to sink into its dark depths—

But instead, my feet landed on solid ground just three feet below.

It wasn't a well at all.

It was a fountain.

Chernobog laughed.

"Did you think you would drown in the deep darkness of a well?"

I looked at him.

"Well, not exactly. You see what I did there?" he laughed. "Well?"

I didn't laugh.

"Oh, come on. Where is your sense of humor?" he asked.

I stared at him.

A thunderous crash erupted from behind the school, shaking the air.

I snapped my head toward the sound.

The thick barrier pulsed with a fiery red glow, but beyond it, I could see.

A grin spread across my face as Lena emerged at the front of a surging wave of Capron Bay's people, charging toward the barrier. Their battle cries and war screams filled the night, a deafening declaration that they were ready to fight

He twisted his face into an exaggerated, mocking expression, flailing his hands dramatically as if imitating a panicked crowd.

"Looks like the cavalry has arrived," he sneered, his voice dripping with sarcasm.

"They're ready to fight you," I hissed.

"You do realize, if they decide to fight, the deal is off, right?"

I glanced at him and then at Lena and her army. They stopped at the barrier, trying to figure out how to get around it.

"Wait, what?" I stammered.

"Yes, you heard me correct. If they fight, there is no deal. They will be destroyed just like the rest of the world."

"You can't," I said.

"It's not up to me," he shrugged.

I glanced back at my friends. Panic setting in.

"Let's get on with this," his patience growing thin.

I dropped barely hovering just above the fountain's water. My vision swam, and a relentless pounding tore through my skull like a jackhammer drilling straight into my brain.

"Arghhh," I groaned, clutching my head, desperate to clear the fog creeping in.

The unseen force constricting me shifted, slithering toward the back of my head.

It felt like a massive, invisible hand had clamped down, locking me in place.

I tried to turn my head, but I couldn't.

351

The unseen hand slammed my head into the water, forcing me under. I thrashed, struggling to break free, but its grip was unrelenting. It shook me violently, twisting and churning, forcing the air from my lungs as bubbles erupted around me, distorting the water. Just as my chest burned with the desperate need for oxygen, the hand yanked me back to the surface.

I gasped, dragging deep, ragged breaths.

And that's when I saw it.

The water beneath me was glowing, shifting through faint, rapidly changing colors.

"The fountain is draining your energy and power," the God of Winter chuckled, stepping into the fountain. "And I will absorb it all."

I stole a quick glance at Dad. He was still down, unmoving. A flicker of movement at the barrier caught my eye. My friends were there, frantically searching for a way through. Mom reached up, trying to climb the thorny vines—

Zap!

The red energy surged, jolting her backward. She stumbled, collapsing into Doc's arms.

"You..." I started, but before I could finish, the invisible force *slammed* me back into the water. More air burst from my lungs as I fought to twist and break free, but I couldn't move.

I felt it now, the energy being ripped from me.

The water pulsed brighter, swirling with an unnatural glow.

I was held under for what felt like an eternity.

My lungs burned, screaming for air.

The invisible force yanked me from the water again, and I gasped desperately, sucking in as much air as my burning lungs could manage.

I tried to fight back, to break free. But I was weaker now. I felt it. My strength was fading. My power was draining away.

Chernobog glowed.

The water from the fountain coiled up his body, pulsing like a living thing, feeding him and making him stronger.

He grinned. "It is an honorable death, Prentice," he chuckled darkly. "You sacrificed yourself to save your friends. They will sing songs of you."

He threw his head back and laughed.

The invisible hand slammed me back into the glowing water. I barely had the strength to resist. My body was too weak, too drained. The last bit of air rushed from my lungs even faster this time, but I clenched my jaw shut, refusing to inhale. I darted my eyes around, searching desperately for a way out.

But there was nothing.

Just cold stone beneath me and the pulsing, glowing water swallowing me whole.

Then...

Lena.

She appeared in my mind, standing beside me at the pond behind our house.

It was the first time I had met her, the moment everything had changed. The first time I saw the colors. I remember looking at her long black hair, her striking crystal-green eyes.

And how the world had shifted.

Everything turned green, wrapping me in its warmth. It was calming. Peaceful. Thrilling.

She reminded me of Spring.

In an instant, I was ripped back up, my body heaving for breath, my lungs burning.

Chernobog's voice slithered through the air.

"Why do you still fight, Prentice?" he mused. "Let go. Join your Poppa."

I barely had a second to react before I was shoved back under.

My body screamed for air.

I was out of time.

Why didn't he just keep me under? Why not hold me there until it was over?

He could.

Maybe I should just...let go.

A memory surfaced.

"C'mon, buddy, let it go. Let Uncle Dak hold you tight."

I heard Dakota's voice, saw him wrapping Cal in a tight hug, comforting him through his tears—until, finally, Cal laughed. It was the night he told us about the Boo Hags.

353

I could feel it, the warmth of that moment, the laughter, the unbreakable bond of friendship back at the clubhouse.

But I couldn't let go.

I wouldn't.

Chernobog yanked me back up.

I gasped, dragging in ragged breaths as my vision swam.

Through the haze, I saw him pulsing with energy, glowing brighter, stronger. And beyond him.

The distant roar of his army.

He followed my gaze and smirked.

"You hear them?" he sneered. "Pretty soon, they'll be in *your* world, ravaging everything in their path."

Then, with a wicked laugh—

He slammed me back into the water.

I was drowning.

Why haven't I drowned yet?

He could have finished it by now. He should have finished it by now.

I was missing something.

The invisible hand shoved me deeper. My lungs burned, barely holding on.

The water pulsed, glowing brighter as its energy funneled into him, strengthening him as he stood in the fountain.

Then...I saw it.

A small symbol, etched into the stone at his feet.

Something familiar.

I knew it. But from where?

Before I could grasp the memory, I was yanked back up, gasping desperately for air.

"See how the energy flows over me?" Chernobog declared, his voice brimming with power. "It feels... unstoppable!"

He stepped toward me, and suddenly, the invisible force vanished—

Replaced by his iron grip.

Before I could react, he slammed me back into the water.

I struggled, forcing my mind to focus.

The symbol. I had seen it before.

Why am I still alive?

The thought clawed at me. He could have drowned me by now. He should have.

Then it hit me—

I had felt this before. Back in the underground chamber of Gruber Chemical. They could have killed me there too. The chamber.

I had been unconscious, trapped. But there was something on the ceiling, a ward. A protective symbol. The same one engraved at the bottom of the fountain.

My vision blurred. My lungs screamed, ready to give up.

Then his grip tightened.

I was dragged back up, gasping desperately for air.

"Why... not... kill... me?" I choked out.

Chernobog tilted his head, studying me for a moment, then grinned.

"Because I want to savor this," he laughed, his body pulsing as my stolen energy crawled over him. "I want to drag it out as long as I can. Don't worry—your time is nearly over."

He shoved me under again.

This time, his strength had grown.

He drove my head deeper, forcing my entire body to sink farther into the fountain's glowing abyss.

And that's when I heard them.

"We love you, Prentice."

The voices came all at once—

Mom. Dad. Carolyn.

"We love you, Crayon Man," Franklin's voice stammered through the darkness.

I was sure this was it. The end.

"Poppa?" I whispered, hoping for an answer—

But none came.

Chernobog shoved me deeper.

I was near his feet when something caught my eye—

They weren't glowing as strongly as the rest of him.

I heard a voice.

"Feel the energy of the dolphins through the water. Absorb it, Prentice."

Jon Kane.

The glow must grow, but that glow must come from sacrifice.

The memory rushed in, Jon and I standing at the edge of the Caribbean, the ocean stretching wide and calm before us.

"The darkness will try to dim your light," his voice echoed. "It will squeeze the life out of you. But you have a gift. Embrace it. Cherish it. Only *you* can supply the conditions to breathe life into your soul."

The words rang as clearly now as they had that night.

"When your body, mind, and soul become one, you will achieve the final level. And when that moment comes, your glow will be a true rainbow of life. In that moment, Prentice, your glow can change everything."

I shot upward, empty gasps.

And now, Chernobog wasn't just glowing.

He was radiating.

Brighter. Stronger. Like he was about to explode.

His eyes burned with triumph.

"Look, Prentice!" he roared. "Look! The barrier between worlds is breaking! The time is upon us! I will finally claim this world, all because you gave it freely to me!"

A violent gust of wind struck me like a hammer.

"Goodbye, Rainbow Warrior," he sneered.

And slammed my head back into the water.

Poppa's voice echoed.

"The big guy and I will be in it when the wind hits you. Until then, remember everything you've been taught. Your power comes from your desire to help others—what you give freely can return to you."

I smiled, holding onto his words.

"Prentice."

Lena's voice echoed in my mind, soft yet heavy with sorrow.

"You can go. You don't have to fight anymore. I'll make sure everyone knows of your sacrifice."

"Are you sure this is what you want, honey?" *Mom's smooth voice whispered, warm and familiar.*

A sudden realization hit me—my lungs were empty.

No.

"No!" I screamed—and let go.

I opened my mouth, welcoming the flood.

Water rushed into my throat, my lungs, my entire body.

Darkness crawled over me.

My muscles failed.

My body collapsed in his grasp and dropping further into the well. My nose brushed the symbol at the bottom and the line broke.

Chernobog let out a triumphant roar.

"Come forth, army of the Dark!" he bellowed, yanking me from the water. He lifted my head, eyes burning with victory.

Then he froze.

I smiled.

His expression twisted in rage. "Impossible!" he snarled.

And shoved me back under.

But this time…

I didn't move.

"Arghhhh!" He shoved with all his strength.

I didn't budge.

Water dripped from my face as I stood firm, unmoving.

Then, in a single motion, I *lashed out*—my left hand *gripping his hair*—and *slammed* him into the water.

Chernobog barely had time to react. His body *crashed* into the glowing pool, his struggles useless against the sheer force of my attack.

And I had to admit.

It was so satisfying to dunk the so-called Dark God.

"I take it all back," I shouted, my voice vibrating with power. "I'm taking back everything you stole from me!"

As he thrashed beneath my grip, I felt it. The energy. The raw power.

It surged into me, rushing through my veins. It was mine again.

But he was strong.

With a furious growl, he forced himself up, ripping free from my hold and throwing my hand aside.

I stumbled back, but I didn't fall.

Chernobog roared in pure fury.

A blood-red glow spiraled up his body, pulsing with rage and dark energy.

He struck, fast, vicious.

But not fast enough.

I caught his attack midair.

His raw power crashing against my glowing golden hand.

"My turn," I said with a grin.

I clenched my fingers tighter around his fist—bone and tendon *crushed* together with a sickening *crack*.

Chernobog howled in agony, his ancient body betraying him as he collapsed to one knee.

The people of Capron Bay erupted with cheers, their voices booming across the battlefield as I held him there—his trembling fist locked in my glowing grip, radiating every color imaginable.

Then—

A sound like hell itself breaking loose.

I looked past him, my stomach dropping as an ear-splitting chorus of howls and screams filled the air.

The army of darkness had breached the gate.

And they were pouring into our world.

A sea of nightmares—monstrous demons clad in full armor, wielding weapons straight from the depths of some unspeakable horror.

Chernobog gritted his teeth, a cruel grin flickering through his pain.

"You're too late," he rasped, forcing a chuckle through the agony. "My army is coming, and there is nothing you can do to stop it."

A piercing screech ripped through the early morning sky behind me.

I spun around just in time to see the glowing red barrier of thorns shrink, slithering back into the earth—clearing the way.

For reinforcements.

I turned back to him, my expression set. "I got an army of my own."

Chernobog followed my gaze, his smirk widening as he saw Lena leading the people of Capron Bay straight toward us.

358

"I have too many soldiers, Prentice," he sneered, nodding toward the charging townspeople. "Your army isn't big enough. They will all die."

And I knew…he was right.

Some of Capron Bay's forces were armed law enforcement officers, but most were just regular people, mothers, fathers, shop owners, teachers, clutching whatever they could as weapons.

The wind exploded from nowhere.

The trees shook like a tornado was ripping through them.

The frozen river lurched, waves slamming against the jagged rocks.

Chernobog's massive tent ripped free of its stakes and hurtled into the sky, lost in the swirling chaos as the storm rattled the earth itself.

I didn't hesitate.

I slammed both hands into his chest, sending him tumbling out of the fountain.

Before he could scramble to his feet, I was already moving.

I leapt over the edge of the fountain and sprinted toward Carolyn.

Her terrified eyes locked onto mine. "PJ!" she cried. "Get me out of here!"

I grabbed the lock, yanking hard.

It didn't budge.

I turned my head.

The horde was closing in fast.

I could have blasted the cage open, but it was too small.

I couldn't risk hurting my sister.

"Prentice!"

I heard my name and turned, Dad was struggling to his knee, wobbling but determined.

"Move!" he shouted, raising his firearm and aiming at the lock.

Bang!

The shot sizzled past me, striking the metal with a sharp crack as the lock split in two.

"What a shot," I murmured, ripping the shattered lock free and swinging the cage door open.

I scooped Carolyn into my arms and turned—

"Wait!" she cried.

"What?"

"She needs help."

I followed her gaze.

A small figure huddled at the back of the cage, wrapped in a thin blanket. She had been hidden in the shadows—I hadn't even seen her before.

I knelt beside Carolyn. "Can you stand?"

She nodded.

Gently, I set her down and stepped inside the cage.

"I can get you out of here," I whispered.

The girl—frail, with long blonde hair and piercing ice-blue eyes—stared at me warily.

"You're Jack's sister, aren't you?" I asked.

Her eyes widened slightly before she gave a cautious nod.

I softened my voice. "I can take you to him. You don't have to be afraid anymore. You can finally be free of Chernobog."

Carolyn placed a reassuring hand on her arm. "He's telling the truth. This is my brother, Prentice."

The girl hesitated, then reached out.

I gently took her hand and eased her out of the cage. She was small, so fragile—

"Can you run?" I asked.

She nodded.

"Then let's go."

I grabbed her hand, and we took off, racing toward the school.

The storm raged around us—wind howling, trees bending, icy water spraying violently against the rocks.

"It doesn't matter where you run, Prentice!"

Chernobog's voice thundered behind us.

"We're coming! We're coming!"

I tried to block him out, but it was impossible.

Above us, the sky screeched—dark figures swooped through the swirling clouds, monstrous flying demons circling like vultures.

Why aren't they attacking yet?

We reached the river's edge, where Dad met us, his eyes scanning me for injuries.

"You, okay?"

I was bloody, bruised, and exhausted—

But I nodded. "I'm good, Dad."

He gave me a look. "What happened to giving up your powers?" he asked, scooping Carolyn into his arms.

I hesitated. "Well… you know… I was kind of wrong about that."

Dad smirked. "Kind of?"

I groaned. "If this is where you say 'I told you so'"

"Of course not." He paused. "But I did tell you so."

"I know," I sighed, forcing a smile as I glanced around, trying to figure out how to cross the river.

Across the water, Lena stood at the head of the Capron Bay battalion.

They had reached the river's edge—only to be stopped cold as a thick fog rolled in, creeping from the tree line and slithering along the rocky banks.

I smiled at her—

But she didn't smile back.

Her expression was hard—anger and disappointment burning in her glare.

Dad chuckled. "You'll have to deal with that later."

I sighed. "I think I'd rather deal with the army of demons charging at us."

Dad gave a low whistle as the ground shook beneath us. "You sure? There's a lot of them."

I jerked my chin toward Lena. "Do you see the look she's giving me?"

Dad followed my gaze—

Then winced. "Yep. You're in trouble."

"Thanks for the support."

I turned to him. "Can you get Carolyn across?"

361

He was already wading into the churning water, holding her close. The current fought him, but he pushed through.

I turned to Jack's sister. "You ready?"

Before she could answer, I felt a presence beside me. "Jack!"

The girl cried out and threw herself into her brother's arms.

Jack lifted her, holding her so tightly it was like he never wanted to let go.

His voice broke. "Why did you save her?"

I didn't answer. I didn't have to.

"Thank You," he whispered and leapt into the air with his sister in his arms and disappeared into the thickening fog that threatened to cover the soon-to-be battlefield. The wind grew heavier as the Dark God's army closed on me.

I surveyed the terrain, deciding whether to stay on this side of the river or go stand with Lena and my friends. Part of me wanted to take on the demon horde on this site to keep them away from the people I cared about.

"Prentice!" Lena's voice cut through the chaos. "Come on!"

I hesitated, wanting to keep them safe—*out* of this fight—but I knew that was impossible.

The creatures charging us were *too many*. My power alone wouldn't be enough. I waded into the river, pushing through the icy current toward the Capron Bay side.

The enemy was close now.

Their monstrous cries and wild whoops echoed through the night, the sound scraping against my nerves like nails on a chalkboard. It wasn't just noise, it was primal, something wrong at its core.

If evil had a sound, this was it.

I reached the other side, stepping onto solid ground.

"Welcome back, Crayon Man," Franklin laughed, flashing a grin.

"Hey, guys," I said, glancing at my friends.

I opened my mouth, ready to apologize, but Chernobog's voice boomed across the battlefield.

"People of Capron Bay!"

Every eye turned toward him.

He stood tall in his true demon form, massive wings raised high, his fanged mouth dripping with saliva, his glowing eyes filled with pure hate.

"This is your last chance to leave the battlefield," he declared. "Walk away now, and I will let you return to your homes. You will live long, happy lives, free from harm."

Not a single person moved.

The ground shook as his army reached the water's edge.

His voice turned cold.

"Leave now," he repeated, his eyes locking onto mine.

I felt the tension building behind me, the silent determination of every person standing ready to fight.

Lena's voice was barely a whisper beside me. "We're all with you, Prentice."

Chernobog's gaze didn't waver.

"Rainbow Warrior," he sneered. "When the horde tears through your friends, your family, your neighbors, when they feast on their flesh, remember this."

His voice was silk, laced with poison.

"Their blood will be on your hands."

The words hit me. Hard.

He was right.

No matter how this ended.

Blood would stain my hands.

I was about to step forward but stopped.

"We'll make our own choices," a voice called out.

I turned.

Through the crowd, Grace pushed her way forward, her frail body standing defiantly at the front of the line.

A tiny old woman, facing down the Dark God and his army of demons.

"What's the matter?" Franklin smirked. "Dog got your tongue?"

I heard Mollie whisper to him. "Its cat got your tongue."

"What cat?" Franklin frowned.

Dakota sighed. "No, it's cat got your tongue. That's the saying."

"That's ridiculous. Who's afraid of a cat?"

As if on cue, a massive winter cat demon emerged beside Chernobog, its glowing blue eyes locking onto Franklin.

His face went pale.

"Uhm… my bad!" Franklin stammered. "That cat will definitely get your… uh… tongue. Probably… eat it too. Actually, it might just eat…your whole body."

"Stop," Mollie chided.

"Right. Yep. I'm… shutting up now."

I nodded at Grace as she came to stand beside me.

She smiled. "I've lived long enough."

Chernobog's army reached his side, their inhuman forms howling and screeching across the river.

"Take a look at what awaits you!" the Winter Lord bellowed. "Even with two Rainbow Warriors, you don't have a chance!"

"Don't forget the Winter Fairy!" Jack's voice rang out.

He stepped forward, standing beside Grace.

Chernobog's wings flared wide.

"FROST!" he roared. "This is even better! I get to destroy all of you at once!"

Jack glanced at me. "There's… a lot of them."

"Yep," I said, not looking at the enemy.

The wind howled, roaring through the valley like a train barreling down the tracks. The fog thickened, curling over the river's surface, crawling up the banks.

Everyone stepped back, wary thinking it was an attack.

But I glanced at Chernobog.

And he looked just as shocked as we were.

"Prentice, what is this?" Rachel asked.

"I…don't know."

The wind exploded.

Fog surged in every direction.

Thunder cracked, shaking the ground.

Lightning ripped through the sky, illuminating the battlefield in stark white light.

I turned my head, looking at the legions behind Chernobog.

It was going to be a slaughter.

The demons felt it too. Their war cries rose, the bloodlust building.

Then…

The fog ignited.

A blinding golden light erupted from its depths, twisting into a funnel of swirling energy. For a moment, I thought it was a tornado about to tear us apart. But the wind stopped. The fog exploded into brilliant white light.

And a figure stepped through.

I knew that silhouette.

I smiled.

"PJ."

The voice was warm. Familiar.

The figure winked.

"Poppa."

Then, another figure stepped forward.

A giant of a man, dressed in full Revolutionary War attire.

The Mountain had returned.

And behind them…

An army poured from the light.

Warriors spread out, taking position beside the people of Capron Bay.

Dozens of Inuit villagers, wrapped in ancient fur garments, rushed to Grace's. Tears filled her eyes as she recognized them, her village. The ones who had been slaughtered a century ago. They had returned for revenge.

A lone figure approached my dad.

Sgt. Jason Donegan.

Dad straightened.

The men and women of Capron Bay PD snapped to attention…and saluted.

Another man emerged, scanning the battle lines. I didn't recognize him.

But Mollie did.

"Daddy!"

She ran to him, and he caught her in a fierce hug.

Fiona joined them, weeping.

"Dude," Franklin whispered. "This is exactly like the scene from Avengers."

I turned to Poppa, my voice barely above a whisper.

"How is this possible?"

Poppa smirked. "When knucklehead over there opened the door for his dead army to come through,"

"All of the dead could come through," Adam finished.

Poppa grinned. "You always were the smart one, Adam."

I turned to Chernobog.

There was a glint of fear in his eyes.

Franklin grinned.

"LET'S GET READY TO RUUUUMMMMMBBBLLLLLEEEE!"

Chernobog's expression twisted into rage.

"CHARGE!" he roared.

And the battle began.

33
THE CAPRON BAY WAR

Bam, bam, bam!

Chernobog raised his arm in a grand, arrogant gesture, commanding his army to charge. For a moment, they hesitated, unsure where to strike first.

Perfect.

I no longer needed to build energy. No more struggling to contain it. For the first time, I had complete control. Power surged through every inch of me, my blazing rockets swirling with the full force of the rainbow's energy.

The dark God never saw it coming.

A supersonic kaleidoscope of pure energy streaked across the river, slamming into his exposed chest with unstoppable force.

He was launched backward, the impact sending him hurtling through the air. His massive tent collapsed beneath him, swallowing him in its tangled canopy. For a heartbeat, silence fell.

My instincts told me otherwise. The Dark God wasn't dead. Sadly, we wouldn't be so lucky, but the suddenness of his fall shocked his troops enough that Lena and her army had an opening. The sight of their leader seemingly destroyed in the first seconds of battle sent a ripple of hesitation through his army.

But my instincts screamed the truth.

Chernobog wasn't dead.

We wouldn't be that **lucky**.

Still, his sudden downfall was enough to stun his troops, giving Lena and her army the opening they needed. And largest man out there, led the charge.

The Mountain let out a bone-rattling war cry and charged straight into the heart of the undead horde. At the sheer sight of him, his towering frame, his wild eyes, the front lines of demons staggered, uncertainty rippling through their ranks. Their commanders glanced at each other, unsure of what to do. And they paid dearly for it.

367

The Mountain plunged into the mass of monsters, swinging his ancient musket like a war hammer. Demons flew in every direction, their helmets cracking, armor crumpling under each devastating blow.

Meanwhile, Grace raised her hands beside me, and unleashed chaos. Waves of rainbow energy flowed from her fingertips in swirling, hypnotic arcs. Her hands moved with stunning speed, faster than Mr. Miyagi could say "wax on, wax off." Every beam of light that burst from her fingers vaporized the undead on contact. Demons crumbled into ash under the brilliance of her power.

The Inuit warriors surged around her. Fierce fishermen and hunters, long denied their vengeance, now roared into battle with a century's worth of fury. Their spears, axes, and pikes tore through the enemy, forcing the demons back, clearing space for Grace to keep firing her radiant magic, leveling wave after wave of the dead.

Shrieking demon cries yanked my attention to another fierce skirmish. There, charging headfirst through the chaos, was a mountain of a man, fists swinging like wrecking balls. Detective Hog Sheridan plowed through anything in his path.
Savage beasts lunged with weapons, but every time they got close, his mighty fists smashed their snarling faces into *oblivion.*

Beside him, the smaller but equally relentless Agent Shane Mason fought with cold precision. A jagged scar ran down his cheek, his expression unreadable as he unleashed arcs of yellow lightning from one hand, frying demons mid-charge. With the other hand, he fired his sidearm. Every bullet perfectly placed, dropping enemy after enemy with surgical accuracy.

A deafening roar from above.

I looked up just as a flaming, dragon-like monster *dove toward me.* Its massive, taloned feet slammed into me before I could react. The claws missed skewering me, barely, but they still snatched me up, flinging me through the air like a rag doll.

The beast ascended rapidly, dragging me into the sky in its crushing grip. I strained, pushing against its thick, burning talons, but they wouldn't budge. It squeezed harder, like it was trying to crack me open.

Breathing became harder.

But so did my resolve.

The pain wasn't breaking me, it was fueling my rage.

BAM, BAM, BAM!

Fiery bolts of energy *exploded* from my hands, searing through the monster's flesh. It shrieked in agony, its grip loosening.

And I was free.

I tumbled through the sky, twisting wildly. Instinct kicked in and I straightened out, arms at my sides, soaring like Iron Man except, I didn't have rockets.

And nothing was stopping me from plummeting straight for the ground.

WHOOSH!

A gust of wind rushed past me.

"Need a lift?" Jack smirked, gripping my arm and guiding me downward.

I exhaled. "Thanks."

Jack shrugged. "No, thank you, Prentice, for getting my sister."

"You can thank me when this is over," I told him.

He gave a nod, then shot back into the sky.

A bloodcurdling roar cut through the battlefield.

I turned.

And froze.

Brother Kiernan stood alone, facing off against a towering ice-blue monster. No armor covered its massive body, so I could *see* the muscles rippling beneath its glowing skin, surging with raw power.

A terrifying double-headed axe crackled in its grip, sparking with streaks of electric energy. The battlefield paused.

Even the raging armies fell silent as the two warriors circled each other—testing, measuring. The Priest unsheathed his sword, mirroring the demon's movements, his feet gliding smoothly across the ground.

He waited.

The beast struck first. With a whoosh of air, the axe whirled toward Thomas's skull. A perfect, unstoppable kill shot. But Thomas side-stepped at the last second.

Smooth, controlled, and deadly.

369

The blade barely missed his face, its icy edge skimming past his cheek. The glowing demon skidded past him. And stopped. It didn't turn. It didn't move.

Thomas straightened, his sword gleaming as he flicked it to the side.

CLANG!

The demon's double-headed axe hit the ground, along with its severed arm. The cut had been fast. No one had even seen it happen. The beast turned, roaring in rage and charging blindly.

But Thomas didn't flinch. At the last second, he dropped to one knee. Blade flashing.

The crowd held its breath.

A moment later, the demon collapsed.

Its upper half slid cleanly off its legs, bisected in a single strike.

For a moment there was silence, then the army roared in fury, surging back into battle.

Thomas's sword became a whirlwind, carving through enemies like they were made of air. I spun around as bolts of red energy slashed through the battlefield, striking down black-clad warriors barreling toward my friends.

Grammy.

She fired relentlessly, taking down foe after foe, her hands glowing with power.

Beyond her, I caught a strange sight. A huddled group of Chernobog's warriors, swinging their weapons wildly at nothing.

At least I thought it was nothing but then, a demon lifted into the air and slammed into the ground with a bone-shattering crunch.

I smirked.

Mollie. The invisible warrior who was systematically wrecking them one by one.

Behind me, a voice rose. "Strike one!" Franklin's voice rang out.

I turned just in time to see him wind up and launch a thick rock straight into the nose of a charging monster. The creature crumpled instantly, out cold.

"Strike two!" he called.

I shook my head.

How was he so accurate in battle, but completely useless when pitching at actual baseball games?

A loud grunt snapped my attention elsewhere. Lena dropped to one knee, swinging a baseball bat hard into a beast's shins. The creature toppled, bellowing in pain. Before it could rise, Rachel and Dakota dropped a massive boulder onto its head. The crunch of metal and bone was sickening.

I winced. "Oof. That had to hurt."

"Prentice! Above you!"

I whipped around and saw two more winged, ancient dragon-dinosaurs zeroing in. I spun my hands in tight circles, energy crackling as I built a rainbow-filled cannonball between my palms.

A humming sound buzzed through the air as a tiny plane zipped between the monsters. Their eyes following the small plane, instead of their target. It was a brief moment, but it was enough to cause them to slam into each other. Their heads collided with such force that they were knocked unconscious and fell to the ground, exploding into a mess of wings and limbs.

"Yes!" Adam shouted as he worked the joystick on his chair, and his small drone attacked another flying demon.

I searched the battlefield for Doc and found him and Chief Tackna standing in front of Mom, Mrs. Sheridan, Ms. Fiona, and Ms. Annie, who were tending to wounded Capron Bay warriors. The Chief's men were wading into the demon army around them, keeping them away from the makeshift medical center.

My sister's cries drew my gaze to the river. She and Dad were surrounded by three demon hounds. Dad tried to put himself between the four-legged monsters and Carolyn, but she kept stepping to his side, holding a thick branch out front of her and ready to defend herself.

One of the creatures roared and lunged at its prey. The horrifying demon hound never reached the target. Druss appeared from nowhere, soaring through the air, slamming into the beast, and driving it to the ground, where he latched onto the neck, shaking his head wildly from side to side. The demon hound howled in pain and fear as my dog showed the pack, who

371

was the Alpha. He let go of the beast, and it limped away into the woods. The remaining two hounds whined, bowed to the raging retriever, and followed their friend into the woods, leaving the battle behind.

The sounds of battle filled the air in every direction as the Capron Bay defenders seemed to be winning the day. Every day citizens fought side by side, joined by Capron Bay police officers, FBI, and FEMA agents who were now free of possession. So far, humans seem to be holding their own against the army of darkness.

Howls and cries in the distance chilled me to the bone. Reinforcements for the demons would soon be joining the fighting while the brave Capron Bay battalion had none. I scanned the whole area, looking for something, anything to defend against the relentless onslaught of the dead.

"P.J.?" the voice said behind me.

I turned to see Poppa standing there. I hugged him.

They keep coming, Poppa," I panted, looking at the many reinforcements charging down the hill.

"So, what are you going to do?" he asked me.

I shook my head, not knowing the answer.

"Pendleton!" the voice raged above the sounds of battle.

Spinning around, I saw Chernobog stepping from the tent that had collapsed around him. He was angry. No, furious.

"He's mad," Poppa hinted.

"You think?" I chuckled.

As we watched him, his human form faded, and he began to grow. I could hear his body stretching as the bone hardened and the muscles and tendons expanded and bulged. His feet morphed into freakishly long and large claws. Ankles and calves contorted into odd-angled joints to support heavy knees and massive thighs rippling with red sparks of energy running along bulging muscles.

I realized the red energy wasn't running along the muscles. It was pulsing beneath the growing quadriceps muscle. I could see the energy throbbing under his entire body as it grew larger and larger until he stood twelve feet tall.

Two massive horns stretched from a bony skull. The horns were thick at the base of the head and grew longer, twisting

372

and rounding into two sharp, thin hooks that looked like a beetle's pinchers. His face changed to a charcoal grey color with hardened cheekbones and pointed ears. Glowing red eyes radiated with hatred and anger.

"I didn't think you could get any uglier," I smirked.

I heard Poppa sigh behind me at my sarcasm.

Chernobog, or whatever he'd become, said nothing, but his fiery gaze revealed his pure hatred for me. Before I could react, two powerful beams of energy shot from his eyes.

The speed caught me off guard—

I barely had time to move before they slammed into the ground at my feet.

The force knocked me off balance, sending us sprawling.

Poppa rolled to his feet just as another blast tore through the air—

BOOM!

The explosion missed his head by inches, the shockwave hurling him down an embankment.

I twisted, firing golden orbs of light at the devilish monster. But he barely flinched. He swatted them away like flies.

I scrambled to my feet just in time to dodge another red-hot energy blast.

The ground erupted beside me, dirt and grass spraying in all directions. I dove behind a boulder, heart pounding, as the next blast roared past.

"Pendleton!" he bellowed, and the boulder shattered from another round of energy. I fell backward, rolling away from his path as he stalked toward me. I stood, trying to get more cover.

BAM!

The energy blasted me in the back, launching me into the air. I struck a massive oak tree so hard I thought I shattered every bone.

"Ughh," I groaned, fighting to stand.

My friends screamed for me, but it sounded so far away.

A massive hand hauled me off the ground. The thick claws squeezed tighter as I rose to face the giant demon's eyes.

"I should eat you," he roared.

"I hope you choke on me," I gurgled.

Crack!

373

A rock pinged off his head.

Crack!

Another.

I twisted my head and saw Lena, Rachel, and Dakota throwing rocks at the Dark God. Their aim was good. The stones cracked off his head, but they only made him angry. His eyes fired at them. The ground exploded in a cloud of smoke, dirt, and rocks. When it cleared, I couldn't see any of them.

"What did," I began to cry out. He turned and threw me across the glade, and I couldn't stop myself. My body tumbled repeatedly, landing with a crunch and rolling on the hard ground. I slammed into another thick oak tree, sure I broke something this time.

"Oh…that hurt," I groaned, turning my head and seeing Lena lying on the ground next to me. Blood flowed from a gash on her head, and her arm was twisted underneath her.

"Lena," I groaned, but she didn't move. I dragged myself over to her and pushed her shoulder.

Nothing.

I got to a knee and took her hand in mine. That's when I saw Dakota and Rachel behind her. They were sprawled on the ground. Dakota's body was half covering Rachel's as if he was trying to protect her from the blast. Now, neither of them moved.

Adam pulled up next to me.

"Is she okay?" he asked.

Before I could answer him, a boulder barreled down the slope, crashing into him and his chair. His chair twisted and shattered as the heavy rock carried him down the hill. When it reached the bottom, I could see his tiny body crumpled on the ground and his chair smashed to pieces.

"Adam," I whispered, fearing the worst.

Franklin and Mollie raced from the tree line to where Adam lay.

"Is he okay? I yelled down to them.

I could see tears in Mollie's eyes as she turned to me.

"Is he?"

"Wendy," came the horrifying scream from the trees, and a horde of wendigos walked from the woods. The leader had one arm and no hair on his body.

"Franklin!" I shouted, knowing I couldn't get to him and Mollie in time.

He looked up at me. Our eyes met, and he nodded.

My hands ignited, and I readied to incinerate them all.

Crack!

The clawed foot slammed into my side. I heard and felt my ribs crack. Pain exploded through me as my body spiraled through the air, flipping over a small rise before crashing onto the hard ground.

I tumbled over and over until the cliff's edge suddenly rushed into view.

Desperate, I snatched a thick root, halting just short of going over.

My chest heaved.

I looked back. Chernobog was stalking toward me, his monstrous form looming larger with every step. Demons marched beside him, dragging my friends like trophies.

My grip slipped.

I tumbled over the edge. And splashed into the freezing water below.

I sank.

Deeper. And deeper.

I didn't fight it.

I couldn't.

And for the first time, I wasn't sure if I even wanted to.

My friends were wounded—or worse. My town was under siege, overwhelmed by an endless tide of demonic soldiers. I felt hopeless, gazing up through the water toward the distant surface.

Far above, silhouetted against the storm-dark sky, stood Chernobog.

Even from deep below, I could see his massive form smirking, arms raised in arrogant triumph at the cliff's edge.

"It didn't have to be like this, Prentice!"

His voice boomed, echoing through the water like thunder.

375

"Your friends don't have to suffer anymore!"

In that moment, I saw them.

My friends.

One by one, dragged into view, forced to their knees beside him.

Shackled. Beaten. But not broken.

Their eyes searched the river below, searching for me.

Chernobog raised his hand.

"Kill them all," he commanded, before launching himself into the sky toward the battlefield below.

No.

I kicked, surging through the river like a missile bursting from the water. Rainbow energy trailed behind me as I rocketed into the air, soaring above the towering god.

And landed with force behind him, on the other side of the cliff.

A demon drew his sword, stepping toward Franklin.

The blade gleamed in the dim light inches from his neck, but Franklin grinned. "You hold that sword like a girl," he snorted.

The demon hesitated, clearly confused.

Until another one leaned in and muttered, "That is a girl."

A beat of awkward silence followed. Even chained and surrounded, my friends hadn't lost their spirit.

"Wait... what?" Franklin blinked. "I didn't think they actually made girl demons."

"You know a lot of demons?" Dakota raised a brow.

"Well... no... but it just seemed like..."

"Like what?" Rachel cut in, arms crossed.

Franklin opened his mouth and wisely said nothing.

"Do it!" one of the demons barked.

"Wait!" Franklin shouted and raised his hand.

The demon paused, confused.

"So... do you go by he or she?" Franklin asked innocently. "I'm just curious. It's 2025, you know?"

The demon stared at him, blinking slowly.

"I... don't... know," it rasped, voice scratchy with uncertainty.

"Enough! Do it!" another demon snarled.

376

But that awkward exchange was all I needed.

"I give all of my power freely!" I declared, stepping forward.

Every eye turned to me.

I wiggled my fingers and thin rainbow strands flared from my hands, arcing toward each of my friends. The energy struck them sinking in, fusing into their bodies.

Each one absorbed the vibrant light of the rainbow, their shackled forms beginning to glow.

"What are you doing?!" Chernobog bellowed from above.

"Giving up my power, you big jerk," I smirked.

Then I fired.

Two red fireballs.

They slammed into his knees.

And the god of death crashed to the ground.

That was the cue.

Franklin snapped his chains off like they were made of string.

As the demon raised its sword, he decked it with a powerful right hook spinning it through the air.

"You just hit a girl," Dakota grinned, ripping his restraints apart.

A one-eyed demon lunged.

But Dakota met it with a solid kick to the chest, launching it over the edge of the cliff.

Franklin turned to the stunned demon on the ground.

"Wait... are you seriously a girl?"

The demon didn't answer. Just groaned.

"Does it matter?" Adam muttered, rolling his eyes.

"I mean...I've never hit a girl before," he muttered as the demon kicked him in the private area.

Franklin grunted and got angry. He slammed a fist into the belly of the beast, grabbed hold of it by the shoulders, spun, and launched it off the cliff.

"Sorry, demon lady," he shouted as the thing tumbled over the side.

Adam, who wasn't handcuffed, rolled away from his captor. The short, fat troll ran after him, trying to stomp on him as he rolled.

377

"Adam," I shouted, realizing he was headed straight for the cliff's edge.

He stopped rolling just as the creepy guard went to stomp on his head. The paralyzed boy caught the thick boot in his hands and twisted as hard as he could. The sound of bone crunching as the knee broke was gut-wrenching. The monster screamed in pain just as Adam rolled into the remaining leg as hard as he could, causing that one to fail. The creature collapsed to the ground next to Adam.

"Not being able to walk sucks, doesn't it?" Adam asked just before headbutting the monster, crushing its nose. There was no cry of pain this time. The beast just lay on the ground, not moving.

Rachel and Lena broke their cuffs as three ogre guards tried to corral them. One of the guards grabbed Lena by the shoulder, spinning her around. She grabbed the wrist, twisted it, and launched the monster to the depths of the water below. Rachel began firing shot after shot of colorful pink lasers like Spider-Man does. One of the demons exploded in a pink mist.

"Pink?" I asked. "Really?"

"It's not like I know what color I'm using. Whoa...wait a minute. We're using the colors," she shouted.

"What did you do, Prentice?" Lena asked.

"He wanted me to give up my powers, so I did," I smiled. "Just not to him."

Chernobog roared in anger as he got to his feet.

"But you still have your powers," Rachel pointed out.

"I guess," I laughed, turning back to the giant Dark God. He fired two red laser beams at me that exploded at my feet. When the dust cleared, he was already in the sky, heading back to the battlefield.

"Come on. Let's go," I ordered, grabbing Adam and shooting into the sky. Franklin bolted, sprinting so fast he was a blur, his legs a whirlwind of motion.

Rachel vanished in a flicker of light, reappearing instantly on the battlefield below, her form already in motion.

Dakota launched into the air with a single leap, soaring hundreds of feet before slamming back down—only to leap again, higher and harder.

Lena soared up beside me, gliding effortlessly through the sky, her arms stretched wide, eyes focused and fierce.

One glance was all it took.

My friends all have power now.

A moment later, we landed amid the battle. The reinforced demon army was pushing the Capron Bay warriors back. Dad, the Mountain, Poppa, Hog, and Mason fought valiantly, but there were simply too many monsters to hold off.

The giant Chernobog was now in the fray, kicking and stomping on the defenders. I put Adam down with my friends and looked at the battle.

"I have to end this now," I said.

"Can you?" Lena asked. "Are you strong enough?"

I shrugged and leaped into the sky towards my enemy.

"Hey... ugly!" I shouted, grabbing his attention.

He turned, just in time to see my fist grow five times its size and slam into his jaw with a vicious right hook. A thick fang popped free from his mouth, spinning through the air as he crashed to the ground.

I grinned.

But I didn't see the backhand coming. The hit landed like a freight train. I flew through the sky, blasting through the thick trees lining the schoolyard and bouncing off every single one before landing face-first in the mud.

I groaned. "Ouch."

No time to sulk.

I rocketed back into the air, bursting through the canopy.

A red laser beam shot from my hands, slamming into the giant's shoulder.

But he didn't even flinch.

Instead, he fired back.

Thick black bolts of energy screamed through the air toward me. I barely dodged the first one but the second struck my feet dead-on. My body spun out of control, tumbling through the **sky**.

And crashing into the raging battle below.

Dazed, I blinked up.

And immediately wished I hadn't.

Towering over me was a tall, lanky nightmare.

Its fingers replaced by gleaming, razor-sharp claws. Its twisted, almost-human face stretched into a wide, unnatural grin. Crazed, soulless eyes locked onto mine.

And it laughed.

"We're not done," a voice roared over me. Hog was standing opposite them, laughing.

"HAHAHA!" it laughed and lunged for Hog. The movement was fast, but the big detective was ready. He caught the clawed hand and twisted violently. The laughing psycho man screamed as the hand snapped backward, causing the bone to break the blue skin. Hog landed a massive kick to the midsection in another swift movement, doubling it over.

I got to my feet just in time to see Hog *hoist* the creature high over his head and slam it down across his bent knee with brutal force. The creature's body snapped backward with a sickening crunch, its spine or whatever passed for one clearly broken.

Hog let the mangled thing slide to the ground, where it lay motionless in the thick mud.

He looked over at me, stone-faced.

"Remember that when you date Lena," he said flatly.

I blinked. "Yes, sir," I muttered, nodding quickly.

"Go finish this," he ordered, turning toward the fight.

I pivoted, ready to launch back into the air.

But a searing red bolt blasted into my chest, driving me backward with violent force.

Before Hog could react a second bolt slammed into him, knocking him to the ground as he tried to step in.

"I am so tired of you, kid," Alpha snarled, looming over me. He raised his hand and fired another crackling bolt of lightning straight into my chest.

"ARGHH!" I screamed, the pain ripping through my body.

"You don't understand anything!" he spat. "You gave your power to your friends, made yourself weak!"

Another bolt shot from his palm.

And I braced for it.

BAM!

A bright yellow blast of electricity slammed into Alpha's side, sending him stumbling.

"That's my son!" dad bellowed, his hands glowing with raw yellow energy.

BAM!

A red-hot bolt of energy struck Alpha again, knocking him to the ground.

"That's my grandson!" Grammy roared, eyes burning with fury.

Golden-white lightning crackled through the air, striking Alpha's twisted body as he lay stunned.

"That's my brother!" Carolyn shouted, everyone froze, startled by her sudden burst of energy.

Then, Poppa stepped into view.

He walked over casually, reached down, and grabbed Alpha by the collar. He tilted his head, gave the man a little slap on the cheek. "You've done it now," Poppa said with a laugh, then nodded behind him.

Alpha turned.

Just in time to catch a wicked right cross to the nose.

CRACK!

Blood flew as he crumpled to the ground.

"That's my SON!" Mom shouted, shaking her sore knuckles.

I rose to my feet, legs trembling, heart pounding, looking at my family, standing strong beside me and smiled.

I gazed down at the pathetic figure of Alpha, groaning in the dirt.

"You don't get it, Alpha," I told him, voice steady. "My power comes from my family and friends. I'm stronger now than I've ever been."

I thought about disintegrating him, but he wasn't the problem now. I turned and launched into the sky, ignoring Alpha. My sights were locked on the real threat.

Chernobog.

He was tearing into my town, firing blasts at the people below, stomping, kicking, throwing them like rag dolls.

Not for long.

I flew straight for his head and tried to make my fist big again, but nothing happened. I punched him in the side of the head with my regular-sized hand. He just grunted and turned angry eyes to me.

He was about to backhand me again when a blast of pink energy burned into his left ear. He glared at Rachel, but before he could do anything, Franklin raced around his feet at super speed, swinging a heavy war club, he must have picked up from a demon.

It hurt Chernobog because he hopped up on a leg for a moment.

Dakota then jumped high and landed a double kick off the giant's forehead, knocking him backward. He tried to catch his balance, but Adam had wrapped a thick rope around his feet, causing him to fall. When he landed, he crushed a bunch of his own men.

He didn't hesitate. When he hit the ground, he lasered the entire area with lightning bolts from his eyes. He didn't care if he cut down his soldiers. He carpet-bombed the whole place.

My friends huddled together, expecting to be burned to death, but the blast never reached them. Mollie appeared, her arms out wide and glowing in a multi-colored wall of energy, shielding my friends from instant death.

Chernobog fumed with anger as he stood.

"Prentice, you need to take your power back," Rachel said.

I glanced at them all and collapsed to a knee. I was exhausted.

"I love having super speed. But you know how to use this stuff. Plus, I'm faster than all of you anyway," Franklin grinned.

"This power is meant for you," Lena said, taking my hand.

"She's right," Dakota and Adam agreed.

"I can't do that again," Mollie grunted, shaking her arms. "It hurt."

All my friends circled around me hugging me. I instantly felt the power surge through me.

"More reinforcements come, Pendleton," he declared. I didn't even bother to look. I shot off the ground like a rocket. My speed caught him off guard, and my body slammed into his jaw like a bullet. A rainbow blast exploded as I made contact.

He staggered back but didn't fall. He swiped at me with massive hands but missed. I kamikazed him again, using my whole body as a punch. This time, I struck him in the cheek. Again, the rainbow energy exploded on contact.

He swung his right fist, but I launched straight into it, striking his arm at the wrist. Colors exploded in all directions, and I felt his power give. I absorbed his power, and he grew smaller each time I hit him.

I cracked him again and again as I floated around his head. Energy crackled and sizzled with each blow.

"Prentice, look!" Lena shouted. I turned to see a giant rainbow taking shape above me.

I smiled and hit him again.

I felt the rainbow pulsing behind me. It was a living and breathing energy flow, and I grabbed it.

I felt Chernobog's fear in that moment.

"Bottom of the ninth, two outs, bases loaded, and we're down by three," I recited.

"Swing away, Prentice," Franklin shouted from below. I stepped up in the box, strode with the front foot, kept my hands inside the target, and launched my hips. The rainbow bat struck Chernobog with a crack, sending him flying across the battlefield into the reinforcements and charging down the hill. He knocked them over like a bowling ball, taking out the pins.

When the Dark God came to a stop, he was once again normal size. I flew across the carnage and slammed my feet into him. The kick knocked him to the ground. He bounced and rolled over rocks and bushes, stopping at the water's edge. He tried to stand but fell to the ground and rolled to his back. As he did, I could feel he was utterly powerless.

"You've lost," I told him.

He rolled over and looked at me. Sweat dripped from his messy hair. Blood flowed from gashes and cuts on each side of his nose. Deep purple formed underneath his sunken eyes and along his jawline. His right shoulder was out of its socket, and his left ankle twisted in the wrong direction. He was a beaten mess.

The glowing energy he had shown moments earlier pulsed in and out, getting weaker with each surge. It pulsed, flashed, sizzled, and then finally vanished.

Chernobog was defeated.

"Kill him!" shouts behind me erupted.

"End him," someone else yelled.

I glanced back at the angry people of Capron Bay. They had endured so much, and now they wanted their revenge.

I'd be lying if I said I didn't *want* to blast him into a million pieces. But I wasn't sure it would make me feel better.

I stared at the broken god before me.

Chernobog had struggled to his knees, barely holding himself up.

Blood trickled from his mouth as he coughed, drawing a ragged breath.

He looked nothing like the towering monster that had threatened to destroy everything.

Jack appeared beside me, quiet.

"Can I kill him?" I murmured.

He didn't answer right away.

"I... I don't know," he said finally. "Is that what you want to do?"

My body felt like a volcano, ready to erupt. My hands pulsed with raw energy, glowing with the power I'd earned. No, the power I'd become. I could end him. Right here.

"I can kill him," I whispered to Jack.

But then I looked at him.

Kneeling.

Helpless.

Defeated.

This was the creature who had ruled with fear for centuries, who had hurt so many.

But killing him?

That wasn't me.

"No," I said at last. "I want lives for a life."

"What?" Jack blinked.

"Bring back everyone who died here today," I told the dark god, "And I'll let you live."

"I... can't do that," he muttered.

I raised my hands, charging in my palms.

"Then you die."

"Wait! Wait!" he stammered, crawling to his feet.

I paused.

"Can you do it or not?"

He hesitated, then nodded.

"It must be done now," he said. "If no bond holds them here, the dead don't stay long. They... move on quickly."

"Do it," I commanded. "And wipe the memory from everyone's minds. No one remembers this."

He turned to the altar.

With a trembling hand, he drew symbols in the dirt surrounding the stone slab.

Then he closed his eyes and began to chant in a language that sounded older than time.

The sky turned black.

Lightning split the horizon in a brilliant web.

The earth quaked, cracking beneath our feet.

Geysers of smoke and mist erupted from the ground, twisting into ghostly shapes.

For a moment, I feared I'd been tricked—

That this was some doom spell.

But then—

It stopped.

The sky cleared.

The air fell still.

And the world was quiet again.

Chernobog looked at me with tired, hollow eyes.

"They will all return to their homes, or wherever they were when the storm began," he said.

"Will they remember?" I asked.

He shrugged.

"Most... will not."

"Some will?" I pressed.

"It depends on each person. Their mental make-up and their willingness to accept what they can't see," he nodded.

I looked at Dad, knowing he was thinking the same thing. Do we want people to remember or not?

"Nothing we can do about it," he shrugged. I knew he was right.

"Now, get rid of the demon army," I ordered Chernobog.

He snapped his fingers, and the legions of dead were gone. The only people remaining on the battlefield were my family, friends, and the ghost army that Poppa brought with him.

"I want them brought back," I said firmly, glancing toward Poppa, the Mountain, Sgt. Donegan, and the rest of the ghost army.

"These people have been dead a long time," Chernobog replied. "It doesn't work that way."

"You said a life for a life. I'm holding you to it," I demanded.

He shook his head. "One life for one life. That's all the balance allows."

"Not good enough!" I shouted.

"Then kill me," he said quietly.

"Prentice," Dad warned gently.

"Do it," I ordered Chernobog, fists glowing.

"I can't," he said, defiant.

"Yes, you can!"

"I can only bring back one. But to do that, another must give up their life. I am bound by that law. I cannot change it."

Dad said my name again, softer this time.

I turned, eyes full of tears, and looked around at Poppa, Grammy, Mollie, the Mountain. Everyone stood silent, waiting.

"A life for a life," a calm voice said.

We all turned to see Grace walking forward.

"Grace..." Jack whispered, eyes wide.

She took the Snow Fairy's hand and smiled. "It's okay. I've lived a long life thanks to you and Chief Pendleton." She glanced at Poppa, who nodded.

"Grace, no," Jack pleaded.

"It's time I go home," she said simply, her voice serene.

"Are you sure?" I asked.

"I am," she said, eyes sparkling with peace. "I'm ready."

Jack broke down, but she gently held his hand. "Thank you for everything."

He nodded, eyes brimming.

Then she turned to me and nodded.

"Who will you bring back?" Chernobog asked.

I looked to Poppa and the Mountain.

"Not today, kid," the Mountain grinned. "I wouldn't last ten minutes in this century. We started a revolution over a three-cent tax, now look at you people."

Poppa just smirked. "Don't even think about it."

"Poppa," I sobbed, running to him and throwing my arms around him.

"P.J., you know what's right," he said, voice gentle. "And I'm okay with it."

Grammy appeared beside him, calm as ever.

"Grammy, I'm sorry."

"No, honey. This isn't even a question."

Poppa kissed my forehead. "I'll always be with you."

"We must hurry," Chernobog warned.

I scanned the area and found her. Mollie, standing beside Fiona and Ms. Annie.

I gestured to her. She hesitated, unsure.

Until Dad walked over, knelt beside her, and whispered something that made her smile through tears.

She stepped forward, passing the Mountain.

"Hey kid," he grinned. "Take care of that one over there." He nodded at Franklin. "He reminds me of me... just, you know, smaller."

"I'm not that much smaller," Franklin muttered.

"See?" the Mountain chuckled. "I like him."

Mollie ran to Grammy and Poppa, hugging them tightly.

"I'm sorry," she cried.

"You've got nothing to be sorry for," Grammy said. "Now go."

Poppa lifted her chin. "You deserve this life, Mollie. I've lived mine. Now, it's your turn."

Chernobog stepped forward. "Young lady, go to the old woman."

Mollie took Grace's hand.

The sun stood high above as Chernobog began chanting in his ancient tongue.

A thick fog swirled around them, building into a misty vortex.

A high-pitched ringing pierced the air, then…

Silence.

The fog vanished.

Both bodies lay still on the ground.

No one breathed.

Suddenly, a joyful cry rose from the Inuit villagers as a young girl appeared before them. Two older villagers rushed forward, embracing her.

Grace had returned home at last.

She turned to Jack, smiling, then waved at me. And vanished with her people.

"Momma…" Mollie coughed as she stood, trembling.

Fiona ran to her, tears streaming, and held her tight.

Nobody spoke. Nobody moved.

The moment belonged to them.

"What happens now?" Dad asked Poppa a long few moments later.

"We all have to go," Poppa said.

Sgt. Donegan stepped forward. "Sir… I believe it's time."

Dad nodded.

Donegan saluted.

But Dad didn't return it. Instead, he extended his hand.

Donegan shook it and turned.

"Ten hut!" Hog barked.

Every Capron Bay officer snapped to attention, saluting Donegan as he passed.

"Hey, rookie," Dad called.

Donegan turned back.

"You were a good cop."

Donegan smiled and vanished.

Poppa turned to Dad. "This job's not easy."

"No, sir," Dad said, hugging him.

Poppa embraced Grammy next. They whispered to each other, just the two of them, and said goodbye without a tear.

Then he came to me.

"You did good, P.J."

"Will I see you again?"

Poppa hesitated. "I don't think so. It's time I move on."

I hugged him tightly. "I love you, Poppa."

"Love you too, kiddo. And remember, great power, great responsibility. Got it,

I nodded. "Yes, sir. I promise."

Poppa turned to Hog. "He'll need you big man."

"He always does," Hog smiled shaking his hand. "It was honor sir."

Poppa nodded and turned to Agent Mason

"And you too, Dumpster Man."

Mason grumbled, rubbing his cheek and glancing at Franklin. "Don't."

"What?" Franklin smiled hand raised.

Poppa moved on to Doc embracing his old friend. "Take care of them Jonathan."

"I will. You have my solemn vow."

To Brother Kiernan: "This is your home now and this is your family."

Thomas nodded in return.

Finally, he looked over at us kids.

"You're a special group of kids. Protect each other. At all costs."

None of us said a word as he turned and walked into a fog that rose from nowhere.

"Read my files," he called back. "You think THIS was bad, just wait."

"Wait... what?" Dad asked.

But he was gone.

"Hey, shorty," Franklin said to the Mountain. "Catch you on the flip side."

"Did you just call me shorty?" the Mountain scowled. "I like you, kid," he laughed, and vanished.

And just like that, Capron Bay High School was quiet once again.

The battlefield. The castle. The river. The demons.

All gone.

"Did he get away?" Brother Kiernan asked looking for Chernobog.

"No," I said.

"Where is he?" Doc asked.

"I don't know," I admitted.

"How do we know he won't return?" Lena asked.

"He has no power. I felt it leave him," I said.

"But that doesn't mean it can't come back," Jack warned.

I nodded. "True. But we'll cross that bridge when it comes."

I looked out toward the woods.

I knew he was out there.

But for now…he was powerless.

"If he ever returns…" Lena said.

"We'll be ready for him," I finished.

"Yes, we will."

34
THE AFTERMATH

Capron Bay Middle School
One Week Later
3:30 P.M.

School had just let out, and we all sat on the freezing snowbank piled high from where the town had plowed the parking lot. It had been nearly a week since the war for Capron Bay, and today was the first day back to school.

"It's a strange thing, isn't it?" Dakota pondered. His voice tinged with confusion. "Those who came back from the dead, they remember nothing of their journey."

He was referring to the fact that most Capron Bay citizens don't remember the events that happened during the eternal storm. Those who did recall some of the details were told it was a result of the storm, a rare meteorological event that impacted people's minds and made people see things in the snow that weren't there.

"It's not a bad thing, though," I added. "We don't need a lot of people knowing about me and the things out there trying to do this town harm."

"Yeah, but it would be nice for everyone to know you saved this town again," Lena sighed.

"We saved this town," I corrected her. "I couldn't have done it without you guys."

"Besides, the people that matter know everything," Adam grinned.

"And we know who Alpha is now," Rachel said.

"Speaking of that, any word on him?" Franklin asked.

"The team was in France looking for him. They got word that Alpha, Senator Bradler, and Agent Byrd were hiding in some ancient castle in the French Alps," I told them.

"I still don't get why you couldn't go," Mollie said.

"I tried to, but Dad shut it down quickly, and even Grammy agreed. So, I figured it was best not to argue about it," I replied.

"What about Chernobog?" Lena asked, squeezing my hand.

"Haven't heard anything about him," I said. "I talked to Jack yesterday. Chernobog has vanished."

"Somehow, I don't believe that" Dakota grimaced.

I nodded. We all knew he was still out there somewhere. He was beaten and probably very weak, but I had a feeling he would be back.

"Should've killed him," Franklin muttered.

"Would you have done it," I asked him.

"I..." he paused for a long moment. "No. I wouldn't have either."

"That's what makes us different from them," I stressed.

Everyone agreed.

Adam's phone buzzed, and he looked down at the text message.

"Hey, Dad says the rink in the backyard is ready. Let's go play some hockey," he grinned.

"You got tires that can go on the ice?" Rachel asked him.

"They're not tires," he smiled. "They're skates."

"Oh, this is going to be good," Franklin laughed. "C'mon, let's go."

Whack!

"Ouch," Rachel shouted as the snowball struck her on the side of her head.

I spun to see Peter and his cousins trudging through the snow.

"I'm going to," Dakota began to say as he stood and stepped toward the newcomers.

I stepped in front of him, holding him back.

"It's Huey, Dewey, and Louie," Franklin challenged.

"You got a smart mouth," Peter said.

"Come and shut it then," Franklin grinned.

"I will," the kid named Hu threatened.

"Who will?" Franklin laughed.

"I will," Hu said again.

"Who?" Franklin cackled.

"I will," the boy said again.

"Hu shut up," Bo ordered. "He's making fun of your name."

"Are they your sheep, Bo Peep?" Mollie chuckled.

Everyone laughed except me. I watched Bo, awaiting her response. She just smiled and said nothing.

Peter tossed another snowball up and down in his hand and glared at Dakota.

"You throw that, and I'm going to make you eat it," Dakota said, standing his ground.

I was proud of him. There was a time when he would have been too scared to stand his ground like that. After everything we had been through, he was stronger and ready for a fight.

"You think you can do that?" Peter smiled.

Dakota stared back.

"I know he can," Adam interrupted.

"Now, now, boys," Bo laughed. "We'll get to that in time, but not now."

"Come on, Bo," Peter urged.

"Let's go," she told him. Her eyes never left mine. "This isn't over."

"Yeah, you can bet on it," Lena added.

"I'm not interested in you, Lena. I want your boyfriend," Bo replied, staring at me.

"Good luck with that," Rachel added.

Bo laughed.

"You won't be laughing for long," Lena smirked.

"Come on, boys," Bo said. "Let's go."

"Really?" Peter asked.

"I said, let's go. Yu will be here soon,' she said as the three of them turned and left.

"Did she say You?" Franklin laughed.

"Probably spelled Yu," Rachel told him.

"Really? Hu, Yu, and Bo?" he cackled.

I said nothing. I watched the three of them leave until they were out of sight.

"What's the matter, Prentice?" Adam asked.

393

"She's got powers," I whispered.

"What?" Lena asked.

"She's touched by the rainbow," I answered, using the term Jon Kane had used.

"Seriously?" Mollie asked.

I nodded.

"We have to be careful with her," I added.

Nobody said a word for a long moment.

"Hey, have you looked at Poppa's files yet?" Adam asked, changing the subject.

"Dad locked it all up really quickly," I told them.

"What do you think is in those files?" Rachel inquired.

"I don't know what's in most of them," I said.

"Wait, you said most of them. Does that mean you know what's in some of them?" Dakota asked.

I opened my backpack and pulled out a manila folder.

"What's in it?" Adam asked.

"Let's wait until we get back to HQ," I smiled.

"Come on, tell us something," Mollie chimed in.

"I haven't looked through it much, but what I did see, I can tell you Capron Bay is a hot spot for other worldly visitors," I smiled.

"We knew that already. We saw Chernobog's world and the demon army," Adam reminded us all.

"I'm not talking about that?" I grinned.

"What did you mean then?" Rachel asked.

"Let's just say, we're not alone in the universe," I declared.

394

Epilogue: The Beacon

The snow had long since stopped falling.

A quiet hush lingered over Capron Bay—the kind that didn't just muffle sound, it swallowed it whole. The storm was gone... or so everyone thought. But the air still crackled with something wicked. And watchful.

Deep in the snow-covered woods, a satellite dish—long abandoned, long decommissioned—shuddered to life. Metal groaned as it creaked and turned, aligning itself slowly, deliberately, with a section of the night sky that appeared on no modern astronomical chart.

There were no stars there.
Just darkness. Endless. Silent.

Then came the static—piercing the cold stillness with a sharp, mechanical shriek.

And within that static... voices. Garbled. Echoing. Not like ours. Not human.

Without warning, a beam of energy erupted from the dish—silent, invisible to all but one. It carved through the sky, faster than light, vanishing into the abyss above.

Down in Capron Bay, Prentice was walking Druss along a snowbank-lined street, breathing in the peace, the silence... the illusion.

But Druss stopped.

Every muscle in the dog's body tensed. His head turned sharply toward the sky.

Prentice followed his gaze. And then he saw it.

The beam. Blazing across the void—not with light, but with a feeling. A pressure behind the eyes. A noise that didn't exist. He clutched his ears as a high-pitched sound sliced through his skull.

And in that moment, he heard it—

His name. Whispered, stretched, repeated in the static...

"Prentice..."
Not a question. Recognition.

The beam flickered.

And vanished.

The night returned to stillness. But Prentice knew—deep in his bones, in the marrow of whatever made him *different*—that the beam had been a message.

A beacon.

Something had heard it.

And it already knew his name.

Prentice Pendleton and The Supernatural Squad will return Soon

Prentice thought the Eternal Storm was over.

He was wrong.

Beneath the snowdrifts and silence, something ancient has awakened—something trapped long ago by Project IRIS, a top-secret Cold War initiative born from the Roswell crash. The government thought the creature they imprisoned beneath the reservation was the real threat.

It wasn't.

Before it was captured, the creature's ally, hidden among the townspeople of Capron Bay, tried to send a message to its home world. The transmission was halted when the creature was sealed. But the storm changed everything. The barrier is gone. The signal is live.

Now, the real monsters are on their way.

As Prentice and his friends begin hearing voices, seeing shadows, and dreaming in languages they don't understand, a strange and awkward ally reawakens with terrible fashion sense, a deep love for pudding, and a decades-old promise to protect Earth. He's quirky, brilliant, and deeply loyal. But he fears the one they call The Culler. The creature that is hunting for a host to summon the others.

The message is traveling through the void.
And the countdown has already begun.

The message that was never sent… was sent.
And the Voidwalkers… are coming.

Coming Christmas 2025...

Prentice Pendleton and The Voidwalkers!

About The Author

I'm Kevin McGee, the mind behind "Prentice Pendleton and the Supernatural Squad of Capron Bay" and the chilling anthology "United States of Scare: Terrifying Tales from the Fifty States." Born in Rhode Island in 1972, my childhood was a tapestry of baseball dreams and vivid storytelling. When the leaves turned and the fields emptied, my imagination took over, filling the gaps with stories and adventures.

Halloween in New England was a magical time, with the Great Pumpkin reigning over a kingdom of fall colors, haunted tales, and the freedom to be anything you wanted. It was a simpler time, a time for stories that became a part of who I am.

As the seasons changed, so did my life. From a history degree to a career in law enforcement, each step honed my imagination, exposing me to stories so wild they couldn't be made up. Eventually, I traded the badge for the classroom, moving south to teach history and coach sports in the Carolinas. Now, after another move and a decade of teaching, I've embraced my lifelong dream: writing. In the past year alone, I've penned five books, diving deep into the supernatural mysteries of Capron Bay and the haunting folklore of America.

I invite you to explore the stories and characters that have sprung from my mind. There's much more to come for our friends in Capron Bay, and I hope you find as much joy in reading these tales as I have in writing them.